I0785101

Sax Rohmer

The Golden Scorpion & The Yellow Claw

OK Publishing 2021

Sax Rohmer
The Golden Scorpion & The Yellow Claw

Published by
MUSAICUM
Books

- Advanced Digital Solutions & High-Quality book Formatting -

musaicumbooks@okpublishing.info

2021 OK Publishing

ISBN 978-80-272-7946-3

Contents

The Yellow Claw

THE LADY OF THE CIVET FURS

Henry Leroux wrote busily on. The light of the table-lamp, softened and enriched by its mosaic shade, gave an appearance of added opulence to the already handsome appointments of the room. The little table-clock ticked merrily from half-past eleven to a quarter to twelve.

Into the cozy, bookish atmosphere of the novelist's study penetrated the muffled chime of Big Ben; it chimed the three-quarters. But, with his mind centered upon his work, Leroux wrote on ceaselessly.

An odd figure of a man was this popular novelist, with patchy and untidy hair which lessened the otherwise striking contour of his brow. A neglected and unpicturesque figure, in a baggy, neutral-colored dressing-gown; a figure more fitted to a garret than to this spacious, luxurious workroom, with the soft light playing upon rank after rank of rare and costly editions, deepening the tones in the Persian carpet, making red morocco more red, purifying the vellum and regilding the gold of the choice bindings, caressing lovingly the busts and statuettes surmounting the book-shelves, and twinkling upon the scantily-covered crown of Henry Leroux. The door bell rang.

Leroux, heedless of external matters, pursued his work. But the door bell rang again and continued to ring.

"Soames! Soames!" Leroux raised his voice irascibly, continuing to write the while. "Where the devil are you! Can't you hear the door bell?"

Soames did not reveal himself; and to the ringing of the bell was added the unmistakable rattling of a letter-box.

"Soames!" Leroux put down his pen and stood up. "Damn it! he's out! I have no memory!"

He retied the girdle of his dressing-gown, which had become unfastened, and opened the study door. Opposite, across the entrance lobby, was the outer door; and in the light from the lobby lamp he perceived two laughing eyes peering in under the upraised flap of the letter-box. The ringing ceased.

"Are you VERY angry with me for interrupting you?" cried a girl's voice.

"My dear Miss Cumberly!" said Leroux without irritation; "on the contrary — er — I am delighted to see you — or rather to hear you. There is nobody at home, you know."...

"I DO know," replied the girl firmly, "and I know something else, also. Father assures me that you simply STARVE yourself when Mrs. Leroux is away! So I have brought down an omelette!"

"Omelette!" muttered Leroux, advancing toward the door; "you have — er — brought an omelette! I understand — yes; you have brought an omelette? Er — that is very good of you."

He hesitated when about to open the outer door, raising his hands to his dishevelled hair and unshaven chin. The flap of the letter-box dropped; and the girl outside could be heard stifling her laughter.

"You must think me — er — very rude," began Leroux; "I mean — not to open the door. But"...

"I quite understand," concluded the voice of the unseen one. "You are a most untidy object! And I shall tell Mira DIRECTLY she returns that she has no right to leave you alone like this! Now I am going to hurry back upstairs; so you may appear safely. Don't let the omelette get cold. Good night!"

"No, certainly I shall not!" cried Leroux. "So good of you — I — er — do like omelette.... Good night!"

Calmly he returned to his writing-table, where, in the pursuit of the elusive character whose exploits he was chronicling and who had brought him fame and wealth, he forgot in the same moment Helen Cumberly and the omelette.

The table-clock ticked merrily on; SCRATCH — SCRATCH — SPLUTTER — SCRATCH — went Henry Leroux's pen; for this up-to-date litterateur, essayist by inclination, creator of "Martin Zeda, Criminal Scientist" by popular clamor, was yet old-fashioned enough, and sufficient of an enthusiast, to pen his work, while lesser men dictated.

So, amidst that classic company, smiling or frowning upon him from the oaken shelves, where Petronius Arbiter, exquisite, rubbed shoulders with Balzac, plebeian; where Omar Khayyam leaned confidentially toward Philostratus; where Mark Twain, standing squarely beside Thomas Carlyle, glared across the room at George Meredith, Henry Leroux pursued the amazing career of "Martin Zeda."

It wanted but five minutes to the hour of midnight, when again the door bell clamored in the silence.

Leroux wrote steadily on. The bell continued to ring, and, furthermore, the ringer could be heard beating upon the outer door.

"Soames!" cried Leroux irritably, "Soames! Why the hell don't you go to the door!"

Leroux stood up, dashing his pen upon the table.

"I shall have to sack that damned man!" he cried; "he takes too many liberties — stopping out until this hour of the night!"

He pulled open the study door, crossed the hallway, and opened the door beyond.

In, out of the darkness — for the stair lights had been extinguished — staggered a woman; a woman whose pale face exhibited, despite the ravages of sorrow or illness, signs of quite unusual beauty. Her eyes were wide opened, and terror-stricken, the pupils contracted almost to vanishing point. She wore a magnificent cloak of civet fur wrapped tightly about her, and, as Leroux opened the door, she tottered past him into the lobby, glancing back over her shoulder.

With his upraised hands plunged pathetically into the mop of his hair, Leroux turned and stared at the intruder. She groped as if a darkness had descended, clutched at the sides of the study doorway, and then, unsteadily, entered — and sank down upon the big chesterfield in utter exhaustion.

Leroux, rubbing his chin, perplexedly, walked in after her. He scarcely had his foot upon the study carpet, ere the woman started up, tremulously, and shot out from the enveloping furs a bare arm and a pointing, quivering finger.

"Close the door!" she cried hoarsely — "close the door!... He has... followed me!"...

The disturbed novelist, as a man in a dream, turned, retraced his steps, and closed the outer door of the flat. Then, rubbing his chin more vigorously than ever and only desisting from this exercise to fumble in his dishevelled hair, he walked back into the study, whose Athenean calm had thus mysteriously been violated.

Two minutes to midnight; the most respectable flat in respectable Westminster; a lonely and very abstracted novelist — and a pale-faced, beautiful woman, enveloped in costly furs, sitting staring with fearful eyes straight before her. This was such a scene as his sense of the proprieties and of the probabilities could never have permitted Henry Leroux to create.

His visitor kept moistening her dry lips and swallowing, emotionally.

Standing at a discreet distance from her: —

"Madam," began Leroux, nervously.

She waved her hand, enjoining him to silence, and at the same time intimating that she would explain herself directly speech became possible. Whilst she sought to recover her composure, Leroux, gradually forcing himself out of the dreamlike state, studied her with a sort of anxious curiosity.

It now became apparent to him that his visitor was no more than twenty-five or twenty-six years of age, but illness or trouble, or both together, had seared and marred her beauty. Amid the auburn masses of her hair, gleamed streaks, not of gray, but of purest white. The low brow was faintly wrinkled, and the big — unnaturally big — eyes were purple shaded; whilst two heavy lines traced their way from the corner of the nostrils to the corner of the mouth — of the drooping mouth with the bloodless lips.

Her pallor became more strange and interesting the longer he studied it; for, underlying the skin was a yellow tinge which he found inexplicable, but which he linked in his mind with the contracted pupils of her eyes, seeking vainly for a common cause.

He had a hazy impression that his visitor, beneath her furs, was most inadequately clothed; and seeking confirmation of this, his gaze strayed downward to where one little slippered foot peeped out from the civet furs.

Leroux suppressed a gasp. He had caught a glimpse of a bare ankle!

He crossed to his writing-table, and seated himself, glancing sideways at this living mystery. Suddenly she began, in a voice tremulous and scarcely audible: —

"Mr. Leroux, at a great — at a very great personal risk, I have come to-night. What I have to ask of you — to entreat of you, will... will"...

Two bare arms emerged from the fur, and she began clutching at her throat and bosom as though choking — dying.

Leroux leapt up and would have run to her; but forcing a ghastly smile, she waved him away again.

"It is all right," she muttered, swallowing noisily. But frightful spasms of pain convulsed her, contorting her pale face.

"Some brandy —!" cried Leroux, anxiously.

"If you please," whispered the visitor.

She dropped her arms and fell back upon the chesterfield, insensible.

II

MIDNIGHT AND MR. KING

Leroux clutched at the corner of the writing-table to steady himself and stood there looking at the deathly face. Under the most favorable circumstances, he was no man of action, although in common with the rest of his kind he prided himself upon the possession of that presence of mind which he lacked. It was a situation which could not have alarmed "Martin Zeda," but it alarmed, immeasurably, nay, struck inert with horror, Martin Zeda's creator.

Then, in upon Leroux's mental turmoil, a sensible idea intruded itself.

"Dr. Cumberly!" he muttered. "I hope to God he is in!"

Without touching the recumbent form upon the chesterfield, without seeking to learn, without daring to learn, if she lived or had died, Leroux, the tempo of his life changed to a breathless gallop, rushed out of the study, across the entrance hail, and, throwing wide the flat door, leapt up the stair to the flat above — that of his old friend, Dr. Cumberly.

The patter of the slippered feet grew faint upon the stair; then, as Leroux reached the landing above, became inaudible altogether.

In Leroux's study, the table-clock ticked merrily on, seeming to hasten its ticking as the hand crept around closer and closer to midnight. The mosaic shade of the lamp mingled reds and blues and greens upon the white ceiling above and poured golden light upon the pages of manuscript strewn about beneath it. This was a typical work-room of a literary man having the ear of the public — typical in every respect, save for the fur-clad figure outstretched upon the settee.

And now the peeping light indiscreetly penetrated to the hem of a silken garment revealed by some disarrangement of the civet fur. To the eye of an experienced observer, had such an observer been present in Henry Leroux's study, this billow of silk and lace behind the sheltering fur must have proclaimed itself the edge of a night-robe, just as the ankle beneath had proclaimed itself to Henry Leroux's shocked susceptibilities to be innocent of stocking.

Thirty seconds were wanted to complete the cycle of the day, when one of the listless hands thrown across the back of the chesterfield opened and closed spasmodically. The fur at the bosom of the midnight visitor began rapidly to rise and fall.

Then, with a choking cry, the woman struggled upright; her hair, hastily dressed, burst free of its bindings and poured in gleaming cascade down about her shoulders.

Clutching with one hand at her cloak in order to keep it wrapped about her, and holding the other blindly before her, she rose, and with that same odd, groping movement, began to approach the writing-table. The pupils of her eyes were mere pin-points now; she shuddered convulsively, and her skin was dewed with perspiration. Her breath came in agonized gasps.

"God! — I…am dying…and I cannot — tell him!" she breathed.

Feverishly, weakly, she took up a pen, and upon a quarto page, already half filled with Leroux's small, neat, illegible writing, began to scrawl a message, bending down, one hand upon the table, and with her whole body shaking.

Some three or four wavering lines she had written, when intimately, for the flat of Henry Leroux in Palace Mansions lay within sight of the clock-face — Big Ben began to chime midnight.

The writer started back and dropped a great blot of ink upon the paper; then, realizing the cause of the disturbance, forced herself to continue her task.

The chime being completed: ONE! boomed the clock; TWO!…THREE! …FOUR!…

The light in the entrance-hall went out!

FIVE! boomed Big Ben; — SIX!…SEVEN!…

A hand, of old ivory hue, a long, yellow, clawish hand, with part of a sinewy forearm, crept in from the black lobby through the study doorway and touched the electric switch!

EIGHT!…

The study was plunged in darkness!

Uttering a sob — a cry of agony and horror that came from her very soul — the woman stood upright and turned to face toward the door, clutching the sheet of paper in one rigid hand.

Through the leaded panes of the window above the writing-table swept a silver beam of moonlight. It poured, searchingly, upon the fur-clad figure swaying by the table; cutting through the darkness of the room like some huge scimitar, to end in a pallid pool about the woman's shadow on the center of the Persian carpet.

Coincident with her sobbing cry — NINE! boomed Big Ben; TEN!…

Two hands — with outstretched, crooked, clutching fingers — leapt from the darkness into the light of the moonbeam.

"God! Oh, God!" came a frenzied, rasping shriek — "MR. KING!"

Straight at the bare throat leapt the yellow hands; a gurgling cry rose — fell — and died away.

Gently, noiselessly, the lady of the civet fur sank upon the carpet by the table; as she fell, a dim black figure bent over her. The tearing of paper told of the note being snatched from her frozen grip; but never for a moment did the face or the form of her assailant encroach upon the moonbeam.

Batlike, this second and terrible visitant avoided the light.

The deed had occupied so brief a time that but one note of the great bell had accompanied it.

TWELVE! rang out the final stroke from the clock-tower. A low, eerie whistle, minor, rising in three irregular notes and falling in weird, unusual cadence to silence again, came from somewhere outside the room.

Then darkness — stillness — with the moon a witness of one more ghastly crime.

Presently, confused and intermingled voices from above proclaimed the return of Leroux with the doctor. They were talking in an excited key, the voice of Leroux, especially, sounding almost hysterical. They created such a disturbance that they attracted the attention of Mr. John Exel, M. P., occupant of the flat below, who at that very moment had returned from the House and was about to insert the key in the lock of his door. He looked up the stairway, but, all being in darkness, was unable to detect anything. Therefore he called out: —

"Is that you, Leroux? Is anything the matter?"

"Matter, Exel!" cried Leroux; "there's a devil of a business! For mercy's sake, come up!"

His curiosity greatly excited, Mr. Exel mounted the stairs, entering the lobby of Leroux's flat immediately behind the owner and Dr. Cumberly — who, like Leroux, was arrayed in a dressing-gown; for he had been in bed when summoned by his friend.

"You are all in the dark, here," muttered Dr. Cumberly, fumbling for the switch.

"Some one has turned the light out!" whispered Leroux, nervously; "I left it on."

Dr. Cumberly pressed the switch, turning up the lobby light as Exel entered from the landing. Then Leroux, entering the study first of the three, switched on the light there, also.

One glance he threw about the room, then started back like a man physically stricken.

"Cumberly!" he gasped, "Cumberly" — and he pointed to the furry heap by the writing-table.

"You said she lay on the chesterfield," muttered Cumberly.

"I left her there."...

Dr. Cumberly crossed the room and dropped upon his knees. He turned the white face toward the light, gently parted the civet fur, and pressed his ear to the silken covering of the breast. He started slightly and looked into the glazing eyes.

Replacing the fur which he had disarranged, the physician stood up and fixed a keen gaze upon the face of Henry Leroux. The latter swallowed noisily, moistening his parched lips.

"Is she"... he muttered; "is she"...

"God's mercy, Leroux!" whispered Mr. Exel — "what does this mean?"

"The woman is dead," said Dr. Cumberly.

In common with all medical men, Dr. Cumberly was a physiognomist; he was a great physician and a proportionately great physiognomist. Therefore, when he looked into Henry Leroux's eyes, he saw there, and recognized, horror and consternation. With no further evidence than that furnished by his own powers of perception, he knew that the mystery of this woman's death was as inexplicable to Henry Leroux as it was inexplicable to himself.

He was a masterful man, with the gray eyes of a diplomat, and he knew Leroux as did few men. He laid both hands upon the novelist's shoulders.

"Brace up, old chap!" he said; "you will want all your wits about you."

"I left her," began Leroux, hesitatingly — "I left"...

"We know all about where you left her, Leroux," interrupted Cumberly; "but what we want to get at is this: what occurred between the time you left her, and the time of our return?"

Exel, who had walked across to the table, and with a horror-stricken face was gingerly examining the victim, now exclaimed: —

"Why! Leroux! she is — she is... UNDRESSED!"

Leroux clutched at his dishevelled hair with both hands.

"My dear Exel!" he cried — "my dear, good man! Why do you use that tone? You say 'she is undressed!' as though I were responsible for the poor soul's condition!"

"On the contrary, Leroux!" retorted Exel, standing very upright, and staring through his monocle; "on the contrary, YOU misconstrue ME! I did not intend to imply — to insinuate — "

"My dear Exel!" broke in Dr. Cumberly — "Leroux is perfectly well aware that you intended nothing unkindly. But the poor chap, quite naturally, is distraught at the moment. You MUST understand that, man!"

"I understand; and I am sorry," said Exel, casting a sidelong glance at the body. "Of course, it is a delicate subject. No doubt Leroux can explain."...

"Damn your explanation!" shrieked Leroux hysterically. "I CANNOT explain! If I could explain, I"...

"Leroux!" said Cumberly, placing his arm paternally about the shaking man — "you are such a nervous subject. DO make an effort, old fellow. Pull yourself together. Exel does not know the circumstances — "

"I am curious to learn them," said the M. P. icily.

Leroux was about to launch some angry retort, but Cumberly forced him into the chesterfield, and crossing to a bureau, poured out a stiff peg of brandy from a decanter which stood there. Leroux sank upon the chesterfield, rubbing his fingers up and down his palms with a curious nervous movement and glancing at the dead woman, and at Exel, alternately, in a mechanical, regular fashion, pathetic to behold.

Mr. Exel, tapping his boot with the head of his inverted cane, was staring fixedly at the doctor.

"Here you are, Leroux," said Cumberly; "drink this up, and let us arrange our facts in decent order before we — "

"Phone for the police?" concluded Exel, his gaze upon the last speaker.

Leroux drank the brandy at a gulp and put down the glass upon a little persian coffee table with a hand which he had somehow contrived to steady.

"You are keen on the official forms, Exel?" he said, with a wry smile. "Please accept my apology for my recent — er — outburst, but picture this thing happening in your place!"

"I cannot," declared Exel, bluntly.

"You lack imagination," said Cumberly. "Take a whisky and soda, and help me to search the flat."

"Search the flat!"

The physician raised a forefinger, forensically.

"Since you, Exel, if not actually in the building, must certainly have been within sight of the street entrance at the moment of the crime, and since Leroux and I descended the stair and met you on the landing, it is reasonable to suppose that the assassin can only be in one place: HERE!"

"HERE!" cried Exel and Leroux, together.

"Did you see anyone leave the lower hall as you entered?"

"No one; emphatically, there was no one there!"

"Then I am right."

"Good God!" whispered Exel, glancing about him, with a new, and keen apprehensiveness.

"Take your drink," concluded Cumberly, "and join me in my search."

"Thanks," replied Exel, nervously proffering a cigar-case; "but I won't drink."

"As you wish," said the doctor, who thus, in his masterful way, acted the host; "and I won't smoke. But do you light up."

"Later," muttered Exel; "later. Let us search, first."

Leroux stood up; Cumberly forced him back.

"Stay where you are, Leroux; it is elementary strategy to operate from a fixed base. This study shall be the base. Ready, Exel?"

Exel nodded, and the search commenced. Leroux sat rigidly upon the settee, his hands resting upon his knees, watching and listening. Save for the merry ticking of the table-clock, and the movements of the searchers from room to room, nothing disturbed the silence. From the table, and that which lay near to it, he kept his gaze obstinately averted.

Five or six minutes passed in this fashion, Leroux expecting each to bring a sudden outcry. He was disappointed. The searchers returned, Exel noticeably holding himself aloof and Cumberly very stern.

Exel, a cigar between his teeth, walked to the writing-table, carefully circling around the dreadful obstacle which lay in his path, to help himself to a match. As he stooped to do so, he perceived that in the closed right hand of the dead woman was a torn scrap of paper.

"Leroux! Cumberly!" he exclaimed; "come here!"

He pointed with the match as Cumberly hurriedly crossed to his side. Leroux, inert, remained where he sat, but watched with haggard eyes. Dr. Cumberly bent down and sought to detach the paper from the grip of the poor cold fingers, without tearing it. Finally he contrived to release the fragment, and, perceiving it to bear some written words, he spread it out beneath the lamp, on the table, and eagerly scanned it, lowering his massive gray head close to the writing.

He inhaled, sibilantly.

"Do you see, Exel?" he jerked — for Exel was bending over his shoulder.

"I do — but I don't understand."

"What is it?" came hollowly from Leroux.

"It is the bottom part of an unfinished note," said Cumberly, slowly. "It is written shakily in a woman's hand, and it reads: — 'Your wife'"...

Leroux sprang to his feet and crossed the room in three strides.

"Wife!" he muttered. His voice seemed to be choked in his throat; "my wife! It says something about my wife?"

"It says," resumed the doctor, quietly, "'your wife.' Then there's a piece torn out, and the two words 'Mr. King.' No stop follows, and the line is evidently incomplete."

"My wife!" mumbled Leroux, staring unseeingly at the fragment of paper. "MY WIFE! MR. KING! Oh! God! I shall go mad!"

"Sit down!" snapped Dr. Cumberly, turning to him; "damn it, Leroux, you are worse than a woman!"

In a manner almost childlike, the novelist obeyed the will of the stronger man, throwing himself into an armchair, and burying his face in his hands.

"My wife!" he kept muttering — "my wife!"...

Exel and the doctor stood staring at one another; when suddenly, from outside the flat, came a metallic clattering, followed by a little suppressed cry. Helen Cumberly, in daintiest deshabille, appeared in the lobby, carrying, in one hand, a chafing-dish, and, in the other, the lid. As she advanced toward the study, from whence she had heard her father's voice: —

"Why, Mr. Leroux!" she cried, "I shall CERTAINLY report you to Mira, now! You have not even touched the omelette!"

"Good God! Cumberly! stop her!" muttered Exel, uneasily. "The door was not latched!"...

But it was too late. Even as the physician turned to intercept his daughter, she crossed the threshold of the study. She stopped short at perceiving Exel; then, with a woman's unerring intuition, divined a tragedy, and, in the instant of divination, sought for, and found, the hub of the tragic wheel.

One swift glance she cast at the fur-clad form, prostrate.

The chafing-dish fell from her hand, and the omelette rolled, a grotesque mass, upon the carpet. She swayed, dizzily, raising one hand to her brow, but had recovered herself even as Leroux sprang forward to support her.

"All right, Leroux!" cried Cumberly; "I will take her upstairs again. Wait for me, Exel."

Exel nodded, lighted his cigar, and sat down in a chair, remote from the writing-table.

"Mira — my wife!" muttered Leroux, standing, looking after Dr. Cumberly and his daughter as they crossed the lobby. "She will report to — my wife."...

In the outer doorway, Helen Cumberly looked back over her shoulder, and her glance met that of Leroux. Hers was a healing glance and a strengthening glance; it braced him up as nothing else could have done. He turned to Exel.

"For Heaven's sake, Exel!" he said, evenly, "give me your advice — give me your help; I am going to 'phone for the police."

Exel looked up with an odd expression.

"I am entirely at your service, Leroux," he said. "I can quite understand how this ghastly affair has shaken you up."

"It was so sudden," said the other, plaintively. "It is incredible that so much emotion can be crowded into so short a period of a man's life."...

Big Ben chimed the quarter after midnight. Leroux, eyes averted, walked to the writing-table, and took up the telephone.

III

INSPECTOR DUNBAR TAKES CHARGE

Detective-Inspector Dunbar was admitted by Dr. Cumberly. He was a man of notable height, large-boned, and built gauntly and squarely. His clothes fitted him ill, and through them one seemed to perceive the massive scaffolding of his frame. He had gray hair retiring above a high brow, but worn long and untidily at the back; a wire-like straight-cut mustache, also streaked with gray, which served to accentuate the grimness of his mouth and slightly undershot jaw. A massive head, with tawny, leonine eyes; indeed, altogether a leonine face, and a frame indicative of tremendous nervous energy.

In the entrance lobby he stood for a moment.

"My name is Cumberly," said the doctor, glancing at the card which the Scotland Yard man had proffered. "I occupy the flat above."

"Glad to know you, Dr. Cumberly," replied the detective in a light and not unpleasant voice —and the fierce eyes momentarily grew kindly.

"This —" continued Cumberly, drawing Dunbar forward into the study, "is my friend, Leroux — Henry Leroux, whose name you will know?"

"I have not that pleasure," replied Dunbar.

"Well," added Cumberly, "he is a famous novelist, and his flat, unfortunately, has been made the scene of a crime. This is Detective-Inspector Dunbar, who has come to solve our difficulties, Leroux." He turned to where Exel stood upon the hearth-rug — toying with his monocle. "Mr. John Exel, M. P."

"Glad to know you, gentlemen," said Dunbar.

Leroux rose from the armchair in which he had been sitting and stared, drearily, at the newcomer. Exel screwed the monocle into his right eye, and likewise surveyed the detective. Cumberly, taking a tumbler from the bureau, said: —

"A scotch-and-soda, Inspector?"

"It is a suggestion," said Dunbar, "that, coming from a medical man, appeals."

Whilst the doctor poured out the whisky and squirted the soda into the glass, Inspector Dunbar, standing squarely in the middle of the room, fixed his eyes upon the still form lying in the shadow of the writing-table.

"You will have been called in, doctor," he said, taking the proffered tumbler, "at the time of the crime?"

"Exactly!" replied Cumberly. "Mr. Leroux ran up to my flat and summoned me to see the woman."

"What time would that be?"

"Big Ben had just struck the final stroke of twelve when I came out on to the landing."

"Mr. Leroux would be waiting there for you?"

"He stood in my entrance-lobby whilst I slipped on my dressing-gown, and we came down together."

"I was entering from the street," interrupted Exel, "as they were descending from above"...

"You can enter from the street, sir, in a moment," said Dunbar, holding up his hand. "One witness at a time, if you please."

Exel shrugged his shoulders and turned slightly, leaning his elbow upon the mantelpiece and flicking off the ash from his cigar.

"I take it you were in bed?" questioned Dunbar, turning again to the doctor.

"I had been in bed about a quarter of an hour when I was aroused by the ringing of the door-bell. This ringing struck me as so urgent that I ran out in my pajamas, and found there Mr. Leroux, in a very disturbed state —"

"What did he say? Give his own words as nearly as you remember them."

Leroux, who had been standing, sank slowly back into the armchair, with his eyes upon Dr. Cumberly as the latter replied: —

"He said 'Cumberly! Cumberly! For God's sake, come down at once; there is a strange woman in my flat, apparently in a dying condition!'"

"What did you do?"

"I ran into my bedroom and slipped on my dressing-gown, leaving Mr. Leroux in the entrance-hall. Then, with the clock chiming the last stroke of midnight, we came out together and I closed my door behind me. There was no light on the stair; but our conversation — Mr. Leroux was speaking in a very high-pitched voice"...

"What was he saying?"

"He was explaining to me how some woman, unknown to him, had interrupted his work a few minutes before by ringing his door-bell."...

Inspector Dunbar held up his hand.

"I won't ask you to repeat what he said, doctor; Mr. Leroux, presently, can give me his own words."

"We had descended to this floor, then," resumed Cumberly, "when Mr. Exel, entering below, called up to us, asking if anything was the matter. Leroux replied, 'Matter, Exel! There's a devil of a business! For mercy's sake, come up!'"

"Well?"

"Mr. Exel thereupon joined us at the door of this flat."

"Was it open?"

"Yes. Mr. Leroux had rushed up to me, leaving the door open behind him. The light was out, both in the lobby and in the study, a fact upon which I commented at the time. It was all the more curious as Mr. Leroux had left both lights on!"...

"Did he say so?"

"He did. The circumstances surprised him to a marked degree. We came in and I turned up the light in the lobby. Then Leroux, entering the study, turned up the light there, too. I entered next, followed by Mr. Exel — and we saw the body lying where you see it now."

"Who saw it first?"

"Mr. Leroux; he drew my attention to it, saying that he had left her lying on the chesterfield and NOT upon the floor."

"You examined her?"

"I did. She was dead, but still warm. She exhibited signs of recent illness, and of being addicted to some drug habit; probably morphine. This, beyond doubt, contributed to her death, but the direct cause was asphyxiation. She had been strangled!"

"My God!" groaned Leroux, dropping his face into his hands.

"You found marks on her throat?"

"The marks were very slight. No great pressure was required in her weak condition."

"You did not move the body?"

"Certainly not; a more complete examination must be made, of course. But I extracted a piece of torn paper from her clenched right hand."

Inspector Dunbar lowered his tufted brows.

"I'm not glad to know you did that," he said. "It should have been left."

"It was done on the spur of the moment, but without altering the position of the hand or arm. The paper lies upon the table, yonder."

Inspector Dunbar took a long drink. Thus far he had made no attempt to examine the victim. Pulling out a bulging note-case from the inside pocket of his blue serge coat, he unscrewed a fountain-pen, carefully tested the nib upon his thumb nail, and made three or four brief entries. Then, stretching out one long arm, he laid the wallet and the pen beside his glass upon the top of a bookcase, without otherwise changing his position, and glancing aside at Exel, said: —

"Now, Mr. Exel, what help can you give us?"

"I have little to add to Dr. Cumberly's account," answered Exel, offhandedly. "The whole thing seemed to me"...

"What it seemed," interrupted Dunbar, "does not interest Scotland Yard, Mr. Exel, and won't interest the jury."

Leroux glanced up for a moment, then set his teeth hard, so that his jaw muscles stood out prominently under the pallid skin.

"What do you want to know, then?" asked Exel.

"I will be wanting to know," said Dunbar, "where you were coming from, to-night?"

"From the House of Commons."

"You came direct?"

"I left Sir Brian Malpas at the corner of Victoria Street at four minutes to twelve by Big Ben, and walked straight home, actually entering here, from the street, as the clock was chiming the last stroke of midnight."

"Then you would have walked up the street from an easterly direction?"

"Certainly."

"Did you meet any one or anything?"

"A taxi-cab, empty — for the hood was lowered — passed me as I turned the corner. There was no other vehicle in the street, and no person."

"You don't know from which door the cab came?"

"As I turned the corner," replied Exel, "I heard the man starting his engine, although when I actually saw the cab, it was in motion; but judging by the sound to which I refer, the cab had been stationary, if not at the door of Palace Mansions, certainly at that of the next block — St. Andrew's Mansions."

"Did you hear, or see anything else?"

"I saw nothing whatever. But just as I approached the street door, I heard a peculiar whistle, apparently proceeding from the gardens in the center of the square. I attached no importance to it at the time."

"What kind of whistle?"

"I have forgotten the actual notes, but the effect was very odd in some way."

"In what way?"

"An impression of this sort is not entirely reliable, Inspector; but it struck me as Oriental."

"Ah!" said Dunbar, and reached out the long arm for his notebook.

"Can I be of any further assistance?" said Exel, glancing at his watch.

"You had entered the hall-way and were about to enter your own flat when the voices of Dr. Cumberly and Mr. Leroux attracted your attention?"

"I actually had the key in my hand," replied Exel.

"Did you actually have the key in the lock?"

"Let me think," mused Exel, and he took out a bunch of keys and dangled them, reflectively, before his eyes. "No! I was fumbling for the right key when I heard the voices above me."

"But were you facing your door?"

"No," averred Exel, perceiving the drift of the inspector's inquiries; "I was facing the stairway the whole time, and although it was in darkness, there is a street lamp immediately outside on the pavement, and I can swear, positively, that no one descended; that there was no one in the hall nor on the stair, except Mr. Leroux and Dr. Cumberly."

"Ah!" said Dunbar again, and made further entries in his book. "I need not trouble you further, sir. Good night!"

Exel, despite his earlier attitude of boredom, now ignored this official dismissal, and, tossing the stump of his cigar into the grate, lighted a cigarette, and with both hands thrust deep in his pockets, stood leaning back against the mantelpiece. The detective turned to Leroux.

"Have a brandy-and-soda?" suggested Dr. Cumberly, his eyes turned upon the pathetic face of the novelist.

But Leroux shook his head, wearily.

"Go ahead, Inspector!" he said. "I am anxious to tell you all I know. God knows I am anxious to tell you."

A sound was heard of a key being inserted in the lock of a door.

Four pairs of curious eyes were turned toward the entrance lobby, when the door opened, and a sleek man of medium height, clean shaven, but with his hair cut low upon the cheek bones, so as to give the impression of short side-whiskers, entered in a manner at once furtive and servile.

He wore a black overcoat and a bowler hat. Reclosing the door, he turned, perceived the group in the study, and fell back as though someone had struck him a fierce blow.

Abject terror was written upon his features, and, for a moment, the idea of flight appeared to suggest itself urgently to him; but finally, he took a step forward toward the study.

"Who's this?" snapped Dunbar, without removing his leonine eyes from the newcomer.

"It is Soames," came the weary voice of Leroux.

"Butler?"

"Yes."

"Where's he been?"

"I don't know. He remained out without my permission."

"He did, eh?"

Inspector Dunbar thrust forth a long finger at the shrinking form in the doorway.

"Mr. Soames," he said, "you will be going to your own room and waiting there until I ring for you."

"Yes, sir," said Soames, holding his hat in both bands, and speaking huskily. "Yes, sir: certainly, sir."

He crossed the lobby and disappeared.

"There is no other way out, is there?" inquired the detective, glancing at Dr. Cumberly.

"There is no other way," was the reply; "but surely you don't suspect"...

"I would suspect the Archbishop of Westminster," snapped Dunbar, "if he came in like that! Now, sir," — he turned to Leroux — "you were alone, here, to-night?"

"Quite alone, Inspector. The truth is, I fear, that my servants take liberties in the absence of my wife."

"In the absence of your wife? Where is your wife?"

"She is in Paris."

"Is she a Frenchwoman?"

"No! oh, no! But my wife is a painter, you understand, and — er — I met her in Paris — er — ...Must you insist upon these — domestic particulars, Inspector?"

"If Mr. Exel is anxious to turn in," replied the inspector, "after his no doubt exhausting duties at the House, and if Dr. Cumberly —"

"I have no secrets from Cumberly!" interjected Leroux. "The doctor has known me almost from boyhood, but — er —" turning to the politician — "don't you know, Exel — no offense, no offense"...

"My dear Leroux," responded Exel hastily, "I am the offender! Permit me to wish you all good night."

He crossed the study, and, at the door, paused and turned.

"Rely upon me, Leroux," he said, "to help in any way within my power."

He crossed the lobby, opened the outer door, and departed.

"Now, Mr. Leroux," resumed Dunbar, "about this matter of your wife's absence."

IV

A WINDOW IS OPENED

Whilst Henry Leroux collected his thoughts, Dr. Cumberly glanced across at the writing-table where lay the fragment of paper which had been clutched in the dead woman's hand, then turned his head again toward the inspector, staring at him curiously. Since Dunbar had not yet attempted even to glance at the strange message, he wondered what had prompted the present line of inquiry.

"My wife," began Leroux, "shared a studio in Paris, at the time that I met her, with an American lady a very talented portrait painter — er — a Miss Denise Ryland. You may know her name? — but of course, you don't, no! Well, my wife is, herself, quite clever with her brush; in fact she has exhibited more than once at the Paris Salon. We agreed at — er — the time of our — of our — engagement, that she should be free to visit her old artistic friends in Paris at any time. You understand? There was to be no let or hindrance.... Is this really necessary, Inspector?"

"Pray go on, Mr. Leroux."

"Well, you understand, it was a give-and-take arrangement; because I am afraid that I, my-self, demand certain — sacrifices from my wife — and — er — I did not feel entitled to — interfere"...

"You see, Inspector," interrupted Dr. Cumberly, "they are a Bohemian pair, and Bohemians, inevitably, bore one another at times! This little arrangement was intended as a safety-valve. Whenever ennui attacked Mrs. Leroux, she was at liberty to depart for a week to her own friends in Paris, leaving Leroux to the bachelor's existence which is really his proper state; to go unshaven and unshorn, to dine upon bread and cheese and onions, to work until all hours of the morning, and generally to enjoy himself!"

"Does she usually stay long?" inquired Dunbar.

"Not more than a week, as a rule," answered Leroux.

"You must excuse me," continued the detective, "if I seem to pry into intimate matters; but on these occasions, how does Mrs. Leroux get on for money?"

"I have opened a credit for her," explained the novelist, wearily, "at the Credit Lyonnais, in Paris."

Dunbar scribbled busily in his notebook.

"Does she take her maid with her?" he jerked, suddenly.

"She has no maid at the moment," replied Leroux; "she has been without one for twelve months or more, now."

"When did you last hear from her?"

"Three days ago."

"Did you answer the letter?"

"Yes; my answer was amongst the mail which Soames took to the post, to-night."

"You said, though, if I remember rightly, that he was out without permission?"

Leroux ran his fingers through his hair.

"I meant that he should only have been absent five minutes or so; whilst he remained out for more than an hour."

Inspector Dunbar nodded, comprehendingly, tapping his teeth with the head of the foun-tain-pen.

"And the other servants?"

"There are only two: a cook and a maid. I released them for the evening — glad to get rid of them — wanted to work."

"They are late?"

"They take liberties, damnable liberties, because I am easy-going."

"I see," said Dunbar. "So that you were quite alone this evening, when" — he nodded in the direction of the writing-table — "your visitor came?"

"Quite alone."

"Was her arrival the first interruption?"

"No — er — not exactly. Miss Cumberly..."

"My daughter," explained Dr. Cumberly, "knowing that Mr. Leroux, at these times, was very neglectful in regard to meals, prepared him an omelette, and brought it down in a chafing-dish."

"How long did she remain?" asked the inspector of Leroux.

"I — er — did not exactly open the door. We chatted, through — er — through the letter-box, and she left the omelette outside on the landing."

"What time would that be?"

"It was a quarter to twelve," declared Cumberly. "I had been supping with some friends, and returned to find Helen, my daughter, engaged in preparing the omelette. I congratulated her upon the happy thought, knowing that Leroux was probably starving himself."

"I see. The omelette, though, seems to be upset here on the floor?" said the inspector.

Cumberly briefly explained how it came to be there, Leroux punctuating his friend's story with affirmative nods.

"Then the door of the flat was open all the time?" cried Dunbar.

"Yes," replied Cumberly; "but whilst Exel and I searched the other rooms — and our search was exhaustive — Mr. Leroux remained here in the study, and in full view of the lobby — as you see for yourself."

"No living thing," said Leroux, monotonously, "left this flat from the time that the three of us, Exel, Cumberly, and I, entered, up to the time that Miss Cumberly came, and, with the doctor, went out again."

"H'm!" said the inspector, making notes; "it appears so, certainly. I will ask you then, for your own account, Mr. Leroux, of the arrival of the woman in the civet furs. Pay special attention" — he pointed with his fountain-pen — "to the TIME at which the various incidents occurred."

Leroux, growing calmer as he proceeded with the strange story, complied with the inspector's request. He had practically completed his account when the door-bell rang.

"It's the servants," said Dr. Cumberly. "Soames will open the door."

But Soames did not appear.

The ringing being repeated: —

"I told him to remain in his room," said Dunbar, "until I rang for him, I remember — "

"I will open the door," said Cumberly.

"And tell the servants to stay in the kitchen," snapped Dunbar.

Dr. Cumberly opened the door, admitting the cook and housemaid.

"There has been an unfortunate accident," he said — "but not to your master; you need not be afraid. But be good enough to remain in the kitchen for the present."

Peeping in furtively as they passed, the two women crossed the lobby and went to their own quarters.

"Mr. Soames next," muttered Dunbar, and, glancing at Cumberly as he returned from the lobby: — "Will you ring for him?" he requested.

Dr. Cumberly nodded, and pressed a bell beside the mantelpiece. An interval followed, in which the inspector made notes and Cumberly stood looking at Leroux, who was beating his palms upon his knees, and staring unseeingly before him.

Cumberly rang again; and in response to the second ring, the housemaid appeared at the door.

"I rang for Soames," said Dr. Cumberly.

"He is not in, sir," answered the girl.

Inspector Dunbar started as though he had been bitten.

"What!" he cried; "not in?"

"No, sir," said the girl, with wide-open, frightened eyes.

Dunbar turned to Cumberly.

"You said there was no other way out!"

"There IS no other way, to my knowledge."

"Where's his room?"

Cumberly led the way to a room at the end of a short corridor, and Inspector Dunbar, entering, and turning up the light, glanced about the little apartment. It was a very neat servants' bedroom; with comfortable, quite simple, furniture; but the chest-of-drawers had been hastily ransacked, and the contents of a trunk — or some of its contents — lay strewn about the floor.

"He has packed his grip!" came Leroux's voice from the doorway. "It's gone!"

The window was wide open. Dunbar sprang forward and leaned out over the ledge, looking to right and left, above and below.

A sort of square courtyard was beneath, and for the convenience of tradesmen, a hand-lift was constructed outside the kitchens of the three flats comprising the house; i. e.: — Mr. Exel's, ground floor, Henry Leroux's second floor, and Dr. Cumberly's, top. It worked in a skeleton shaft which passed close to the left of Soames' window.

For an active man, this was a good enough ladder, and the inspector withdrew his head shrugging his square shoulders, irritably.

"My fault entirely!" he muttered, biting his wiry mustache. "I should have come and seen for myself if there was another way out."

Leroux, in a new flutter of excitement, now craned from the window.

"It might be possible to climb down the shaft," he cried, after a brief survey, "but not if one were carrying a heavy grip, such as that which he has taken!"

"H'm!" said Dunbar. "You are a writing gentleman, I understand, and yet it does not occur to you that he could have lowered the bag on a cord, if he wanted to avoid the noise of dropping it!"

"Yes — er — of course!" muttered Leroux. "But really — but really — oh, good God! I am bewildered! What in Heaven's name does it all mean!"

"It means trouble," replied Dunbar, grimly; "bad trouble."

They returned to the study, and Inspector Dunbar, for the first time since his arrival, walked across and examined the fragmentary message, raising his eyebrows when he discovered that it was written upon the same paper as Leroux's MSS. He glanced, too, at the pen lying on a page of "Martin Zeda" near the lamp and at the inky splash which told how hastily the pen had been dropped.

Then — his brows drawn together — he stooped to the body of the murdered woman. Partially raising the fur cloak, he suppressed a gasp of astonishment.

"Why! she only wears a silk night-dress, and a pair of suede slippers!"

He glanced back over his shoulder.

"I had noted that," said Cumberly. "The whole business is utterly extraordinary."

"Extraordinary is no word for it!" growled the inspector, pursuing his examination.…"Marks of pressure at the throat — yes; and generally unhealthy appearance."

"Due to the drug habit," interjected Dr. Cumberly.

"What drug?"

"I should not like to say out of hand; possibly morphine."

"No jewelry," continued the detective, musingly; "wedding ring — not a new one. Finger nails well cared for, but recently neglected. Hair dyed to hide gray patches; dye wanted renewing. Shoes, French. Night-robe, silk; good lace; probably French, also. Faint perfume — don't know what it is — apparently proceeding from civet fur. Furs, magnificent; very costly."…

He slightly moved the table-lamp in order to direct its light upon the white face. The blood-less lips were parted and the detective bent, closely peering at the teeth thus revealed.

"Her teeth were oddly discolored, doctor," he said, taking out a magnifying glass and examining them closely. "They had been recently scaled, too; so that she was not in the habit of neglecting them."

Dr. Cumberly nodded.

"The drug habit, again," he said guardedly; "a proper examination will establish the full facts."

The inspector added brief notes to those already made, ere he rose from beside the body. Then: —

"You are absolutely certain," he said, deliberately, facing Leroux, "that you had never set eyes on this woman prior to her coming here, to-night?"

"I can swear it!" said Leroux.

"Good!" replied the detective, and closed his notebook with a snap. "Usual formalities will have to be gone through, but I don't think I need trouble you, gentlemen, any further, to-night."

V
DOCTORS DIFFER

Dr. Cumberly walked slowly upstairs to his own flat, a picture etched indelibly upon his mind, of Henry Leroux, with a face of despair, sitting below in his dining-room and listening to the ominous sounds proceeding from the study, where the police were now busily engaged. In the lobby he met his daughter Helen, who was waiting for him in a state of nervous suspense.

"Father!" she began, whilst rebuke died upon the doctor's lips — "tell me quickly what has happened."

Perceiving that an explanation was unavoidable, Dr. Cumberly outlined the story of the night's gruesome happenings, whilst Big Ben began to chime the hour of one.

Helen, eager-eyed, and with her charming face rather pale, hung upon every word of the narrative.

"And now," concluded her father, "you must go to bed. I insist."

"But father!" cried the girl — "there is some thing"...

She hesitated, uneasily.

"Well, Helen, go on," said the doctor.

"I am afraid you will refuse."

"At least give me the opportunity."

"Well — in the glimpse, the half-glimpse, which I had of her, I seemed"...

Dr. Cumberly rested his hands upon his daughter's shoulders characteristically, looking into the troubled gray eyes.

"You don't mean," he began...

"I thought I recognized her!" whispered the girl.

"Good God! can it be possible?"

"I have been trying, ever since, to recall where we had met, but without result. It might mean so much"...

Dr. Cumberly regarded her, fixedly.

"It might mean so much to — Mr. Leroux. But I suppose you will say it is impossible?"

"It IS impossible," said Dr. Cumberly firmly; "dismiss the idea, Helen."

"But father," pleaded the girl, placing her hands over his own, "consider what is at stake"...

"I am anxious that you should not become involved in this morbid business."

"But you surely know me better than to expect me to faint or become hysterical, or anything silly like that! I was certainly shocked when I came down to-night, because — well, it was all so frightfully unexpected"...

Dr. Cumberly shook his head. Helen put her arms about his neck and raised her eyes to his.

"You have no right to refuse," she said, softly: "don't you see that?"

Dr. Cumberly frowned. Then: —

"You are right, Helen," he agreed. "I should know your pluck well enough. But if Inspector Dunbar is gone, the police may refuse to admit us"...

"Then let us hurry!" cried Helen. "I am afraid they will take away"...

Side by side they descended to Henry Leroux's flat, ringing the bell, which, an hour earlier, the lady of the civet furs had rung.

A sergeant in uniform opened the door.

"Is Detective-Inspector Dunbar here?" inquired the physician.

"Yes, sir."

"Say that Dr. Cumberly wishes to speak to him. And" — as the man was about to depart — "request him not to arouse Mr. Leroux."

Almost immediately the inspector appeared, a look of surprise upon his face, which increased on perceiving the girl beside her father.

"This is my daughter, Inspector," explained Cumberly; "she is a contributor to the Planet, and to various magazines, and in this journalistic capacity, meets many people in many walks of life. She thinks she may be of use to you in preparing your case."

Dunbar bowed rather awkwardly.

"Glad to meet you, Miss Cumberly," came the inevitable formula. "Entirely at your service."

"I had an idea, Inspector," said the girl, laying her hand confidentially upon Dunbar's arm, "that I recognized, when I entered Mr. Leroux's study, tonight" — Dunbar nodded — "that I recognized — the — the victim!"

"Good!" said the inspector, rubbing his palms briskly together. His tawny eyes sparkled. "And you would wish to see her again before we take her away. Very plucky of you, Miss Cumberly! But then, you are a doctor's daughter."

They entered, and the inspector closed the door behind them.

"Don't arouse poor Leroux," whispered Cumberly to the detective. "I left him on a couch in the dining-room.".…

"He is still there," replied Dunbar; "poor chap! It is".…

He met Helen's glance, and broke off shortly.

In the study two uniformed constables, and an officer in plain clothes, were apparently engaged in making an inventory — or such was the impression conveyed. The clock ticked merrily on; its ticking a desecration, where all else was hushed in deference to the grim visitor. The body of the murdered woman had been laid upon the chesterfield, and a little, dark, bearded man was conducting an elaborate examination; when, seeing the trio enter, he hastily threw the coat of civet fur over the body, and stood up, facing the intruders.

"It's all right, doctor," said the inspector; "and we shan't detain you a moment." He glanced over his shoulder. "Mr. Hilton, M. R. C. S." he said, indicating the dark man — "Dr. Cumberly and Miss Cumberly."

The divisional surgeon bowed to Helen and eagerly grasped the hand of the celebrated physician.

"I am fortunate in being able to ask your opinion," he began.…

Dr. Cumberly nodded shortly, and with upraised hand, cut him short.

"I shall willingly give you any assistance in my power," he said; "but my daughter has voluntarily committed herself to a rather painful ordeal, and I am anxious to get it over."

He stooped and raised the fur from the ghastly face.

Helen, her hand resting upon her father's shoulder, ventured one rapid glance and then looked away, shuddering slightly. Dr. Cumberly replaced the coat and gazed anxiously at his daughter. But Helen, with admirable courage, having closed her eyes for a moment, reopened them, and smiled at her father's anxiety. She was pale, but perfectly composed.

"Well, Miss Cumberly?" inquired the inspector, eagerly; whilst all in the room watched this slim girl in her charming deshabille, this dainty figure so utterly out of place in that scene of morbid crime.

She raised her gray eyes to the detective.

"I still believe that I have seen the face, somewhere, before. But I shall have to reflect a while — I meet so many folks, you know, in a casual way — before I can commit myself to any statement."

In the leonine eyes looking into hers gleamed the light of admiration and approval. The canny Scotsman admired this girl for her beauty, as a matter of course, for her courage, because courage was a quality standing high in his estimation, but, above all, for her admirable discretion.

"Very proper, Miss Cumberly," he said; "very proper and wise on your part. I don't wish to hurry you in any way, but" — he hesitated, glancing at the man in plain clothes, who had now resumed a careful perusal of a newspaper — "but her name doesn't happen to be Vernon —"

"Vernon!" cried the girl, her eyes lighting up at sound of the name. "Mrs. Vernon! it is! it is! She was pointed out to me at the last Arts Ball — where she appeared in a most monstrous Chinese costume —"

"Chinese?" inquired Dunbar, producing the bulky notebook.

"Yes. Oh! poor, poor soul!"

"You know nothing further about her, Miss Cumberly?"

"Nothing, Inspector. She was merely pointed out to me as one of the strangest figures in the hall. Her husband, I understand, is an art expert —"

"He WAS!" said Dunbar, closing the book sharply. "He died this afternoon; and a paragraph announcing his death appears in the newspaper which we found in the victim's fur coat!"

"But how —"

"It was the only paragraph on the half-page folded outwards which was in any sense PER-SONAL. I am greatly indebted to you, Miss Cumberly; every hour wasted on a case like this means a fresh plait in the rope around the neck of the wrong man!"

Helen Cumberly grew slowly quite pallid.

"Good night," she said; and bowing to the detective and to the surgeon, she prepared to depart.

Mr. Hilton touched Dr. Cumberly's arm, as he, too, was about to retire.

"May I hope," he whispered, "that you will return and give me the benefit of your opinion in making out my report?"

Dr. Cumberly glanced at his daughter; and seeing her to be perfectly composed: — "For the moment, I have formed no opinion, Mr. Hilton," he said, quietly, "not having had an opportunity to conduct a proper examination."

Hilton bent and whispered, confidentially, in the other's ear: —

"She was drugged!"

The innuendo underlying the words struck Dr. Cumberly forcibly, and he started back with his brows drawn together in a frown.

"Do you mean that she was addicted to the use of drugs?" he asked, sharply; "or that the drugging took place to-night."

"The drugging DID take place to-night!" whispered the other. "An injection was made in the left shoulder with a hypodermic syringe; the mark is quite fresh."

Dr. Cumberly glared at his fellow practitioner, angrily.

"Are there no other marks of injection?" he asked.

"On the left forearm, yes. Obviously self-administered. Oh, I don't deny the habit! But my point is this: the injection in the shoulder was NOT self-administered."

"Come, Helen," said Cumberly, taking his daughter's arm; for she had drawn near, during the colloquy — "you must get to bed."

His face was very stern when he turned again to Mr. Hilton.

"I shall return in a few minutes," he said, and escorted his daughter from the room.

VI

AT SCOTLAND YARD

Matters of vital importance to some people whom already we have met, and to others whom thus far we have not met, were transacted in a lofty and rather bleak looking room at Scotland Yard between the hours of nine and ten A. M.; that is, later in the morning of the fateful day whose advent we have heard acclaimed from the Tower of Westminster.

The room, which was lighted by a large French window opening upon a balcony, commanded an excellent view of the Thames Embankment. The floor was polished to a degree of brightness, almost painful. The distempered walls, save for a severe and solitary etching of a former Commissioner, were nude in all their unloveliness. A heavy deal table (upon which rested a blotting-pad, a pewter ink-pot, several newspapers and two pens) together with three deal chairs, built rather as monuments of durability than as examples of art, constituted the only furniture, if we except an electric lamp with a green glass shade, above the table.

This was the room of Detective-Inspector Dunbar; and Detective-Inspector Dunbar, at the hour of our entrance, will be found seated in the chair, placed behind the table, his elbows resting upon the blotting-pad.

At ten minutes past nine, exactly, the door opened, and a thick-set, florid man, buttoned up in a fawn colored raincoat and wearing a bowler hat of obsolete build, entered. He possessed a black mustache, a breezy, bustling manner, and humorous blue eyes; furthermore, when he took off his hat, he revealed the possession of a head of very bristly, upstanding, black hair. This was Detective-Sergeant Sowerby, and the same who was engaged in examining a newspaper in the study of Henry Leroux when Dr. Cumberly and his daughter had paid their second visit to that scene of an unhappy soul's dismissal.

"Well?" said Dunbar, glancing up at his subordinate, inquiringly.

"I have done all the cab depots," reported Sergeant Sowerby, "and a good many of the private owners; but so far the man seen by Mr. Exel has not turned up."

"The word will be passed round now, though," said Dunbar, "and we shall probably have him here during the day."

"I hope so," said the other good-humoredly, seating himself upon one of the two chairs ranged beside the wall. "If he doesn't show up."...

"Well?" jerked Dunbar — "if he doesn't?"

"It will look very black against Leroux."

Dunbar drummed upon the blotting-pad with the fingers of his left hand.

"It beats anything of the kind that has ever come my way," he confessed. "You get pretty cautious at weighing people up, in this business; but I certainly don't think — mind you, I go no further — but I certainly don't think Mr. Henry Leroux would willingly kill a fly; yet there is circumstantial evidence enough to hang him."

Sergeant Sowerby nodded, gazing speculatively at the floor.

"I wonder," he said, slowly, "why the girl — Miss Cumberly — hesitated about telling us the woman's name?"

"I am not wondering about that at all," replied Dunbar, bluntly. "She must meet thousands in the same way. The wonder to me is that she remembered at all. I am open to bet half-a-crown that YOU couldn't remember the name of every woman you happened to have pointed out to you at an Arts Ball?"

"Maybe not," agreed Sowerby; "she's a smart girl, I'll allow. I see you have last night's papers there?"

"I have," replied Dunbar; "and I'm wondering"...

"If there's any connection?"

"Well," continued the inspector, "it looks on the face of it as though the news of her husband's death had something to do with Mrs. Vernon's presence at Leroux's flat. It's not a natural thing for a woman, on the evening of her husband's death, to rush straight away to another man's place"...

"It's strange we couldn't find her clothes"...

"It's not strange at all! You're simply obsessed with the idea that this was a love intrigue! Think, man! the most abandoned woman wouldn't run to keep an appointment with a lover at a time like that! And remember she had the news in her pocket! She came to that flat dressed — or undressed — just as we found her; I'm sure of it. And a point like that sometimes means the difference between hanging and acquittal."

Sergeant Sowerby digested these words, composing his jovial countenance in an expression of unnatural profundity. Then: —

"THE point to my mind," he said, "is the one raised by Mr. Hilton. By gum! didn't Dr. Cumberly tell him off!"

"Dr. Cumberly," replied Dunbar, "is entitled to his opinion, that the injection in the woman's shoulder was at least eight hours old; whilst Mr. Hilton is equally entitled to maintain that it was less than ONE hour old. Neither of them can hope to prove his case."

"If either of them could?"...

"It might make a difference to the evidence — but I'm not sure."

"What time is your appointment?"

"Ten o'clock," replied Dunbar. "I am meeting Mr. Debnam — the late Mr. Vernon's solicitor. There is something in it. Damme! I am sure of it!"

"Something in what?"

"The fact that Mr. Vernon died yesterday evening, and that his wife was murdered at midnight."

"What have you told the press?"

"As little as possible, but you will see that the early editions will all be screaming for the arrest of Soames."

"I shouldn't wonder. He would be a useful man to have; but he's probably out of London now."

"I think not. He's more likely to wait for instructions from his principal."

"His principal?"

"Certainly. You don't think Soames did the murder, do you?"

"No; but he's obviously an accessory."

"I'm not so sure even of that."

"Then why did he bolt?"

"Because he had a guilty conscience."

"Yes," agreed Sowerby; "it does turn out that way sometimes. At any rate, Stringer is after him, but he's got next to nothing to go upon. Has any reply been received from Mrs. Leroux in Paris?"

"No," answered Dunbar, frowning thoughtfully. "Her husband's wire would reach her first thing this morning; I am expecting to hear of a reply at any moment."

"They're a funny couple, altogether," said Sowerby. "I can't imagine myself standing for Mrs. Sowerby spending her week-ends in Paris. Asking for trouble, I call it!"

"It does seem a daft arrangement," agreed Dunbar; "but then, as you say, they're a funny couple."

"I never saw such a bundle of nerves in all my life!"...

"Leroux?"

Sowerby nodded.

"I suppose," he said, "it's the artistic temperament! If Mrs. Leroux has got it, too, I don't wonder that they get fed up with one another's company."

"That's about the secret of it. And now, I shall be glad, Sowerby, if you will be after that taxi-man again. Report at one o'clock. I shall be here."

With his hand on the door-knob: "By the way," said Sowerby, "who the blazes is Mr. King?"

Inspector Dunbar looked up.

"Mr. King," he replied slowly, "is the solution of the mystery."

VII

THE MAN IN THE LIMOUSINE

The house of the late Horace Vernon was a modern villa of prosperous appearance; but, on this sunny September morning, a palpable atmosphere of gloom seemed to overlie it. This made itself perceptible even to the toughened and unimpressionable nerves of Inspector Dunbar. As he mounted the five steps leading up to the door, glancing meanwhile at the lowered blinds at the windows, he wondered if, failing these evidences and his own private knowledge of the facts, he should have recognized that the hand of tragedy had placed its mark upon this house. But when the door was opened by a white-faced servant, he told himself that he should, for a veritable miasma of death seemed to come out to meet him, to envelop him.

Within, proceeded a subdued activity: somber figures moved upon the staircase; and Inspector Dunbar, having presented his card, presently found himself in a well-appointed library.

At the table, whereon were spread a number of documents, sat a lean, clean-shaven, sallow-faced man, wearing gold-rimmed pince-nez; a man whose demeanor of business-like gloom was most admirably adapted to that place and occasion. This was Mr. Debnam, the solicitor. He gravely waved the detective to an armchair, adjusted his pince-nez, and coughed, introductorily.

"Your communication, Inspector," he began (he had the kind of voice which seems to be buried in sawdust packing), "was brought to me this morning, and has disturbed me immeasurably, unspeakably."

"You have been to view the body, sir?"

"One of my clerks, who knew Mrs. Vernon, has just returned to this house to report that he has identified her."

"I should have preferred you to have gone yourself, sir," began Dunbar, taking out his notebook.

"My state of health, Inspector," said the solicitor, "renders it undesirable that I should submit myself to an ordeal so unnecessary — so wholly unnecessary."

"Very good!" muttered Dunbar, making an entry in his book; "your clerk, then, whom I can see in a moment, identifies the murdered woman as Mrs. Vernon. What was her Christian name?"

"Iris — Iris Mary Vernon."

Inspector Dunbar made a note of the fact.

"And now," he said, "you will have read the copy of that portion of my report which I submitted to you this morning — acting upon information supplied by Miss Helen Cumberly?"

"Yes, yes, Inspector, I have read it — but, by the way, I do not know Miss Cumberly."

"Miss Cumberly," explained the detective, "is the daughter of Dr. Cumberly, the Harley Street physician. She lives with her father in the flat above that of Mr. Leroux. She saw the body by accident — and recognized it as that of a lady who had been named to her at the last Arts Ball."

"Ah!" said Debnam, "yes — I see — at the Arts Ball, Inspector. This is a mysterious and a very ghastly case."

"It is indeed, sir," agreed Dunbar. "Can you throw any light upon the presence of Mrs. Vernon at Mr. Leroux's flat on the very night of her husband's death?"

"I can — and I cannot," answered the solicitor, leaning back in the chair and again adjusting his pince-nez, in the manner of a man having important matters — and gloomy, very gloomy, matters — to communicate.

"Good!" said the inspector, and prepared to listen.

"You see," continued Debnam, "the late Mrs. Vernon was not actually residing with her husband at the date of his death."

"Indeed!"

"Ostensibly" — the solicitor shook a lean forefinger at his vis-a-vis — "ostensibly, Inspector, she was visiting her sister in Scotland."

Inspector Dunbar sat up very straight, his brows drawn down over the tawny eyes.

"These visits were of frequent occurrence, and usually of about a week's duration. Mr. Vernon, my late client, a man — I'll not deny it — of inconstant affections (you understand me, Inspector?), did not greatly concern himself with his wife's movements. She belonged to a smart Bohemian set, and — to use a popular figure of speech — burnt the candle at both ends; late dances, night clubs, bridge parties, and other feverish pursuits, possibly taken up as a result of the — shall I say cooling? — of her husband's affections"...

"There was another woman in the case?"

"I fear so, Inspector; in fact, I am sure of it: but to return to Mrs. Vernon. My client provided her with ample funds; and I, myself, have expressed to him astonishment respecting her expenditures in Scotland. I understand that her sister was in comparatively poor circumstances, and I went so far as to point out to Mr. Vernon that one hundred pounds was — shall I say an excessive? — outlay upon a week's sojourn in Auchterander, Perth."

"A hundred pounds!"

"One hundred pounds!"

"Was it queried by Mr. Vernon?"

"Not at all."

"Was Mr. Vernon personally acquainted with this sister in Perth?"

"He was not, Inspector. Mrs. Vernon, at the time of her marriage, did not enjoy that social status to which my late client elevated her. For many years she held no open communication with any member of her family, but latterly, as I have explained, she acquired the habit of recuperating — recuperating from the effects of her febrile pleasures — at this obscure place in Scotland. And Mr. Vernon, his interest in her movements having considerably — shall I say abated? — offered no objection: even suffered it gladly, counting the cost but little against"...

"Freedom?" suggested Dunbar, scribbling in his notebook.

"Rather crudely expressed, perhaps," said the solicitor, peering over the top of his glasses, "but you have the idea. I come now to my client's awakening. Four days ago, he learned the truth; he learned that he was being deceived!"

"Deceived!"

"Mrs. Vernon, thoroughly exhausted with irregular living, announced that she was about to resort once more to the healing breezes of the heather-land" — Mr. Debnam was thoroughly warming to his discourse and thoroughly enjoying his own dusty phrases.

"Interrupting you for a moment," said the inspector, "at what intervals did these visits take place?"

"At remarkably regular intervals, Inspector: something like six times a year."

"For how long had Mrs. Vernon made a custom of these visits?"

"Roughly, for two years."

"Thank you. Will you go on, sir?"

"She requested Mr. Vernon, then, on the last occasion to give her a check for eighty pounds; and this he did, unquestioningly. On Thursday, the second of September, she left for Scotland"...

"Did she take her maid?"

"Her maid always received a holiday on these occasions; Mrs. Vernon wired her respecting the date of her return."

"Did any one actually see her off?"

"No, not that I am aware of, Inspector."

"To put the whole thing quite bluntly, Mr. Debnam," said Dunbar, fixing his tawny eyes upon the solicitor, "Mr. Vernon was thoroughly glad to get rid of her for a week?"

Mr. Debnam shifted uneasily in his chair; the truculent directness of the detective was unpleasing to his tortuous mind. However: —

"I fear you have hit upon the truth," he confessed, "and I must admit that we have no legal evidence of her leaving for Scotland on this, or on any other occasion. Letters were received from Perth, and letters sent to Auchterander from London were answered. But the truth, the painful truth came to light, unexpectedly, dramatically, on Monday last"...

"Four days ago?"

"Exactly; three days before the death of my client." Mr. Debnam wagged his finger at the inspector again. "I maintain," he said, "that this painful discovery, which I am about to mention, precipitated my client's end; although it is a fact that there was — hereditary heart trouble. But I admit that his neglect of his wife (to give it no harsher name) contributed to the catastrophe."

He paused to give dramatic point to the revelation.

"Walking homeward at a late hour on Monday evening from a flat in Victoria Street — the flat of — shall I employ the term a particular friend? — Mr. Vernon was horrified — horrified beyond measure, to perceive, in a large and well-appointed car — a limousine — his wife!"...

"The inside lights of the car were on, then?"

"No; but the light from a street lamp shone directly into the car. A temporary block in the traffic compelled the driver of the car, whom my client described to me as an Asiatic — to pull up for a moment. There, within a few yards of her husband, Mrs. Vernon reclined in the car — or rather in the arms of a male companion!"

"What!"

"Positively!" Mr. Debnam was sedately enjoying himself. "Positively, my dear Inspector, in the arms of a man of extremely dark complexion. Mr. Vernon was unable to perceive more than this, for the man had his back toward him. But the light shone fully upon the face of Mrs. Vernon, who appeared pale and exhausted. She wore a conspicuous motor-coat of civet fur, and it was this which first attracted Mr. Vernon's attention. The blow was a very severe one to a man in my client's state of health; and although I cannot claim that his own conscience was clear, this open violation of the marriage vows outraged the husband — outraged him. In fact he was so perturbed, that he stood there shaking, quivering, unable to speak or act, and the car drove away before he had recovered sufficient presence of mind to note the number."

"In which direction did the car proceed?"

"Toward Victoria Station."

"Any other particulars?"

"Not regarding the car, its driver, or its occupants; but early on the following morning, Mr. Vernon, very much shaken, called upon me and instructed me to despatch an agent to Perth immediately. My agent's report reached me at practically the same time as the news of my client's death"...

"And his report was?"...

"His report, Inspector, telegraphic, of course, was this: that no sister of Mrs. Vernon resided at the address; that the place was a cottage occupied by a certain Mrs. Fry and her husband; that the husband was of no occupation, and had no visible means of support" — he ticked off the points on the long forefinger — "that the Frys lived better than any of their neighbors; and — most important of all — that Mrs. Fry's maiden name, which my agent discovered by recourse to the parish register of marriages — was Ann Fairchild."

"What of that?"

"Ann Fairchild was a former maid of Mrs. Vernon!"

"In short, it amounts to this, then: Mrs. Vernon, during these various absences, never went to Scotland at all? It was a conspiracy?"

"Exactly — exactly, Inspector! I wired instructing my agent to extort from the woman, Fry, the address to which she forwarded letters received by her for Mrs. Vernon. The lady's death, news of which will now have reached him, will no doubt be a lever, enabling my representative to obtain the desired information."

"When do you expect to hear from him?"

"At any moment. Failing a full confession by the Frys, you will of course know how to act, Inspector?"

"Damme!" cried Dunbar, "can your man be relied upon to watch them? They mustn't slip away! Shall I instruct Perth to arrest the couple?"

"I wired my agent this morning, Inspector, to communicate with the local police respecting the Frys."

Inspector Dunbar tapped his small, widely-separated teeth with the end of his fountain-pen.

"I have had one priceless witness slip through my fingers," he muttered. "I'll hand in my resignation if the Frys go!"

"To whom do you refer?"

Inspector Dunbar rose.

"It is a point with which I need not trouble you, sir," he said. "It was not included in the extract of report sent to you. This is going to be the biggest case of my professional career, or my name is not Robert Dunbar!"

Closing his notebook, he thrust it into his pocket, and replaced his fountain-pen in the little leather wallet.

"Of course," said the solicitor, rising in turn, and adjusting the troublesome pince-nez, "there was some intrigue with Leroux? So much is evident."

"You will be thinking that, eh?"

"My dear Inspector" — Mr. Debnam, the wily, was seeking information — "my dear Inspector, Leroux's own wife was absent in Paris — quite a safe distance; and Mrs. Vernon (now proven to be a woman conducting a love intrigue) is found dead under most compromising circumstances — MOST compromising circumstances — in his flat! His servants, even, are got safely out of the way for the evening"...

"Quite so," said Dunbar, shortly, "quite so, Mr. Debnam." He opened the door. "Might I see the late Mrs. Vernon's maid?"

"She is at her home. As I told you, Mrs. Vernon habitually released her for the period of these absences."

The notebook reappeared.

"The young woman's address?"

"You can get it from the housekeeper. Is there anything else you wish to know?"

"Nothing beyond that, thank you."

Three minutes later, Inspector Dunbar had written in his book: — Clarice Goodstone, c/o Mrs. Herne, 134a Robert Street, Hampstead Road, N. W.

He departed from the house whereat Death the Gleaner had twice knocked with his Scythe.

VIII
CABMAN TWO

Returning to Scotland Yard, Inspector Dunbar walked straight up to his own room. There he found Sowerby, very red faced and humid, and a taximan who sat stolidly surveying the Embankment from the window.

"Hullo!" cried Dunbar; "he's turned up, then?"

"No, he hasn't," replied Sowerby with a mild irritation. "But we know where to find him, and he ought to lose his license."

The taximan turned hurriedly. He wore a muffler so tightly packed between his neck and the collar of his uniform jacket, that it appeared materially to impair his respiration. His face possessed a bluish tinge, suggestive of asphyxia, and his watery eyes protruded remarkably; his breathing was noisily audible.

"No, chuck it, mister!" he exclaimed. "I'm only tellin' you 'cause it ain't my line to play tricks on the police. You'll find my name in the books downstairs more'n any other driver in London! I reckon I've brought enough umbrellas, cameras, walkin' sticks, hopera cloaks, watches and sicklike in 'ere, to set up a blarsted pawnbroker's!"

"That's all right, my lad!" said Dunbar, holding up his hand to silence the voluble speaker. "There's going to be no license-losing. You did not hear that you were wanted before?"

The watery eyes of the cabman protruded painfully; he respired like a horse.

"ME, guv'nor!" he exclaimed. "Gor'blime! I ain't the bloke! I was drivin' back from takin' the Honorable 'Erbert 'Arding 'ome — same as I does almost every night, when the 'ouse is a-sittin' — when I see old Tom Brian drawin' away from the door o' Palace Man —"

Again Dunbar held up his hand.

"No doubt you mean well," he said; "but damme! begin at the beginning! Who are you, and what have you come to tell us?"

"'Oo are I? — 'Ere's 'oo I ham!" wheezed the cabman, proffering a greasy license. "Richard 'Amper, number 3 Breams Mews, Dulwich Village"...

"That's all right," said Dunbar, thrusting back the proffered document; "and last night you had taken Mr. Harding the member of Parliament, to his residence in?" —

"In Peers' Chambers, Westminister — that's it, guv'nor! Comin' back, I 'ave to pass along the north side o' the Square, an' just a'ead o' me, I see old Tom Brian a-pullin' round the Johnny 'Orner, — 'im comin' from Palace Mansions."

"Mr. Exel only mentioned seeing ONE cab," muttered Dunbar, glancing keenly aside at Sowerby.

"Wotcher say, guv'nor?" asked the cabman.

"I say — did you see a gentleman approaching from the corner?" asked Dunbar.

"Yus," declared the man; "I see 'im, but 'e 'adn't got as far as the Johnny 'Orner. As I passed outside old Tom Brian, wot's changin' 'is gear, I see a bloke blowin' along on the pavement — a bloke in a high 'at, an' wearin' a heye-glass."

"At this time, then," pursued Dunbar, "you had actually passed the other cab, and the gentleman on the pavement had not come up with it?"

"'E couldn't see it, guv'nor! I'm tellin' you 'e 'adn't got to the Johnny 'Orner!"

"I see," muttered Sowerby. "It's possible that Mr. Exel took no notice of the first cab — especially as it did not come out of the Square."

"Wotcher say, guv'nor?" queried the cabman again, turning his bleared eyes upon Sergeant Sowerby.

"He said," interrupted Dunbar, "was Brian's cab empty?"

"'Course it was," rapped Mr. Hamper, "'e 'd just dropped 'is fare at Palace Mansions."...

"How do you know?" snapped Dunbar, suddenly, fixing his fierce eyes upon the face of the speaker.

The cabman glared in beery truculence.

"I got me blarsted senses, ain't I?" he inquired. "There's only two lots o' flats on that side o' the Square — Palace Mansions, an' St. Andrew's Mansions."

"Well?"

"St. Andrew's Mansions," continued Hamper, "is all away!"

"All away?"

"All away! I know, 'cause I used to have a reg'lar fare there. 'E's in Egyp'; flat shut up. Top floor's to let. Bottom floor's two old unmarried maiden ladies what always travels by 'bus. So does all their blarsted friends an' relations. Where can old Tom Brian 'ave been comin' from, if it wasn't Palace Mansions?"

"H'm!" said Dunbar, "you are a loss to the detective service, my lad! And how do you account for the fact that Brian has not got to hear of the inquiry?"

Hamper bent to Dunbar and whispered, beerily, in his ear: "P'r'aps 'e don't want to 'ear, guv'nor!"

"Oh! Why not?"

"Well, 'e knows there's something up there!"

"Therefore it's his plain duty to assist the police."

"Same as what I does?" cried Hamper, raising his eyebrows. "Course it is! but 'ow d'you know 'e ain't been got at?"

"Our friend, here, evidently has one up against Mr. Tom Brian!" muttered Dunbar aside to Sowerby.

"Wotcher say, guv'nor?" inquired the cabman, looking from one to the other.

"I say, no doubt you can save us the trouble of looking out Brian's license, and give us his private address?" replied Dunbar.

"Course I can. 'E lives hat num'er 36 Forth Street, Brixton, and 'e's out o' the big Brixton depot."

"Oh!" said Dunbar, dryly. "Does he owe you anything?"

"Wotcher say, guv'nor?"

"I say, it's very good of you to take all this trouble and whatever it has cost you in time, we shall be pleased to put right."

Mr. Hamper spat in his right palm, and rubbed his hands together, appreciatively.

"Make it five bob!" he said.

"Wait downstairs," directed Dunbar, pressing a bell-push beside the door. "I'll get it put through for you."

"Right 'o!" rumbled the cabman, and went lurching from the room as a constable in uniform appeared at the door. "Good mornin', guv'nor. Good mornin'!"

The cabman having departed, leaving in his wake a fragrant odor of fourpenny ale: —

"Here you are, Sowerby!" cried Dunbar. "We are moving at last! This is the address of the late Mrs. Vernon's maid. See her; feel your ground, carefully, of course; get to know what clothes Mrs. Vernon took with her on her periodical visits to Scotland."

"What clothes?"

"That's the idea; it is important. I don't think the girl was in her mistress's confidence, but I leave it to you to find out. If circumstances point to my surmise being inaccurate — you know how to act."

"Just let me glance over your notes, bearing on the matter," said Sowerby, "and I'll be off."

Dunbar handed him the bulging notebook, and Sergeant Sowerby lowered his inadequate eyebrows, thoughtfully, whilst he scanned the evidence of Mr. Debnam. Then, returning the book to his superior, and adjusting the peculiar bowler firmly upon his head, he set out.

Dunbar glanced through some papers — apparently reports — which lay upon the table, penciled comments upon two of them, and then, consulting his notebook once more in order to refresh his memory, started off for Forth Street, Brixton.

Forth Street, Brixton, is a depressing thoroughfare. It contains small, cheap flats, and a number of frowsy looking houses which give one the impression of having run to seed. A hostelry of sad aspect occupies a commanding position midway along the street, but inspires the traveler not with cheer, but with lugubrious reflections upon the horrors of inebriety. The odors, unpleasantly mingled, of fried bacon and paraffin oil, are wafted to the wayfarer from the porches of these family residences.

Number 36 proved to be such a villa, and Inspector Dunbar contemplated it from a distance, thoughtfully. As he stood by the door of the public house, gazing across the street, a tired looking woman, lean and anxious-eyed, a poor, dried up bean-pod of a woman, appeared from the door of number 36, carrying a basket. She walked along in the direction of the neighboring highroad, and Dunbar casually followed her.

For some ten minutes he studied her activities, noting that she went from shop to shop until her basket was laden with provisions of all sorts. When she entered a wine-and-spirit merchant's, the detective entered close behind her, for the place was also a post-office. Whilst he purchased a penny stamp and fumbled in his pocket for an imaginary letter, he observed, with interest, that the woman had purchased, and was loading into the hospitable basket, a bottle of whisky, a bottle of rum, and a bottle of gin.

He left the shop ahead of her, sure, now, of his ground, always provided that the woman proved to be Mrs. Brian. Dunbar walked along Forth Street slowly enough to enable the woman to overtake him. At the door of number 36, he glanced up at the number, questioningly, and turned in the gate as she was about to enter.

He raised his hat.

"Have I the pleasure of addressing Mrs. Brian?"

Momentarily, a hard look came into the tired eyes, but Dunbar's gentleness of manner and voice, together with the kindly expression upon his face, turned the scales favorably.

"I am Mrs. Brian," she said; "yes. Did you want to see me?"

"On a matter of some importance. May I come in?"

She nodded and led the way into the house; the door was not closed.

In a living-room whereon was written a pathetic history — a history of decline from easy circumstance and respectability to poverty and utter disregard of appearances — she confronted him, setting down her basket on a table from which the remains of a fish breakfast were not yet removed.

"Is your husband in?" inquired Dunbar with a subtle change of manner.

"He's lying down."

The hard look was creeping again into the woman's eyes.

"Will you please awake him, and tell him that I have called in regard to his license?"

He thrust a card into her hand: —

DETECTIVE-INSPECTOR DUNBAR, C. I. D. NEW SCOTLAND YARD. S. W.

IX
THE MAN IN BLACK

Mrs. Brian started back, with a wild look, a trapped look, in her eyes.

"What's he done?" she inquired. "What's he done? Tom's not done anything!"

"Be good enough to waken him," persisted the inspector. "I wish to speak to him."

Mrs. Brian walked slowly from the room and could be heard entering one further along the passage. An angry snarling, suggesting that of a wild animal disturbed in its lair, proclaimed the arousing of Taximan Thomas Brian. A thick voice inquired, brutally, why the sanguinary hell he (Mr. Brian) had had his bloodstained slumbers disturbed in this gory manner and who was the vermilion blighter responsible.

Then Mrs. Brian's voice mingled with that of her husband, and both became subdued. Finally, a slim man, who wore a short beard, or had omitted to shave for some days, appeared at the door of the living-room. His face was another history upon the same subject as that which might be studied from the walls, the floor, and the appointments of the room. Inspector Dunbar perceived that the shadow of the neighboring hostelry overlay this home.

"What's up?" inquired the new arrival.

The tone of his voice, thickened by excess, was yet eloquent of the gentleman. The barriers passed, your pariah gentleman can be the completest blackguard of them all. He spoke coarsely, and the infectious Cockney accent showed itself in his vowels; but Dunbar, a trained observer, summed up his man in a moment and acted accordingly.

"Come in and shut the door!" he directed. "No" — as Mrs. Brian sought to enter behind her husband — "I wish to speak with you, privately."

"Hop it!" instructed Brian, jerking his thumb over his shoulder — and Mrs. Brian obediently disappeared, closing the door.

"Now," said Dunbar, looking the man up and down, "have you been into the depot, to-day?"

"No."

"But you have heard that there's an inquiry?"

"I've heard nothing. I've been in bed."

"We won't argue about that. I'll simply put a question to you: Where did you pick up the fare that you dropped at Palace Mansions at twelve o'clock last night?"

"Palace Mansions!" muttered Brian, shifting uneasily beneath the unflinching stare of the tawny eyes. "What d'you mean? What Palace Mansions?"

"Don't quibble!" warned Dunbar, thrusting out a finger at him. "This is not a matter of a loss of license; it's a life job!"

"Life job!" whispered the man, and his weak face suddenly relaxed, so that, oddly, the old refinement shone out through the new, vulgar veneer.

"Answer my questions straight and square and I'll take your word that you have not seen the inquiry!" said Dunbar.

"Dick Hamper's done this for me!" muttered Brian. "He's a dirty, low swine! Somebody'll do for him one night!"

"Leave Hamper out of the question," snapped Dunbar. "You put down a fare at Palace Mansions at twelve o'clock last night?"

For one tremendous moment, Brian hesitated, but the good that was in him, or the evil — a consciousness of wrongdoing, or of retribution pending — respect for the law, or fear of its might — decided his course.

"I did."

"It was a man?"

Again Brian, with furtive glance, sought to test his opponent; but his opponent was too strong for him. With Dunbar's eyes upon his face, he chose not to lie.

"It was a woman."

"How was she dressed?"

"In a fur motor-coat — civet fur."

The man of culture spoke in those two words, "civet fur"; and Dunbar nodded quickly, his eyes ablaze at the importance of the evidence.

"Was she alone?"

"She was."

"What fare did she pay you?"

"The meter only registered eightpence, but she gave me half-a-crown."

"Did she appear to be ill?"

"Very ill. She wore no hat, and I supposed her to be in evening dress. She almost fell as she got out of the cab, but managed to get into the hall of Palace Mansions quickly enough, looking behind her all the time."

Inspector Dunbar shot out the hypnotic finger again.

"She told you to wait!" he asserted, positively. Brian looked to right and left, up and down, thrusting his hands into his coat pockets, and taking them out again to stroke his collarless neck. Then: —

"She did — yes," he admitted.

"But you were bribed to drive away? Don't deny it! Don't dare to trifle with me, or by God! you'll spend the night in Brixton Jail!"

"It was made worth my while," muttered Brian, his voice beginning to break, "to hop it."

"Who paid you to do it?"

"A man who had followed all the way in a big car."

"That's it! Describe him!"

"I can't! No, no! you can threaten as much as you like, but I can't describe him. I never saw his face. He stood behind me on the near side of the cab, and just reached forward and pushed a flyer under my nose."

Inspector Dunbar searched the speaker's face closely — and concluded that he was respecting the verity.

"How was he dressed?"

"In black, and that's all I can tell you about him."

"You took the money?"

"I took the money, yes"...

"What did he say to you?"

"Simply: 'Drive off.'"

"Did you take him to be an Englishman from his speech?"

"No; he was not an Englishman. He had a foreign accent."

"French? German?"

"No," said Brian, looking up and meeting the glance of the fierce eyes. "Asiatic!"

Inspector Dunbar, closely as he held himself in hand, started slightly.

"Are you sure?"

"Certainly. Before I — when I was younger — I traveled in the East, and I know the voice and intonation of the cultured Oriental."

"Can you place him any closer than that?"

"No, I can't venture to do so." Brian's manner was becoming, momentarily, more nearly that of a gentleman. "I might be leading you astray if I ventured a guess, but if you asked me to do so, I should say he was a Chinaman."

"A CHINAMAN?" Dunbar's voice rose excitedly.

"I think so."

"What occurred next?"

"I turned my cab and drove off out of the Square."

"Did you see where the man went?"

"I didn't. I saw nothing of him beyond his hand."

"And his hand?"

"He wore a glove."

"And now," said Dunbar, speaking very slowly, "where did you pick up your fare?"

"In Gillingham Street, near Victoria Station."

"From a house?"

"Yes, from Nurse Proctor's."

"Nurse Proctor's! Who is Nurse Proctor?"

Brian shrugged his shoulders in a nonchalant manner, which obviously belonged to an earlier phase of existence.

"She keeps a nursing home," he said — "for ladies."

"Do you mean a maternity home?"

"Not exactly; at least I don't think so. Most of her clients are society ladies, who stay there periodically."

"What are you driving at?" demanded Dunbar. "I have asked you if it is a maternity home."

"And I have replied that it isn't. I am only giving you facts; you don't want my surmises."

"Who hailed you?"

"The woman did — the woman in the fur coat. I was just passing the door very slowly when it was flung open with a bang, and she rushed out as though hell were after her. Before I had time to pull up, she threw herself into my cab and screamed: 'Palace Mansions! Westminster!' I reached back and shut the door, and drove right away."

"When did you see that you were followed?"

"We were held up just outside the music hall, and looking back, I saw that my fare was dreadfully excited. It didn't take me long to find out that the cause of her excitement was a big limousine, three or four back in the block of traffic. The driver was some kind of an Oriental, too, although I couldn't make him out very clearly."

"Good!" snapped Dunbar; "that's important! But you saw nothing more of this car?"...

"I saw it follow me into the Square."

"Then where did it wait?"

"I don't know; I didn't see it again."

Inspector Dunbar nodded rapidly.

"Have you ever driven women to or from this Nurse Proctor's before?"

"On two other occasions, I have driven ladies who came from there. I knew they came from there, because it got about amongst us that the tall woman in nurse's uniform who accompanied them was Nurse Proctor."

"You mean that you didn't take these women actually from the door of the house in Gillingham Street, but from somewhere adjacent?"

"Yes; they never take a cab from the door. They always walk to the corner of the street with a nurse, and a porter belonging to the house brings their luggage along."

"The idea is secrecy?"

"No doubt. But as I have said, the word was passed round."

"Did you know either of these other women?"

"No; but they were obviously members of good society."

"And you drove them?"

"One to St. Pancras, and one to Waterloo," said Brian, dropping back somewhat into his coarser style, and permitting a slow grin to overspread his countenance.

"To catch trains, no doubt?"

"Not a bit of it! To MEET trains!"

"You mean?"

"I mean that their own private cars were waiting for them at the ARRIVAL platform as I drove 'em up to the DEPARTURE platform, and that they simply marched through the station and pretended to have arrived by train!"

Inspector Dunbar took out his notebook and fountain-pen, and began to tap his teeth with the latter, nodding his head at the same time.

"You are sure of the accuracy of your last statement?" he said, raising his eyes to the other.

"I followed one of them," was the reply, "and saw her footman gravely take charge of the luggage which I had just brought from Victoria; and a pal of mine followed the other — the Waterloo one, that was."

Inspector Dunbar scribbled busily. Then: —

"You have done well to make a clean breast of it," he said. "Take a straight tip from me. Keep off the drink!"

X

THE GREAT UNDERSTANDING

It was in the afternoon of this same day — a day so momentous in the lives of more than one of London's millions — that two travelers might have been seen to descend from a first-class compartment of the Dover boat-train at Charing Cross.

They had been the sole occupants of the compartment, and, despite the wide dissimilarity of character to be read upon their countenances, seemed to have struck up an acquaintance based upon mutual amiability and worldly common sense. The traveler first to descend and gallantly to offer his hand to his companion in order to assist her to the platform, was the one whom a casual observer would first have noted.

He was a man built largely, but on good lines; a man past his youth, and somewhat too fleshy; but for all his bulk, there was nothing unwieldy, and nothing ungraceful in his bearing or carriage. He wore a French traveling-coat, conceived in a style violently Parisian, and composed of a wonderful check calculated to have blinded any cutter in Savile Row. From beneath its gorgeous folds protruded the extremities of severely creased cashmere trousers, turned up over white spats which nestled coyly about a pair of glossy black boots. The traveler's hat was of velour, silver gray and boasting a partridge feather thrust in its silken band. One glimpse of the outfit must have brought the entire staff of the Tailor and Cutter to an untimely grave.

But if ever man was born who could carry such a make-up, this traveler was he. The face was cut on massive lines, on fleshy lines, clean-shaven, and inclined to pallor. The hirsute blue tinge about the jaw and lips helped to accentuate the virile strength of the long, flexible mouth, which could be humorous, which could be sorrowful, which could be grim. In the dark eyes of the man lay a wealth of experience, acquired in a lifelong pilgrimage among many peoples, and to many lands. His dark brows were heavily marked, and his close-cut hair was splashed with gray.

Let us glance at the lady who accepted his white-gloved hand, and who sprang alertly onto the platform beside him.

She was a woman bordering on the forties, with a face of masculine vigor, redeemed and effeminized, by splendid hazel eyes, the kindliest imaginable. Obviously, the lady was one who had never married, who despised, or affected to despise, members of the other sex, but who had never learned to hate them; who had never grown soured, but who found the world a garden of heedless children — of children who called for mothering. Her athletic figure was clothed in a "sensible" tweed traveling dress, and she wore a tweed hat pressed well on to her head, and brown boots with the flattest heels conceivable. Add to this a Scotch woolen muffler, and a pair of woolen gloves, and you have a mental picture of the second traveler — a truly incongruous companion for the first.

Joining the crowd pouring in the direction of the exit gates, the two chatted together animatedly, both speaking English, and the man employing that language with a perfect ease and command of words which nevertheless failed to disguise his French nationality. He spoke with an American accent; a phenomenon sometimes observable in one who has learned his English in Paris.

The irritating formalities which beset the returning traveler — and the lady distinctly was of the readily irritated type — were smoothed away by the magic personality of her companion. Porters came at the beck of his gloved hand; guards, catching his eye, saluted and were completely his servants; ticket inspectors yielded to him the deference ordinarily reserved for directors of the line.

Outside the station, then, her luggage having been stacked upon a cab, the lady parted from her companion with assurances, which were returned, that she should hope to improve the acquaintance.

The address to which the French gentleman politely requested the cabman to drive, was that of a sound and old-established hotel in the neighborhood of the Strand, and at no great distance from the station.

Then, having stood bareheaded until the cab turned out into the traffic stream of that busy thoroughfare, the first traveler, whose baggage consisted of a large suitcase, hailed a second cab and drove to the Hotel Astoria — the usual objective of Americans.

Taking leave of him for the moment, let us follow the lady.

Her arrangements were very soon made at the hotel, and having removed some of the travel-stains from her person and partaken of one cup of China tea, respecting the quality whereof she delivered herself of some caustic comments, she walked down into the Strand and mounted to the top of a Victoria bound 'bus.

That she was not intimately acquainted with London, was a fact readily observable by her fellow passengers; for as the 'bus went rolling westward, from the large pocket of her Norfolk jacket she took out a guide-book provided with numerous maps, and began composedly to consult its complexities.

When the conductor came to collect her fare, she had made up her mind, and was replacing the guidebook in her pocket.

"Put me down by the Storis, Victoria Street, conductor," she directed, and handed him a penny — the correct fare.

It chanced that at about the time, within a minute or so, of the American lady's leaving the hotel, and just as red rays, the harbingers of dusk, came creeping in at the latticed widow of her cozy work-room, Helen Cumberly laid down her pen with a sigh. She stood up, mechanically rearranging her hair as she did so, and crossed the corridor to her bedroom, the window whereof overlooked the Square.

She peered down into the central garden. A common-looking man sat upon a bench, apparently watching the labors of the gardener, which consisted at the moment of the spiking of scraps of paper which disfigured the green carpet of the lawn.

Helen returned to her writing-table and reseated herself. Kindly twilight veiled her, and a chatty sparrow who perched upon the window-ledge pretended that he had not noticed two tears which trembled, quivering, upon the girl's lashes. Almost unconsciously, for it was an established custom, she sprinkled crumbs from the tea-tray beside her upon the ledge, whilst the tears dropped upon a written page and two more appeared in turn upon her lashes.

The sparrow supped enthusiastically, being joined in his repast by two talkative companions. As the last fragments dropped from the girl's white fingers, she withdrew her hand, and slowly — very slowly — her head sank down, pillowed upon her arms.

For some five minutes she cried silently; the sparrows, unheeded, bade her good night, and flew to their nests in the trees of the Square. Then, very resolutely, as if inspired by a settled purpose, she stood up and recrossed the corridor to her bedroom.

She turned on the lamp above the dressing-table and rapidly removed the traces of her tears, contemplating in dismay a redness of her pretty nose which did not prove entirely amenable to treatment with the powder-puff. Finally, however, she switched off the light, and, going out on to the landing, descended to the door of Henry Leroux's flat.

In reply to her ring, the maid, Ferris, opened the door. She wore her hat and coat, and beside her on the floor stood a tin trunk.

"Why, Ferris!" cried Helen —"are you leaving?"

"I am indeed, miss!" said the girl, independently.

"But why? whatever will Mr. Leroux do?"

"He'll have to do the best he can. Cook's goin' too!"

"What! cook is going?"

"I am!" announced a deep, female voice.

And the cook appeared beside the maid.

"But whatever —" began Helen; then, realizing that she could achieve no good end by such an attitude: "Tell Mr. Leroux," she instructed the maid, quietly, "that I wish to see him."

Ferris glanced rapidly at her companion, as a man appeared on the landing, to inquire in an abysmal tone, if "them boxes was ready to be took?" Helen Cumberly forestalled an insolent refusal which the cook, by furtive wink, counseled to the housemaid.

"Don't trouble," she said, with an easy dignity reminiscent of her father. "I will announce myself."

She passed the servants, crossed the lobby, and rapped upon the study door.

"Come in," said the voice of Henry Leroux.

Helen opened the door. The place was in semidarkness, objects being but dimly discernible. Leroux sat in his usual seat at the writing-table. The room was in the utmost disorder, evidently having received no attention since its overhauling by the police. Helen pressed the switch, lighting the two lamps.

Leroux, at last, seemed in his proper element: he exhibited an unhealthy pallor, and it was obvious that no razor had touched his chin for at least three days. His dark blue eyes the eyes of a dreamer — were heavy and dull, with shadows pooled below them. A biscuit-jar, a decanter and a syphon stood half buried in papers on the table.

"Why, Mr. Leroux!" said Helen, with a deep note of sympathy in her voice — "you don't mean to say"...

Leroux rose, forcing a smile to his haggard face.

"You see — much too good," he said. "Altogether — too good."...

"I thought I should find you here," continued the girl, firmly; "but I did not anticipate" — she indicated the chaos about — "this! The insolence, the disgraceful, ungrateful insolence, of those women!"

"Dear, dear, dear!" murmured Leroux, waving his hand vaguely; "never mind — never mind! They — er — they... I don't want them to stop... and, believe me, I am — er — perfectly comfortable!"

"You should not be in — THIS room, at all. In fact, you should go right away."...

"I cannot... my wife may — return — at any moment." His voice shook. "I — am expecting her return — hourly."...

His gaze sought the table-clock; and he drew his lips very tightly together when the pitiless hands forced upon his mind the fact that the day was marching to its end.

Helen turned her head aside, inhaling deeply, and striving for composure.

"Garnham shall come down and tidy up for you," she said, quietly; "and you must dine with us."

The outer door was noisily closed by the departing servants.

"You are much too good," whispered Leroux, again; and the weary eyes glistened with a sudden moisture. "Thank you! Thank you! But — er — I could not dream of disturbing"...

"Mr. Leroux," said Helen, with all her old firmness — "Garnham is coming down IMMEDIATELY to put the place in order! And, whilst he is doing so, you are going to prepare yourself for a decent, Christian dinner!"

Henry Leroux rested one hand upon the table, looking down at the carpet. He had known for a long time, in a vague fashion, that he lacked something; that his success — a wholly inartistic one — had yielded him little gratification; that the comfort of his home was a purely monetary product and not in any sense atmospheric. He had schooled himself to believe that he liked loneliness — loneliness physical and mental, and that in marrying a pretty, but pleasure-loving girl, he had insured an ideal menage. Furthermore, he honestly believed that he worshiped his wife; and with his present grief at her unaccountable silence was mingled no atom of reproach.

But latterly he had begun to wonder — in his peculiarly indefinite way he had begun to doubt his own philosophy. Was the void in his soul a product of thwarted ambition? — for, whilst he slaved, scrupulously, upon "Martin Zeda," he loathed every deed and every word of that Old Man of the Sea. Or could it be that his own being — his nature of Adam — lacked something which wealth, social position, and Mira, his wife, could not yield to him?

Now, a new tone in the voice of Helen Cumberly — a tone different from that compound of good-fellowship and raillery, which he knew — a tone which had entered into it when she had exclaimed upon the state of the room — set his poor, anxious heart thrumming like a lute. He felt a hot flush creeping upon him; his forehead grew damp. He feared to raise his eyes.

"Is that a bargain?" asked Helen, sweetly.

Henry Leroux found a lump in his throat; but he lifted his untidy head and took the hand which the girl had extended to him. She smiled a bit unnaturally; then every tinge of color faded from her cheeks, and Henry Leroux, unconsciously holding the white hand in a vice-like grip, looked hungrily into the eyes grown suddenly tragic whilst into his own came the light of a great and sorrowful understanding.

"God bless you," he said. "I will do anything you wish."

Helen released her hand, turned, and ran from the study. Not until she was on the landing did she dare to speak. Then: —

"Garnham shall come down immediately. Don't be late for dinner!" she called — and there was a hint of laughter and of tears in her voice, of the restraint of culture struggling with rebellious womanhood.

XI

PRESENTING M. GASTON MAX

Not venturing to turn on the light, not daring to look upon her own face in the mirror, Helen Cumberly sat before her dressing-table, trembling wildly. She wanted to laugh, and wanted to cry; but the daughter of Seton Cumberly knew what those symptoms meant and knew how to deal with them. At the end of an interval of some four or five minutes, she rang.

The maid opened the door.

"Don't light up, Merton," she said, composedly. "I want you to tell Garnham to go down to Mr. Leroux's and put the place in order. Mr. Leroux is dining with us."

The girl withdrew; and Helen, as the door closed, pressed the electric switch. She stared at her reflection in the mirror as if it were the face of an enemy, then, turning her head aside, sat deep in reflection, biting her lip and toying with the edge of the white doily.

"You little traitor!" she whispered, through clenched teeth. "You little traitor — and hypocrite" — sobs began to rise in her throat — "and fool!"

Five more minutes passed in a silent conflict. A knock announced the return of the maid; and the girl reentered, placing upon the table a visiting-card: —

DENISE RYLAND ATELIER 4, RUE DU COQ D'OR, MONTMARTRE, PARIS.

Helen Cumberly started to her feet with a stifled exclamation and turned to the maid; her face, to which the color slowly had been returning, suddenly blanched anew.

"Denise Ryland!" she muttered, still holding the card in her hand, "why — that's Mrs. Leroux's friend, with whom she had been staying in Paris! Whatever can it mean?"

"Shall I show her in here, please?" asked the maid.

"Yes, in here," replied Helen, absently; and, scarcely aware that she had given instructions to that effect, she presently found herself confronted by the lady of the boat-train!

"Miss Cumberly?" said the new arrival in a pleasant American voice.

"Yes — I am Helen Cumberly. Oh! I am so glad to know you at last! I have often pictured you; for Mira — Mrs. Leroux — is always talking about you, and about the glorious times you have together! I have sometimes longed to join you in beautiful Paris. How good of you to come back with her!"

Miss Ryland unrolled the Scotch muffler from her throat, swinging her head from side to side in a sort of spuriously truculent manner, quite peculiarly her own. Her keen hazel eyes were fixed upon the face of the girl before her. Instinctively and immediately she liked Helen Cumberly; and Helen felt that this strong-looking, vaguely masculine woman, was an old, intimate friend, although she had never before set eyes upon her.

"H'm!" said Miss Ryland. "I have come from Paris" — she punctuated many of her sentences with wags of the head as if carefully weighing her words — "especially" (pause) "to see you" (pause and wag of head) "I am glad... to find that... you are the thoroughly sensible... kind of girl that I... had imagined, from the accounts which... I have had of you."...

She seated herself in an armchair.

"Had of me from Mira?" asked Helen.

"Yes... from Mrs. Leroux."

"How delightful it must be for you to have her with you so often! Marriage, as a rule, puts an end to that particular sort of good-time, doesn't it?"

"It does... very properly... too. No MAN... no MAN in his ... right senses... would permit... his wife... to gad about in Paris with another... girl" (she presumably referred to herself) "whom HE had only met... casually... and did not like"...

"What! do you mean that Mr. Leroux doesn't like you? I can't believe that!"

"Then the sooner... you believe it... the better."

"It can only be that he does not know you, properly?"

"He has no wish... to know me... properly; and I have no desire... to cultivate... the... friendship of such... a silly being."

Helen Cumberly was conscious that a flush was rising from her face to her brow, and tingling in the very roots of her hair. She was indignant with herself and turned, aside, bending over her table in order to conceal this ill-timed embarrassment from her visitor.

"Poor Mr. Leroux!" she said, speaking very rapidly; "I think it awfully good of him, and sporty, to allow his wife so much liberty."

"Sporty!" said Miss Ryland, head wagging and nostrils distended in scorn. "Idi-otic…I should call it."

"Why?"

Helen Cumberly, perfectly composed again, raised her clear eyes to her visitor.

"You seem so…thoroughly sensible, except in regard to…Harry Leroux; — and ALL women, with a few…exceptions, are FOOLS where the true…character of a MAN is concerned — that I will take you right into my confidence."

Her speech lost its quality of syncopation; the whole expression of her face changed; and in the hazel eyes a deep concern might be read.

"My dear," she stood up, crossed to Helen's side, and rested her artistic looking hands upon the girl's shoulder. "Harry Leroux stands upon the brink of a great tragedy — a life's tragedy!"

Helen was trembling slightly again.

"Oh, I know!" she whispered — "I know —"

"You know?"

There was surprise in Miss Ryland's voice.

"Yes, I have seen them — watched them — and I know that the police think"…

"Police! What are you talking about — the police?"

Helen looked up with a troubled face.

"The murder!" she began…

Miss Ryland dropped into a chair which, fortunately, stood close behind her, with a face suddenly set in an expression of horror. She began to understand, now, a certain restraint, a certain ominous shadow, which she had perceived, or thought she had perceived, in the atmosphere of this home, and in the manner of its occupants.

"My dear girl," she began, and the old nervous, jerky manner showed itself again, momentarily, — "remember that…I left Paris by …the first train, this morning, and have simply been… traveling right up to the present moment."…

"Then you have not heard? You don't know that a — murder — has been committed?"

"MURDER! Not — not"…

"Not any one connected with Mr. Leroux; no, thank God! but it was done in his flat."…

Miss Ryland brushed a whisk of straight hair back from her brow with a rough and ungraceful movement.

"My dear," she began, taking a French telegraphic form from her pocket, "you see this message? It's one which reached me at an unearthly hour this morning from Harry Leroux. It was addressed to his wife at my studio; therefore, as her friend, I opened it. Mira Leroux has actually visited me there twice since her marriage —"

"Twice!" Helen rose slowly to her feet, with horrified eyes fixed upon the speaker.

"Twice I said! I have not seen her, and have rarely heard from her, for nearly twelve months, now! Therefore I packed up post-haste and here I am! I came to you, because, from what little I have heard of you, and of your father, I judged you to be the right kind of friends to consult."…

"You have not seen her for twelve months?"

Helen's voice was almost inaudible, and she was trembling dreadfully.

"That's a fact, my dear. And now, what are we going to tell Harry Leroux?"

It was a question, the answer to which was by no means evident at a glance; and leaving Helen Cumberly face to face with this new and horrible truth which had brought Denise Ryland hotfoot from Paris to London, let us glance, for a moment, into the now familiar room of Detective-Inspector Dunbar at Scotland Yard.

He had returned from his interrogation of Brian; and he received the report of Sowerby, respecting the late Mrs. Vernon's maid. The girl, Sergeant Sowerby declared, was innocent of complicity, and could only depose to the fact that her late mistress took very little luggage with her on the occasions of her trips to Scotland. With his notebook open before him upon the table, Dunbar was adding this slight item to his notes upon the case, when the door opened, and the uniformed constable entered, saluted, and placed an envelope in the Inspector's hand.

"From the commissioner!" said Sowerby, significantly.

With puzzled face, Dunbar opened the envelope and withdrew the commissioner's note. It was very brief: —

"M. Gaston Max, of the Paris Police, is joining you in the Palace Mansions murder case. You will cooperate with him from date above."

"MAX!" said Dunbar, gazing astoundedly at his subordinate.

Certainly it was a name which might well account for the amazement written upon the inspector's face; for it was the name of admittedly the greatest criminal investigator in Europe!

"What the devil has the case to do with the French police?" muttered Sowerby, his ruddy countenance exhibiting a whole history of wonderment.

The constable, who had withdrawn, now reappeared, knocking deferentially upon the door, throwing it open, and announcing:

"Mr. Gaston Max, to see Detective-Inspector Dunbar."

Bowing courteously upon the threshold, appeared a figure in a dazzling check traveling-coat — a figure very novel, and wholly unforgettable.

"I am honored to meet a distinguished London colleague," he said in perfect English, with a faint American accent.

Dunbar stepped across the room with outstretched hand, and cordially shook that of the famous Frenchman.

"I am the more honored," he declared, gallantly playing up to the other's courtesy. "This is Detective-Sergeant Sowerby, who is acting with me in the case."

M. Gaston Max bowed low in acknowledgment of the introduction.

"It is a pleasure to meet Detective-Sergeant Sowerby," he declared.

These polite overtures being concluded then, and the door being closed, the three detectives stood looking at one another in momentary silence. Then Dunbar spoke with blunt directness:

"I am very pleased to have you with us, Mr. Max," he said; "but might I ask what your presence in London means?"

M. Gaston Max shrugged in true Gallic fashion.

"It means, monsieur," he said, " — murder — and MR. KING!"

XII

MR. GIANAPOLIS

It will prove of interest at this place to avail ourselves of an opportunity denied to the police, and to inquire into the activities of Mr. Soames, whilom employee of Henry Leroux.

Luke Soames was a man of unpleasant character; a man ever seeking advancement — advancement to what he believed to be an ideal state, viz.: the possession of a competency; and to this ambition he subjugated all conflicting interests — especially the interests of others. From narrow but honest beginnings, he had developed along lines ever growing narrower until gradually honesty became squeezed out. He formed the opinion that wealth was unobtainable by dint of hard work; and indeed in a man of his limited intellectual attainments, this was no more than true.

At the period when he becomes of interest, he had just discovered himself a gentleman-at-large by reason of his dismissal from the services of a wealthy bachelor, to whose establishment in Piccadilly he had been attached in the capacity of valet. There was nothing definite against his character at this time, save that he had never remained for long in any one situation.

His experience was varied, if his references were limited; he had served not only as valet, but also as chauffeur, as steward on an ocean liner, and, for a limited period, as temporary butler in an American household at Nice.

Soames' banking account had increased steadily, but not at a rate commensurate with his ambitions; therefore, when entering his name and qualifications in the books of a certain exclusive employment agency in Mayfair he determined to avail himself, upon this occasion, of his comparative independence by waiting until kindly Fate should cast something really satisfactory in his path.

Such an opening occurred very shortly after his first visit to the agent. He received a card instructing him to call at the office in order to meet a certain Mr. Gianapolis. Quitting his rooms in Kennington, Mr. Soames, attired in discreet black, set out to make the acquaintance of his hypothetical employer.

He found Mr. Gianapolis to be a little and very swarthy man, who held his head so low as to convey the impression of having a pronounced stoop; a man whose well-cut clothes and immaculate linen could not redeem his appearance from a constitutional dirtiness. A jet black mustache, small, aquiline features, an engaging smile, and very dark brown eyes, viciously crossed, made up a personality incongruous with his sheltering silk hat, and calling aloud for a tarboosh and a linen suit, a shop in a bazaar, or a part in the campaign of commercial brigandage which, based in the Levant, spreads its ramifications throughout the Orient, Near and Far.

Mr. Gianapolis had the suave speech and smiling manner. He greeted Soames not as one greets a prospective servant, but as one welcomes an esteemed acquaintance. Following a brief chat, he proposed an adjournment to a neighboring saloon bar; and there, over cocktails, he conversed with Mr. Soames as one crook with another.

Soames was charmed, fascinated, yet vaguely horrified; for this man smilingly threw off the cloak of hypocrisy from his companion's shoulders, and pretended, with the skill of his race, equally to nudify his own villainy.

"My dear Mr. Soames!" he said, speaking almost perfect English, but with the sing-song intonation of the Greek, and giving all his syllables an equal value — "you are the man I am looking for; and I can make your fortune."

This was entirely in accordance with Mr. Soames' own views, and he nodded, respectfully.

"I know," continued Gianapolis, proffering an excellent Egyptian cigarette, "that you were cramped in your last situation — that you were misunderstood"...

Soames, cigarette in hand, suppressed a start, and wondered if he were turning pale. He selected a match with nervous care.

"The little matter of the silver spoons," continued Gianapolis, smiling fraternally, "was perhaps an error of judgment. Although" — patting the startled Soames upon the shoulder — "they were a legitimate perquisite; I am not blaming you. But it takes so long to accumulate a really useful balance in that petty way. Now" — he glanced cautiously about him — "I can offer you a post under conditions which will place you above the consideration of silver spoons!"

Soames, hastily finishing his cocktail, sought for words; but Gianapolis, finishing his own, blandly ordered two more, and, tapping Soames upon the knee, continued:

"Then that matter of the petty cash, and those trifling irregularities in the wine-bill, you remember? — when you were with Colonel Hewett in Nice?"...

Soames gripped the counter hard, staring at the newly arrived cocktail as though it were hypnotizing him.

"These little matters," added Gianapolis, appreciatively sipping from his own glass, "which would weigh heavily against your other references, in the event of their being mentioned to any prospective employer"...

Soames knew beyond doubt that his face was very pale indeed.

"These little matters, then," pursued Gianapolis, "all go to prove to ME that you are a man of enterprise and spirit — that you are the very man I require. Now I can offer you a post in the establishment of Mr. Henry Leroux, the novelist. The service will be easy. You will be required to attend to callers and to wait at table upon special occasions. There will be no valeting, and you will have undisputed charge of the pantry and wine-cellar. In short, you will enjoy unusual liberty. The salary, you would say? It will be the same as that which you received from Mr. Mapleson"...

Soames raised his head drearily; he felt himself in the toils; he felt himself a mined man.

"It isn't a salary," he began, "which"...

"My dear Mr. Soames," said Gianapolis, tapping him confidentially upon the knee again — "my dear Soames, it isn't the salary, I admit, which you enjoyed whilst in the services of Colonel Hewett in a similar capacity. But this is not a large establishment, and the duties are light. Furthermore, there will be — extras."

"Extras?"

Mr. Soames' eye brightened, and under the benignant influence of the cocktails his courage began to return.

"I do not refer," smiled Mr. Gianapolis, "to perquisites! The extras will be monetary. Another two pounds per week"...

"Two pounds!"

"Bringing your salary up to a nice round figure; the additional amount will be paid to you from another source. You will receive the latter payment quarterly"...

"From — from"...

"From me!" said Mr. Gianapolis, smiling radiantly. "Now, I know you are going to accept; that is understood between us. I will give you the address — Palace Mansions, Westminster — at which you must apply; and I will tell you what little services will be required from you in return for this additional emolument."

Mr. Soames hurriedly finished his second cocktail. Mr. Gianapolis, in true sporting fashion, kept pace with him and repeated the order.

"You will take charge of the mail!" he whispered softly, one irregular eye following the movements of the barmaid, and the other fixed almost fiercely upon the face of Soames. "At certain times — of which you will be notified in advance — Mrs. Leroux will pay visits to Paris. At such times, all letters addressed to her, or re-addressed to her, will not be posted! You will ring me up when such letters come into your possession — they must ALL come into your possession! — and I will arrange to meet you, say at the corner of Victoria Street, to receive them. You understand?"

Mr. Soames understood, and thus far found his plastic conscience marching in step with his inclinations.

"Then," resumed Gianapolis, "prior to her departure on these occasions, Mrs. Leroux will hand you a parcel. This also you will bring to me at the place arranged. Do you find anything onerous in these conditions?"

"Not at all," muttered Soames, a trifle unsteadily; "it seems all right" — the cocktails were beginning to speak now, and his voice was a duet — "simply perfectly all right — all square."

"Good!" said Mr. Gianapolis with his radiant smile; and the gaze of his left eye, crossing that of its neighbor, observed the entrance of a stranger into the bar. He drew his stool closer and lowered his voice:

"Mrs. Leroux," he continued, "will be in your confidence. Mr. Leroux and every one else — EVERY ONE else — must not suspect the arrangement"...

"Certainly — I quite understand"...

"Mrs. Leroux will engage you this afternoon — her husband is a mere cipher in the household — and you will commence your duties on Monday. Later in the week, Wednesday or Thursday, we will meet by appointment, and discuss further details."

"Where can I see you?"

"Ring up this number: 18642 East, and ask for Mr. King. No! don't write it down; remember it! I will come to the telephone, and arrange a meeting."

Shortly after this, then, the interview concluded; and later in the afternoon of that day Mr. Soames presented himself at Palace Mansions.

He was received by Mrs. Leroux — a pretty woman with a pathetically weak mouth. She had fair hair, not very abundant, and large eyes; which, since they exhibited the unusual phenomenon, in a blonde, of long dark lashes (Mr. Soames judged their blackness to be natural), would have been beautiful had they not been of too light a color, too small in the pupils, and utterly expressionless. Indeed, her whole face lacked color, as did her personality, and the exquisite tea-gown which she wore conveyed that odd impression of slovenliness, which is often an indication of secret vice. She was quite young and indisputably pretty, but this malproprete, together with a certain aimlessness of manner, struck an incongruous note; for essentially she was of a type which for its complement needs vivacity.

Mr. Soames, a man of experience, scented an intrigue and a neglectful husband. Since he was engaged on the spot without reference to the invisible Leroux, he was immediately confirmed in the latter part of his surmise. He departed well satisfied with his affairs, and with the promise of the future, over which Mr. Gianapolis, the cherubic, radiantly presided.

XIII
THE DRAFT ON PARIS

For close upon a month Soames performed the duties imposed upon him in the household of Henry Leroux. He was unable to discover, despite a careful course of inquiry from the cook and the housemaid, that Mrs. Leroux frequently absented herself. But the servants were newly engaged, for the flat in Palace Mansions had only recently been leased by the Leroux. He gathered that they had formerly lived much abroad, and that their marriage had taken place in Paris. Mrs. Leroux had been to visit a friend in the French capital once, he understood, since the housemaid had been in her employ.

The mistress (said the housemaid) did not care twopence-ha'penny for her husband; she had married him for his money, and for nothing else. She had had an earlier love (declared the cook) and was pining away to a mere shadow because of her painful memories. During the last six months (the period of the cook's service) Mrs. Leroux had altered out of all recognition. The cook was of opinion that she drank secretly.

Of Mr. Leroux, Soames formed the poorest opinion. He counted him a spiritless being, whose world was bounded by his book-shelves, and whose wife would be a fool if she did not avail herself of the liberty which his neglect invited her to enjoy. Soames felt himself, not a snake in the grass, but a benefactor — a friend in need — a champion come to the defense of an unhappy and persecuted woman.

He wondered when an opportunity should arise which would enable him to commence his chivalrous operations; almost daily he anticipated instructions to the effect that Mrs. Leroux would be leaving for Paris immediately. But the days glided by and the weeks glided by, without anything occurring to break the monotony of the Leroux household.

Mr. Soames sought an opportunity to express his respectful readiness to Mrs. Leroux; but the lady was rarely visible outside her own apartments until late in the day, when she would be engaged in preparing for the serious business of the evening: one night a dance, another, a bridge-party; so it went. Mr. Leroux rarely joined her upon these festive expeditions, but clung to his study like Diogenes to his tub.

Great was Mr. Soames' contempt; bitter were the reproaches of the cook; dark were the predictions of the housemaid.

At last, however, Soames, feeling himself neglected, seized an opportunity which offered to cement the secret bond (the TOO secret bond) existing between himself and the mistress of the house.

Meeting her one afternoon in the lobby, which she was crossing on the way from her bedroom to the drawing-room, he stood aside to let her pass, whispering:

"At your service, whenever you are ready, madam!"

It was a non-committal remark, which, if she chose to keep up the comedy, he could explain away by claiming it to refer to the summoning of the car from the garage — for Mrs. Leroux was driving out that afternoon.

She did not endeavor to evade the occult meaning of the words, however. In the wearily dreamy manner which, when first he had seen her, had aroused Soames' respectful interest, she raised her thin hand to her hair, slowly pressing it back from her brow, and directed her big eyes vacantly upon him.

"Yes, Soames," she said (her voice had a faraway quality in keeping with the rest of her personality), "Mr. King speaks well of you. But please do not refer again to" — she glanced in a manner at once furtive and sorrowful, in the direction of the study-door — "to the ... little arrangement of"...

She passed on, with the slow, gliding gait, which, together with her fragility, sometimes lent her an almost phantomesque appearance.

This was comforting, in its degree; since it proved that the smiling Gianapolis had in no way misled him (Soames). But as a man of business, Mr. Soames was not fully satisfied. He selected an evening when Mrs. Leroux was absent — and indeed she was absent almost every evening, for Leroux entertained but little. The cook and the housemaid were absent, also; therefore, to all intents and purposes, Soames had the flat to himself; since Henry Leroux counted in that establishment, not as an entity, but rather as a necessary, if unornamental, portion of the fittings.

Standing in the lobby, Soames raised the telephone receiver, and having paused with closed eyes preparing the exact form of words in which he should address his invisible employer, he gave the number: East 18642.

Following a brief delay: —

"Yes," came a nasal voice, "who is it?"

"Soames! I want to speak to Mr. King!"

The words apparently surprised the man at the other end of the wire, for he hesitated ere inquiring: —

"What did you say your name was?"

"Soames — Luke Soames."

"Hold on!"

Soames, with closed eyes, and holding the receiver to his ear, silently rehearsed again the exact wording of his speech. Then: —

"Hullo!" came another voice — "is that Mr. Soames?"

"Yes! Is that Mr. Gianapolis speaking?"

"It is, my dear Soames!" replied the sing-song voice; and Soames, closing his eyes again, had before him a mental picture of the radiantly smiling Greek.

"Yes, my dear Soames," continued Gianapolis; "here I am. I hope you are quite well — perfectly well?"

"I am perfectly well, thank you; but as a man of business, it has occurred to me that failing a proper agreement — which in this case I know would be impossible — a trifling advance on the first quarter's"...

"On your salary, my dear Soames! On your salary? Payment for the first quarter shall be made to you to-morrow, my dear Soames! Why ever did you not express the wish before? Certainly, certainly!"...

"Will it be sent to me?"

"My dear fellow! How absurd you are! Can you get out to-morrow evening about nine o'clock?"

"Yes, easily."

"Then I will meet you at the corner of Victoria Street, by the hotel, and hand you your first quarter's salary. Will that be satisfactory?"

"Perfectly," said Soames, his small eyes sparkling with avarice. "Most decidedly, Mr. Gianapolis. Many thanks."...

"And by the way," continued the other, "it is rather fortunate that you rang me up this evening, because it has saved me the trouble of ringing you up."

"What?" — Soames' eyes half closed, from the bottom lids upwards: — "there is something"...

"There is a trifling service which I require of you — yes, my dear Soames."

"Is it?"...

"We will discuss the matter to-morrow evening. Oh! it is a mere trifle. So good-by for the present."

Soames, with the fingers of his two hands interlocked before him, and his thumbs twirling rapidly around one another, stood in the lobby, gazing reflectively at the rug-strewn floor. He was working out in his mind how handsomely this first payment would show up on the welcome side of his passbook. Truly, he was fortunate in having met the generous Gianapolis....

He thought of a trifling indiscretion committed at the expense of one Mr. Mapleson, and of the wine-bill of Colonel Hewett; and he thought of the apparently clairvoyant knowledge of the Greek. A cloud momentarily came between his perceptive and the rosy horizon.

But nearer to the foreground of the mental picture, uprose a left-hand page of his pass book; and its tidings of great joy, written in clerkly hand, served to dispel the cloud.

Soames sighed in gentle rapture, and, soft-footed, passed into his own room.

Certainly his duties were neither difficult nor unpleasant. The mistress of the house lived apparently in a hazy dream-world of her own, and Mr. Leroux was the ultimate expression of the non-commercial. Mr. Soames could have robbed him every day had he desired to do so; but he had refrained from availing himself even of those perquisites which he considered justly his; for it was evident, to his limited intelligence, that greater profit was to be gained by establishing himself in this household than by weeding-out five shillings here, and half-a-sovereign there, at the risk of untimely dismissal.

Yet — it was a struggle! All Mr. Soames' commercial instincts were up in arms against this voice of a greater avarice which counseled abstention. For instance: he could have added half-a-sovereign a week to his earnings by means of a simple arrangement with the local wine merchant. Leroux's cigars he could have sold by the hundreds; for Leroux, when a friend called, would absently open a new box, entirely forgetful of the fact that a box from which but two — or at most three — cigars had been taken, lay already on the bureau.

Mr. Soames, in order to put his theories to the test, had temporarily abstracted half-a-dozen such boxes from the study and the dining-room and had hidden them. Leroux, finding, as he supposed, that he was out of cigars, had simply ordered Soames to get him some more.

"Er — about a dozen boxes — er — Soames," he had said; "of the same sort!"

Was ever a man of business submitted to such an ordeal? After receiving those instructions, Soames had sat for close upon an hour in his own room, contemplating the six broken boxes, containing in all some five hundred and ninety cigars; but the voice within prevailed; he must court no chance of losing his situation; therefore, he "discovered" these six boxes in a cupboard — much to Henry Leroux's surprise!

Then, Leroux regularly sent him to the Charing Cross branch of the London County and Suburban Bank with open checks! Sometimes, he would be sent to pay in, at other times to withdraw; the amounts involved varying from one guinea to 150 pounds! But, as he told himself, on almost every occasion that he went to Leroux's bank, he was deliberately throwing money away, deliberately closing his eyes to the good fortune which this careless and gullible man cast in his path. He observed a scrupulous honesty in all these dealings, with the result that the bank manager came to regard him as a valuable and trustworthy servant, and said as much to the assistant manager, expressing his wonder that Leroux — whose account occasioned the bank more anxiety, and gave it more work, than that of any other two depositors — had at last engaged a man who would keep his business affairs in order!

And these were but a few of the golden apples which Mr. Soames permitted to slip through his fingers, so steadfast was he in his belief that Gianapolis would be as good as his word, and make his fortune.

Leroux employed no secretary; and his MSS. were typed at his agent's office. A most slovenly man in all things, and in business matters especially, he was the despair, not only of his banker, but of his broker; he was a man who, in professional parlance, "deserved to be robbed." It is improbable that he had any but the haziest ideas, at any particular time, respecting the state of his bank balance and investments. He detested the writing of business letters, and was always at great pains to avoid anything in the nature of a commercial rendezvous. He would sign any document which his lawyer or his broker cared to send him, with simple, unquestioned faith.

His bank he never visited, and his appearance was entirely unfamiliar to the staff. True, the manager knew him slightly, having had two interviews with him: one when the account was opened, and the second when Leroux introduced his solicitor and broker — in order that in the future he might not be troubled in any way with business affairs.

Mr. Soames perceived more and more clearly that the mild deception projected was unlikely to be discovered by its victim; and, at the appointed time, he hastened to the corner of Victoria Street, to his appointment with Gianapolis. The latter was prompt, for Soames perceived his radiant smile afar off.

The saloon bar of the Red Lion was affably proposed by Mr. Gianapolis as a suitable spot to discuss the business. Soames agreed, not without certain inward qualms; for the proximity of the hostelry to New Scotland Yard was a disquieting circumstance.

However, since Gianapolis affected to treat their negotiations in the light of perfectly legitimate business, he put up no protest, and presently found himself seated in a very cozy corner of the saloon bar, with a glass of whisky-and-soda on a little table before him, bubbling in a manner which rendered it an agreeable and refreshing sight in the eyes of Mr. Soames.

"You know," said Gianapolis, the gaze of his left eye bisecting that of his right in a most bewildering manner, "they call this 'the 'tec's tabernacle!'"

"Indeed," said Soames, without enthusiasm; "I suppose some of the Scotland Yard men do drop in now and then?"

"Beyond doubt, my dear Soames."

Soames responded to his companion's radiant smile with a smile of his own by no means so pleasant to look upon. Soames had the type of face which, in repose, might be the face of an honest man; but his smile would have led to his instant arrest on any racecourse in Europe: it was the smile of a pick-pocket.

"Now," continued Gianapolis, "here is a quarter's salary in advance."

From a pocket-book, he took a little brown paper envelope and from the brown paper envelope counted out four five-pound notes, five golden sovereigns, one half-sovereign, and ten shillings' worth of silver. Soames' eyes glittered, delightedly.

"A little informal receipt?" smiled Gianapolis, raising his eyebrows, satanically. "Here on this page of my notebook I have written: 'Received from Mr. King for service rendered, 26 pounds, being payment, in advance, of amount due on 31st October 19 — ' I have attached a stamp to the page, as you will see," continued Gianapolis, "and here is a fountain-pen. Just sign across the stamp, adding to-day's date."

Soames complied with willing alacrity; and Gianapolis having carefully blotted the signature, replaced the notebook in his pocket, and politely acknowledged the return of the fountain-pen. Soames, glancing furtively about him, replaced the money in the envelope, and thrust the latter carefully into a trouser pocket.

"Now," resumed Gianapolis, "we must not permit our affairs of business to interfere with our amusements."

He stepped up to the bar and ordered two more whiskies with soda. These being sampled, business was resumed.

"To-morrow," said Gianapolis, leaning forward across the table so that his face almost touched that of his companion, "you will be entrusted by Mr. Leroux with a commission."...

Soames nodded eagerly, his eyes upon the speaker's face.

"You will accompany Mrs. Leroux to the bank," continued Gianapolis, "in order that she may write a specimen signature, in the presence of the manager, for transmission to the Credit Lyonnais in Paris."...

Soames nearly closed his little eyes in his effort to comprehend.

"A draft in her favor," continued the Greek, "has been purchased by Mr. Leroux's bank from the Paris bank, and, on presentation of this, a checkbook will be issued to Mrs. Leroux by the Credit Lyonnais in Paris to enable her to draw at her convenience upon that establishment against the said order. Do you follow me?"

Soames nodded rapidly, eager to exhibit an intelligent grasp of the situation.

"Now" — Gianapolis lowered his voice impressively — "no one at the Charing Cross branch of the London County and Suburban Bank has ever seen Mrs. Leroux! — Oh! we have been careful of that, and we shall be careful in the future. You are known already as an accredited agent of Leroux; therefore" — he bent yet closer to Soames' ear — "you will direct the chauffeur to drop you, not at the Strand entrance, but at the side entrance. You follow?"

Soames, almost holding his breath, nodded again.

"At the end of the court, in which the latter entrance is situated, a lady dressed in the same manner as Mrs. Leroux (this is arranged) will be waiting. Mrs. Leroux will walk straight up the court, into the corridor of Bank Chambers by the back entrance, and from thence out into the Strand. YOU will escort the second lady into the manager's office, and she will sign 'Mira Leroux' instead of the real Mira Leroux."...

Soames became aware that he was changing color. This was a superior felony, and as such it awed his little mind. It was tantamount to burning his boats. Missing silver spoons and cooked petty cash were trivialities usually expiable at the price of a boot-assisted dismissal; but this — !

"You understand?" Gianapolis was not smiling, now. "There is not the slightest danger. The signature of the lady whom you will meet will be an exact duplicate of the real one; that is, exact enough to deceive a man who is not looking for a forgery. But it would not be exact enough to deceive the French banker — he WILL be looking for a forgery. You follow me? The signature on the checks drawn against the Credit Lyonnais will be the SAME as the specimen forwarded by the London County and Suburban, since they will be written by the same lady — the duplicate Mrs. Leroux. Therefore, the French bank will have no means of detecting the harmless little deception practised upon them, and the English bank, if it should ever see those checks, will raise no question, since the checks will have been honored by the Credit Lyonnais."

Soames finished his whisky-and-soda at a gulp.

"Finally," concluded Gianapolis, "you will escort the lady out by the front entrance to the Strand. She will leave you and walk in an easterly direction — making some suitable excuse if the manager should insist upon seeing her to the door; and the real Mrs. Leroux will come out by the Strand end of Bank Chambers' corridor, and walk back with you around the corner to where the car will be waiting. Perfect?"

"Quite," said Soames, huskily....

But when, some twenty minutes later, he returned to Palace Mansions, he was a man lost in thought; and he did not entirely regain his wonted composure, and did not entirely shake off the incubus, Doubt, until in his own room he had re-counted the contents of the brown paper envelope. Then: —

"It's safe enough," he muttered; "and it's worth it!"

Thus it came about that, on the following morning, Leroux called him into the study and gave him just such instructions as Gianapolis had outlined the evening before.

"I am — er — too busy to go myself, Soames," said Leroux, "and — er — Mrs. Leroux will shortly be paying a visit to friends in — er — in Paris. So that I am opening a credit there for her. Save so much trouble — and — such a lot of — correspondence — international money orders — and such worrying things. Mr. Smith, the manager, knows you and you will take this letter of authority. The draft I understand has already been purchased."

Mr. Soames was bursting with anxiety to learn the amount of this draft, but could find no suitable opportunity to inquire. The astonishing deception, then, was carried out without anything resembling a hitch. Mrs. Leroux went through with her part in the comedy, in the dreamy manner of a somnambulist; and the duplicate Mrs. Leroux, who waited at the appointed spot, had achieved so startling a resemblance to her prototype, that Mr. Soames became conscious of a craving for a peg of brandy at the moment of setting eyes upon her. However, he braced himself up and saw the business through.

As was to be expected, no questions were raised and no doubts entertained. The bank manager was very courteous and very reserved, and the fictitious Mrs. Leroux equally reserved, indeed, cold. She avoided raising her motor veil, and, immediately the business was concluded, took her departure, Mr. Smith escorting her as far as the door.

She walked away toward Fleet Street, and the respectful attendant, Soames, toward Charing Cross; he rejoined Mrs. Leroux at the door of Bank Chambers, and the two turned the corner and entered the waiting car. Soames was rather nervous; Mrs. Leroux quite apathetic.

Shortly after this event, Soames learnt that the date of Mrs. Leroux's departure to Paris was definitely fixed. He received from her hands a large envelope.

"For Mr. King," she said, in her dreamy fashion; and he noticed that she seemed to be in poorer health than usual. Her mouth twitched strangely; she was a nervous wreck.

Then came her departure, attended by a certain bustle, an appointment with Mr. Gianapolis; and the delivery of the parcel into that gentleman's keeping.

Mrs. Leroux was away for six days on this occasion. Leroux sent her three postcards during that time, and re-addressed some ten or twelve letters which arrived for her. The address in all cases was:

> c/o Miss Denise Ryland,
>   Atelier 4, Rue du Coq d'Or,
>   Montmartre,
>   Paris.

East 18642 was much in demand that week; and there were numerous meetings between Soames and Gianapolis at the corner of Victoria Street, and numerous whiskies-and-sodas in the Red Lion; for Gianapolis persisted in his patronage of that establishment, apparently for no other reason than because it was dangerously near to Scotland Yard, and an occasional house of call for members of the Criminal Investigation Department.

Thus did Mr. Soames commence his career of duplicity at the flat of Henry Leroux; and for some twelve months before the events which so dramatically interfered with the delightful scheme, he drew his double salary and performed his perfidious work with great efficiency and contentment. Mrs. Leroux paid four other visits to Paris during that time, and always returned in much better spirits, although pale and somewhat haggard looking. It fell to the lot of Soames always to meet her at Charing Cross; but never once, by look or by word, did she proffer, or invite, the slightest exchange of confidence. She apathetically accepted his aid in conducting this intrigue as she would have accepted his aid in putting on her opera-cloak.

The curious Soames had read right through the telephone directory from A to Z in quest of East 18642 — only to learn that no such number was published. His ingenuity not being great, he could think of no means to learn the address of the mysterious Mr. King. So keenly had he been impressed with the omniscience of that shadowy being who knew all his past, that he feared to inquire of the Eastern Exchange. His banking account was growing handsomely, and, above all things, he dreaded to kill the goose that laid the golden eggs.

Then came the night which shattered all. Having rung up East 18642 and made an appointment with Gianapolis in regard to some letters for Mrs. Leroux, he had been surprised, on reaching the corner of Victoria Street, to find that Gianapolis was not there! He glanced up at the face of Big Ben. Yes — for the first time during their business acquaintance, Mr. Gianapolis was late!

For close upon twenty minutes, Soames waited, walking slowly up and down. When, at last, coming from the direction of Westminster, he saw the familiar spruce figure.

Eagerly he hurried forward to meet the Greek; but Gianapolis — to the horror and amazement of Soames — affected not to know him! He stepped aside to avoid the stupefied butler, and passed. But, in passing, he hissed these words at Soames: —

"Follow to Victoria Street Post Office! Pretend to post letters at next box to me and put them in my hand!"

He was gone!

Soames, dazed at this new state of affairs, followed him at a discreet distance. Gianapolis ran up the Post Office steps briskly, and Soames, immediately afterwards, ascended also — furtively. Gianapolis was taking out a number of letters from his pocket.

Soames walked across to the "Country" box on his right, and affected to scrutinize the addresses on the envelopes of Mrs. Leroux's correspondence.

Gianapolis, on the pretense of posting a country letter, reached out and snatched the correspondence from Soames' hand. The gaze of his left eye crookedly sought the face of the butler.

"Go home!" whispered Gianapolis; "be cautious!"

XIV
EAST 18642

In a pitiable state of mind, Soames walked away from the Post Office. Gianapolis had hurried off in the direction of Victoria Station. Something was wrong! Some part of the machine, of the dimly divined machine whereof he formed a cog, was out of gear. Since the very nature of this machine — its construction and purpose, alike — was unknown to Soames, he had no basis upon which to erect surmises for good or ill.

His timid inquiries into the identity of East 18642 had begun and terminated with his labored perusal of the telephone book, a profitless task which had occupied him for the greater part of an evening.

The name, Gianapolis, did not appear at all; whereas there proved to be some two hundred and ninety Kings. But, oddly, only four of these were on the Eastern Exchange; one was a veterinary surgeon; one a boat-builder; and a third a teacher of dancing. The fourth, an engineer, seemed a "possible" to Soames, although his published number was not 18642; but a brief — a very brief — conversation, convinced the butler that this was not his man.

He had been away from the flat for over an hour, and he doubted if even the lax sense of discipline possessed by Mr. Leroux would enable that gentleman to overlook this irregularity. Soames had a key of the outer door, and he built his hopes upon the possibility that Leroux had not noticed his absence and would not hear his return.

He opened the door very quietly, but had scarcely set his foot in the lobby ere the dreadful, unforgettable scene met his gaze.

For more years than he could remember, he had lived in dread of the law; and, in Luke Soames' philosophy, the words Satan and Detective were interchangeable. Now, before his eyes, was a palpable, unmistakable police officer; and on the floor...

Just one glimpse he permitted himself — and, in a voice that seemed to reach him from a vast distance, the detective was addressing HIM!...

Slinking to his room, with his craven heart missing every fourth beat, and his mind in chaos, Soames sank down upon the bed, locked his hands together and hugged them, convulsively, between his knees.

It was come! He had overstepped that almost invisible boundary-line which divides indiscretion from crime. He knew now that the voice within him, the voice which had warned him against Gianapolis and against becoming involved in what dimly he had perceived to be an elaborate scheme, had been, not the voice of cowardice (as he had supposed) but that of prudence.

And it was too late. The dead woman, he told himself — he had been unable to see her very clearly — undoubtedly was Mrs. Leroux. What in God's name had happened! Probably her husband had killed her...which meant? It meant that proofs — PROOFS — were come into his possession; and who should be involved, entangled in the meshes of this fallen conspiracy, but himself, Luke Soames!

As must be abundantly evident, Soames was not a criminal of the daring type; he did not believe in reaching out for anything until he was well assured that he could, if necessary, draw back his hand. This last venture, this regrettable venture — this ruinous venture — had been a mistake. He had entered into it under the glamour of Gianapolis' personality. Of what use, now, to him was his swelling bank balance?

But in justice to the mental capacity of Soames, it must be admitted that he had not entirely overlooked such a possibility as this; he had simply refrained, for the good of his health, from contemplating it.

Long before, he had observed, with interest, that, should an emergency arise (such as a fire), a means of egress had been placed by the kindly architect adjacent to his bedroom window. Thus, his departure on the night of the murder was not the fruit of a sudden scheme, but of one well matured.

Closing and locking his bedroom door, Soames threw out upon the bed the entire contents of his trunk; selected those things which he considered indispensable, and those which might constitute clues. He hastily packed his grip, and, with a last glance about the room and some seconds of breathless listening at the door, he attached to the handle a long piece of cord, which at some time had been tied about his trunk, and, gently opening the window, lowered the grip into the courtyard beneath. The light he had already extinguished, and with the conviction dwelling in his bosom that in some way he was become accessory to a murder — that he was a man shortly to be pursued by the police of the civilized world — he descended the skeleton lift-shaft, picked up his grip, and passed out under the archway into the lane at the back of Palace Mansions and St. Andrew's Mansions.

He did not proceed in the direction which would have brought him out into the Square, but elected to emerge through the other end. At exactly the moment that Inspector Dunbar rushed into his vacated room, Mr. Soames, grip in hand, was mounting to the top of a southward bound 'bus at the corner of Parliament Street!

He was conscious of a need for reflection. He longed to sit in some secluded spot in order to think. At present, his brain was a mere whirligig, and all things about him seemingly danced to the same tune. Stationary objects were become unstable in the eyes of Soames, and the solid earth, burst free of its moorings, no longer afforded him a safe foothold. There was a humming in his ears; and a mist floated before his eyes. By the time that the motor-'bus was come to the south side of the bridge, Soames had succeeded in slowing down his mental roundabout in some degree; and now he began grasping at the flying ideas which the diminishing violence of his brain storm enabled him, vaguely, to perceive.

The first fruits of his reflections were bitter. He viewed the events of the night in truer focus; he saw that by his flight he had sealed his fate — had voluntarily outlawed himself. It became frightfully evident to him that he dared not seek to draw from his bank, that he dared not touch even his modest Post Office account. With the exception of some twenty-five shillings in his pocket, he was penniless!

How could he hope to fly the country, or even to hide himself, without money?

He glanced suspiciously about the 'bus; for he perceived that an old instinct had prompted him to mount one which passed the Oval — a former point of debarkation when he lived in rooms near Kennington Park. Someone might recognize him!

Furtively, he scanned his fellow passengers, but perceived no acquaintance.

What should he do — where should he go? It was a desperate situation.

The inspector who had cared to study that furtive, isolated figure, could not have failed to mark it for that of a hunted man.

At Kennington Gate the 'bus made a halt. Soames glanced at the clock on the corner. It was close upon one A. M. Where in heaven's name should he go? What a fool he had been to come to this district where he was known!

Stay! There was one man in London, surely, who must be almost as keenly interested in the fate of Luke Soames as Luke Soames himself ... Gianapolis!

Soames sprang up and hurried off the 'bus. No public telephone box would be available at that hour, but dire need spurred his slow mind and also lent him assurance. He entered the office of the taxicab depot on the next corner, and, from the man whom he found in charge, solicited and obtained the favor of using the telephone. Lifting the receiver, he asked for East 18642.

The seconds that elapsed, now, were as hours of deathly suspense to the man at the telephone. If the number should be engaged!...If the exchange could get no reply!...

"Hullo!" said a nasal voice — "who is it?"

"It is Soames — and I want to speak to Mr. King!"

He lowered his tone as much as possible, almost whispering his own name. He knew the voice which had answered him; it was the same that he always heard when ringing up East 18642. But would Gianapolis come to the telephone? Suddenly —

"Is that Soames?" spoke the sing-song voice of the Greek.

"Yes, yes!"

"Where are you?"

"At Kennington."

"Are they following you?"

"No — I don't think so, at least; what am I to do? Where am I to go?"

"Get to Globe Road — near Stratford Bridge, East, without delay. But whatever you do, see that you are not followed! Globe Road is the turning immediately beyond the Railway Station. It is not too late, perhaps, to get a 'bus or tram, for some part of the way, at any rate. But even if the last is gone, don't take a cab; walk. When you get to Globe Road, pass down on the left-hand side, and, if necessary, right to the end. Make sure you are not followed, then walk back again. You will receive a signal from an open door. Come right in. Good-by."

Soames replaced the receiver on the hook, uttering a long-drawn sigh of relief. The arbiter of his fortunes had not failed him!

"Thank you very much!" he said to the man in charge of the office, who had been bending over his books and apparently taking not the slightest interest in the telephone conversation. Soames placed twopence, the price of the call, on the desk. "Good night."

"Good night."

He hastened out of the gate and across the road. An electric tramcar which would bear him as far as the Elephant-and-Castle was on the point of starting from the corner. Grip in hand, Soames boarded the car and mounted to the top deck. He was in some doubt respecting his mode of travel from the next point onward, but the night was fine, even if he had to walk, and his reviving spirits would cheer him with visions of a golden future!

His money! — That indeed was a bitter draught: the loss of his hardly earned savings! But he was now established — linked by a common secret — in partnership with Gianapolis; he was one of that mysterious, obviously wealthy group which arranged drafts on Paris — which could afford to pay him some hundreds of pounds per annum for such a trifling service as juggling the mail!

Mr. King! — If Gianapolis were only the servant, what a magnificent man of business must be hidden beneath the cognomen, Mr. King! And he was about to meet that lord of mystery. Fear and curiosity were oddly blended in the anticipation.

By great good fortune, Soames arrived at the Elephant-and-Castle in time to catch an eastward bound motor-'bus, a 'bus which would actually carry him to the end of Globe Road. He took his seat on top, and with greater composure than he had known since his dramatic meeting with Gianapolis in Victoria Street, lighted one of Mr. Leroux's cabanas (with which he invariably kept his case filled) and settled down to think about the future.

His reflections served apparently to shorten the journey; and Soames found himself proceeding along Globe Road — a dark and uninviting highway — almost before he realized that London Bridge had been traversed. It was now long past one o'clock; and that part of the east-end showed dreary and deserted. Public houses had long since ejected their late guests, and even those argumentative groups, which, after closing-time, linger on the pavements, within the odor Bacchanalian, were dispersed. The jauntiness was gone, now, from Soames' manner, and aware of a marked internal depression, he passed furtively along the pavement with its long shadowy reaches between the islands of light formed by the street lamps. From patch to patch he passed, and each successive lamp that looked down upon him found him more furtive, more bent in his carriage.

Not a shop nor a house exhibited any light. Sleeping Globe Road, East, served to extinguish the last poor spark of courage within Soames' bosom. He came to the extreme end of the road without having perceived a beckoning hand, without having detected a sound to reveal that his advent was observed. In the shadow of a wall he stopped, resting his grip upon the pavement and looking back upon his tracks.

No living thing moved from end to end of Globe Road.

Shivering slightly, Soames picked up the bag and began to walk back. Less than half-way along, an icy chill entered into his veins, and his nerves quivered like piano wires, for a soft crying of his name came, eerie, through the silence, and terrified the hearer.

"SOAMES!... SOAMES!"...

Soames stopped dead, breathing very rapidly, and looking about him right and left. He could hear the muted pulse of sleeping London. Then, in the dark doorway of the house before which he stood, he perceived, dimly, a motionless figure. His first sensation was not of relief, but of fear. The figure raised a beckoning hand. Soames, conscious that his course was set and that he must navigate it accordingly, opened the iron gate, passed up the path and entered the house to which he thus had been summoned....

He found himself surrounded by absolute darkness, and the door was closed behind him.

"Straight ahead, Soames!" said the familiar voice of Gianapolis out of the darkness.

Soames, with a gasp of relief, staggered on. A hand rested upon his shoulder, and he was guided into a room on the right of the passage. Then an electric lamp was lighted, and he found himself confronting the Greek.

But Gianapolis was no longer radiant; all the innate evil of the man shone out through the smirking mask.

"Sit down, Soames!" he directed.

Soames, placing his bag upon the floor, seated himself in a cane armchair. The room was cheaply furnished as an office, with a roll-top desk, a revolving chair, and a filing cabinet. On a side-table stood a typewriter, and about the room were several other chairs, whilst the floor was covered with cheap linoleum. Gianapolis sat in the revolving chair, staring at the lowered blinds of the window, and brushing up the points of his black mustache.

With a fine white silk handkerchief Soames gently wiped the perspiration from his forehead and from the lining of his hat-band. Gianapolis began abruptly: —

"There has been an — accident" (he continued to brush his mustache, with increasing rapidity). "Tell me all that took place after you left the Post Office."

Soames nervously related his painful experiences of the evening, whilst Gianapolis drilled his mustache to a satanic angle. The story being concluded:

"Whatever has happened?" groaned Soames; "and what am I to do?"

"What you are to do," replied Gianapolis, "will be arranged, my dear Soames, by — Mr. King. Where you are to go, is a problem shortly settled: you are to go nowhere; you are to stay here."...

"Here!"

Soames gazed drearily about the room.

"Not exactly here — this is merely the office; but at our establishment proper in Limehouse."...

"Limehouse!"

"Certainly. Although you seem to be unaware of the fact, Soames, there are some charming resorts in Limehouse; and your duties, for the present, will confine you to one of them."

"But — but," hesitated Soames, "the police"...

"Unless my information is at fault," said Gianapolis, "the police have no greater chance of paying us a visit, now, than they had formerly."...

"But Mrs. Leroux"...

"Mrs. Leroux!"

Gianapolis twirled around in the chair, his eyes squinting demoniacally: — "Mrs. Leroux!"

"She — she"...

"What about Mrs. Leroux?"

"Isn't she dead?"

"Dead! Mrs. Leroux! You are laboring under a strange delusion, Soames. The lady whom you saw was not Mrs. Leroux."

Soames' brain began to fail him again.

"Then who," he began....

"That doesn't concern you in the least, Soames. But what does concern you is this: your connection, and my connection, with the matter cannot possibly be established by the police. The incident is regrettable, but the emergency was dealt with — in time. It represents a serious deficit, unfortunately, and your own usefulness, for the moment, becomes nil; but we shall have to look after you, I suppose, and hope for better things in the future."

He took up the telephone.

"East 39951," he said, whilst Soames listened, attentively. Then: —

"Is that Kan-Suh Concessions?" he asked. "Yes — good! Tell Said to bring the car past the end of the road at a quarter-to-two. That's all."

He hung up the receiver.

"Now, my dear Soames," he said, with a faint return to his old manner, "you are about to enter upon new duties. I will make your position clear to you. Whilst you do your work, and keep yourself to yourself, you are in no danger; but one indiscretion — just one — apart from what it may mean for others, will mean, for YOU, immediate arrest as accessory to a murder!"

Soames shuddered, coldly.

"You can rely upon me, Mr. Gianapolis," he protested, "to do absolutely what you wish — absolutely. I am a ruined man, and I know it — I know it. My only hope is that you will give me a chance."...

"You shall have every chance, Soames," replied Gianapolis — "every chance."

XV

CAVE OF THE GOLDEN DRAGON

When the car stopped at the end of a short drive, Soames had not the slightest idea of his whereabouts. The blinds at the window of the limousine had been lowered during the whole journey, and now he descended from the step of the car on to the step of a doorway. He was in some kind of roofed-in courtyard, only illuminated by the headlamps of the car. Mr. Gianapolis pushed him forward, and, as the door was closed, he heard the gear of the car reversed; then — silence fell.

"My grip!" he began, nervously.

"It will be placed in your room, Soames."

The voice of the Greek answered him from the darkness.

Guided by the hand of Gianapolis, he passed on and descended a flight of stone steps. Ahead of him a light shone out beneath a door, and, as he stumbled on the steps, the door was thrown suddenly open.

He found himself looking into a long, narrow apartment.... He pulled up short with a smothered, gasping cry.

It was a cavern! — but a cavern the like of which he had never seen, never imagined. The walls had the appearance of being rough-hewn from virgin rock — from black rock — from rock black as the rocks of Shellal — black as the gates of Erebus.

Placed at regular intervals along the frowning walls, to right and left, were spiral, slender pillars, gilded and gleaming. They supported an archwork of fancifully carven wood, which curved gently outward to the center of the ceiling, forming, by conjunction with a similar, opposite curve, a pointed arch.

In niches of the wall were a number of grotesque Chinese idols. The floor was jet black and polished like ebony. Several tiger-skin rugs were strewn about it. But, dominating the strange place, in the center of the floor stood an ivory pedestal, supporting a golden dragon of exquisite workmanship; and before it, as before a shrine, an enormous Chinese vase was placed, of the hue, at its base, of deepest violet, fading, upward, through all the shades of rose pink seen in an Egyptian sunset, to a tint more elusive than a maiden's blush. It contained a mass of exotic poppies of every shade conceivable, from purple so dark as to seem black, to poppies of the whiteness of snow.

Just within the door, and immediately in front of Soames, stood a slim man of about his own height, dressed with great nicety in a perfectly fitting morning-coat, his well-cut cashmere trousers falling accurately over glossy boots having gray suede uppers. His linen was immaculate, and he wore a fine pearl in his black poplin cravat. Between two yellow fingers smoldered a cigarette.

Soames, unconsciously, clenched his fists: this slim man embodied the very spirit of the outre. The fantastic surroundings melted from the ken of Soames, and he seemed to stand in a shadow-world, alone with an incarnate shadow.

For this was a Chinaman! His jet black lusterless hair was not shaven in the national manner, but worn long, and brushed back from his slanting brow with no parting, so that it fell about his white collar behind, lankly. He wore gold-rimmed spectacles, which magnified his oblique eyes and lent him a terrifying beetle-like appearance. His mephistophelean eyebrows were raised interrogatively, and he was smiling so as to exhibit a row of uneven yellow teeth.

Soames, his amazement giving place to reasonless terror, fell back a step — into the arms of Gianapolis.

"This is our friend from Palace Mansions," said the Greek. He squeezed Soames' arm, reassuringly. "Your new principal, Soames, Mr. Ho-Pin, from whom you will take your instructions."

"I have these instructions for Mr. Soames," said Ho-Pin, in a metallic, monotonous voice. (He gave to r half the value of w, with a hint of the presence of l.) "He will wremain here as valet until the search fowr him becomes less wrigowrous."

Soames, scarce believing that he was awake, made no reply. He found himself unable to meet the glittering eyes of the Chinaman; he glanced furtively about the room, prepared at any moment to wake up from what seemed to him an absurd, a ghostly dream.

"Said will change his appeawrance," continued Ho-Pin, smoothly, "so that he will not wreadily be wrecognized. Said will come now."

Ho-Pin clapped his hands three times.

The door at the end of the room immediately opened, and a thick-set man of a pronounced Arabian type, entered. He wore a chauffeur's livery of dark blue; and Soames recognized him for the man who had driven the car.

"Said," said Ho-Pin very deliberately, turning to face the new arrival, "ahu hina — Lucas Effendi — Mr. Lucas. Waddi el — shenta ila beta oda. Fehimt?"

Said bowed his head.

"Fahim, effendi," he muttered rapidly.

"Ma fihsh."…

Again Said bowed his head, then, glancing at Soames: —

"Ta'ala wayyaya!" he said.

Soames, looking helplessly at Gianapolis — who merely pointed to the door — followed Said from the room.

He was conducted along a wide passage, thickly carpeted and having its walls covered with a kind of matting kept in place by strips of bamboo. Its roof was similarly concealed. A door near to the end, and on the right, proved to open into a square room quite simply furnished in the manner of a bed-sitting room. A little bathroom opened out of it in one corner. The walls were distempered white, and there was no window. Light was furnished by an electric lamp, hanging from the center of the ceiling.

Soames, glancing at his bag, which Said had just placed beside the white-enameled bedstead, turned to his impassive guide.

"This is a funny go!" he began, with forced geniality. "Am I to live here?"

"Ma'lesh!" muttered Said — "ma'lesh!"

He indicated, by gestures, that Soames should remove his collar; he was markedly unemotional. He crossed to the bathroom, and could be heard filling the hand-basin with water.

"Kursi!" he called from within.

Soames, seriously doubting his own sanity, and so obsessed with a sense of the unreal that his senses were benumbed, began to take off his collar; he could not feel the contact of his fingers with his neck in the act. Collarless, he entered the little bathroom.…

"Kursi!" repeated Said; then: "Ah! ana nesit! ma'lesh!"

Said — whilst Soames, docile in his stupor, watched him — went back, picked up the solitary cane chair which the apartment boasted, and brought it into the bathroom. Soames perceived that he was to be treated to something in the nature of a shampoo; for Said had ranged a number of bottles, a cake of soap, and several towels, along a shelf over the bath.

In a curious state of passivity, Soames submitted to the operation. His hair was vigorously toweled, then fanned in the most approved fashion; but this was no more than the beginning of the operation. As he leaned back in the chair:

"Am I dreaming?" he said aloud. "What's all this about?"

"Uskut!" muttered Said — "Uskut!"

Soames, at no time an aggressive character, resigned himself to the incredible.

Some lotion, which tingled slightly upon the scalp, was next applied by Said from a long-necked bottle. Then, fresh water having been poured into the basin, a dark purple liquid was added, and Soames' head dipped therein by the operating Eastern. This time no rubbing followed, but after some minutes of vigorous fanning, he was thrust back into the chair, and a dry towel tucked firmly into his collar-band. He anticipated that he was about to be shaved, and in this was not disappointed.

Said, filling a shaving-mug from the hot-water tap, lathered Soames' chin and the abbreviated whiskers upon which he had prided himself. Then the razor was skilfully handled, and Soames' face shaved until his chin was as smooth as satin.

Next, a dark brown solution was rubbed over the skin, and even upon his forehead and right into the roots of the hair; upon his throat, his ears, and the back of his neck. He was now past the putting of questions or the raising of protest; he was as clay in the hands of the silent

Oriental. Having fanned his wet face again for some time, Said, breaking the long silence, muttered:

"Ikfil'iyyun!"

Soames stared. Said indicated, by pantomime, that he desired him to close his eyes, and Soames obeyed mechanically. Thereupon the Oriental busied himself with the ex-butler's not very abundant lashes for five minutes or more. Then the busy fingers were at work with his inadequate eyebrows: finally: —

"Khalas!" muttered Said, tapping him on the shoulder.

Soames wearily opened his eyes, wondering if his strange martyrdom were nearly at its end. He discovered his hair to be still rather damp, but, since it was sparse, it was rapidly drying. His eyes smarted painfully.

Removing all trace of his operations, Said, with no word of farewell, took up his towels, bottles and other paraphernalia and departed.

Soames watched the retreating figure crossing the outer room, but did not rise from the chair until the door had closed behind Said. Then, feeling strangely like a man who has drunk too heavily, he stood up and walked into the bedroom. There was a small shaving-glass upon the chest-of-drawers, and to this he advanced, filled with the wildest apprehensions.

One glance he ventured, and started back with a groan.

His apprehensions had fallen short of the reality. With one hand clutching the bedrail, he stood there swaying from side to side, and striving to screw up his courage to the point whereat he might venture upon a second glance in the mirror. At last he succeeded, looking long and pitifully.

"Oh, Lord!" he groaned, "what a guy!"

Beyond doubt he was strangely changed. By nature, Luke Soames had hair of a sandy color; now it was of so dark a brown as to seem black in the lamplight. His thin eyebrows and scanty lashes were naturally almost colorless; but they were become those of a pronounced brunette. He was of pale complexion, but to-night had the face of a mulatto, or of one long in tropical regions. In short, he was another man — a man whom he detested at first sight!

This was the price, or perhaps only part of the price, of his indiscretion. Mr. Soames was become Mr. Lucas. Clutching the top of the chest-of-drawers with both hands, he glared at his own reflection, dazedly.

In that pose, he was interrupted. Said, silently opening the door behind him, muttered:

"Ta'ala wayyaya!"

Soames whirled around in a sudden panic, his heart leaping madly. The immobile brown face peered in at the door.

"Ta'ala wayyaya!" repeated Said, his face expressionless as a mask. He pointed along the corridor. "Ho-Pin Effendi!" he explained.

Soames, raising his hands to his collarless neck, made a swallowing noise, and would have spoken; but:

"Ta'ala wayyaya!" reiterated the Oriental.

Soames hesitated no more. Reentering the corridor, with its straw-matting walls, he made a curious discovery. Away to the left it terminated in a blank, matting-covered wall. There was no indication of the door by which he had entered it. Glancing hurriedly to the right, he failed also to perceive any door there. The bespectacled Ho-Pin stood halfway along the passage, awaiting him. Following Said in that direction, Soames was greeted with the announcement:

"Mr. King will see you."

The words taught Soames that his capacity for emotion was by no means exhausted. His endless conjectures respecting the mysterious Mr. King were at last to be replaced by facts; he was to see him, to speak with him. He knew now that it was a fearful privilege which gladly he would have denied himself.

Ho-Pin opened a door almost immediately behind him, a door the existence of which had not hitherto been evident to Soames. Beyond, was a dark passage.

"You will follow me, closely," said Ho-Pin with one of his piercing glances.

Soames, finding his legs none too steady, entered the passage behind Ho-Pin. As he did so, the door was closed by Said, and he found himself in absolute darkness.

"Keep close behind me," directed the metallic voice.

Soames could not see the speaker, since no ray of light penetrated into the passage. He stretched out a groping hand, and, although he was conscious of an odd revulsion, touched the shoulder of the man in front of him and maintained that unpleasant contact whilst they walked on and on through apparently endless passages, extensive as a catacomb. Many corners they turned; they turned to the right, they turned to the left. Soames was hopelessly bewildered. Then, suddenly, Ho-Pin stopped.

"Stand still," he said.

Soames became vaguely aware that a door was being closed somewhere near to him. A lamp lighted up directly over his head... he found himself in a small library!

Its four walls were covered with book-shelves from floor to ceiling, and the shelves were packed to overflowing with books in most unusual and bizarre bindings. A red carpet was on the floor and a red-shaded lamp hung from the ceiling, which was conventionally white-washed. Although there was no fireplace, the room was immoderately hot, and heavy with the perfume of roses. On three little tables were great bowls filled with roses, and there were other bowls containing roses in gaps between the books on the open shelves.

A tall screen of beautifully carved sandalwood masked one corner of the room, but beyond it protruded the end of a heavy writing-table upon which lay some loose papers, and, standing amid them, an enormous silver rose-bowl, brimming with sulphur-colored blooms.

Soames, obeying a primary instinct, turned, as the light leaped into being, to seek the door by which he had entered. As he did so, the former doubts of his own sanity returned with renewed vigor.

The book-lined wall behind him was unbroken by any opening.

Slowly, as a man awaking from a stupor, Soames gazed around the library.

It contained no door.

He rested his hand upon one of the shelves and closed his eyes. Beyond doubt he was going mad! The tragic events of that night had proved too much for him; he had never disguised from himself the fact that his mental capacity was not of the greatest. He was assured, now, that his brain had lost its balance shortly after his flight from Palace Mansions, and that the events of the past two hours had been phantasmal. He would presently return to sanity (or, blasphemously, he dared to petition heaven that he would) and find himself...? Perhaps in the hands of the police!

"Oh, God!" he groaned — "Oh, God!"

He opened his eyes...

A woman stood before the sandalwood screen! She had the pallidly dusky skin of a Eurasian, but, by virtue of nature or artifice, her cheeks wore a peachlike bloom. Her features were flawless in their chiseling, save for the slightly distended nostrils, and her black eyes were magnificent.

She was divinely petite, slender and girlish; but there was that in the lines of her figure, so seductively defined by her clinging Chinese dress, in the poise of her small head, with the blush rose nestling amid the black hair — above all in the smile of her full red lips — which discounted the youth of her body; which whispered "Mine is a soul old in strange sins — a soul for whom dead Alexandria had no secrets, that learnt nothing of Athenean Thais and might have tutored Messalina"...

In her fanciful robe of old gold, with her tiny feet shod in ridiculously small, gilt slippers, she stood by the screen watching the stupefied man — an exquisite, fragrantly youthful casket of ancient, unnameable evils.

"Good evening, Soames!" she said, stumbling quaintly with her English, but speaking in a voice musical as a silver bell. "You will here be known as Lucas. Mr. King he wishing me to say that you to receive two pounds, at each week."...

Soames, glassy-eyed, stood watching her. A horror, the horror of insanity, had descended upon him — a clammy, rose-scented mantle. The room, the incredible, book-lined room, was a red blur, surrounding the black, taunting eyes of the Eurasian. Everything was out of focus; past, present, and future were merged into a red, rose-haunted nothingness...

"You will attend to Block A," resumed the girl, pointing at him with a little fan. "You will also attend to the gentlemen."...

She laughed softly, revealing tiny white teeth; then paused, head tilted coquettishly, and appeared to be listening to someone's conversation — to the words of some person seated behind the screen. This fact broke in upon Soames' disordered mind and confirmed him in his opinion that he was a man demented. For only one slight sound broke the silence of the room. The red carpet below the little tables was littered with rose petals, and, in the super-heated atmosphere, other petals kept falling — softly, with a gentle rustling. Just that sound there was...and no other. Then:

"Mr. King he wishing to point out to you," said the girl, "that he hold receipts of you, which bind you to him. So you will be free man, and have liberty to go out sometimes for your own business. Mr. King he wishing to hear you say you thinking to agree with the conditions and be satisfied."

She ceased speaking, but continued to smile; and so complete was the stillness, that Soames, whose sense of hearing had become nervously stimulated, heard a solitary rose petal fall upon the corner of the writing-table.

"I...agree," he whispered huskily; "and...I am...satisfied."

He looked at the carven screen as a lost soul might look at the gate of Hades; he felt now that if a sound should come from beyond it he would shriek out, he would stop up his ears; that if the figure of the Unseen should become visible, he must die at the first glimpse of it.

The little brown girl was repeating the uncanny business of listening to that voice of silence; and Soames knew that he could not sustain his part in this eerie comedy for another half-minute without breaking out into hysterical laughter. Then:

"Mr. King he releasing you for to-night," announced the silver bell voice.

The light went out.

Soames uttered a groan of terror, followed by a short, bubbling laugh, but was seized firmly by the arm and led on into the blackness — on through the solid, book-laden walls, presumably; and on — on — on, along those interminable passages by which he had come. Here the air was cooler, and the odor of roses no longer perceptible, no longer stifling him, no longer assailing his nostrils, not as an odor of sweetness, but as a perfume utterly damnable and unholy.

With his knees trembling at every step, he marched on, firmly supported by his unseen companion.

"Stop!" directed a metallic, guttural voice.

Soames pulled up, and leaned weakly against the wall. He heard the clap of hands close behind him; and a door opened within twelve inches of the spot whereat he stood.

He tottered out into the matting-lined corridor from which he had started upon that nightmare journey; Ho-Pin appeared at his elbow, but no door appeared behind Ho-Pin!

"This is your wroom," said the Chinaman, revealing his yellow teeth in a mirthless smile.

He walked across the corridor, threw open a door — a real, palpable door...and there was Soames' little white room!

Soames staggered across, for it seemed a veritable haven of refuge — entered, and dropped upon the bed. He seemed to see the rose-petals fall — fall — falling in that red room in the labyrinth — the room that had no door; he seemed to see the laughing eyes of the beautiful Eurasian.

"Good night!" came the metallic voice of Ho-Pin.

The light in the corridor went out.

XVI
HO-PIN'S CATACOMBS

The newly-created Mr. Lucas entered upon a sort of cave-man existence in this fantastic abode where night was day and day was night; where the sun never shone.

He was awakened on the first morning of his sojourn in the establishment of Ho-Pin by the loud ringing of an electric bell immediately beside his bed. He sprang upright with a catching of the breath, peering about him at the unfamiliar surroundings and wondering, in the hazy manner of a sleeper newly awakened, where he was, and how come there. He was fully dressed, and his strapped-up grip lay beside him on the floor; for he had not dared to remove his clothes, had not dared to seek slumber after that terrifying interview with Mr. King. But outraged nature had prevailed, and sleep had come unbeckoned, unbidden.

The electric light was still burning in the room, as he had left it, and as he sat up, looking about him, a purring whistle drew his attention to a speaking-tube which protruded below the bell.

Soames rolled from the bed, head throbbing, and an acrid taste in his mouth, and spoke into the tube:

"Hullo!"

"You will pwrepare for youwr duties," came the metallic gutturals of Ho-Pin. "Bwreakfast will be bwrought to you in a quawrter-of-an-hour."

He made no reply, but stood looking about him dully. It had not been a dream, then, nor was he mad. It was a horrible reality; here, in London, in modern, civilized London, he was actually buried in some incredible catacomb; somewhere near to him, very near to him, was the cave of the golden dragon, and, also adjacent — terrifying thought — was the doorless library, the rose-scented haunt where the beautiful Eurasian spoke, oracularly, the responses of Mr. King!

Soames could not understand it all; he felt that such things could not be; that there must exist an explanation of those seeming impossibilities other than that they actually existed. But the instructions were veritable enough, and would not be denied.

Rapidly he began to unpack his grip. His watch had stopped, since he had neglected to wind it, and he hurried with his toilet, fearful of incurring the anger of Ho-Pin — of Ho-Pin, the beetlesque.

He observed, with passive interest, that the operation of shaving did not appreciably lighten the stain upon his skin, and, by the time that he was shaved, he had begun to know the dark-haired, yellow-faced man grimacing in the mirror for himself; but he was far from being reconciled to his new appearance.

Said peeped in at the door. He no longer wore his chauffeur's livery, but was arrayed in a white linen robe, red-sashed, and wore loose, red slippers; a tarboosh perched upon his shaven skull.

Pushing the door widely open, he entered with a tray upon which was spread a substantial breakfast.

"Hurryup!" he muttered, as one word; wherewith he departed again.

Soames seated himself at the little table upon which the tray rested, and endeavored to eat. His usual appetite had departed with his identity; Mr. Lucas was a poor, twitching being of raw nerves and internal qualms. He emptied the coffee-pot, however, and smoked a cigarette which he found in his case.

Said reappeared.

"Ta'ala!" he directed.

Soames having learnt that that term was evidently intended as an invitation to follow Said, rose and followed, dumbly.

He was conducted along the matting-lined corridor to the left; and now, where formerly he had seen a blank wall, he saw an open door! Passing this, he discovered himself in the cave of the golden dragon. Ho-Pin, dressed in a perfectly fitting morning coat and its usual accompaniments, received him with a mirthless smile.

"Good mowrning!" he said; "I twrust your bwreakfast was satisfactowry?"

"Quite, sir," replied Soames, mechanically, and as he might have replied to Mr. Leroux.

"Said will show you to a wroom," continued Ho-Pin, "where you will find a gentleman awaiting you. You will valet him and perfowrm any other services which he may wrequire of you. When he departs, you will clean the wroom and adjoining bath-wroom, and put it into thowrough order for an incoming tenant. In short, your duties in this wrespect will be identical to those which formerly you perfowrmed at sea. There is one important diffewrence: your name is Lucas, and you will answer no questions."

The metallic voice seemed to reach Soames' comprehension from some place other than the room of the golden dragon — from a great distance, or as though he were fastened up in a box and were being addressed by someone outside it.

"Yes, sir," he replied.

Said opened the yellow door upon the right of the room, and Soames followed him into another of the matting-lined corridors, this one running right and left and parallel with the wall of the apartment which he had just quitted. Six doors opened out of this corridor; four of them upon the side opposite to that by which he had entered, and one at either end.

These doors were not readily to be detected; and the wall, at first glance, presented an unbroken appearance. But from experience, he had learned that where the strips of bamboo which overlay the straw matting formed a rectangular panel, there was a door, and by the light of the electric lamp hung in the center of the corridor, he counted six of these.

Said, selecting a key from a bunch which he carried, opened one of the doors, held it ajar for Soames to enter, and permitted it to reclose behind him.

Soames entered nervously. He found himself in a room identical in size with his own private apartment; a bathroom, etc., opened out of it in one corner after the same fashion. But there similarity ended.

The bed in this apartment was constructed more on the lines of a modern steamer bunk; that is, it was surrounded by a rail, and was raised no more than a foot from the floor. The latter was covered with a rich carpet, worked in many colors, and the wall was hung with such paper as Soames had never seen hitherto in his life. The scheme of this mural decoration was distinctly Chinese, and consisted in an intricate design of human and animal figures, bewilderingly mingled; its coloring was brilliant, and the scheme extended, unbroken, over the entire ceiling. Cushions, most fancifully embroidered, were strewn about the floor, and the bed coverlet was a piece of heavy Chinese tapestry. A lamp, shaded with silk of a dull purple, swung in the center of the apartment, and an ebony table, inlaid with ivory, stood on one side of the bed; on the other was a cushioned armchair figured with the eternal, chaotic Chinese design, and being littered, at the moment, with the garments of the man in the bed. The air of the room was disgusting, unbreathable; it caught Soames by the throat and sickened him. It was laden with some kind of fumes, entirely unfamiliar to his nostrils. A dainty Chinese tea-service stood upon the ebony table.

For fully thirty seconds Soames, with his back to the door, gazed at the man in the bed, and fought down the nausea which the air of the place had induced in him.

This sleeper was a man of middle age, thin to emaciation and having lank, dark hair. His face was ghastly white, and he lay with his head thrown back and with his arms hanging out upon either side of the bunk, so that his listless hands rested upon the carpet. It was a tragic face; a high, intellectual brow and finely chiseled features; but it presented an indescribable aspect of decay; it was as the face of some classic statue which has long lain buried in humid ruins.

Soames shook himself into activity, and ventured to approach the bed. He moistened his dry lips and spoke:

"Good morning, sir" — the words sounded wildly, fantastically out of place. "Shall I prepare your bath?"

The sleeper showed no signs of awakening.

Soames forced himself to touch one of the thrown-back shoulders. He shook it gently.

The man on the bed raised his arms and dropped them back again into their original position, without opening his eyes.

"They... are hiding," he murmured thickly... "in the... orange grove.... If the felucca sails... closer... they will"...

Soames, finding something very horrifying in the broken words, shook the sleeper more urgently.

"Wake up, sir!" he cried; "I am going to prepare your bath."

"Don't let them... escape," murmured the man, slowly opening his eyes — "I have not"...

He struggled upright, glaring madly at the intruder. His light gray eyes had a glassiness as of long sickness, and his pupils, which were unnaturally dilated, began rapidly to contract; became almost invisible. Then they expanded again — and again contracted.

"Who — the deuce are you?" he murmured, passing his hand across his unshaven face.

"My name is — Lucas, sir," said Soames, conscious that if he remained much longer in the place he should be physically sick. "At your service — shall I prepare the bath?"

"The bath?" said the man, sitting up more straightly — "certainly, yes — of course"...

He looked at Soames, with a light of growing sanity creeping into his eyes; a faint flush tinged the pallid face, and his loose mouth twitched sensitively.

"Then, Said," he began, looking Soames up and down... "let me see, whom did you say you were?"

"Lucas, sir — at your service."

"Ah," muttered the man, lowering his eyes in unmistakable shame —"yes, yes, of course. You are new here?"

"Yes, sir. Shall I prepare your bath?"

"Yes, please. This is Wednesday morning?"

"Wednesday morning, sir; yes."

"Of course — it is Wednesday. You said your name was?"

"Lucas, sir," reiterated Soames, and, crossing the fantastic apartment, he entered the bath-room beyond.

This contained the most modern appointments and was on an altogether more luxurious scale than that attached to his own quarters. He noted, without drawing any deduction from the circumstance, that the fittings were of American manufacture. Here, as in the outer room, there was no window; an electric light hung from the center of the ceiling. Soames busied himself in filling the bath, and laying out the towels upon the rack.

"Fairly warm, sir?" he asked.

"Not too warm, thank you," replied the other, now stumbling out of bed and falling into the armchair — "not too warm."

"If you will take your bath, sir," said Soames, returning to the outer room, "I will brush your clothes and be ready to shave you."

"Yes, yes," said the man, rubbing his hands over his face wearily. "You are new here?"

Soames, who was becoming used to answering this question, answered it once more without irritation.

"Yes, sir, will you take your bath now? It is nearly full, I think."

The man stood up unsteadily and passed into the bathroom, closing the door behind him. Soames, seeking to forget his surroundings, took out from a small hand-bag which he found beneath the bed, a razor-case and a shaving stick. The clothes-brush he had discovered in the bathroom; and now he set to work to brush the creased garments stacked in the armchair. He noted that they were of excellent make, and that the linen was of the highest quality. He was thus employed when the outer door silently opened and the face of Said looked in.

"Gazm," said the Oriental; and he placed inside, upon the carpet, a pair of highly polished boots.

The door was reclosed.

Soames had all the garments in readiness by the time that the man emerged from the bathroom, looking slightly less ill, and not quite so pallid. He wore a yellow silk kimono; and, with greater composure than he had yet revealed, he seated himself in the armchair that Soames might shave him.

This operation Soames accomplished, and the subject, having partially dressed, returned to the bathroom to brush his hair. When his toilet was practically completed:

"Shall I pack the rest of the things in the bag, sir?" asked Soames.

The man nodded affirmatively.

Five minutes later he was ready to depart, and stood before the ex-butler a well-dressed, intellectual, but very debauched-looking gentleman. Being evidently well acquainted with the regime of the establishment, he pressed an electric bell beside the door, presented Soames with half-a-sovereign, and, as Said reappeared, took his departure, leaving Soames more reconciled to his lot than he could ever have supposed possible.

The task of cleaning the room was now commenced by Soames. Said returned, bringing him the necessary utensils; and for fifteen minutes or so he busied himself between the outer apartment and the bathroom. During this time he found leisure to study the extraordinary mural decorations; and, as he looked at them, he learned that they possessed a singular property.

If one gazed continuously at any portion of the wall, the intertwined figures thereon took shape — nay, took life; the intricate, elaborate design ceased to be a design, and became a procession, a saturnalia; became a sinister comedy, which, when first visualized, shocked Soames immoderately. The horrors presented by these devices of evil cunning, crowding the walls, appalled the narrow mind of the beholder, revolted him in an even greater degree than they must have revolted a man of broader and cleaner mind. He became conscious of a quality of evil which pervaded the room; the entire place seemed to lie beneath a spell, beneath the spell of an invisible, immeasurably wicked intelligence.

His reflections began to terrify him, and he hastened to complete his duties. The stench of the place was sickening him anew, and when at last Said opened the door, Soames came out as a man escaping from some imminent harm.

"Di," muttered Said.

He pointed to the opened door of a second room, identical in every respect with the first; and Soames started back with a smothered groan. Had his education been classical he might have likened himself to Hercules laboring for Augeus; but his mind tending scripturally, he wondered if he had sold his soul to Satan in the person of the invisible Mr. King!

XVII
KAN-SUH CONCESSIONS

Soames' character was of a pliable sort, and ere many days had passed he had grown accustomed to this unnatural existence among the living corpses in the catacombs of Ho-Pin.

He rarely saw Ho-Pin, and desired not to see him at all; as for Mr. King, he even endeavored to banish from his memory the name of that shadowy being. The memory of the Eurasian he could not banish, and was ever listening for the silvery voice, but in vain. He had no particular duties, apart from the care of the six rooms known as Block A, and situated in the corridor to the left of the cave of the golden dragon; this, and the valeting of departing occupants. But the hours at which he was called upon to perform these duties varied very greatly. Sometimes he would attend to four human wrecks in the same morning; whilst, perhaps on the following day, he would not be called upon to officiate until late in the evening. One fact early became evident to him. There was a ceaseless stream of these living dead men pouring into the catacombs of Ho-Pin, coming he knew not whence, and issuing forth again, he knew not whither.

Twice in the first week of his new and strange service he recognized the occupants of the rooms as men whom he had seen in the upper world. On entering the room of one of these (at ten o'clock at night) he almost cried out in his surprise; for the limp, sallow-faced creature extended upon the bed before him was none other than Sir Brian Malpas — the brilliant politician whom his leaders had earmarked for office in the next Cabinet!

As Soames stood contemplating him stretched there in his stupor, he found it hard to credit the fact that this was the same man whom political rivals feared for his hard brilliance, whom society courted, and whose engagement to the daughter of a peer had been announced only a few months before.

Throughout this time, Soames had made no attempt to seek the light of day: he had not seen a newspaper; he knew nothing of the hue and cry raised throughout England, of the hunt for the murderer of Mrs. Vernon. He suffered principally from lack of companionship. The only human being with whom he ever came in contact was Said, the Egyptian; and Said, at best, was uncommunicative. A man of very limited intellect, Luke Soames had been at a loss for many days to reconcile Block A and its temporary occupants with any comprehensible scheme of things. Whereas some of the rooms would be laden with nauseating fumes, others would be free of these; the occupants, again, exhibited various symptoms.

That he was a servant of an opium-den de luxe did not for some time become apparent to him; then, when first the theory presented itself, he was staggered by a discovery so momentous.

But it satisfied his mind only partially. Some men whom he valeted might have been doped with opium, certainly, but all did not exhibit those indications which, from hearsay, he associated with the resin of the white poppy.

Knowing nothing of the numerous and exotic vices which have sprung from the soil of the Orient, he was at a loss for a full explanation of the facts as he saw them.

Finding himself unmolested, and noting, in the privacy of his own apartment, how handsomely his tips were accumulating, Soames was rapidly becoming reconciled to his underground existence, more especially as it spelt safety to a man wanted by the police. His duties thus far had never taken him beyond the corridor known as Block A; what might lie on the other side of the cave of the golden dragon he knew not. He never saw any of the habitues arrive, or actually leave; he did not know whether the staff of the place consisted of himself, Said, Ho-Pin, the Eurasian girl — and...the other, or if there were more servants of this unseen master. But never a day passed by that the clearance of at least one apartment did not fall to his lot, and never an occupant quitted those cells without placing a golden gratuity in the valet's palm.

His appetite returned, and he slept soundly enough in his clean white bedroom, content to lose the upper world, temporarily, and to become a dweller in the catacombs — where tips were large and plentiful. His was the mind of a domestic animal, neither learning from the past nor questioning the future; but dwelling only in the well-fed present.

No other type of European, however lowly, could have supported existence in such a place.

Thus the days passed, and the nights passed, the one merged imperceptibly in the other. At the end of the first week, two sovereigns appeared upon the breakfast tray which Said brought to Soames' room; and, some little time later, Said reappeared with his bottles and paraphernalia to renew the ex-butler's make-up. As he was leaving the room:

"Ahu hina — G'nap'lis effendi!" he muttered, and went out as Mr. Gianapolis entered.

At sight of the Greek, Soames realized, in one emotional moment, how really lonely he had been and how in his inmost heart he longed for a sight of the sun, for a breath of unpolluted air, for a glimpse of gray, homely London.

All the old radiance had returned to Gianapolis; his eyes were crossed in an amiable smile.

"My dear Soames!" he cried, greeting the really delighted man. "How well your new complexion suits you! Sit down, Soames, sit down, and let us talk."

Soames placed a chair for Gianapolis, and seated himself upon the bed, twirling his thumbs in the manner which was his when under the influence of excitement.

"Now, Soames," continued Gianapolis — "I mean Lucas! — my anticipations, which I mentioned to you on the night of — the accident...you remember?"

"Yes," said Soames rapidly, "yes."

"Well, they have been realized. Our establishment, here, continues to flourish as of yore. Nothing has come to light in the press calculated to prejudice us in the eyes of our patrons, and although your own name, Soames"...

Soames started and clutched at the bedcover.

"Although your own name has been freely mentioned on all sides, it is not generally accepted that you perpetrated the deed."

Soames discovered his hair to be bristling; his skin tingled with a nervous apprehension.

"That I," he began dryly, paused and swallowed — "that I perpetrated....Has it been"...

"It has been hinted at by one or two Fleet Street theorists — yes, Soames! But the post-mortem examination of — the victim, revealed the fact that she was addicted to drugs"...

"Opium?" asked Soames, eagerly.

Gianapolis smiled.

"What an observant mind you have, Soames!" he said. "So you have perceived that these groves are sacred to our Lady of the Poppies? Well, in part that is true. Here, under the auspices of Mr. Ho-Pin, fretful society seeks the solace of the brass pipe; yes, Soames, that is true. Have you ever tried opium?"

"Never!" declared Soames, with emphasis, "never!"

"Well, it is a delight in store for you! But the reason of our existence as an institution, Soames, is not far to seek. Once the joys of Chandu become perceptible to the neophyte, a great need is felt — a crying need. One may drink opium or inject morphine; these, and other crude measures, may satisfy temporarily, but if one would enjoy the delights of that fairyland, of that enchanted realm which bountiful nature has concealed in the heart of the poppy, one must retire from the ken of goths and vandals who do not appreciate such exquisite delights; one must dedicate, not an hour snatched from grasping society, but successive days and nights to the goddess"...

Soames, barely understanding this discourse, listened eagerly to every word of it, whilst Gianapolis, waxing eloquent upon his strange thesis, seemed to be addressing, not his solitary auditor, but an invisible concourse.

"In common with the lesser deities," he continued, "our Lady of the Poppies is exacting. After a protracted sojourn at her shrine, so keen are the delights which she opens up to her worshipers, that a period of lassitude, of exhaustion, inevitably ensues. This precludes the proper worship of the goddess in the home, and necessitates — I say NECESSITATES the presence, in such a capital as London, of a suitable Temple. You have the honor, Soames, to be a minor priest of that Temple!"

Soames brushed his dyed hair with his fingers and endeavored to look intelligent.

"A branch establishment — merely a sacred caravanserai where votaries might repose ere reentering the ruder world," continued Gianapolis — "has unfortunately been raided by the police!"

With that word, POLICE, he seemed to come to earth again.

"Our arrangements, I am happy to say, were such that not one of the staff was found on the premises and no visible link existed between that establishment and this. But now let us talk about yourself. You may safely take an evening off, I think"...

He scrutinized Soames attentively.

"You will be discreet as a matter of course, and I should not recommend your visiting any of your former haunts. I make this proposal, of course, with the full sanction of Mr. King."

The muscles of Soames' jaw tightened at sound of the name, and he avoided the gaze of the crossed eyes.

"And the real purpose of my visit here this morning is to acquaint you with the little contrivance by which we ensure our privacy here. Once you are acquainted with it, you can take the air every evening at suitable hours, on application to Mr. Ho-Pin."

Soames coughed dryly.

"Very good," he said in a strained voice; "I am glad of that."

"I knew you would be glad, Soames," declared the smiling Gianapolis; "and now, if you will step this way, I will show you the door by which you must come and go." He stood up, then bent confidentially to Soames' ear. "Mr. King, very wisely," he whispered, "has retained you on the premises hitherto, because some doubt, some little doubt, remained respecting the information which had come into the possession of the police."

Again that ominous word! But ere Soames had time to reflect, Gianapolis led the way out of the room and along the matting-lined corridor into the apartment of the golden dragon. Soames observed, with a nervous tremor, that Mr. Ho-Pin sat upon one of the lounges, smoking a cigarette, and arrayed in his usual faultless manner. He did not attempt to rise, however, as the pair entered, but merely nodded to Gianapolis and smiled mirthlessly at Soames.

They quitted the room by the door opening on the stone steps — the door by which Soames had first entered into that evil Aladdin's cave. Gianapolis went ahead, and Soames, following him, presently emerged through a low doorway into a concrete-paved apartment, having walls of Portland stone and a white-washed ceiling. One end consisted solely of a folding gate, evidently designed to admit the limousine.

Gianapolis turned, as Soames stepped up beside him.

"If you will glance back," he said, "you will see exactly where the door is situated."

Soames did as directed, and suppressed a cry of surprise. Four of the stone blocks were fictitious — were, in verity, a heavy wooden door, faced in some way with real, or imitation granite — a door communicating with the steps of the catacombs.

"Observe!" said Gianapolis.

He closed the door, which opened outward, and there remained nothing to show the keenest observer — unless he had resorted to sounding — that these four blocks differed in any way from their fellows.

"Ingenious, is it not?" said Gianapolis, genially. "And now, my dear Soames, observe again!"

He rolled back the folding gates; and beyond was a garage, wherein stood the big limousine.

"I keep my car here, Soames, for the sake of — convenience! And now, my dear Soames, when you go out this evening, Said will close this entrance after you. When you return, which, I understand, you must do at ten o'clock, you will enter the garage by the side door yonder, which will not be locked, and you will press the electric button at the back of the petrol cans here — look! you can see it! — the inner door will then be opened for you. Step this way."

He passed between the car and the wall of the garage, opened the door at the left of the entrance gates, and, Soames following, came out into a narrow lane. For the first time in many days Soames scented the cleaner air of the upper world, and with it he filled his lungs gratefully.

Behind him was the garage, before him the high wall of a yard, and, on his right, for a considerable distance, extended a similar wall; in the latter case evidently that of a wharf — for beyond it flowed the Thames.

Proceeding along beside this wall, the two came to the gates of a warehouse. They passed these, however, and entered a small office. Crossing the office, they gained the interior of the warehouse, where chests bearing Chinese labels were stacked in great profusion.

"Then this place," began Soames...

"Is a ginger warehouse, Soames! There is a very small office staff, but sufficiently large to cope with the limited business done — in the import and export of ginger! The firm is known as Kan-Suh Concessions and imports preserved Chinese ginger from its own plantations in that province of the Celestial Empire. There is a small wharf attached, as you may have noted. Oh! it is a going concern and perfectly respectable!"

Soames looked about him with wide-opened eyes.

"The ginger staff," said Gianapolis, "is not yet arrived. Mr. Ho-Pin is the manager. The lane, in which the establishment is situated, communicates with Limehouse Causeway, and, being a cul-de-sac, is little frequented. Only this one firm has premises actually opening into it and I have converted the small corner building at the extremity of the wharf into a garage for my car. There are no means of communication between the premises of Kan-Suh Concessions and those of the more important enterprise below — and I, myself, am not officially associated with the ginger trade. It is a precaution which we all adopt, however, never to enter or leave the garage if anyone is in sight."...

Soames became conscious of a new security. He set about his duties that morning with a greater alacrity than usual, valeting one of the living dead men — a promising young painter whom he chanced to know by sight — with a return to the old affable manner which had rendered him so popular during his career as cabin steward.

He felt that he was now part and parcel of Kan-Suh Concessions; that Kan-Suh Concessions and he were at one. He had yet to learn that his sense of security was premature, and that his added knowledge might be an added danger.

When Said brought his lunch into his room, he delivered also a slip of paper bearing the brief message:

"Go out 6.30 — return 10."

Mr. Soames uncorked his daily bottle of Bass almost gaily, and attacked his lunch with avidity.

XVIII
THE WORLD ABOVE

The night had set in grayly, and a drizzle of fine rain was falling. West India Dock Road presented a prospect so uninviting that it must have damped the spirits of anyone but a cave-dweller.

Soames, buttoned up in a raincoat kindly lent by Mr. Gianapolis, and of a somewhat refined fit, with a little lagoon of rainwater forming within the reef of his hat-brim, trudged briskly along. The necessary ingredients for the manufacture of mud are always present (if invisible during dry weather) in the streets of East-end London, and already Soames' neat black boots were liberally bedaubed with it. But what cared Soames? He inhaled the soot-laden air rapturously; he was glad to feel the rain beating upon his face, and took a childish pleasure in ducking his head suddenly and seeing the little stream of water spouting from his hat-brim. How healthy they looked, these East-end workers, these Italian dock-hands, these Jewish tailors, these nondescript, greasy beings who sometimes saw the sun. Many of them, he knew well, labored in cellars; but he had learnt that there are cellars and cellars. Ah! it was glorious, this gray, murky London!

Yet, now that temporarily he was free of it, he realized that there was that within him which responded to the call of the catacombs; there was a fascination in the fume-laden air of those underground passages; there was a charm, a mysterious charm, in the cave of the golden dragon, in that unforgettable place which he assumed to mark the center of the labyrinth; in the wicked, black eyes of the Eurasian. He realized that between the abstraction of silver spoons and deliberate, organized money-making at the expense of society, a great chasm yawned; that there may be romance even in felony.

Soames at last felt himself to be a traveler on the highroad to fortune; he had become almost reconciled to the loss of his bank balance, to the loss of his place in the upper world. His was the constitution of a born criminal, and, had he been capable of subtle self-analysis, he must have known now that fear, and fear only, hitherto had held him back, had confined him to the ranks of the amateurs. Well, the plunge was taken.

Deep in such reflections, he trudged along through the rain, scarce noting where his steps were leading him, for all roads were alike to-night. His natural inclinations presently dictated a halt at a brilliantly lighted public house; and, taking off his hat to shake some of the moisture from it, he replaced it on his head and entered the saloon lounge.

The place proved to be fairly crowded, principally with local tradesmen whose forefathers had toiled for Pharaoh; and conveying his glass of whisky to a marble-topped table in a corner comparatively secluded, Soames sat down for a consideration of past, present, and future; an unusual mental exercise. Curiously enough, he had lost something of his old furtiveness; he no longer examined, suspiciously, every stranger who approached his neighborhood; for as the worshipers of old came by the gate of Fear into the invisible presence of Moloch, so he — of equally untutored mind — had entered the presence of Mr. King! And no devotee of the Ammonite god had had greater faith in his potent protection than Soames had in that of his unseen master. What should a servant of Mr. King fear from the officers of the law? How puny a thing was the law in comparison with the director of that secret, powerful, invulnerable organization whereof to-day he (Soames) formed an unit!

Then, oddly, the old dormant cowardice of the man received a sudden spurring, and leaped into quickness. An evening paper lay upon the marble top of the table, and carelessly taking it up, Soames, hitherto lost in imaginings, was now reminded that for more than a week he had lain in ignorance of the world's doings. Good Heavens! how forgetful he had been! It was the nepenthe of the catacombs. He must make up for lost time and get in touch again with passing events: especially he must post himself up on the subject of... the murder....

The paper dropped from his hands, and, feeling himself blanch beneath his artificial tan, Soames, in his old furtive manner, glanced around the saloon to learn if he were watched. Apparently no one was taking the slightest notice of him, and, with an unsteady hand, he raised his glass and drained its contents. There, at the bottom of the page before him, was the cause of this sudden panic; a short paragraph conceived as follows: —

REPORTED ARREST OF SOAMES

It is reported that a man answering to the description of Soames, the butler wanted in connection with the Palace Mansions outrage, has been arrested in Birmingham. He was found sleeping in an outhouse belonging to Major Jennings, of Olton, and as he refused to give any account of himself, was handed over, by the gentleman's gardener, to the local police. His resemblance to the published photograph being observed, he was closely questioned, and although he denies being Luke Soames, he is being held for further inquiry.

Soames laid down the paper, and, walking across to the bar, ordered a second glass of whisky. With this he returned to the table and began more calmly to re-read the paragraph. From it he passed to the other news. He noted that little publicity was given to the Palace Mansions affair, from which he judged that public interest in the matter was already growing cold. A short summary appeared on the front page, and this he eagerly devoured. It read as follows: —

PALACE MANSIONS MYSTERY

The police are following up an important clue to the murderer of Mrs. Vernon, and it is significant in this connection that a man answering to the description of Soames was apprehended at Olton (Birmingham) late last night. (See Page 6). The police are very reticent in regard to the new information which they hold, but it is evident that at last they are confident of establishing a case. Mr. Henry Leroux, the famous novelist, in whose flat the mysterious outrage took place, is suffering from a nervous breakdown, but is reported to be progressing favorably by Dr. Cumberly, who is attending him. Dr. Cumberly, it will be remembered, was with Mr. Leroux, and Mr. John Exel, M. P., at the time that the murder was discovered. The executors of the late Mr. Horace Vernon are faced with extraordinary difficulties in administering the will of the deceased, owing to the tragic coincidence of his wife's murder within twenty-four hours of his own demise.

Public curiosity respecting the nursing home in Gillingham Street, with its electric baths and other modern appliances, has by no means diminished, and groups of curious spectators regularly gather outside the former establishment of Nurse Proctor, and apparently derive some form of entertainment from staring at the windows and questioning the constable on duty. The fact that Mrs. Vernon undoubtedly came from this establishment on the night of the crime, and that the proprietors of the nursing home fled immediately, leaving absolutely no clue behind them, complicates the mystery which Scotland Yard is engaged in unraveling.

It is generally believed that the woman, Proctor, and her associates had actually no connection with the crime, and that realizing that the inquiry might turn in their direction, they decamped. The obvious inference, of course, is that the nursing home was conducted on lines which would not bear official scrutiny.

The flight of the butler, Soames, presents a totally different aspect, and in this direction the police are very active.

Soames searched the remainder of the paper scrupulously, but failed to find any further reference to the case. The second Scottish stimulant had served somewhat to restore his failing courage; he congratulated himself upon taking the only move which could have saved him from arrest; he perceived that he owed his immunity entirely to the protective wings of Mr. King. He trembled to think that his fate might indeed have been that of the man arrested at Olton; for, without money and without friends, he would have become, ere this, just such an outcast and natural object of suspicion.

He noted, as a curious circumstance, that throughout the report there was no reference to the absence of Mrs. Leroux; therefore — a primitive reasoner — he assumed that she was back again at Palace Mansions. He was mentally incapable of fitting Mrs. Leroux into the secret machine engineered by Mr. King through the visible agency of Ho-Pin. On the whole, he was disposed to believe that her several absences — ostensibly on visits to Paris — had nothing to do with the catacombs of Ho-Pin, but were to be traced to the amours of the radiant Gianapolis. Taking into consideration his reception by the Chinaman in the cave of the golden dragon, he determined, to his own satisfaction, that this had been dictated by prudence, and by Mr. Gianapolis. In short he believed that the untimely murder of Mrs. Vernon had threatened to direct attention to the commercial enterprise of the Greek, and that he, Soames, had become incorporated in the latter in this accidental fashion. He believed himself to have been employed in a private intrigue during the time that he was at Palace Mansions, and counted it a freak of fate that Mr. Gianapolis' affairs of the pocket had intruded upon his affairs of the heart.

It was all very confusing, and entirely beyond Soames' mental capacity to unravel.

He treated himself to a third scotch whisky, and sallied out into the rain. A brilliantly lighted music hall upon the opposite side of the road attracted his attention. The novelty of freedom having worn off, he felt no disposition to spend the remainder of the evening in the street, for the rain was now falling heavily, but determined to sample the remainder of the program offered by the "first house," and presently was reclining in a plush-covered, tip-up seat in the back row of the stalls.

The program was not of sufficient interest wholly to distract his mind, and during the performance of a very tragic comedian, Soames found his thoughts wandering far from the stage. His seat was at the extreme end of the back row, and, quite unintentionally, he began to listen to the conversation of two men, who, standing just inside the entrance door and immediately behind him to the right, were talking in subdued voices.

"There are thousands of Kings in London," said one...

Soames slowly lowered his hands to the chair-arms on either side of him and clutched them tightly. Every nerve in his body seemed to be strung up to the ultimate pitch of tensity. He was listening, now, as a man arraigned might listen for the pronouncement of a judgment.

"That's the trouble," replied a second voice; "but you know Max's ideas on the subject? He has his own way of going to work; but my idea, Sowerby, is that if we can find the one Mr. Soames — and I am open to bet he hasn't left London — we shall find the right Mr. King."

The comedian finished, and the orchestra noisily chorded him off. Soames, his forehead wet with perspiration, began to turn his head, inch by inch. The lights in the auditorium were partially lowered, and he prayed, devoutly, that they would remain so; for now, glancing out of the corner of his right eye, he saw the speakers.

The taller of the two, a man wearing a glistening brown overall and rain-drenched tweed cap, was the detective who had been in Leroux's study and who had ordered him to his room on the night of the murder!

Then commenced for Soames such an ordeal as all his previous life had not offered him; an ordeal beside which even the interview with Mr. King sank into insignificance. His one hope was in the cunning of Said's disguise; but he knew that Scotland Yard men judged likenesses, not by complexions, which are alterable, not by the color of the hair, which can be dyed, but by certain features which are measurable, and which may be memorized because nature has fashioned them immutable.

What should he do? — What should he do? In the silence:

"No good stopping any longer," came the whispered voice of the shorter detective; "I have had a good look around the house, and there is nobody here.".…

Soames literally held his breath.

"We'll get along down to the Dock Gate," was the almost inaudible reply; "I am meeting Stringer there at nine o'clock."

Walking softly, the Scotland Yard men passed out of the theater.

XIX
THE LIVING DEAD

The night held yet another adventure in store for Soames. His encounter with the two Scotland Yard men had finally expelled all thoughts of pleasure from his mind. The upper world, the free world, was beset with pitfalls; he realized that for the present, at any rate, there could be no security for him, save in the catacombs of Ho-Pin. He came out of the music-hall and stood for a moment just outside the foyer, glancing fearfully up and down the rain-swept street. Then, resuming the drenched raincoat which he had taken off in the theater, and turning up its collar about his ears, he set out to return to the garage adjoining the warehouse of Kan-Suh Concessions.

He had fully another hour of leave if he cared to avail himself of it, but, whilst every pedestrian assumed, in his eyes, the form of a detective, whilst every dark corner seemed to conceal an ambush, whilst every passing instant he anticipated feeling a heavy hand upon his shoulder, and almost heard the words: — "Luke Soames, I arrest you".… Whilst this was his case, freedom had no joys for him.

No light guided him to the garage door, and he was forced to seek for the handle by groping along the wall. Presently, his hand came in contact with it, he turned it — and the way was open before him.

Being far from familiar with the geography of the place, he took out a box of matches, and struck one to light him to the shelf above which the bell-push was concealed.

Its feeble light revealed, not only the big limousine near which he was standing and the usual fixtures of a garage, but, dimly penetrating beyond into the black places, it also revealed something else.…

The door in the false granite blocks was open!

Soames, who had advanced to seek the bell-push, stopped short. The match burnt down almost to his fingers, whereupon he blew it out and carefully crushed it under his foot. A faint reflected light rendered perceptible the stone steps below. At the top, Soames stood looking down. Nothing stirred above, below, or around him. What did it mean? Dimly to his ears came the hooting of some siren from the river — evidently that of a large vessel. Still he hesitated; why he did so, he scarce knew, save that he was afraid — vaguely afraid.

Then, he asked himself what he had to fear, and conjuring up a mental picture of his white bedroom below, he planted his foot firmly upon the first step, and from thence, descended to the bottom, guided by the faint light which shone out from the doorway beneath.

But the door proved to be only partly opened, and Soames knocked deferentially. No response came to his knocking, and he so greatly ventured as to push the door fully open.

The cave of the golden dragon was empty. Half frightfully, Soames glanced about the singular apartment, in amid the mountainous cushions of the leewans, behind the pedestal of the dragon; to the right and to the left of the doorway wherein he stood.

There was no one there; but the door on the right — the door inlaid with ebony and green stone, which he had never yet seen open was open now, widely opened. He glided across the floor, his wet boots creaking unmusically, and peeped through. He saw a matting-lined corridor identical with that known as Block A. The door of one apartment, that on the extreme left, was opened. Sickly fumes were wafted out to him, and these mingled with the incense-like odor which characterized the temple of the dragon.

A moment he stood so, then started back, appalled.

An outcry — the outcry of a woman, of a woman whose very soul is assailed — split the stillness. Not from the passageway before him, but from somewhere behind him — from the direction of Block A — it came.

"For God's sake — oh! for God's sake, have mercy! Let me go!...let me go!" Higher, shriller, more fearful and urgent, grew the voice — "LET ME GO!"...

Soames' knees began to tremble beneath him; he clutched at the black wall for support; then turned, and with unsteady footsteps crossed to the door communicating with the corridor which contained his room. It had a lever handle of the Continental pattern, and, trembling with apprehension that it might prove to be locked, Soames pressed down this handle.

The door opened...

"Hina, effendi! — hina!"

The voice sounded like that of Said....

"Oh! God in Heaven help me!...Help! — help!"...

"Imsik!"...

Footsteps were pattering upon the stone stairs; someone was descending from the warehouse! The frenzied shrieks of the woman continued. Soames broke into a cold perspiration; his heart, which had leaped wildly, seemed now to have changed to a cold stone in his breast. Just at the entrance to the corridor he stood, frozen with horror at those cries.

"Ikfil el-bab!" came now, in the voice of Ho-Pin, — and nearer.

"Let me go!...only let me go, and I will never breathe a word. ...Ah! Ah! Oh! God of mercy! not the needle again! You are killing me!...not the needle!"...

Soames staggered on to his own room and literally fell within — as across the cave of the golden dragon, behind him, SOMEONE — one whom he did not see but only heard, one whom with all his soul he hoped had not seen HIM — passed rapidly.

Another shriek, more frightful than any which had preceded it, struck the trembling man as an arrow might have struck him. He dropped upon his knees at the side of the bed and thrust his fingers firmly into his ears. He had never swooned in his life, and was unfamiliar with the symptoms, but now he experienced a sensation of overpowering nausea; a blood-red mist floated before his eyes, and the floor seemed to rock beneath him like the deck of a ship....

That soul-appalling outcry died away, merged into a sobbing, moaning sound which defied Soames' efforts to exclude it....He rose to his feet, feeling physically ill, and turned to close his door....

They were dragging someone — someone who sighed, shudderingly, and whose sighs sank to moans, and sometimes rose to sobs, — across the apartment of the dragon. In a faint, dying voice, the woman spoke again: —

"Not Mr. King!...NOT MR. KING!...Is there no God in Heaven!...AH! spare me...spare"...

Soames closed the door and stood propped up against it, striving to fight down the deathly sickness which assailed him. His clothes were sticking to his clammy body, and a cold perspiration was trickling down his forehead and into his eyes. The sensation at his heart was unlike anything that he had ever known; he thought that he must be dying.

The awful sounds died away... then a muffled disturbance drew his attention to a sort of square trap which existed high up on one wall of the room, but which admitted no light, and which hitherto had never admitted any sound. Now, in the utter darkness, he found himself listening — listening...

He had learnt, during his duties in Block A, that each of the minute suites was rendered sound-proof in some way, so that what took place in one would be inaudible to the occupant of the next, provided that both doors were closed. He perceived, now, that some precaution hitherto exercised continuously had been omitted to-night, and that the sounds which he could hear came from the room next to his own — the room which opened upon the corridor that he had never entered, and which now he classified, mentally, as Block B.

What did it mean?

Obviously there had been some mishap in the usually smooth conduct of Ho-Pin's catacombs. There had been a hurried outgoing in several directions... a search?

And by the accident of his returning an hour earlier than he was expected, he was become a witness of this incident, or of its dreadful, concluding phases. He had begun to move away from the door, but now he returned, and stood leaning against it.

That stifling room where roses shed their petals, had been opened to-night; a chill touched the very center of his being and told him so. The occupant of that room — the Minotaur of this hideous labyrinth — was at large to-night, was roaming the passages about him, was perhaps outside his very door....

Dull moaning sounds reached him through the trap. He realized that if he had the courage to cross the room, stand upon a chair and place his ear to the wall, he might be able to detect more of what was passing in the next apartment. But craven fear held him in its grip, and in vain he strove to shake it off. Trembling wildly, he stood with his back to the door, whilst muttered words, and moans, ever growing fainter, reached him from beyond. A voice, a harsh, guttural voice — surely not that of Ho-Pin — was audible, above the moaning.

For two minutes — three minutes — four minutes — he stood there, tottering on the brink of insensibility, then... a faint sound — a new sound, — drew his gaze across the room, and up to the corner where the trap was situated.

A very dim light was dawning there; he could just detect the outline of an opening — a half-light breaking the otherwise impenetrable darkness.

He felt that his capacity for fear was strained to its utmost; that he could support nothing more, yet a new horror was in store for him; for, as he watched that gray patch, in it, as in a frame, a black silhouette appeared — the silhouette of a human head... a woman's head!

Soames convulsively clenched his jaws, for his teeth were beginning to chatter.

A whistle, an eerie, minor whistle, subscribed the ultimate touch of terror to the night. The silhouette disappeared, and, shortly afterwards, the gray luminance. A faint click told of some shutter being fastened; complete silence reigned.

Soames groped his way to the bed and fell weakly upon it, half lying down and burying his face in the pillow. For how long, he had no idea, but for some considerable time, he remained so, fighting to regain sufficient self-possession to lie to Ho-Pin, who sooner or later must learn of his return.

At last he managed to sit up. He was not trembling quite so wildly, but he still suffered from a deathly sickness. A faint streak of light from the corridor outside shone under his door. As he noted it, it was joined by a second streak, forming a triangle.

There was a very soft rasping of metal. Someone was opening the door!

Soames lay back upon the bed. This time he was past further panic and come to a stage of sickly apathy. He lay, now, because he could not sit upright, because stark horror had robbed him of physical strength, and had drained the well of his emotions dry.

Gradually — so that the operation seemed to occupy an interminable time, the door opened, and in the opening a figure appeared.

The switch clicked, and the room was flooded with electric light.

Ho-Pin stood watching him.

Soames — in his eyes that indescribable expression seen in the eyes of a bird placed in a cobra's den — met the Chinaman's gaze. This gaze was no different from that which habitually he directed upon the people of the catacombs. His yellow face was set in the same mirthless smile, and his eyebrows were raised interrogatively. For the space of ten seconds, he stood watching the man on the bed. Then: —

"You wreturn vewry soon, Mr. Soames?" he said, softly.

Soames groaned like a dying man, whispering:

"I was... taken ill — very ill."...

"So you wreturn befowre the time awranged for you?"

His metallic voice was sunk in a soothing hiss. He smiled steadily: he betrayed no emotion.

"Yes... sir," whispered Soames, his hair clammily adhering to his brow and beads of perspiration trickling slowly down his nose.

"And when you wreturn, you see and you hear — stwrange things, Mr. Soames?"

Soames, who was in imminent danger of becoming physically ill, gulped noisily.

"No, sir," he whispered, — tremulously, "I've been — in here all the time."

Ho-Pin nodded, slowly and sympathetically, but never removed the glittering eyes from the face of the man on the bed.

"So you hear nothing, and see nothing?"

The words were spoken even more softly than he had spoken hitherto.

"Nothing," protested Soames. He suddenly began to tremble anew, and his trembling rattled the bed. "I have been — very ill indeed, sir."

Ho-Pin nodded again slowly, and with deep sympathy.

"Some medicine shall be sent to you, Mr. Soames," he said.

He turned and went out slowly, closing the door behind him.

XX
ABRAHAM LEVINSKY BUTTS IN

At about the time that this conversation was taking place in Ho-Pin's catacombs, Detective-Inspector Dunbar and Detective-Sergeant Sowerby were joined by a third representative of New Scotland Yard at the appointed spot by the dock gates. This was Stringer, the detective to whom was assigned the tracing of the missing Soames; and he loomed up through the rain-mist, a glistening but dejected figure.

"Any luck?" inquired Sowerby, sepulchrally.

Stringer, a dark and morose looking man, shook his head.

"I've beaten up every 'Chink' in Wapping and Limehouse, I should reckon," he said, plaintively. "They're all as innocent as babes unborn. You can take it from me: Chinatown hasn't got a murder on its conscience at present. BRR! it's a beastly night. Suppose we have one?"

Dunbar nodded, and the three wet investigators walked back for some little distance in silence, presently emerging via a narrow, dark, uninviting alleyway into West India Dock Road. A brilliantly lighted hostelry proved to be their objective, and there, in a quiet corner of the deserted billiard room, over their glasses, they discussed this mysterious case, which at first had looked so simple of solution if only because it offered so many unusual features, but which, the deeper they probed, merely revealed fresh complications.

"The business of those Fry people, in Scotland, was a rotten disappointment," said Dunbar, suddenly. "They were merely paid by the late Mrs. Vernon to re-address letters to a little newspaper shop in Knightsbridge, where an untraceable boy used to call for them! Martin has just reported this evening. Perth wires for instructions, but it's a dead-end, I'm afraid."

"You know," said Sowerby, fishing a piece of cork from the brown froth of a fine example by Guinness, "to my mind our hope's in Soames; and if we want to find Soames, to my mind we want to look, not east, but west."

"Hear, hear!" concorded Stringer, gloomily sipping hot rum.

"It seems to me," continued Sowerby, "that Limehouse is about the last place in the world a man like Soames would think of hiding in."

"It isn't where he'll be THINKING of hiding," snapped Dunbar, turning his fierce eyes upon the last speaker. "You can't seem to get the idea out of your head, Sowerby, that Soames is an independent agent. He ISN'T an independent agent. He's only the servant; and through the servant we hope to find the master."

"But why in the east-end?" came the plaintive voice of Stringer; "for only one reason, that I can see — because Max says that there's a Chinaman in the case."

"There's opium in the case, isn't there?" said Dunbar, adding more water to his whisky, "and where there's opium there is pretty frequently a Chinaman."

"But to my mind," persisted Sowerby, his eyebrows drawn together in a frown of concentration, "the place where Mrs. Vernon used to get the opium was the place we raided in Gillingham Street."

"Nurse Proctor's!" cried Stringer, banging his fist on the table. "Exactly my idea! There may have been a Chinaman concerned in the management of the Gillingham Street stunt, or there may not, but I'll swear that was where the opium was supplied. In fact I don't think that there's any doubt about it. Medical evidence (opinions differed a bit, certainly) went to show that she had been addicted to opium for some years. Other evidence — you got it yourself, Inspector — went to show that she came from Gillingham Street on the night of the murder. Gillingham Street crowd vanished like a beautiful dream before we had time to nab them! What more do you want? What are we up to, messing about in Limehouse and Wapping?"

Sowerby partook of a long drink and turned his eyes upon Dunbar, awaiting the inspector's reply.

"You both have the wrong idea!" said Dunbar, deliberately; "you are all wrong! You seem to be under the impression that if we could lay our hands upon the missing staff of the so-called Nursing Home, we should find the assassin to be one of the crowd. It doesn't follow at all. For a long time, you, Sowerby," — he turned his tawny eyes upon the sergeant — "had the idea that Soames was the murderer, and I'm not sure that you have got rid of it yet! You, Stringer, appear to think that Nurse Proctor is responsible. Upon my word, you are a hopeless pair! Suppose Soames had nothing whatever to do with the matter, but merely realized that he could not prove an alibi? Wouldn't YOU bolt? I put it to you."

Sowerby stared hard, and Stringer scratched his chin, reflectively.

"The same reasoning applies to the Gillingham Street people," continued Dunbar. "We haven't the slightest idea of THEIR whereabouts because we don't even know who they were; but we do know something about Soames, and we're looking for him, not because we think he did the murder, but because we think he can tell us who did."

"Which brings us back to the old point," interrupted Stringer, softly beating his fist upon the table at every word; "why are we looking for Soames in the east-end?"

"Because," replied Dunbar, "we're working on the theory that Soames, though actually not accessory to the crime, was in the pay of those who were"...

"Well?" — Stringer spoke the word eagerly, his eyes upon the inspector's face.

"And those who WERE accessory," — continued Dunbar, "were servants of Mr. King."

"Ah!" Stringer brought his fist down with a bang — "Mr. King! That's where I am in the dark, and where Sowerby, here, is in the dark." He bent forward over the table. "Who the devil is Mr. King?"

Dunbar twirled his whisky glass between his fingers.

"We don't know," he replied quietly, "but Soames does, in all probability; and that's why we're looking for Soames."

"Is it why we're looking in Limehouse?" persisted Stringer, the argumentative.

"It is," snapped Dunbar. "We have only got one Chinatown worthy of the name, in London, and that's not ten minutes' walk from here."

"Chinatown — yes," said Sowerby, his red face glistening with excitement; "but why look for Mr. King in Chinatown?"

"Because," replied Dunbar, lowering his voice, "Mr. King in all probability is a Chinaman."

"Who says so?" demanded Stringer.

"Max says so…"

"MAX!" — again Stringer beat his fist upon the table. "Now we have got to it! We're working, then, not on our own theories, but on those of Max?"

Dunbar's sallow face flushed slightly, and his eyes seemed to grow brighter.

"Mr. Gaston Max obtained information in Paris," he said, "which he placed, unreservedly, at my disposal. We went into the matter thoroughly, with the result that our conclusions were identical. A certain Mr. King is at the bottom of this mystery, and, in all probability, Mr. King is a Chinaman. Do I make myself clear?"

Sowerby and Stringer looked at one another, perplexedly. Each man finished his drink in silence. Then:

"What took place in Paris?" began Sowerby.

There was an interruption. A stooping figure in a shabby, black frock-coat, the figure of a man who wore a dilapidated bowler pressed down upon his ears, who had a greasy, Semitic countenance, with a scrubby, curling, sandy colored beard, sparse as the vegetation of a desert, appeared at Sowerby's elbow.

He carried a brimming pewter pot. This he set down upon a corner of the table, depositing himself in a convenient chair and pulling out a very dirty looking letter from an inside pocket. He smoothed it carefully. He peered, little-eyed, from the frowning face of Dunbar to the surprised countenance of Sowerby, and smiled with native amiability at the dangerous-looking Stringer.

"Excuthe me," he said, and his propitiatory smile was expansive and dazzling, "excuthe me buttin' in like thith. It theemth rude, I know — it doth theem rude; but the fact of the matter ith I'm a tailor — thath's my pithneth, a tailor. When I thay a tailor, I really mean a breecheth-maker — tha'th what I mean, a breecheth-maker. Now thethe timeth ith very hard timeth for breecheth-makerth."…

Dunbar finished his whisky, and quietly replaced the glass upon the table, looking from Sowerby to Stringer with unmistakable significance. Stringer emptied his glass of rum, and Sowerby disposed of his stout.

"I got thith letter lath night," continued the breeches-maker, bending forward confidentially over the table. (The document looked at least twelve months old.) "I got thith letter latht night with thethe three fiverth in it; and not havin' no friendth in London — I'm an American thitithen, by birth, — Levinthky, my name ith — Abraham Levinthky — I'm a Noo Englander. Well, not havin' no friendth in London, and theein' you three gentlemen thittin' here, I took the liberty"…

Dunbar stood up, glared at Levinsky, and stalked out of the billiard-room, followed by his equally indignant satellites. Having gained the outer door:

"Of all the blasted impudence!" he said, turning to Sowerby and Stringer; but there was a glint of merriment in the fierce eyes. "Can you beat that? Did you tumble to his game?"

Sowerby stared at Stringer, and Stringer stared at Sowerby.

"Except," began the latter in a voice hushed with amazement, "that he's got the coolest cheek of any mortal being I ever met."…

Dunbar's grim face relaxed, and he laughed boyishly, his square shoulders shaking.

"He was leading up to the confidence trick!" he said, between laughs. "Damn it all, man, it was the old confidence trick! The idea of a confidence-merchant spreading out his wares before three C. I. D. men!"

He was choking with laughter again; and now, Sowerby and Stringer having looked at one another for a moment, the surprised pair joined him in his merriment. They turned up their collars and went out into the rain, still laughing.

"That man," said Sowerby, as they walked across to the stopping place of the electric trains, "is capable of calling on the Commissioner and asking him to 'find the lady'!"

XXI
THE STUDIO IN SOHO

Certainly, such impudence as that of Mr. Levinsky is rare even in east-end London, and it may be worth while to return to the corner of the billiard-room and to study more closely this remarkable man.

He was sitting where the detectives had left him, and although their departure might have been supposed to have depressed him, actually it had had a contrary effect; he was chuckling with amusement, and, between his chuckles, addressing himself to the contents of the pewter with every mark of appreciation. Three gleaming golden teeth on the lower row, and one glittering canine, made a dazzling show every time that he smiled; he was a very greasy and a very mirthful Hebrew.

Finishing his tankard of ale, he shuffled out into the street, the line of his bent shoulders running parallel with that of his hat-brim. His hat appeared to be several sizes too large for his head, and his skull was only prevented from disappearing into the capacious crown by the intervention of his ears, which, acting as brackets, supported the whole weight of the rain-sodden structure. He mounted a tram proceeding in the same direction as that which had borne off the Scotland Yard men. Quitting this at Bow Road, he shuffled into the railway station, and from Bow Road proceeded to Liverpool Street. Emerging from the station at Liverpool Street, he entered a motor-'bus bound westward.

His neighbors, inside, readily afforded him ample elbow room; and, smiling agreeably at every one, including the conductor (who resented his good-humor) and a pretty girl in the corner seat (who found it embarrassing) he proceeded to Charing Cross. Descending from the 'bus, he passed out into Leicester Square and plunged into the network of streets which complicates the map of Soho. It will be of interest to follow him.

In a narrow turning off Greek Street, and within hail of the popular Bohemian restaurants, he paused before a doorway sandwiched between a Continental newsagent's and a tiny French cafe; and, having fumbled in his greasy raiment he presently produced a key, opened the door, carefully closed it behind him, and mounted the dark stair.

On the top floor he entered a studio, boasting a skylight upon which the rain was drumming steadily and drearily. Lighting a gas burner in one corner of the place which bore no evidence of being used for its legitimate purpose — he entered a little adjoining dressing-room. Hot and cold water were laid on there, and a large zinc bath stood upon the floor. With the aid of an enamel bucket, Mr. Abraham Levinsky filled the bath.

Leaving him to his ablutions, let us glance around the dressing-room. Although there was no easel in the studio, and no indication of artistic activity, the dressing-room was well stocked with costumes. Two huge dress-baskets were piled in one corner, and their contents hung upon hooks around the three available walls. A dressing table, with a triplicate mirror and a suitably shaded light, presented a spectacle reminiscent less of a model's dressing-room than of an actor's.

At the expiration of some twenty-five minutes, the door of this dressing-room opened; and although Abraham Levinsky had gone in, Abraham Levinsky did not come out!

Carefully flicking a particle of ash from a fold of his elegant, silk-lined cloak, a most distinguished looking gentleman stepped out onto the bleak and dirty studio. He wore, in addition to a graceful cloak, which was lined with silk of cardinal red, a soft black hat, rather wide brimmed and dented in a highly artistic manner, and irreproachable evening clothes; his linen was immaculate; and no valet in London could have surpassed the perfect knotting of his tie. His pearl studs were elegant and valuable; and a single eyeglass was swung about his neck by a thin, gold chain. The white gloves, which fitted perfectly, were new; and if the glossy boots were rather long in the toe-cap from an English point of view, the gold-headed malacca cane which the newcomer carried was quite de rigeur.

The strong clean-shaven face calls for no description here; it was the face of M. Gaston Max.

M. Max, having locked the study door, and carefully tried it to make certain of its security, descended the stairs. He peeped out cautiously into the street ere setting foot upon the pavement; but no one was in sight at the moment, and he emerged quickly, closing the door behind him, and taking shelter under the newsagent's awning. The rain continued its steady downpour, but M. Max stood there softly humming a little French melody until a taxi-cab crawled into view around the Greek Street corner.

He whistled shrilly through his teeth — the whistle of a gamin; and the cabman, glancing up and perceiving him, pulled around into the turning, and drew up by the awning.

M. Max entered the cab.

"To Frascati's," he directed.

The cabman backed out into Greek Street and drove off. This was the hour when the theaters were beginning to eject their throngs, and outside one of them, where a popular comedy had celebrated its three-hundred-and-fiftieth performance, the press of cabs and private cars was so great that M. Max found himself delayed within sight of the theater foyer.

Those patrons of the comedy who had omitted to order vehicles or who did not possess private conveyances, found themselves in a quandary tonight, and amongst those thus unfortunately situated, M. Max, watching the scene with interest, detected a lady whom he knew — none other than the delightful American whose conversation had enlivened his recent journey from Paris — Miss Denise Ryland. She was accompanied by a charming companion, who, although she was wrapped up in a warm theater cloak, seemed to be shivering disconsolately as she and her friend watched the interminable stream of vehicles filing up before the theater, and cutting them off from any chance of obtaining a cab for themselves.

M. Max acted promptly.

"Drive into that side turning!" he directed the cabman, leaning out of the window. The cabman followed his directions, and M. Max, heedless of the inclement weather, descended from the cab, dodged actively between the head lamps of a big Mercedes and the tail-light of a taxi, and stood bowing before the two ladies, his hat pressed to his bosom with one gloved hand, the other, ungloved, resting upon the gold knob of the malacca.

"Why!" cried Miss Ryland, "if it isn't...M. Gaston! My dear ...M. Gaston! Come under the awning, or" — her head was wagging furiously — "you will be...simply drowned."

M. Max smilingly complied.

"This is M. Gaston," said Denise Ryland, turning to her companion, "the French gentleman... whom I met...in the train from...Paris. This is Miss Helen Cumberly, and I know you two will get on...famously."

M. Max acknowledged the presentation with a few simple words which served to place the oddly met trio upon a mutually easy footing. He was, par excellence, the polished cosmopolitan man of the world.

"Fortunately I saw your dilemma," he explained. "I have a cab on the corner yonder, and it is entirely at your service."

"Now that...is real good of you," declared Denise Ryland. "I think you're...a brick."...

"But, my dear Miss Ryland!" cried Helen, "we cannot possibly deprive M. Gaston of his cab on a night like this!"

"I had hoped," said the Frenchman, bowing gallantly, "that this most happy reunion might not be allowed to pass uncelebrated. Tell me if I intrude upon other plans, because I am speaking selfishly; but I was on my way to a lonely supper, and apart from the great pleasure which your company would afford me, you would be such very good Samaritans if you would join me."

Helen Cumberly, although she was succumbing rapidly to the singular fascination of M. Max, exhibited a certain hesitancy. She was no stranger to Bohemian customs, and if the distinguished Frenchman had been an old friend of her companion's, she should have accepted without demur; but she knew that the acquaintance had commenced in a Continental railway train, and her natural prudence instinctively took up a brief for the prosecution. But Denise Ryland had other views.

"My dear girl," she said, "you are not going to be so…crack-brained…as to stand here…arguing and contracting…rheumatism, lumbago…and other absurd complaints…when you know PERFECTLY well that we had already arranged to go…to supper!" She turned to the smiling Max. "This girl needs…DRAGGING out of…her morbid self…M. Gaston! We'll accept…your cab, on the distinct…understanding that YOU are to accept OUR invitation…to supper."

M. Max bowed agreeably.

"By all means let MY cab take us to YOUR supper," he said, laughing.

XXII
M. MAX MOUNTS CAGLIOSTRO'S STAIRCASE

At a few minutes before midnight, Helen Cumberly and Denise Ryland, escorted by the attentive Frenchman, arrived at Palace Mansions. Any distrust which Helen had experienced at first was replaced now by the esteem which every one of discrimination (criminals excluded) formed of M. Max. She perceived in him a very exquisite gentleman, and although the acquaintance was but one hour old, counted him a friend. Denise Ryland was already quite at home in the Cumberly household, and she insisted that Dr. Cumberly would be deeply mortified should M. Gaston take his departure without making his acquaintance. Thus it came about that M. Gaston Max was presented (as "M. Gaston") to Dr. Cumberly.

Cumberly, who had learned to accept men and women upon his daughter's estimate, welcomed the resplendent Parisian hospitably; the warm, shaded lights made convivial play in the amber deeps of the decanters, and the cigars had a fire-side fragrance which M. Max found wholly irresistible.

The ladies being momentarily out of ear-shot, M. Gaston glancing rapidly about him, said: "May I beg a favor, Dr. Cumberly?"

"Certainly, M. Gaston," replied the physician — he was officiating at the syphon. "Say when."

"When!" said Max. "I should like to see you in Harley Street to-morrow morning."

Cumberly glanced up oddly. "Nothing wrong, I hope?"

"Oh, not professionally," smiled Max; "or perhaps I should say only semi-professionally. Can you spare me ten minutes?"

"My book is rather full in the morning, I believe," said Cumberly, frowning thoughtfully, "and without consulting it — which, since it is in Harley Street, is impossible — I scarcely know when I shall be at liberty. Could we not lunch together?"

Max blew a ring of smoke from his lips and watched it slowly dispersing.

"For certain reasons," he replied, and his odd American accent became momentarily more perceptible, "I should prefer that my visit had the appearance of being a professional one."

Cumberly was unable to conceal his surprise, but assuming that his visitor had good reason for the request, he replied after a moment's reflection:

"I should propose, then, that you come to Harley Street at, shall we say, 9.30? My earliest professional appointment is at 10. Will that inconvenience you?"

"Not at all," Max assured him; "it will suit me admirably."

With that the matter dropped for the time, since Helen and her new friend now reentered; and although Helen's manner was markedly depressed, Miss Ryland energetically turned the conversation upon the subject of the play which they had witnessed that evening.

M. Max, when he took his departure, found that the rain had ceased, and accordingly he walked up Whitehall, interesting himself in those details of midnight London life so absorbing to the visitor, though usually overlooked by the resident.

Punctually at half-past nine, a claret-colored figure appeared in sedate Harley Street. M. Gaston Max pressed the bell above which appeared:

DR. BRUCE CUMBERLY.

He was admitted by Garnham, who attended there daily during the hours when Dr. Cumberly was visible to patients, and presently found himself in the consulting room of the physician.

"Good morning, M. Gaston!" said Cumberly, rising and shaking his visitor by the hand. "Pray sit down, and let us get to business. I can give you a clear half-hour."

Max, by way of reply, selected a card from one of the several divisions of his card-case, and placed it on the table. Cumberly glanced at it and started slightly, turning and surveying his visitor with a new interest.

"You are M. Gaston Max!" he said, fixing his gray eyes upon the face of the man before him. "I understood my daughter to say"...

Max waved his hands, deprecatingly.

"It is in the first place to apologize," he explained, "that I am here. I was presented to your daughter in the name of Gaston — which is at least part of my own name — and because other interests were involved I found myself in the painful position of being presented to you under the same false colors"...

"Oh, dear, dear!" began Cumberly. "But — "

"Ah! I protest, it is true," continued Max with an inimitable movement of the shoulder; "and I regret it; but in my profession"...

"Which you adorn, monsieur," injected Cumberly.

"Many thanks — but in my profession these little annoyances sometimes occur. At the earliest suitable occasion, I shall reveal myself to Miss Cumberly and Miss Ryland, but at present," — he spread his palms eloquently, and raised his eyebrows — "morbleu! it is impossible."

"Certainly; I quite understand that. Your visit to London is a professional one? I am more than delighted to have met you, M. Max; your work on criminal anthroposcopy has an honored place on my shelves."

Again M. Max delivered himself of the deprecatory wave.

"You cover me with confusion," he protested; "for I fear in that book I have intruded upon sciences of which I know nothing, and of which you know much."

"On the contrary, you have contributed to those sciences, M. Max," declared the physician; "and now, do I understand that the object of your call this morning?"...

"In the first place it was to excuse myself — but in the second place, I come to ask your help."

He seated himself in a deep armchair — bending forward, and fixing his dark, penetrating eyes upon the physician. Cumberly, turning his own chair slightly, evinced the greatest interest in M. Max's disclosures.

"If you have been in Paris lately," continued the detective, "you will possibly have availed yourself of the opportunity — since another may not occur — of visiting the house of the famous magician, Cagliostro, on the corner of Rue St. Claude, and Boulevard Beaumarchais"...

"I have not been in Paris for over two years," said Cumberly, "nor was I aware that a house of that celebrated charlatan remained extant."

"Ah! Dr. Cumberly, your judgment of Cagliostro is a harsh one. We have no time for such discussion now, but I should like to debate with you this question: was Cagliostro a charlatan? However, the point is this: Owing to alterations taking place in the Boulevard Beaumarchais, some of the end houses in Rue St. Claude are being pulled down, among them Number 1, formerly occupied by the Comte de Cagliostro. At the time that the work commenced, I availed myself of a little leisure to visit that house, once so famous. I was very much interested, and found it fascinating to walk up the Grande Staircase where so many historical personages once walked to consult the seer. But great as was my interest in the apartments of Cagliostro, I was even more interested in one of the apartments in a neighboring house, into which — quite accidentally, you understand — I found myself looking."

XXIII
RAID IN THE RUE ST. CLAUDE

"I perceived," said M. Gaston Max, "that owing to the progress of the work of demolition, and owing to the carelessness of the people in charge — nom d'un nom! they were careless, those! — I was able, from a certain point, to look into a small room fitted up in a way very curious. There was a sort of bunk somewhat similar to that in a steamer berth, and the walls were covered with paper of a Chinese pattern most bizarre. No one was in the room when I first perceived it, but I had not been looking in for many moments before a Chinaman entered and closed the shutters. He was hasty, this one.

"Eh bien! I had seen enough. I perceived that my visit to the house of Cagliostro had been dictated by a good little angel. It happened that for many months I had been in quest of the headquarters of a certain group which I knew, beyond any tiny doubt, to have its claws deep in Parisian society. I refer to an opium syndicate"...

Dr. Cumberly started and seemed about to speak; but he restrained himself, bending forward and awaiting the detective's next words with even keener interest than hitherto.

"I had been trying — all vainly — to trace the source from which the opium was obtained, and the place where it was used. I have devoted much attention to the subject, and have spent some twelve months in the opium provinces of China, you understand. I know how insidious a thing it is, this opium, and how dreadful a curse it may become when it gets a hold upon a community. I was formerly engaged upon a most sensational case in San Francisco; and the horrors of the discoveries which we made there — the American police and myself — have remained with me ever since. Pardieu! I cannot forget them! Therefore when I learnt that an organized attempt was being made to establish elaborate opium dens upon a most up-to-date plan, in Paris, I exerted myself to the utmost to break up this scheme in its infancy"...

Dr. Cumberly was hanging upon every word.

"Apart from the physical and moral ruin attendant upon the vice," continued Max, "the methods of this particular organization have brought financial ruin to many." He shook his finger at Dr. Cumberly as if to emphasize his certainty upon this point. "I will not go into particulars now, but there is a system of wholesale robbery — sapristi! of most ingenious brigandage — being practised by this group. Therefore I congratulated myself upon the inspiration which had led me to mount Cagliostro's staircase. The way in which these people had conducted their sinister trade from so public a spot as this was really wonderful, but I had already learned to respect the ingenuity of the group, or of the man at the head of it. I wasted no time; not I! We raided the house that evening"...

"And what did you find?" asked Dr. Cumberly, eagerly.

"We found this establishment elaborately fitted, and the whole of the fittings were American. Eh bien! This confirmed me in my belief that the establishment was a branch of the wealthy concern I have mentioned in San Francisco. There was also a branch in New York, apparently. We found six or eight people in the place in various stages of coma; and I cannot tell you their names because — among them, were some well-known in the best society"...

"Good Heavens, M. Max, you surprise and shock me!"

"What I tell you is but the truth. We apprehended two low fellows who acted as servants sometimes in the place. We had records of both of them at the Bureau. And there was also a woman belonging to the same class. None of these seemed to me very important, but we were fortunate enough to capture, in addition, a Chinaman — Sen — and a certain Madame Jean — the latter the principal of the establishment!"

"What! a woman?"

"Morbleu! a woman — exactly! You are surprised? Yes; and I was surprised, but full inquiry convinced me that Madame Jean was the chief of staff. We had conducted the raid at night, of course, and because of the big names, we hushed it up. We can do these things in Paris so much more easily than is possible here in London." He illustrated, delivering a kick upon the person of an imaginary malefactor. "Cochon! Va!" he shrugged. "It is finished!

"The place was arranged with Oriental magnificence. The reception-room — if I can so term that apartment — was like the scene of Rimsky Korsakov's Sheherezade; I could see that very heavy charges were made at this establishment. I will not bore you with further particulars, but I will tell you of my disappointment."

"Your disappointment?"

"Yes, I was disappointed. True, I had brought about the closing of that house, but of the huge sums of money fraudulently obtained from victims, I could find no trace in the accounts of Madame Jean. She defied me with silence, simply declining to give any account of herself beyond admitting that she conducted an hotel at which opium might be smoked if desired. Blagueur! Sen, the Chinaman, who professed to speak nothing but Chinese — ah! cochon! — was equally a difficult case, Nom d'un nom! I was in despair, for apart from frauds connected with the concern, I had more than small suspicions that at least one death — that of a wealthy banker — could be laid at the doors of the establishment in Rue St. Claude."...

Dr. Cumberly bent yet lower, watching the speaker's face.

"A murder!" he whispered.

"I do not say so," replied Max, "but it certainly might have been. The case then must, indeed, have ended miserably, as far as I was concerned, if I had not chanced upon a letter which the otherwise prudent Madame Jean had forgotten to destroy. Triomphe! It was a letter of instruction, and definitely it proved that she was no more than a kind of glorified concierge, and that the chief of the opium group was in London."

"Undoubtedly in London. There was no address on the letter, and no date, and it was curiously signed: Mr. King."

"Mr. King!"

Dr. Cumberly rose slowly from his chair, and took a step toward M. Max.

"You are interested?" said the detective, and shrugged his shoulders, whilst his mobile mouth shaped itself in a grim smile. "Pardieu! I knew you would be! Acting upon another clue which the letter — priceless letter — contained, I visited the Credit Lyonnais. I discovered that an account had been opened there by Mr. Henry Leroux of London on behalf of his wife, Mira Leroux, to the amount of a thousand pounds."

"A thousand pounds — really!" cried Dr. Cumberly, drawing his heavy brows together — "as much as that?"

"Certainly. It was for a thousand pounds," repeated Max, "and the whole of that amount had been drawn out."

"The whole thousand?"

"The whole thousand; nom d'un p'tit bonhomme! The whole thousand! Acting, as I have said, upon the information in this always priceless letter, I confronted Madame Jean and the manager of the bank with each other. Morbleu! 'This,' he said, 'is Mira Leroux of London!'"...

"What!" cried Cumberly, seemingly quite stupefied by this last revelation.

Max spread wide his palms, and the flexible lips expressed sympathy with the doctor's stupefaction.

"It is as I tell you," he continued. "This Madame Jean had been posing as Mrs. Leroux, and in some way, which I was unable to understand, her signature had been accepted by the Credit Lyonnais. I examined the specimen signature which had been forwarded to them by the London County and Suburban Bank, and I perceived, at once, that it was not a case of common forgery. The signatures were identical"...

"Therefore," said Cumberly, and he was thinking of Henry Leroux, whom Fate delighted in buffeting — "therefore, the Credit Lyonnais is not responsible?"

"Most decidedly not responsible," agreed Max. "So you see I now have two reasons for coming to London: one, to visit the London County and Suburban Bank, and the other to find... Mr. King. The first part of my mission I have performed successfully; but the second"... again he shrugged, and the lines of his mouth were humorous.

Dr. Cumberly began to walk up and down the carpet.

"Poor Leroux!" he muttered — "poor Leroux."

"Ah! poor Leroux, indeed," said Max. "He is so typical a victim of this most infernal group!"

"What!" Dr. Cumberly turned in his promenade and stared at the detective — "he's not the only one?"

"My dear sir," said Max, gently, "the victims of Mr. King are truly as the sands of Arabia."

"Good heavens!" muttered Dr. Cumberly; "good heavens!"

"I came immediately to London," continued Max, "and presented myself at New Scotland Yard. There I discovered that my inquiry was complicated by a ghastly crime which had been committed in the flat of Mr. Leroux; but I learned, also, that Mr. King was concerned in this crime — his name had been found upon a scrap of paper clenched in the murdered woman's hand!"

"I was present when it was found," said Dr. Cumberly.

"I know you were," replied Max. "In short, I discovered that the Palace Mansions murder case was my case, and that my case was the Palace Mansions case. Eh bien! the mystery of the Paris draft did not detain me long. A call upon the manager of the London County and Suburban Bank at Charing Cross revealed to me the whole plot. The real Mrs. Leroux had never visited that bank; it was Madame Jean, posing as Mrs. Leroux, who went there and wrote the specimen signature, accompanied by a certain Soames, a butler"...

"I know him!" said Dr. Cumberly, grimly, "the blackguard!"

"Truly a blackguard, truly a big, dirty blackguard! But it is such canaille as this that Mr. King discovers and uses for his own ends. Paris society, I know for a fact; has many such a cankerworm in its heart. Oh! it is a big case, a very big case. Poor Mr. Leroux being confined to his bed — ah! I pity him — I took the opportunity to visit his flat in Palace Mansions with Inspector Dunbar, and I obtained further evidence showing how the conspiracy had been conducted; yes. For instance, Dunbar's notebook showed me that Mr. Leroux was accustomed to receive letters from Mrs. Leroux whilst she was supposed to be in Paris. I actually discovered some of those letters, and they bore no dates. This, if they came from a woman, was not remarkable, but, upon one of them I found something that WAS remarkable. It was still in its envelope, you must understand, this letter, its envelope bearing the Paris post-mark. But impressed upon the paper I discovered a second post-mark, which, by means of a simple process, and the use of a magnifying glass, I made out to be Bow, East!"

"What!"

"Do you understand? This letter, and others doubtless, had been enclosed in an envelope and despatched to Paris from Bow, East? In short, Mrs. Leroux wrote those letters before she left London; Soames never posted them, but handed them over to some representative of Mr. King; this other, in turn, posted them to Madame Jean in Paris! Morbleu! these are clever rogues! This which I was fortunate enough to discover had been on top, you understand, this billet, and the outer envelope being very heavily stamped, that below retained the impress of the post-mark."

"Poor Leroux!" said Cumberly again, with suppressed emotion. "That unsuspecting, kindly soul has been drawn into the meshes of this conspiracy. How they have been wound around him, until..."

"He knows the truth about his wife?" asked Max, suddenly glancing up at the physician, "that she is not in Paris?"

"I, myself, broke the painful news to him," replied Cumberly — "after a consultation with Miss Ryland and my daughter. I considered it my duty to tell him, but I cannot disguise from myself that it hastened, if it did not directly occasion, his breakdown."

"Yes, yes," said Max; "we have been very fortunate however in diverting the attention of the press from the absence of Mrs. Leroux throughout this time. Nom d'un nom! Had they got to know about the scrap of paper found in the dead woman's hand, I fear that this would have been impossible."

"I do not doubt that it would have been impossible, knowing the London press," replied Dr. Cumberly, "but I, too, am glad that it has been achieved; for in the light of your Paris discoveries, I begin at last to understand."

"You were not Mrs. Leroux's medical adviser?"

"I was not," replied Cumberly, glancing sharply at Max. "Good heavens, to think that I had never realized the truth!"

"It is not so wonderful at all. Of course, as I have seen from the evidence which you gave to the police, you knew that Mrs. Vernon was addicted to the use of opium?"

"It was perfectly evident," replied Cumberly; "painfully evident. I will not go into particulars, but her entire constitution was undermined by the habit. I may add, however, that I did not associate the vice with her violent end, except"...

"Ah!" interrupted Max, shaking his finger at the physician, "you are coming to the point upon which you disagreed with the divisional surgeon! Now, it is an important point. You are of opinion that the injection in Mrs. Vernon's shoulder — which could not have been self-administered"...

"She was not addicted to the use of the needle," interrupted Cumberly; "she was an opium SMOKER."

"Quite so, quite so," said Max: "it makes the point all the more clear. You are of opinion that this injection was made at least eight hours before the woman's death?"

"At least eight hours — yes."

"Eh bien!" said Max; "and have you had extensive experience of such injections?"

Dr. Cumberly stared at him in some surprise.

"In a general way," he said, "a fair number of such cases have come under my notice; but it chances that one of my patients, a regular patient — is addicted to the vice."

"Injections?"

"Only as a makeshift. He has periodical bouts of opium smoking — what I may term deliberate debauches."

"Ah!" Max was keenly interested. "This patient is a member of good society?"

"He's a member of Parliament," replied Cumberly, a faint, humorous glint creeping into his gray eyes; "but, of course, that is not an answer to your question! Yes, he is of an old family, and is engaged to the daughter of a peer."

"Dr. Cumberly," said Max, "in a case like the present — apart from the fact that the happiness — pardieu! the life — of one of your own friends is involved... should you count it a breach of professional etiquette to divulge the name of that patient?"

It was a disturbing question; a momentous question for a fashionable physician to be called upon to answer thus suddenly. Dr. Cumberly, who had resumed his promenade of the carpet, stopped with his back to M. Max, and stared out of the window into Harley Street.

M. Max, a man of refined susceptibilities, came to his aid, diplomatically.

"It is perhaps overmuch to ask you," he said. "I can settle the problem in a more simple manner. Inspector Dunbar will ask you for this gentleman's name, and you, as witness in the case, cannot refuse to give it."

"I can refuse until I stand in the witness-box!" replied Cumberly, turning, a wry smile upon his face.

"With the result," interposed Max, "that the ends of justice might be defeated, and the wrong man hanged!"

"True," said Cumberly; "I am splitting hairs. It is distinctly a breach of professional etiquette, nevertheless, and I cannot disguise the fact from myself. However, since the knowledge will never go any further, and since tremendous issues are at stake, I will give you the name of my opium patient. It is Sir Brian Malpas!"

"I am much indebted to you, Dr. Cumberly," said Max; "a thousand thanks;" but in his eyes there was a far-away look. "Malpas — Malpas! Where in this case have I met with the name of Malpas?"

"Inspector Dunbar may possibly have mentioned it to you in reference to the evidence of Mr. John Exel, M. P. Mr. Exel, you may remember"...

"I have it!" cried Max; "Nom d'un nom! I have it! It was from Sir Brian Malpas that he had parted at the corner of Victoria Street on the night of the murder, is it not so?"

"Your memory is very good, M. Max!"

"Then Mr. Exel is a personal friend of Sir Brian Malpas?"

"Excellent! Kismet aids me still! I come to you hoping that you may be acquainted with the constitution of Mrs. Leroux, but no! behold me disappointed in this. Then — morbleu! among your patients I find a possible client of the opium syndicate!"

"What! Malpas? Good God! I had not thought of that! Of course, he must retire somewhere from the ken of society to indulge in these opium orgies"...

"Quite so. I have hopes. Since it would never do for Sir Brian Malpas to know who I am and what I seek, a roundabout introduction is provided by kindly Providence — Ah! that good little angel of mine! — in the person of Mr. John Exel, M. P."

"I will introduce you to Mr. Exel with pleasure."

"Eh bien! Let it be arranged as soon as possible," said M. Max. "To Mr. John Exel I will be, as to Miss Ryland (morbleu! I hate me!) and Miss Cumberly (pardieu! I loathe myself!), M. Gaston! It is ten o'clock, and already I hear your first patient ringing at the front-door bell. Good morning, Dr. Cumberly."

Dr. Cumberly grasped his hand cordially.

"Good morning, M. Max!"

The famous detective was indeed retiring, when:

"M. Max!"

He turned — and looked into the troubled gray eyes of Dr. Cumberly.

"You would ask me where is she — Mrs. Leroux?" he said. "My friend — I may call you my friend, may I not? — I cannot say if she is living or is dead. Some little I know of the Chinese, quite a little; nom de dieu!...I hope she is dead!"...

XXIV
OPIUM

Denise Ryland was lunching that day with Dr. Cumberly and his daughter at Palace Mansions; and as was usually the case when this trio met, the conversation turned upon the mystery.

"I have just seen Leroux," said the physician, as he took his seat, "and I have told him that he must go for a drive to-morrow. I have released him from his room, and given him the run of the place again, but until he can get right away, complete recovery is impossible. A little cheerful company might be useful, though. You might look in and see him for a while, Helen?"

Helen met her father's eyes, gravely, and replied, with perfect composure, "I will do so with pleasure. Miss Ryland will come with me."

"Suppose," said Denise Ryland, assuming her most truculent air, "you leave off...talking in that...frigid manner...my dear. Considering that Mira...Leroux and I were...old friends, and that you...are old friends of hers, too, and considering that I spend...my life amongst...people who very sensibly call...one another...by their Christian names, forget that my name is Ryland, and call me...Denise!"

"I should love to!" cried Helen Cumberly; "in fact, I wanted to do so the very first time I saw you; perhaps because Mira Leroux always referred to you as Denise"...

"May I also avail myself of the privilege?" inquired Dr. Cumberly with gravity, "and may I hope that you will return the compliment?"

"I cannot...do it!" declared Denise Ryland, firmly. "A doctor ...should never be known by any other name than...Doctor. If I heard any one refer to my own...physician as Jack or...Bill, or Dick...I should lose ALL faith in him at once!"

As the lunch proceeded, Dr. Cumberly gradually grew more silent, seeming to be employed with his own thoughts; and although his daughter and Denise Ryland were discussing the very matter that engaged his own attention, he took no part in the conversation for some time. Then:

"I agree with you!" he said, suddenly, interrupting Helen; "the greatest blow of all to Leroux was the knowledge that his wife had been deceiving him."

"He invited...deceit!" proclaimed Denise Ryland, "by his...criminal neglect."

"Oh! how can you say so!" cried Helen, turning her gray eyes upon the speaker reproachfully; "he deserves — "

"He certainly deserves to know the real truth," concluded Dr. Cumberly; "but would it relieve his mind or otherwise?"

Denise Ryland and Helen looked at him in silent surprise.

"The truth?" began the latter — "Do you mean that you know — where she is"...

"If I knew that," replied Dr. Cumberly, "I should know everything; the mystery of the Palace Mansions murder would be a mystery no longer. But I know one thing: Mrs. Leroux's absence has nothing to do with any love affair."

"What!" exclaimed Denise Ryland. "There isn't another man...in the case? You can't tell me"...

"But I DO tell you!" said Dr. Cumberly; "I ASSURE you."

"And you have not told — Mr. Leroux?" said Helen incredulously. "You have NOT told him — although you know that the thought — of THAT is?"...

"Is practically killing him? No, I have not told him yet. For — would my news act as a palliative or as an irritant?"

"That depends," pronounced Denise Ryland, "on the nature of...your news."

"I suppose I have no right to conceal it from him. Therefore, we will tell him to-day. But although, beyond doubt, his mind will be relieved upon one point, the real facts are almost, if not quite, as bad."

"I learnt, this morning," he continued, lighting a cigarette, "certain facts which, had I been half as clever as I supposed myself, I should have deduced from the data already in my possession. I was aware, of course, that the unhappy victim — Mrs. Vernon — was addicted to the use of opium, and if a tangible link were necessary, it existed in the form of the written fragment which I myself took from the dead woman's hand."...

"A link!" said Denise Ryland.

"A link between Mrs. Vernon and Mrs. Leroux," explained the physician. "You see, it had never occurred to me that they knew one another."...

"And did they?" questioned his daughter, eagerly.

"It is almost certain that they were acquainted, at any rate; and in view of certain symptoms, which, without giving them much consideration, I nevertheless had detected in Mrs. Leroux, I am disposed to think that the bond of sympathy which existed between them was"...

He seemed to hesitate, looking at his daughter, whose gray eyes were fixed upon him intently, and then at Denise Ryland, who, with her chin resting upon her hands, and her elbows propped upon the table, was literally glaring at him.

"Opium!" he said.

A look of horror began slowly to steal over Helen Cumberly's face; Denise Ryland's head commenced to sway from side to side. But neither woman spoke.

"By the courtesy of Inspector Dunbar," continued Dr. Cumberly, "I have been enabled to keep in touch with the developments of the case, as you know; and he had noted as a significant fact that the late Mrs. Vernon's periodical visits to Scotland corresponded, curiously, with those of Mrs. Leroux to Paris. I don't mean in regard to date; although in one or two instances (notably Mrs. Vernon's last journey to Scotland, and that of Mrs. Leroux to Paris), there was similarity even in this particular. A certain Mr. Debnam — the late Horace Vernon's solicitor — placed an absurd construction upon this"...

"Do you mean," interrupted Helen in a strained voice, "that he insinuated that Mrs. Vernon"...

"He had an idea that she visited Leroux — yes," replied her father hastily. "It was one of those absurd and irritating theories, which, instinctively, we know to be wrong, but which, if asked for evidence, we cannot hope to PROVE to be wrong."

"It is outrageous!" cried Helen, her eyes flashing indignantly; "Mr. Debnam should be ashamed of himself!"

Dr. Cumberly smiled rather sadly.

"In this world," he said, "we have to count with the Debnams. One's own private knowledge of a man's character is not worth a brass farthing as legal evidence. But I am happy to say that Dunbar completely pooh-poohed the idea."

"I like Inspector Dunbar!" declared Helen; "he is so strong — a splendid man!"

Denise Ryland stared at her cynically, but made no remark.

"The inspector and myself," continued Dr. Cumberly, "attached altogether a different significance to the circumstances. I am pleased to tell you that Debnam's unpleasant theories are already proved fallacious; the case goes deeper, far deeper, than a mere intrigue of that kind. In short, I am now assured — I cannot, unfortunately, name the source of my new information — but I am assured, that Mrs. Leroux, as well as Mrs. Vernon, was addicted to the opium vice."...

"Oh, my God! how horrible!" whispered Helen.

"A certain notorious character," resumed Dr. Cumberly...

"Soames!" snapped Denise Ryland. "Since I heard... that man's name I knew him for... a villain... of the worst possible... description... imaginable."

"Soames," replied Dr. Cumberly, smiling slightly, "was one of the group, beyond doubt — for I may as well explain that we are dealing with an elaborate organization; but the chief member, to whom I have referred, is a greater one than Soames. He is a certain shadowy being, known as Mr. King."

"The name on the paper!" said Helen, quickly. "But of course the police have been looking for Mr. King all along?"

"In a general way — yes; but as we have thousands of Kings in London alone, the task is a stupendous one. The information which I received this morning narrows down the search immensely; for it points to Mr. King being the chief, or president, of a sort of opium syndicate, and, furthermore, it points to his being a Chinaman."

"A Chinaman!" cried Denise and Helen together.

"It is not absolutely certain, but it is more than probable. The point is that Mrs. Leroux has not eloped with some unknown lover; she is in one of the opium establishments of Mr. King."

"Do you mean that she is detained there?" asked Helen.

"It appears to me, now, to be certain that she is. My hypothesis is that she was an habitue of this place, as also was Mrs. Vernon. These unhappy women, by means of elaborate plans, made on their behalf by the syndicate, indulged in periodical opium orgies. It was a game well worth the candle, as the saying goes, from the syndicate's standpoint; for Mrs. Leroux, alone, has paid no less than a thousand pounds to the opium group!"

"A thousand pounds!" cried Denise Ryland. "You don't mean to tell me that that... silly fool... of a man, Harry Leroux... has allowed himself to be swindled of... all that money?"

"There is not the slightest doubt about it," Dr. Cumberly assured her; "he opened a credit to that amount in Paris, and the entire sum has been absorbed by Mr. King!"

"It's almost incredible!" said Helen.

"I quite agree with you," replied her father. "Of course, most people know that there are opium dens in London, as in almost every other big city, but the existence of these palatial establishments, conducted by Mr. King, although undoubtedly a fact, is a fact difficult to accept. It doesn't seem possible that such a place can be conducted secretly; whereas I am assured that all the efforts of Scotland Yard thus far have failed to locate the site of the London branch."

"But surely," cried Denise Ryland, nostrils dilated indignantly, "some of the…customers of this…disgusting place…can be followed?"…

"The difficulty is to identify them," explained Cumberly. "Opium smoking is essentially a secret vice; a man does not visit an opium den openly as he would visit his club; and the elaborate precautions adopted by the women are illustrated in the case of Mrs. Vernon, and in the case of Mrs. Leroux. It is a pathetic fact almost daily brought home to me, that women who acquire a drug habit become more rapidly and more entirely enslaved by it than does a man. It becomes the center of the woman's existence; it becomes her god: all other claims, social and domestic, are disregarded. Upon this knowledge, Mr. King has established his undoubtedly extensive enterprise."…

Dr. Cumberly stood up.

"I will go down and see Leroux," he announced quietly. "His sorrow hitherto has been secondary to his indignation. Possibly ignorance in this case is preferable to the truth, but nevertheless I am determined to tell him what I know. Give me ten minutes or so, and then join me. Are you agreeable?"

"Quite," said Helen.

Dr. Cumberly departed upon his self-imposed mission.

XXV
FATE'S SHUTTLECOCK

Some ten minutes later, Helen Cumberly and Denise Ryland were in turn admitted to Henry Leroux's flat. They found him seated on a couch in his dining-room, wearing the inevitable dressing-gown. Dr. Cumberly, his hands clasped behind him, stood looking out of the window.

Leroux's pallor now was most remarkable; his complexion had assumed an ivory whiteness which lent his face a sort of statuesque beauty. He was cleanly shaven (somewhat of a novelty), and his hair was brushed back from his brow. But the dark blue eyes were very tragic.

He rose at sight of his new visitors, and a faint color momentarily tinged his cheeks. Helen Cumberly grasped his outstretched hand, then looked away quickly to where her father was standing.

"I almost thought," said Leroux, "that you had deserted me."

"No," said Helen, seeming to speak with an effort — "we — my father, thought — that you needed quiet."

Denise Ryland nodded grimly.

"But now," she said, in her most truculent manner, "we are going to…drag you out of…your morbid…self…for a change…which you need…if ever a man…needed it."

"I have just prescribed a drive," said Dr. Cumberly, turning to them, "for to-morrow morning; with lunch at Richmond and a walk across the park, rejoining the car at the Bushey Gate, and so home to tea."

Henry Leroux looked eagerly at Helen in silent appeal. He seemed to fear that she would refuse.

"Do you mean that you have included us in the prescription, father?" she asked.

"Certainly; you are an essential part of it."

"It will be fine," said the girl quietly; "I shall enjoy it."

"Ah!" said Leroux, with a faint note of contentment in his voice; and he reseated himself.

There was an interval of somewhat awkward silence, to be broken by Denise Ryland.

"Dr. Cumberly has told you the news?" she asked, dropping for the moment her syncopated and pugnacious manner.

Leroux closed his eyes and leant back upon the couch.

"Yes," he replied. "And to think that I am a useless wreck — a poor parody of a man — whilst — Mira is... Oh, God! help me! — God help HER!"

He was visibly contending with his emotions; and Helen Cumberly found herself forced to turn her head aside.

"I have been blind," continued Leroux, in a forced, monotonous voice. "That Mira has not — deceived me, in the worst sense of the word, is in no way due to my care of her. I recognize that, and I accept my punishment; for I deserved it. But what now overwhelms me is the knowledge, the frightful knowledge, that in a sense I have misjudged her, that I have remained here inert, making no effort, thinking her absence voluntary, whilst — God help her! — she has been"...

"Once again, Leroux," interrupted Dr. Cumberly, "I must ask you not to take too black a view. I blame myself more than I blame you, for having failed to perceive what as an intimate friend I had every opportunity to perceive; that your wife was acquiring the opium habit. You have told me that you count her as dead" — he stood beside Leroux, resting both hands upon the bowed shoulders — "I have not encouraged you to change that view. One who has cultivated — the — vice, to a point where protracted absences become necessary — you understand me? — is, so far as my experience goes"...

"Incurable! I quite understand," jerked Leroux. "A thousand times better dead, indeed."

"The facts as I see them," resumed the physician, "as I see them, are these: by some fatality, at present inexplicable, a victim of the opium syndicate met her death in this flat. Realizing that the inquiries brought to bear would inevitably lead to the cross-examination of Mrs. Leroux, the opium syndicate has detained her; was forced to detain her."

"Where is the place," began Leroux, in a voice rising higher with every syllable — "where is the infamous den to which — to which"...

Dr. Cumberly pressed his hands firmly upon the speaker's shoulders.

"It is only a question of time, Leroux," he said, "and you will have the satisfaction of knowing that — though at a great cost to yourself — this dreadful evil has been stamped out, that this yellow peril has been torn from the heart of society. Now, I must leave you for the present; but rest assured that everything possible is being done to close the nets about Mr. King."

"Ah!" whispered Leroux, "MR. KING!"

"The circle is narrowing," continued the physician. "I may not divulge confidences; but a very clever man — the greatest practical criminologist in Europe — is devoting the whole of his time, night and day, to this object."

Helen Cumberly and Denise Ryland exhibited a keen interest in the words, but Leroux, with closed eyes, merely nodded in a dull way. Shortly, Dr. Cumberly took his departure, and, Helen looking at her companion interrogatively: —

"I think," said Denise Ryland, addressing Leroux, "that you should not over-tax your strength at present." She walked across to where he sat, and examined some proofslips lying upon the little table beside the couch. "'Martin Zeda,'" she said, with a certain high disdain. "Leave 'Martin Zeda' alone for once, and read a really cheerful book!"

Leroux forced a smile to his lips.

"The correction of these proofs," he said diffidently, "exacts no great mental strain, but is sufficient to — distract my mind. Work, after all, is nature's own sedative."

"I rather agree with Mr. Leroux, Denise," said Helen; — "and really you must allow him to know best."

"Thank you," said Leroux, meeting her eyes momentarily. "I feared that I was about to be sent to bed like a naughty boy!"

"I hope it's fine to-morrow," said Helen rapidly. "A drive to Richmond will be quite delightful."

"I think, myself," agreed Leroux, "that it will hasten my recovery to breathe the fresh air once again."

Knowing how eagerly he longed for health and strength, and to what purpose, the girl found something very pathetic in the words.

"I wish you were well enough to come out this afternoon," she said; "I am going to a private view at Olaf van Noord's studio. It is sure to be an extraordinary afternoon. He is the god of the Soho futurists, you know. And his pictures are the weirdest nightmares imaginable. One always meets such singular people there, too, and I am honored in receiving an invitation to represent the Planet!"

"I consider," said Denise Ryland, head wagging furiously again, "that the man is...mad. He had an exhibition...in Paris ...and everybody...laughed at him...simply LAUGHED at him."

"But financially, he is very successful," added Helen.

"Financially!" exclaimed Denise Ryland, "FINANCIALLY! To criticize a man's work...financially, is about as...sensible as...to judge the Venus...de Milo...by weight! — or to sell the works...of Leonardo...da Vinci by the...yard! Olaf van Noord is nothing but...a fool...of the worst possible...description...imaginable."

"He is at least an entertaining fool!" protested Helen, laughingly.

"A mountebank!" cried Denise Ryland; "a clown...a pantaloon...a whole family of...idiots... rolled into one!"

"It seems unkind to run away and leave you here — in your loneliness," said Helen to Leroux; "but really I must be off to the wilds of Soho."...

"To-morrow," said Leroux, standing up and fixing his eyes upon her lingeringly, "will be a red-letter day. I have no right to complain, whilst such good friends remain to me — such true friends."...

XXVI
"OUR LADY OF THE POPPIES"

A number of visitors were sprinkled about Olaf van Noord's large and dirty studio, these being made up for the most part of those weird and nondescript enthusiasts who seek to erect an apocryphal Montmartre in the plains of Soho. One or two ordinary mortals, representing the Press, leavened the throng, but the entire gathering — "advanced" and unenlightened alike — seemed to be drawn to a common focus: a large canvas placed advantageously in the southeast corner of the studio, where it enjoyed all the benefit of a pure and equably suffused light.

Seated apart from his worshipers upon a little sketching stool, and handling a remarkably long, amber cigarette-holder with much grace, was Olaf van Noord. He had hair of so light a yellow as sometimes to appear white, worn very long, brushed back from his brow and cut squarely all around behind, lending him a medieval appearance. He wore a slight mustache carefully pointed; and his scanty vandyke beard could not entirely conceal the weakness of his chin. His complexion had the color and general appearance of drawing-paper, and in his large blue eyes was an eerie hint of sightlessness. He was attired in a light tweed suit cut in an American pattern, and out from his low collar flowed a black French knot.

Olaf van Noord rose to meet Helen Cumberly and Denise Ryland, advancing across the floor with the measured gait of a tragic actor. He greeted them aloofly, and a little negro boy proffered tiny cups of China tea. Denise Ryland distended her nostrils as her gaze swept the picture-covered walls; but she seemed to approve of the tea.

The artist next extended to them an ivory box containing little yellow-wrapped cigarettes. Helen Cumberly smilingly refused, but Denise Ryland took one of the cigarettes, sniffed at it superciliously — and then replaced it in the box.

"It has a most… egregiously horrible… odor," she commented.

"They are a special brand," explained Olaf van Noord, distractedly, "which I have imported for me from Smyrna. They contain a small percentage of opium."

"Opium!" exclaimed Denise Ryland, glaring at the speaker and then at Helen Cumberly, as though the latter were responsible in some way for the vices of the painter.

"Yes," he said, reclosing the box, and pacing somberly to the door to greet a new arrival.

"Did you ever in all your life," said Denise Ryland, glancing about her, "see such an exhibition… of nightmares?"

Certainly, the criticism was not without justification; the dauby-looking oil-paintings, incomprehensible water-colors, and riotous charcoal sketches which formed the mural decoration of the studio were distinctly "advanced." But, since the center of interest seemed to be the large canvas on the easel, the two moved to the edges of the group of spectators and began to examine this masterpiece. A very puzzled newspaperman joined them, bending and whispering to Helen Cumberly:

"Are you going to notice the thing seriously? Personally, I am writing it up as a practical joke! We are giving him half a column — Lord knows what for! — but I can't see how to handle it except as funny stuff."

"But, for heaven's sake… what does he… CALL it?" muttered Denise Ryland, holding a pair of gold rimmed pince-nez before her eyes, and shifting them to and fro in an endeavor to focus the canvas.

"'Our Lady of the Poppies,'" replied the journalist. "Do you think it's intended to mean anything in particular?"

The question was no light one; it embodied a problem not readily solved. The scene depicted, and depicted with a skill, with a technical mastery of the bizarre that had in it something horrible — was a long narrow room — or, properly, cavern. The walls apparently were hewn from black rock, and at regular intervals, placed some three feet from these gleaming walls, uprose slender golden pillars supporting a kind of fretwork arch which entirely masked the ceiling. The point of sight adopted by the painter was peculiar. One apparently looked down into this apartment from some spot elevated fourteen feet or more above the floor level. The floor, which was black and polished, was strewn with tiger skins; and little, inlaid tables and garishly colored cushions were spread about in confusion, whilst cushioned divans occupied the visible corners of the place. The lighting was very "advanced": a lamp, having a kaleidoscopic shade, swung from the center of the roof low into the room and furnished all the illumination.

Three doors were visible; one, directly in line at the further end of the place, apparently of carved ebony inlaid with ivory; another, on the right, of lemon wood or something allied to it, and inlaid with a design in some emerald hued material; with a third, corresponding door, on the left, just barely visible to the spectator.

Two figures appeared. One was that of a Chinaman in a green robe scarcely distinguishable from the cushions surrounding him, who crouched upon the divan to the left of the central door, smoking a long bamboo pipe. His face was the leering face of a yellow satyr. But, dominating the composition, and so conceived in form, in color, and in lighting, as to claim the attention centrally, so that the other extravagant details became but a setting for it, was another figure.

Upon a slender ivory pedestal crouched a golden dragon, and before the pedestal was placed a huge Chinese vase of the indeterminate pink seen in the heart of a rose, and so skilfully colored as to suggest an internal luminousness. The vase was loaded with a mass of exotic poppies, a riotous splash of color; whilst beside this vase, and slightly in front of the pedestal, stood the figure presumably intended to represent the Lady of the Poppies who gave title to the picture.

The figure was that of an Eastern girl, slight and supple, and possessing a devilish and forbidding grace. Her short hair formed a black smudge upon the canvas, and cast a dense shadow upon her face. The composition was infinitely daring; for out of this shadow shone the great black eyes, their diablerie most cunningly insinuated; whilst with a brilliant exclusion of detail — by means of two strokes of the brush steeped in brightest vermilion, and one seemingly haphazard splash of dead white — an evil and abandoned smile was made to greet the spectator.

To the waist, the figure was a study in satin nudity, whence, from a jeweled girdle, light draperies swept downward, covering the feet and swinging, a shimmering curve out into the foreground of the canvas, the curve being cut off in its apogee by the gold frame.

Above her head, this girl of demoniacal beauty held a bunch of poppies seemingly torn from the vase: this, with her left hand; with her right she pointed, tauntingly, at her beholder.

In comparison with the effected futurism of the other pictures in the studio, "Our Lady of the Poppies," beyond question was a great painting. From a point where the entire composition might be taken in by the eye, the uncanny scene glowed with highly colored detail; but, exclude the scheme of the composition, and focus the eye upon any one item — the golden dragon — the seated Chinaman — the ebony door — the silk-shaded lamp; it had no detail whatever: one beheld a meaningless mass of colors. Individually, no one section of the canvas had life, had meaning; but, as a whole, it glowed, it lived — it was genius. Above all, it was uncanny.

This, Denise Ryland fully realized, but critics had grown so used to treating the work of Olaf van Noord as a joke, that "Our Lady of the Poppies" in all probability would never be judged seriously.

"What does it mean, Mr. van Noord?" asked Helen Cumberly, leaving the group of worshipers standing hushed in rapture before the canvas and approaching the painter. "Is there some occult significance in the title?"

"It is a priestess," replied the artist, in his dreamy fashion....

"A priestess?"

"A priestess of the temple."...

Helen Cumberly glanced again at the astonishing picture.

"Do you mean," she began, "that there is a living original?"

Olaf van Noord bowed absently, and left her side to greet one who at that moment entered the studio. Something magnetic in the personality of the newcomer drew all eyes from the canvas to the figure on the threshold. The artist was removing garish tiger skin furs from the shoulders of the girl — for the new arrival was a girl, a Eurasian girl.

She wore a tiger skin motor-coat, and a little, close-fitting, turban-like cap of the same. The coat removed, she stood revealed in a clinging gown of silk; and her feet were shod in little amber colored slippers with green buckles. The bodice of her dress opened in a surprising V, displaying the satin texture of her neck and shoulders, and enhancing the barbaric character of her appearance. Her jet black hair was confined by no band or comb, but protruded Bishareen-like around the shapely head. Without doubt, this was the Lady of the Poppies — the original of the picture.

"Dear friends," said Olaf van Noord, taking the girl's hand, and walking into the studio, "permit me to present my model!"

Following, came a slightly built man who carried himself with a stoop; an olive faced man, who squinted frightfully, and who dressed immaculately.

"What a most...EXTRAORDINARY-looking creature!" whispered Denise Ryland to Helen. "She has undoubted attractions of...a hellish sort...if I may use...the term."

"She is the strangest looking girl I have ever seen in my life," replied Helen, who found herself unable to turn her eyes away from Olaf van Noord's model. "Surely she is not a professional model!"

The chatty reporter (his name was Crockett) confided to Helen Cumberly:

"She is not exactly a professional model, I think, Miss Cumberly, but she is one of the van Noord set, and is often to be seen in the more exclusive restaurants, and sometimes in the Cafe Royal."

"She is possibly a member of the theatrical profession?"

"I think not. She is the only really strange figure (if we exclude Olaf) in this group of poseurs. She is half Burmese, I believe, and a native of Moulmein."

"Most EXTRAORDINARY creature!" muttered Denise Ryland, focussing upon the Eurasian her gold rimmed glasses — "MOST extraordinary." She glanced around at the company in general. "I really begin to feel... more and more as though I were... in a private lunatic... asylum. That picture... beyond doubt is the work ... of a madman... a perfect... madman!"

"I, also, begin to be conscious of an uncomfortable sensation," said Helen, glancing about her almost apprehensively. "Am I dreaming, or did SOME ONE ELSE enter the studio, immediately behind that girl?"

"A squinting man... yes!"

"But a THIRD person?"

"No, my dear... look for yourself. As you say... you are ... dreaming. It's not to be wondered... at!"

Helen laughed, but very uneasily. Evidently it had been an illusion, but an unpleasant illusion; for she should have been prepared to swear that not two, but THREE people had entered! Moreover, although she was unable to detect the presence of any third stranger in the studio, the persuasion that this third person actually was present remained with her, unaccountably, and uncannily.

The lady of the tiger skins was surrounded by an admiring group of unusuals, and Helen, who had turned again to the big canvas, suddenly became aware that the little cross-eyed man was bowing and beaming radiantly before her.

"May I be allowed," said Olaf van Noord who stood beside him, "to present my friend Mr. Gianapolis, my dear Miss Cumberly?"...

Helen Cumberly found herself compelled to acknowledge the introduction, although she formed an immediate, instinctive distaste for Mr. Gianapolis. But he made such obvious attempts to please, and was so really entertaining a talker, that she unbent towards him a little. His admiration, too, was unconcealed; and no pretty woman, however great her common sense, is entirely admiration-proof.

"Do you not think 'Our Lady of the Poppies' remarkable?" said Gianapolis, pleasantly.

"I think," replied Denise Ryland, — to whom, also, the Greek had been presented by Olaf van Noord, "that it indicates... a disordered... imagination on the part of... its creator."

"It is a technical masterpiece," replied the Greek, smiling, "but hardly a work of imagination; for you have seen the original of the principal figure, and" — he turned to Helen Cumberly — "one need not go very far East for such an interior as that depicted."

"What!" Helen knitted her brows, prettily — "you do not suggest that such an apartment actually exists either East or West?"

Gianapolis beamed radiantly.

"You would, perhaps, like to see such an apartment?" he suggested.

"I should, certainly," replied Helen Cumberly. "Not even in a stage setting have I seen anything like it."

"You have never been to the East?"

"Never, unfortunately. I have desired to go for years, and hope to go some day."

"In Smyrna you may see such rooms; possibly in Port Said — certainly in Cairo. In Constantinople — yes! But perhaps in Paris; and — who knows? — Sir Richard Burton explored Mecca, but who has explored London?"

Helen Cumberly watched him curiously.

"You excite my curiosity," she said. "Don't you think" — turning to Denise Ryland — "he is most tantalizing?"

Denise Ryland distended her nostrils scornfully.

"He is telling... fairy tales," she declared. "He thinks... we are... silly!"

"On the contrary," declared Gianapolis; "I flatter myself that I am too good a judge of character to make that mistake."

Helen Cumberly absorbed his entire attention; in everything he sought to claim her interest; and when, ere taking their departure, the girl and her friend walked around the studio to view the other pictures, Gianapolis was the attendant cavalier, and so well as one might judge, in his case, his glance rarely strayed from the piquant beauty of Helen.

When they departed, it was Gianapolis, and not Olaf van Noord, who escorted them to the door and downstairs to the street. The red lips of the Eurasian smiled upon her circle of adulators, but her eyes — her unfathomable eyes — followed every movement of the Greek.

XXVII
GROVE OF A MILLION APES

Four men sauntered up the grand staircase and entered the huge smoking-room of the Radical Club as Big Ben was chiming the hour of eleven o'clock. Any curious observer who had cared to consult the visitor's book in the hall, wherein the two lines last written were not yet dry, would have found the following entries:

VISITOR RESIDENCE INTROD'ING
  MEMBER
  Dr. Bruce Cumberly London John Exel
  M. Gaston Paris Brian Malpas

The smoking-room was fairly full, but a corner near the big open grate had just been vacated, and here, about a round table, the four disposed themselves. Our French acquaintance being in evening dress had perforce confined himself in his sartorial eccentricities to a flowing silk knot in place of the more conventional, neat bow. He was already upon delightfully friendly terms with the frigid Exel and the aristocratic Sir Brian Malpas. Few natures were proof against the geniality of the brilliant Frenchman.

Conversation drifted, derelict, from one topic to another, now seized by this current of thought, now by that; and M. Gaston Max made no perceptible attempt to steer it in any given direction. But presently:

"I was reading a very entertaining article," said Exel, turning his monocle upon the physician, "in the Planet to-day, from the pen of Miss Cumberly; Ah! dealing with Olaf van Noord."

Sir Brian Malpas suddenly became keenly interested.

"You mean in reference to his new picture, 'Our Lady of the Poppies'?" he said.

"Yes," replied Exel, "but I was unaware that you knew van Noord?"

"I do not know him," said Sir Brian, "I should very much like to meet him. But directly the picture is on view to the public I shall certainly subscribe my half-crown."

"My own idea," drawled Exel, "was that Miss Cumberly's article probably was more interesting than the picture or the painter. Her description of the canvas was certainly most vivid; and I, myself, for a moment, experienced an inclination to see the thing. I feel sure, however, that I should be disappointed."

"I think you are wrong," interposed Cumberly. "Helen is enthusiastic about the picture, and even Miss Ryland, whom you have met and who is a somewhat severe critic, admits that it is out of the ordinary."

Max, who covertly had been watching the face of Sir Brian Malpas, said at this point:

"I would not miss it for anything, after reading Miss Cumberly's account of it. When are you thinking of going to see it, Sir Brian? I might arrange to join you."

"Directly the exhibition is opened," replied the baronet, lapsing again into his dreamy manner. "Ring me up when you are going, and I will join you."

"But you might be otherwise engaged?"

"I never permit business," said Sir Brian, "to interfere with pleasure."

The words sounded absurd, but, singularly, the statement was true. Sir Brian had won his political position by sheer brilliancy. He was utterly unreliable and totally indifferent to that code of social obligations which ordinarily binds his class. He held his place by force of intellect, and it was said of him that had he possessed the faintest conception of his duties toward his fellow men, nothing could have prevented him from becoming Prime Minister. He was a puzzle to all who knew him. Following a most brilliant speech in the House, which would win admiration and applause from end to end of the Empire, he would, perhaps on the following day, exhibit something very like stupidity in debate. He would rise to address the House and take his seat again without having uttered a word. He was eccentric, said his admirers, but there were others who looked deeper for an explanation, yet failed to find one, and were thrown back upon theories.

M. Max, by strategy, masterful because it was simple, so arranged matters that at about twelve o'clock he found himself strolling with Sir Brian Malpas toward the latter's chambers in Piccadilly.

A man who wore a raincoat with the collar turned up and buttoned tightly about his throat, and whose peculiar bowler hat seemed to be so tightly pressed upon his head that it might have been glued there, detached himself from the shadows of the neighboring cab rank as M. Gaston Max and Sir Brian Malpas quitted the Club, and followed them at a discreet distance.

It was a clear, fine night, and both gentlemen formed conspicuous figures, Sir Brian because of his unusual height and upright military bearing, and the Frenchman by reason of his picturesque cloak and hat. Up Northumberland Avenue, across Trafalgar Square and so on up to Piccadilly Circus went the two, deep in conversation; with the tireless man in the raincoat always dogging their footsteps. So the procession proceeded on, along Piccadilly. Then Sir Brian and M. Max turned into the door of a block of chambers, and a constable, who chanced to be passing at the moment, touched his helmet to the baronet.

As the two were entering the lift, the follower came up level with the doorway and abreast of the constable; the top portion of a very red face showed between the collar of the raincoat and the brim of the hat, together with a pair of inquiring blue eyes.

"Reeves!" said the follower, addressing the constable.

The latter turned and stared for a moment at the speaker; then saluted hurriedly.

"Don't do that!" snapped the proprietor of the bowler; "you should know better! Who was that gentleman?"

"Sir Brian Malpas, sir."

"Sir Brian Malpas?"

"Yes, sir."

"And the other?"

"I don't know, sir. I have never seen him before."

"H'm!" grunted Detective-Sergeant Sowerby, walking across the road toward the Park with his hands thrust deep in his pockets; "I have! What the deuce is Max up to? I wonder if Dunbar knows about this move?"

He propped himself up against the railings, scarcely knowing what he expected to gain by remaining there, but finding the place as well suited to reflection as any other. He shared with Dunbar a dread that the famous Frenchman would bring the case to a successful conclusion unaided by Scotland Yard, thus casting professional discredit upon Dunbar and himself.

His presence at that spot was largely due to accident. He had chanced to be passing the Club when Sir Brian and M. Max had come out, and, fearful that the presence of the tall stranger portended some new move on the Frenchman's part, Sowerby had followed, hoping to glean something by persistency when clues were unobtainable by other means. He had had no time to make inquiries of the porter of the Club respecting the identity of M. Max's companion, and thus, as has appeared, he did not obtain the desired information until his arrival in Piccadilly.

Turning over these matters in his mind, Sowerby stood watching the block of buildings across the road. He saw a light spring into being in a room overlooking Piccadilly, a room boasting a handsome balcony. This took place some two minutes after the departure of the lift bearing Sir Brian and his guest upward; so that Sowerby permitted himself to conclude that the room with the balcony belonged to Sir Brian Malpas.

He watched the lighted window aimlessly and speculated upon the nature of the conversation then taking place up there above him. Had he possessed the attributes of a sparrow, he thought, he might have flown up to that balcony and have "got level" with this infernally clever Frenchman who was almost certainly going to pull off the case under the very nose of Scotland Yard.

In short, his reflections were becoming somewhat bitter; and persuaded that he had nothing to gain by remaining there any longer he was about to walk off, when his really remarkable persistency received a trivial reward.

One of the windows communicating with the balcony was suddenly thrown open, so that Sowerby had a distant view of the corner of a picture, of the extreme top of a book-case, and of a patch of white ceiling in the room above; furthermore he had a clear sight of the man who had opened the window, and who now turned and reentered the room. The man was Sir Brian Malpas.

Heedless of the roaring traffic stream, upon the brink of which he stood, heedless of all who passed him by, Sowerby gazed aloft, seeking to project himself, as it were, into that lighted room. Not being an accomplished clairvoyant, he remained in all his component parts upon the pavement of Piccadilly; but ours is the privilege to succeed where Sowerby failed, and the comedy being enacted in the room above should prove well deserving of study.

To the tactful diplomacy of M. Gaston Max, the task of securing from Sir Brian an invitation to step up into his chambers in order to smoke a final cigar was no heavy one. He seated himself in a deep armchair, at the baronet's invitation, and accepted a very fine cigar, contentedly, sniffing at the old cognac with the appreciation of a connoisseur, ere holding it under the syphon.

He glanced around the room, noting the character of the ornaments, and looked up at the big bookshelf which was near to him; these rapid inquiries dictated the following remark: "You have lived in China, Sir Brian?"

Sir Brian surveyed him with mild surprise.

"Yes," he replied; "I was for some time at the Embassy in Pekin."

His guest nodded, blowing a ring of smoke from his lips and tracing its hazy outline with the lighted end of his cigar.

"I, too, have been in China," he said slowly.

"What, really! I had no idea."

"Yes — I have been in China... I"...

M. Gaston grew suddenly deathly pale and his fingers began to twitch alarmingly. He stared before him with wide-opened eyes and began to cough and to choke as if suffocating — dying.

Sir Brian Malpas leapt to his feet with an exclamation of concern. His visitor weakly waved him away, gasping: "It is nothing... it will... pass off. Oh! mon dieu!"...

Sir Brian ran and opened one of the windows to admit more air to the apartment. He turned and looked back anxiously at the man in the armchair.

M. Gaston, twitching in a pitiful manner and still frightfully pale, was clutching the chair-arms and glaring straight in front of him. Sir Brian started slightly and advanced again to his visitor's side.

The burning cigar lay upon the carpet beside the chair, and Sir Brian took it up and tossed it into the grate. As he did so he looked searchingly into the eyes of M. Gaston. The pupils were extraordinary dilated....

"Do you feel better?" asked Sir Brian.

"Much better," muttered M. Gaston, his face twitching nervously — "much better."

"Are you subject to these attacks?"

"Since — I was in China — yes, unfortunately."

Sir Brian tugged at his fair mustache and seemed about to speak, then turned aside, and, walking to the table, poured out a peg of brandy and offered it to his guest.

"Thanks," said M. Gaston; "many thanks indeed, but already I recover. There is only one thing that would hasten my recovery, and that, I fear, is not available."

"What is that?"

He looked again at M. Gaston's eyes with their very dilated pupils.

"Opium!" whispered M. Gaston.

"What! you... you"...

"I acquired the custom in China," replied the Frenchman, his voice gradually growing stronger; "and for many years, now, I have regarded opium, as essential to my well-being. Unfortunately business has detained me in London, and I have been forced to fast for an unusually long time. My outraged constitution is protesting — that is all."

He shrugged his shoulders and glanced up at his host with an odd smile.

"You have my sympathy," said Sir Brian....

"In Paris," continued the visitor, "I am a member of a select and cozy little club; near the Boulevard Beaumarchais...."

"I have heard of it," interjected Malpas — "on the Rue St. Claude?"

"That indeed is its situation," replied the other with surprise. "You know someone who is a member?"

Sir Brian Malpas hesitated for ten seconds or more; then, crossing the room and reclosing the window, he turned, facing his visitor across the large room.

"I was a member, myself, during the time that I lived in Paris," he said, in a hurried manner which did not entirely serve to cover his confusion.

"My dear Sir Brian! We have at least one taste in common!"

Sir Brian Malpas passed his hand across his brow with a weary gesture well-known to fellow Members of Parliament, for it often presaged the abrupt termination of a promising speech.

"I curse the day that I was appointed to Pekin," he said; "for it was in Pekin that I acquired the opium habit. I thought to make it my servant; it has made me"...

"What! you would give it up?"

Sir Brian surveyed the speaker with surprise again.

"Do you doubt it?"

"My dear Sir Brian!" cried the Frenchman, now completely restored, "my real life is lived in the land of the poppies; my other life is but a shadow! Morbleu! to be an outcast from that garden of bliss is to me torture excruciating. For the past three months I have regularly met in my trances."...

Sir Brian shuddered coldly.

"In my explorations of that wonderland," continued the Frenchman, "a most fascinating Eastern girl. Ah! I cannot describe her; for when, at a time like this, I seek to conjure up her image, — nom d'un nom! do you know, I can think of nothing but a serpent!"

"A serpent!"

"A serpent, exactly. Yet, when I actually meet her in the land of the poppies, she is a dusky Cleopatra in whose arms I forget the world — even the world of the poppy. We float down the stream together, always in an Indian bark canoe, and this stream runs through orange groves. Numberless apes — millions of apes, inhabit these groves, and as we two float along, they hurl orange blossoms — orange blossoms, you understand — until the canoe is filled with them. I assure you, monsieur, that I perform these delightful journeys regularly, and to be deprived of the key which opens the gate of this wonderland, is to me like being exiled from a loved one. Pardieu! that grove of the apes! Morbleu! my witch of the dusky eyes! Yet, as I have told you, owing to some trick of my brain, whilst I can experience an intense longing for that companion of my dreams, my waking attempts to visualize her provide nothing but the image"...

"Of a serpent," concluded Sir Brian, smiling pathetically. "You are indeed an enthusiast, M. Gaston, and to me a new type. I had supposed that every slave of the drug cursed his servitude and loathed and despised himself.".…

"Ah, monsieur! to ME those words sound almost like a sacrilege!"

"But," continued Sir Brian, "your remarks interest me strangely; for two reasons. First, they confirm your assertion that you are, or were, an habitue of the Rue St. Claude, and secondly, they revive in my mind an old fancy — a superstition."

"What is that, Sir Brian?" inquired M. Max, whose opium vision was a faithful imitation of one related to him by an actual frequenter of the establishment near the Boulevard Beaumarchais.

"Only once before, M. Gaston, have I compared notes with a fellow opium-smoker, and he, also, was a patron of Madame Jean; he, also, met in his dreams that Eastern Circe, in the grove of apes, just as I".…

"Morbleu! Yes?"

"As I meet her!"

"But this is astounding!" cried Max, who actually thought it so. "Your fancy — your superstition — was this: that only habitues of Rue St. Claude met, in poppyland, this vision? And in your fancy you are now confirmed?"

"It is singular, at least."

"It is more than that, Sir Brian! Can it be that some intelligence presides over that establishment and exercises — shall I call it a hypnotic influence upon the inmates?"

M. Max put the question with sincere interest.

"One does not ALWAYS meet her," murmured Sir Brian. "But — yes, it is possible. For I have since renewed those experiences in London."

"What! in London?"

"Are you remaining for some time longer in London?"

"Alas! for several weeks yet."

"Then I will introduce you to a gentleman who can secure you admission to an establishment in London — where you may even hope sometimes to find the orange grove — to meet your dream-bride!"

"What!" cried M. Gaston, rising to his feet, his eyes bright with gratitude, "you will do that?"

"With pleasure," said Sir Brian Malpas, wearily; "nor am I jealous! But — no! do not thank me, for I do not share your views upon the subject, monsieur. You are a devout worshiper; I, an unhappy slave!"

XXVIII
THE OPIUM AGENT

Into the Palm Court of the Hotel Astoria, Mr. Gianapolis came, radiant and bowing. M. Gaston rose to greet his visitor. M. Gaston was arrayed in a light gray suit and wore a violet tie of very chaste design; his complexion had assumed a quality of sallowness, and the pupils of his eyes had acquired (as on the occasion of his visit to the chambers of Sir Brian Malpas) a chatoyant quality; they alternately dilated and contracted in a most remarkable manner — in a manner which attracted the immediate attention of Mr. Gianapolis.

"My dear sir," he said, speaking in French, "you suffer. I perceive how grievously you suffer; and you have been denied that panacea which beneficent nature designed for the service of mankind. A certain gentleman known to both of us (we brethren of the poppy are all nameless) has advised me of your requirements — and here I am."

"You are welcome," declared M. Gaston.

He rose and grasped eagerly the hand of the Greek, at the same time looking about the Palm Court suspiciously. "You can relieve my sufferings?"

Mr. Gianapolis seated himself beside the Frenchman.

"I perceive," he said, "that you are of those who abjure the heresies of De Quincey. How little he knew, that De Quincey, of the true ritual of the poppy! He regarded it as the German regards his lager, whereas we know — you and I — that it is an Eleusinian mystery; that true communicants must retreat to the temple of the goddess if they would partake of Paradise with her."

"It is perhaps a question of temperament," said M. Gaston, speaking in a singularly tremulous voice. "De Quincey apparently possessed the type of constitution which is cerebrally stimulated by opium. To such a being the golden gates are closed; and the Easterners, whom he despised for what he termed their beastly lethargies, have taught me the real secret of the poppy. I do not employ opium as an aid to my social activities; I regard it as nepenthe from them and as a key to a brighter realm. It has been my custom, M. Gianapolis, for many years, periodically to visit that fairyland. In Paris I regularly arranged my affairs in such a manner that I found myself occasionally at liberty to spend two or three days, as the case might be, in the company of my bright friends who haunted the Boulevard Beaumarchais."

"Ah! Our acquaintance has mentioned something of this to me, Monsieur. You knew Madame Jean?"

"The dear Madame Jean! Name of a name! She was the hierophant of my Paris Temple"...

"And Sen?"

"Our excellent Sen! Splendid man! It was from the hands of the worthy Sen, the incomparable Sen, that I received the key to the gate! Ah! how I have suffered since the accursed business has exiled me from the"...

"I feel for you," declared Gianapolis, warmly; "I, too, have worshiped at the shrine; and although I cannot promise that the London establishment to which I shall introduce you is comparable with that over which Madame Jean formerly presided"...

"Formerly?" exclaimed M. Gaston, with lifted eyebrows. "You do not tell me"...

"My friend," said Gianapolis, "in Europe we are less enlightened upon certain matters than in Smyrna, in Constantinople — in Cairo. The impertinent police have closed the establishment in the Rue St. Claude!"

"Ah!" exclaimed M. Gaston, striking his brow, "misery! I shall return to Paris, then, only to die?"

"I would suggest, monsieur," said Gianapolis, tapping him confidentially upon the breast, "that you periodically visit London in future. The journey is a short one, and already, I am happy to say, the London establishment (conducted by Mr. Ho-Pin of Canton — a most accomplished gentleman, and a graduate of London) — enjoys the patronage of several distinguished citizens of Paris, of Brussels, of Vienna, and elsewhere."

"You offer me life!" declared M. Gaston, gratefully. "The commoner establishments, for the convenience of sailors and others of that class, at Dieppe, Calais," — he shrugged his shoulders, comprehensively — "are impossible as resorts. In catering for the true devotees — for those who, unlike De Quincey, plunge and do not dabble — for those who seek to explore the ultimate regions of poppyland, for those who have learnt the mystery from the real masters in Asia and not in Europe — the enterprise conducted by Madame Jean supplied a want long and bitterly experienced. I rejoice to know that London has not been neglected"...

"My dear friend!" cried Gianapolis enthusiastically, "no important city has been neglected! A high priest of the cult has arisen, and from a parent lodge in Pekin he has extended his offices to kindred lodges in most of the capitals of Europe and Asia; he has not neglected the Near East, and America owes him a national debt of gratitude."

"Ah! the great man!" murmured M. Gaston, with closed eyes. "As an old habitue of the Rue St. Claude, I divine that you refer to Mr. King?"

"Beyond doubt," whispered Gianapolis, imparting a quality of awe to his voice. "From you, my friend, I will have no secrets; but" — he glanced about him crookedly, and lowered his voice to an impressive whisper — "the police, as you are aware"...

"Curse their interference!" said M. Gaston.

"Curse it indeed; but the police persist in believing, or in pretending to believe, that any establishment patronized by lovers of the magic resin must necessarily be a resort of criminals."

"Pah!"

"Whilst this absurd state of affairs prevails, it is advisable, it is more than advisable, it is imperative, that all of us should be secret. The…raid — unpleasant word! — upon the establishment in Paris — was so unexpected that there was no time to advise patrons; but the admirable tact of the French authorities ensured the suppression of all names. Since — always as a protective measure — no business relationship exists between any two of Mr. King's establishments (each one being entirely self-governed) some difficulty is being experienced, I believe, in obtaining the names of those who patronized Madame Jean. But I am doubly glad to have met you, M. Gaston, for not only can I put you in touch with the London establishment, but I can impress upon you the necessity of preserving absolute silence"…

M. Gaston extended his palms eloquently.

"To me," he declared, "the name of Mr. King is a sacred symbol."

"It is to all of us!" responded the Greek, devoutly.

M. Gaston in turn became confidential, bending toward Gianapolis so that, as the shadow of the Greek fell upon his face, his pupils contracted catlike.

"How often have I prayed," he whispered, "for a sight of that remarkable man!"

A look of horror, real or simulated, appeared upon the countenance of Gianapolis.

"To see — Mr. King!" he breathed. "My dear friend, I declare to you by all that I hold sacred that I — though one of the earliest patrons of the first establishment, that in Pekin — have never seen Mr. King!"

"He is so cautious and so clever as that?"

"Even as cautious and even as clever — yes! Though every branch of the enterprise in the world were destroyed, no man would ever see Mr. King; he would remain but a NAME!"

"You will arrange for me to visit the house of — Ho-Pin, did you say? — immediately?"

"To-day, if you wish," said Gianapolis, brightly.

"My funds," continued M. Gaston, shrugging his shoulders, "are not limitless at the moment; and until I receive a remittance from Paris"…

The brow of Mr. Gianapolis darkened slightly.

"Our clientele here," he replied, "is a very wealthy one, and the fees are slightly higher than in Paris. An entrance fee of fifty guineas is charged, and an annual subscription of the same amount"…

"But," exclaimed M. Gaston, "I shall not be in London for so long as a year! In a week or a fortnight from now, I shall be on my way to America!"

"You will receive an introduction to the New York representative, and your membership will be available for any of the United States establishments."

"But I am going to South America."

"At Buenos Aires is one of the largest branches."

"But I am not going to Buenos Aires! I am going with a prospecting party to Yucatan."

"You must be well aware, monsieur, that to go to Yucatan is to exile yourself from all that life holds for you."

"I can take a supply"…

"You will die, monsieur! Already you suffer abominably"…

"I do not suffer because of any lack of the specific," said M. Gaston wearily; "for if I were entirely unable to obtain possession of it, I should most certainly die. But I suffer because, living as I do at present in a public hotel, I am unable to embark upon a protracted voyage into those realms which hold so much for me"…

"I offer you the means"…

"But to charge me one hundred guineas, since I cannot possibly avail myself of the full privileges, is to rob me — is to trade upon my condition!" M. Gaston was feebly indignant.

"Let it be twenty-five guineas, monsieur," said the Greek, reflectively, "entitling you to two visits."

"Good! good!" cried M. Gaston. "Shall I write you a check?"

"You mistake me," said Gianapolis. "I am in no way connected with the management of the establishment. You will settle this business matter with Mr. Ho-Pin"...

"Yes, yes!"

"To whom I will introduce you this evening. Checks, as you must be aware, are unacceptable. I will meet you at Piccadilly Circus, outside the entrance to the London Pavilion, at nine o'clock this evening, and you will bring with you the twenty-five guineas in cash. You will arrange to absent yourself during the following day?"

"Of course, of course! At nine o'clock at Piccadilly Circus?"

"Exactly."

M. Gaston, this business satisfactorily completed, made his way to his own room by a somewhat devious route, not wishing to encounter anyone of his numerous acquaintances whilst in an apparent state of ill-health so calculated to excite compassion. He avoided the lift and ascended the many stairs to his small apartment.

Here he rectified the sallowness of his complexion, which was due, not to outraged nature, but to the arts of make-up. His dilated pupils (a phenomenon traceable to drops of belladonna) he was compelled to suffer for the present; but since their condition tended temporarily to impair his sight, he determined to remain in his room until the time for the appointment with Gianapolis.

"So!" he muttered — "we have branches in Europe, Asia, Africa and America! Eh, bien! to find all those would occupy five hundred detectives for a whole year. I have a better plan: crush the spider and the winds of heaven will disperse his web!"

XXIX
M. MAX OF LONDON AND M. MAX OF PARIS

He seated himself in a cane armchair and, whilst the facts were fresh in his memory, made elaborate notes upon the recent conversation with the Greek. He had achieved almost more than he could have hoped for; but, knowing something of the elaborate organization of the opium group, he recognized that he owed some part of his information to the sense of security which this admirably conducted machine inspired in its mechanics. The introduction from Sir Brian Malpas had worked wonders, without doubt; and his own intimate knowledge of the establishment adjoining the Boulevard Beaumarchais, far from arousing the suspicions of Gianapolis, had evidently strengthened the latter's conviction that he had to deal with a confirmed opium slave.

The French detective congratulated himself upon the completeness of his Paris operation. It was evident that the French police had succeeded in suppressing all communication between the detained members of the Rue St. Claude den and the head office — which he shrewdly suspected to be situated in London. So confident were the group in the self-contained properties of each of their branches that the raid of any one establishment meant for them nothing more than a temporary financial loss. Failing the clue supplied by the draft on Paris, the case, so far as he was concerned, indeed, must have terminated with the raiding of the opium house. He reflected that he owed that precious discovery primarily to the promptness with which he had conducted the raid — to the finding of the letter (the ONE incriminating letter) from Mr. King.

Evidently the group remained in ignorance of the fact that the little arrangement at the Credit Lyonnais had been discovered. He surveyed — and his eyes twinkled humorously — a small photograph which was contained in his writing-case.

It represented a very typical Parisian gentleman, with a carefully trimmed square beard and well brushed mustache, wearing pince-nez and a white silk knot at his neck. The photograph was cut from a French magazine, and beneath it appeared the legend:

"M. Gaston Max, Service de Surete."

There was marked genius in the conspicuous dressing of M. Gaston Max, who, as M. Gaston, was now patronizing the Hotel Astoria. For whilst there was nothing furtive, nothing secret, about this gentleman, the closest scrutiny (and because he invited it, he was never subjected to it) must have failed to detect any resemblance between M. Gaston of the Hotel Astoria and M. Gaston Max of the Service de Surete.

And which was the original M. Gaston Max? Was the M. Max of the magazine photograph a disguised M. Max? or was that the veritable M. Max, and was the patron of the Astoria a disguised M. Max? It is quite possible that M. Gaston Max, himself, could not have answered that question, so true an artist was he; and it is quite certain that had the occasion arisen he would have refused to do so.

He partook of a light dinner in his own room, and having changed into evening dress, went out to meet Mr. Gianapolis. The latter was on the spot punctually at nine o'clock, and taking the Frenchman familiarly by the arm, he hailed a taxi-cab, giving the man the directions, "To Victoria-Suburban." Then, turning to his companion, he whispered: "Evening dress? And you must return in daylight."

M. Max felt himself to be flushing like a girl. It was an error of artistry that he had committed; a heinous crime! "So silly of me!" he muttered.

"No matter," replied the Greek, genially.

The cab started. M. Max, though silently reproaching himself, made mental notes of the destination. He had not renewed his sallow complexion, for reasons of his own, and his dilated pupils were beginning to contract again, facts which were not very evident, however, in the poor light. He was very twitchy, nevertheless, and the face of the man beside him was that of a sympathetic vulture, if such a creature can be imagined. He inquired casually if the new patron had brought his money with him, but for the most part his conversation turned upon China, with which country he seemed to be well acquainted. Arrived at Victoria, Mr. Gianapolis discharged the cab, and again taking the Frenchman by the arm, walked with him some twenty paces away from the station. A car suddenly pulled up almost beside them.

Ere M. Max had time to note those details in which he was most interested, Gianapolis had opened the door of the limousine, and the Frenchman found himself within, beside Gianapolis, and behind drawn blinds, speeding he knew not in what direction!

"I suppose I should apologize, my dear M. Gaston," said the Greek; and, although unable to see him, for there was little light in the car, M. Max seemed to FEEL him smiling — "but this little device has proved so useful hitherto. In the event of any of those troubles — wretched police interferences — arising, and of officious people obtaining possession of a patron's name, he is spared the necessity of perjuring himself in any way"...

"Perhaps I do not entirely understand you, monsieur?" said M. Max.

"It is so simple. The police are determined to raid one of our establishments: they adopt the course of tracking an habitue. This is not impossible. They question him; they ask, 'Do you know a Mr. King?' He replies that he knows no such person, has never seen, has never spoken with him! I assure you that official inquiries have gone thus far already, in New York, for example; but to what end? They say, 'Where is the establishment of a Mr. King to which you have gone on such and such an occasion?' He replies with perfect truth, 'I do not know.' Believe me this little device is quite in your own interest, M. Gaston."

"But when again I feel myself compelled to resort to the solace of the pipe, how then?"

"So simple! You will step to the telephone and ask for this number: East 18642. You will then ask for Mr. King, and an appointment will be made; I will meet you as I met you this evening — and all will be well."

M. Max began to perceive that he had to deal with a scheme even more elaborate than hitherto he had conjectured. These were very clever people, and through the whole complicated network, as through the petal of a poppy one may trace the veins, he traced the guiding will — the power of a tortuous Eastern mind. The system was truly Chinese in its elaborate, uncanny mystifications.

In some covered place that was very dark, the car stopped, and Gianapolis, leaping out with agility, assisted M. Max to descend.

This was a covered courtyard, only lighted by the head-lamps of the limousine.

"Take my hand," directed the Greek.

M. Max complied, and was conducted through a low doorway and on to descending steps.

Dimly, he heard the gear of the car reversed, and knew that the limousine was backing out from the courtyard. The door behind him was closed, and he heard no more. A dim light shone out below.

He descended, walking more confidently now that the way was visible. A moment later he stood upon the threshold of an apartment which calls for no further description at this place; he stood in the doorway of the incredible, unforgettable cave of the golden dragon; he looked into the beetle eyes of Ho-Pin!

Ho-Pin bowed before him, smiling his mirthless smile. In his left hand he held an amber cigarette tube in which a cigarette smoldered gently, sending up a gray pencil of smoke into the breathless, perfumed air.

"Mr. Ho-Pin," said Gianapolis, indicating the Chinaman, "who will attend to your requirements. This is our new friend from Paris, introduced by Sir B. M — — , M. Gaston."

"You are vewry welcome," said the Chinaman in his monotonous, metallic voice. "I understand that a fee of twenty-five guineas" — he bowed again, still smiling.

The visitor took out his pocket-book and laid five notes, one sovereign, and two half-crowns upon a little ebony table beside him. Ho-Pin bowed again and waved his hand toward the lemon-colored door on the left.

"Good night, M. Gaston!" said Gianapolis, in radiant benediction.

"Au revoir, monsieur!"

M. Max followed Ho-Pin to Block A and was conducted to a room at the extreme right of the matting-lined corridor. He glanced about it curiously.

"If you will pwrepare for your flight into the subliminal," said Ho-Pin, bowing in the doorway, "I shall pwresently wreturn with your wings."

In the cave of the golden dragon, Gianapolis sat smoking upon one of the divans. The silence of the place was extraordinary; unnatural, in the very heart of busy commercial London. Ho-Pin reappeared and standing in the open doorway of Block A sharply clapped his hands three times.

Said, the Egyptian, came out of the door at the further end of the place, bearing a brass tray upon which were a little brass lamp of Oriental manufacture wherein burned a blue spirituous flame, a Japanese, lacquered box not much larger than a snuff-box, and a long and most curiously carved pipe of wood inlaid with metal and having a metal bowl. Bearing this, he crossed the room, passed Ho-Pin, and entered the corridor beyond.

"You have, of course, put him in the observation room?" said Gianapolis.

Ho-Pin regarded the speaker unemotionally.

"Assuwredly," he replied; "for since he visits us for the first time, Mr. King will wish to see him"...

A faint shadow momentarily crossed the swarthy face of the Greek at mention of that name — MR. KING. The servants of Mr. King, from the highest to the lowest, served him for gain... and from fear.

XXX

Utter silence had claimed again the cave of the golden dragon. Gianapolis sat alone in the place, smoking a cigarette, and gazing crookedly at the image on the ivory pedestal. Then, glancing at his wrist-watch, he stood up, and, stepping to the entrance door, was about to open it...

"Ah, so! You go — already?" —

Gianapolis started back as though he had put his foot upon a viper, and turned.

The Eurasian, wearing her yellow, Chinese dress, and with a red poppy in her hair, stood watching him through half-shut eyes, slowly waving her little fan before her face. Gianapolis attempted the radiant smile, but its brilliancy was somewhat forced tonight.

"Yes, I must be off," he said hurriedly; "I have to see someone — a future client, I think!"

"A future client — yes!" — the long black eyes were closed almost entirely now. "Who is it — this future client, that you have to see?"

"My dear Mahara! How odd of you to ask that"...

"It is odd of me? — so!...It is odd of me that I thinking to wonder why you alway running away from me now?"

"Run away from you! My dear little Mahara!" — He approached the dusky beauty with a certain timidity as one might seek to caress a tiger-cat — "Surely you know"...

She struck down his hand with a sharp blow of her closed fan, darting at him a look from the brilliant eyes which was a living flame.

Resting one hand upon her hip, she stood with her right foot thrust forward from beneath the yellow robe and pivoting upon the heel of its little slipper. Her head tilted, she watched him through lowered lashes.

"It was not so with you in Moulmein," she said, her silvery voice lowered caressingly. "Do you remember with me a night beside the Irawaddi? — where was that I wonder? Was it in Prome? — Perhaps, yes?...you threatened me to leap in, if...and I think to believe you! — I believing you!"

"Mahara!" cried Gianapolis, and sought to seize her in his arms.

Again she struck down his hand with the little fan, watching him continuously and with no change of expression. But the smoldering fire in those eyes told of a greater flame which consumed her slender body and was potent enough to consume many a victim upon its altar. Gianapolis' yellow skin assumed a faintly mottled appearance.

"Whatever is the matter?" he inquired plaintively.

"So you must be off — yes? I hear you say it; I asking you who to meet?"

"Why do you speak in English?" said Gianapolis with a faint irritation. "Let us talk..."

She struck him lightly on the face with her fan; but he clenched his teeth and suppressed an ugly exclamation.

"Who was it?" she asked, musically, "that say to me, 'to hear you speaking English — like rippling water'?"

"You are mad!" muttered Gianapolis, beginning to drill the points of his mustache as was his manner in moments of agitation. His crooked eyes were fixed upon the face of the girl. "You go too far."

"Be watching, my friend, that you also go not too far."

The tones were silvery as ever, but the menace unmistakable. Gianapolis forced a harsh laugh and brushed up his mustache furiously.

"What are you driving at?" he demanded, with some return of self-confidence. "Am I to be treated to another exhibition of your insane jealousies?"...

"AH!" The girl's eyes opened widely; she darted another venomous glance at him. "I am sure now, I am SURE!"

"My dear Mahara, you talk nonsense!"

"Ah!"

She glided sinuously toward him, still with one hand resting upon her hip, stood almost touching his shoulder and raised her beautiful wicked face to his, peering at him through half-closed eyes, and resting the hand which grasped the fan lightly upon his arm.

"You think I do not see? You think I do not watch?" — softer and softer grew the silvery voice — "at Olaf van Noord's studio you think I do not hear? Perhaps you not thinking to care if I see and hear — for it seem you not seeing nor hearing ME. I watch and I see. Is it her so soft brown hair? That color of hair is so more prettier than ugly black! Is it her English eyes? Eyes that born in the dark forests of Burma so hideous and so like the eyes of the apes! Is it her white skin and her red cheeks? A brown skin — though someone, there was, that say it is satin of heaven — is so tiresome; when no more it is a new toy it does not interest"...

"Really," muttered Gianapolis, uneasily, "I think you must be mad! I don't know what you are talking about."

"LIAR!"

One lithe step forward the Eurasian sprang, and, at the word, brought down the fan with all her strength across Gianapolis' eyes!

He staggered away from her, uttering a hoarse cry and instinctively raising his arms to guard himself from further attack; but the girl stood poised again, her hand upon her hip; and swinging her right toe to and fro. Gianapolis, applying his handkerchief to his eyes, squinted at her furiously.

"Liar!" she repeated, and her voice had something of a soothing whisper. "I say to you, be so careful that you go not too far — with me! I do what I do, not because I am a poor fool"...

"It's funny," declared Gianapolis, an emotional catch in his voice — "it's damn funny for you — for YOU — to adopt these airs with me! Why, you went to Olaf van"...

"Stop!" cried the girl furiously, and sprang at him panther-like so that he fell back again in confusion, stumbled and collapsed upon a divan, with upraised, warding arms. "You Greek rat! you skinny Greek rat! Be careful what you think to say to me — to ME! to ME! Olaf van Noord — the poor, white-faced corpse-man! He is only one of Said's mummies! Be careful what you think to say to me... Oh! be careful — be very careful! It is dangerous of any friend of — MR. KING"...

Gianapolis glanced at her furtively.

"It is dangerous of anyone in a house of — MR. KING to think to make attachments," — she hissed the words beneath her breath — "outside of ourselves. MR. KING would not be glad to hear of it... I do not like to tell it to MR. KING"...

Gianapolis rose to his feet, unsteadily, and stretched out his arms in supplication.

"Mahara!" he said, "don't treat me like this! dear little Mahara! what have I done to you? Tell me! — only tell me!"

"Shall I tell it in English?" asked the Eurasian softly. Her eyes now were nearly closed; "or does it worry you that I speak so ugly"...

"Mahara!"...

"I only say, be so very careful."

He made a final, bold attempt to throw his arms about her, but she slipped from his grasp and ran lightly across the room.

"Go! hurry off!" she said, bending forward and pointing at him with her fan, her eyes widely opened and blazing — "but remember — there is danger! There is Said, who creeps silently, like the jackal"...

She opened the ebony door and darted into the corridor beyond, closing the door behind her.

Gianapolis looked about him in a dazed manner, and yet again applied his handkerchief to his stinging eyes. Whoever could have seen him now must have failed to recognize the radiant Gianapolis so well-known in Bohemian society, the Gianapolis about whom floated a halo of mystery, but who at all times was such a good fellow and so debonair. He took up his hat and gloves, turned, and resolutely strode to the door. Once he glanced back over his shoulder, but shrugged with a sort of self-contempt, and ascended to the top of the steps.

With a key which he selected from a large bunch in his pocket, he opened the door, and stepped out into the garage, carefully closing the door behind him. An electric pocket-lamp served him with sufficient light to find his way out into the lane, and very shortly he was proceeding along Limehouse Causeway. At the moment, indignation was the major emotion ruling his mind; he resented the form which his anger assumed, for it was a passion of rebellion, and rebellion is only possible in servants. It is the part of a slave resenting the lash. He was an unscrupulous, unmoral man, not lacking in courage of a sort; and upon the conquest of Mahara, the visible mouthpiece of Mr. King, he had entered in much the same spirit as that actuating a Kanaka who dives for pearls in a shark-infested lagoon. He had sought a slave, and lo! the slave was become the master! Otherwise whence this spirit of rebellion... this fear?

He occupied himself with such profitless reflections up to the time that he came to the electric trains; but, from thence onward, his mind became otherwise engaged. On his way to Piccadilly Circus that same evening, he had chanced to find himself upon a crowded pavement walking immediately behind Denise Ryland and Helen Cumberly. His esthetic, Greek soul had been fired at first sight of the beauty of the latter; and now, his heart had leaped ecstatically. His first impulse, of course, had been to join the two ladies; but Gianapolis had trained himself to suspect all impulses.

Therefore he had drawn near — near enough to overhear their conversation without proclaiming himself. What he had learned by this eavesdropping he counted of peculiar value.

Helen Cumberly was arranging to dine with her friend at the latter's hotel that evening. "But I want to be home early," he had heard the girl say, "so if I leave you at about ten o'clock I can walk to Palace Mansions. No! you need not come with me; I enjoy a lonely walk through the streets of London in the evening"...

Gianapolis registered a mental vow that Helen's walk should not be a lonely one. He did not flatter himself upon the possession of a pleasing exterior, but, from experience, he knew that with women he had a winning way.

Now, his mind aglow with roseate possibilities, he stepped from the tram in the neighborhood of Shoreditch, and chartered a taxi-cab. From this he descended at the corner of Arundel Street and strolled along westward in the direction of the hotel patronized by Miss Ryland. At a corner from which he could command a view of the entrance, he paused and consulted his watch.

It was nearly twenty minutes past ten. Mentally, he cursed Mahara, who perhaps had caused him to let slip this golden opportunity. But his was not a character easily discouraged; he lighted a cigarette and prepared himself to wait, in the hope that the girl had not yet left her friend.

Gianapolis was a man capable of the uttermost sacrifices upon either of two shrines; that of Mammon, or that of Eros. His was a temperament (truly characteristic of his race) which can build up a structure painfully, year by year, suffering unutterable privations in the cause of its growth, only to shatter it at a blow for a woman's smile. He was a true member of that brotherhood, represented throughout the bazaars of the East, of those singular shopkeepers who live by commercial rapine, who, demanding a hundred piastres for an embroidered shawl from a plain woman, will exchange it with a pretty one for a perfumed handkerchief. Externally of London, he was internally of the Levant.

His vigil lasted but a quarter of an hour. At twenty-five minutes to eleven, Helen Cumberly came running down the steps of the hotel and hurried toward the Strand. Like a shadow, Gianapolis, throwing away a half-smoked cigarette, glided around the corner, paused and so timed his return that he literally ran into the girl as she entered the main thoroughfare.

He started back.

"Why!" he cried, "Miss Cumberly!"

Helen checked a frown, and hastily substituted a smile.

"How odd that I should meet you here, Mr. Gianapolis," she said.

"Most extraordinary! I was on my way to visit a friend in Victoria Street upon a rather urgent matter. May I venture to hope that your path lies in a similar direction?"

Helen Cumberly, deceived by his suave manner (for how was she to know that the Greek had learnt her address from Crockett, the reporter?), found herself at a loss for an excuse. Her remarkably pretty mouth was drawn down to one corner, inducing a dimple of perplexity in her left cheek. She had that breadth between the eyes which, whilst not an attribute of perfect beauty, indicates an active mind, and is often found in Scotch women; now, by the slight raising of her eyebrows, this space was accentuated. But Helen's rapid thinking availed her not at all.

"Had you proposed to walk?" inquired Gianapolis, bending deferentially and taking his place beside her with a confidence which showed that her opportunity for repelling his attentions was past.

"Yes," she said, hesitatingly; "but — I fear I am detaining you"...

Of two evils she was choosing the lesser; the idea of being confined in a cab with this ever-smiling Greek was unthinkable.

"Oh, my dear Miss Cumberly!" cried Gianapolis, beaming radiantly, "it is a greater pleasure than I can express to you, and then for two friends who are proceeding in the same direction to walk apart would be quite absurd, would it not?"

The term "friend" was not pleasing to Helen's ears; Mr. Gianapolis went far too fast. But she recognized her helplessness, and accepted this cavalier with as good a grace as possible.

He immediately began to talk of Olaf van Noord and his pictures, whilst Helen hurried along as though her life depended upon her speed. Sometimes, on the pretense of piloting her at crossings, Gianapolis would take her arm; and this contact she found most disagreeable; but on the whole his conduct was respectful to the point of servility.

A pretty woman who is not wholly obsessed by her personal charms, learns more of the ways of mankind than it is vouchsafed to her plainer sister ever to know; and in the crooked eyes of Gianapolis, Helen Cumberly read a world of unuttered things, and drew her own conclusions. These several conclusions dictated a single course; avoidance of Gianapolis in future.

Fortunately, Helen Cumberly's self-chosen path in life had taught her how to handle the nascent and undesirable lover. She chatted upon the subject of art, and fenced adroitly whenever the Greek sought to introduce the slightest personal element into the conversation. Nevertheless, she was relieved when at last she found herself in the familiar Square with her foot upon the steps of Palace Mansions.

"Good night, Mr. Gianapolis!" she said, and frankly offered her hand.

The Greek raised it to his lips with exaggerated courtesy, and retained it, looking into her eyes in his crooked fashion.

"We both move in the world of art and letters; may I hope that this meeting will not be our last?"

"I am always wandering about between Fleet Street and Soho," laughed Helen. "It is quite certain we shall run into each other again before long. Good night, and thank you so much!"

She darted into the hallway, and ran lightly up the stairs. Opening the flat door with her key, she entered and closed it behind her, sighing with relief to be free of the over-attentive Greek. Some impulse prompted her to enter her own room, and, without turning up the light, to peer down into the Square.

Gianapolis was descending the steps. On the pavement he stood and looked up at the windows, lingeringly; then he turned and walked away.

Helen Cumberly stifled an exclamation.

As the Greek gained the corner of the Square and was lost from view, a lithe figure — kin of the shadows which had masked it — became detached from the other shadows beneath the trees of the central garden and stood, a vague silhouette seemingly looking up at her window as Gianapolis had looked.

Helen leaned her hands upon the ledge and peered intently down. The figure was a vague blur in the darkness, but it was moving away along by the rails...following Gianapolis. No clear glimpse she had of it, for bat-like, it avoided the light, this sinister shape — and was gone.

XXXI
MUSK AND ROSES

It is time to rejoin M. Gaston Max in the catacombs of Ho-Pin. Having prepared himself for drugged repose in the small but luxurious apartment to which he had been conducted by the Chinaman, he awaited with interest the next development. This took the form of the arrival of an Egyptian attendant, white-robed, red-slippered, and wearing the inevitable tarboosh. Upon the brass tray which he carried were arranged the necessities of the opium smoker. Placing the tray upon a little table beside the bed, he extracted from the lacquered box a piece of gummy substance upon the end of a long needle. This he twisted around, skilfully, in the lamp flame until it acquired a blue spirituous flame of its own. He dropped it into the bowl of the carven pipe and silently placed the pipe in M. Max's hand.

Max, with simulated eagerness, rested the mouthpiece between his lips and EXHALED rapturously.

Said stood watching him, without the slightest expression of interest being perceptible upon his immobile face. For some time the Frenchman made pretense of inhaling, gently, the potent vapor, lying propped upon one elbow; then, allowing his head gradually to droop, he closed his eyes and lay back upon the silken pillow.

Once more he exhaled feebly ere permitting the pipe to drop from his listless grasp. The mouthpiece yet rested between his lips, but the lower lip was beginning to drop. Finally, the pipe slipped through his fingers on to the rich carpet, and he lay inert, head thrown back, and revealing his lower teeth. The nauseating fumes of opium loaded the atmosphere.

Said silently picked up the pipe, placed it upon the tray and retired, closing the door in the same noiseless manner that characterized all his movements.

For a time, M. Max lay inert, glancing about the place through the veil of his lashes. He perceived no evidence of surveillance, therefore he ventured fully to open his eyes; but he did not move his head.

With the skill in summarizing detail at a glance which contributed largely to make him the great criminal investigator that he was, he noted those particulars which at an earlier time had occasioned the astonishment of Soames.

M. Max was too deeply versed in his art to attempt any further investigations, yet; he contented himself with learning as much as was possible without moving in any way; and whilst he lay there awaiting whatever might come, the door opened noiselessly — to admit Ho-Pin.

He was about to be submitted to a supreme test, for which, however, he was not unprepared. He lay with closed eyes, breathing nasally.

Ho-Pin, his face a smiling, mirthless mask, bent over the bed. Adeptly, he seized the right eyelid of M. Max, and rolled it back over his forefinger, disclosing the eyeball. M. Max, anticipating this test of the genuineness of his coma, had rolled up his eyes at the moment of Ho-Pin's approach, so that now only the white of the sclerotic showed. His trained nerves did not betray him. He lay like a dead man, never flinching.

Ho-Pin, releasing the eyelid, muttered something gutturally, and stole away from the bed as silently as he had approached it. Very methodically he commenced to search through M. Max's effects, commencing with the discarded garments. He examined the maker's marks upon these, and scrutinized the buttons closely. He turned out all the pockets, counted the contents of the purse, and of the notecase, examined the name inside M. Max's hat, and explored the lining in a manner which aroused the detective's professional admiration. Watch and pocket-knife, Ho-Pin inspected with interest. The little hand-bag which M. Max had brought with him, containing a few toilet necessaries, was overhauled religiously. So much the detective observed through his lowered lashes.

Then Ho-Pin again approached the bed and M. Max became again a dead man.

The silken pyjamas which the detective wore were subjected to gentle examination by the sensitive fingers of the Chinaman, and those same fingers crept beetle-like beneath the pillow.

Silently, Ho-Pin stole from the room and silently closed the door.

M. Max permitted himself a long breath of relief. It was an ordeal through which few men could have passed triumphant.

The SILENCE of the place next attracted the inquirer's attention. He had noted this silence at the moment that he entered the cave of the golden dragon, but here it was even more marked; so that he divined, even before he had examined the walls, that the apartment was rendered sound-proof in the manner of a public telephone cabinet. It was a significant circumstance to which he allotted its full value.

But the question uppermost in his mind at the moment was this: Was the time come yet to commence his explorations?

Patience was included in his complement, and, knowing that he had the night before him, he preferred to wait. In this he did well. Considerable time elapsed, possibly half-an-hour... and again the door opened.

M. Max was conscious of a momentary nervous tremor; for now a WOMAN stood regarding him. She wore a Chinese costume; a huge red poppy was in her hair. Her beauty was magnificently evil; she had the grace of a gazelle and the eyes of a sorceress. He had deceived Ho-Pin, but could he deceive this Eurasian with the witch-eyes wherein burnt ancient wisdom?

He felt rather than saw her approach; for now he ventured to peep no more. She touched him lightly upon the mouth with her fingers and laughed a little low, rippling laugh, the sound of which seemed to trickle along his sensory nerves, icily. She bent over him — lower — lower — and lower yet; until, above the nauseating odor of the place he could smell the musk perfume of her hair. Yet lower she bent; with every nerve in his body he could feel her nearing presence....

She kissed him on the lips.

Again she laughed, in that wicked, eerie glee.

M. Max was conscious of the most singular, the maddest impulses; it was one of the supreme moments of his life. He knew that all depended upon his absolute immobility; yet something in his brain was prompting him — prompting him — to gather the witch to his breast; to return that poisonous, that vampirish kiss, and then to crush out life from the small lithe body.

Sternly he fought down these strange promptings, which he knew to emanate hypnotically from the brain of the creature bending over him.

"Oh, my beautiful dead-baby," she said, softly, and her voice was low, and weirdly sweet. "Oh, my new baby, how I love you, my dead one!" Again she laughed, a musical peal. "I will creep to you in the poppyland where you go...and you shall twine your fingers in my hair and pull my red mouth down to you, kissing me...kissing me, until you stifle and you die of my love.... Oh! my beautiful mummy-baby...my baby."...

The witch-crooning died away into a murmur; and the Frenchman became conscious of the withdrawal of that presence from the room. No sound came to tell of the reclosing of the door; but the obsession was removed, the spell raised.

Again he inhaled deeply the tainted air, and again he opened his eyes.

He had no warranty to suppose that he should remain unmolested during the remainder of the night. The strange words of the Eurasian he did not construe literally; yet could he be certain that he was secure?...Nay! he could be certain that he was NOT!

The shaded lamp was swung in such a position that most of the light was directed upon him where he lay, whilst the walls of the room were bathed in a purple shadow. Behind him and above him, directly over the head of the bunk, a faint sound — a sound inaudible except in such a dead silence as that prevailing — told of some shutter being raised or opened. He had trained himself to watch beneath lowered lids without betraying that he was doing so by the slightest nervous twitching. Now, as he watched the purple shaded lamp above him, he observed that it was swaying and moving very gently, whereas hitherto it had floated motionless in the still air.

No other sound came to guide him, and to have glanced upward would have been to betray all.

For the second time that night he became aware of one who watched him, became conscious of observation without the guaranty of his physical senses. And beneath this new surveillance, there grew up such a revulsion of his inner being as he had rarely experienced. The perfume of ROSES became perceptible; and for some occult reason, its fragrance DISGUSTED.

It was as though a faint draught from the opened shutter poured into the apartment an impalpable cloud of evil; the very soul of the Eurasian, had it taken vapory form and enveloped him, could not have created a greater turmoil of his senses than this!

Some sinister and definitely malignant intelligence was focussed upon him; or was this a chimera of his imagination? Could it be that now he was become en rapport with the thought-forms created in that chamber by its successive occupants?

Scores, perhaps hundreds of brains had there partaken of the unholy sacrament of opium; thousands, millions of evil carnivals had trailed in impish procession about that bed. He knew enough of the creative power of thought to be aware that a sensitive mind coming into contact with such an atmosphere could not fail to respond in some degree to the suggestions, to the elemental hypnosis, of the place.

Was he, owing to his self-induced receptivity of mind, redreaming the evil dreams of those who had occupied that bed before him?

It might be so, but, whatever the explanation, he found himself unable to shake off that uncanny sensation of being watched, studied, by a powerful and inimical intelligence.

Mr. King!...Mr. King was watching him!

The director of that group, whose structure was founded upon the wreckage of human souls, was watching him! Because of a certain sympathy which existed between his present emotions and those which had threatened to obsess him whilst the Eurasian was in the room, he half believed that it was she who peered down at him, now...or she, and another.

The lamp swung gently to and fro, turning slowly to the right and then revolving again to the left, giving life in its gyrations to the intermingled figures on the walls. The atmosphere of the room was nauseating; it was beginning to overpower him....

Creative power of thought...what startling possibilities it opened up. Almost it seemed, if Sir Brian Malpas were to be credited, that the collective mind-force of a group of opium smokers had created the "glamor" of a woman — an Oriental woman — who visited them regularly in their trances. Or had that vision a prototype in the flesh — whom he had seen?...

Creative power of thought...MR. KING! He was pursuing Mr. King; whilst Mr. King might be nothing more than a thought-form — a creation of cumulative thought — an elemental spirit which became visible to his subjects, his victims, which had power over them; which could slay them as the "shell" slew Frankenstein, his creator; which could materialize:...Mr. King might be the Spirit of Opium....

The faint clicking sound was repeated.

Beads of perspiration stood upon M. Max's forehead; his imagination had been running away with him. God! this was a house of fear! He controlled himself, but only by dint of a tremendous effort of will.

Stealthily watching the lamp, he saw that the arc described by its gyrations was diminishing with each successive swing, and, as he watched, its movements grew slighter and slighter, until finally it became quite stationary again, floating, purple and motionless, upon the stagnant air.

Very slowly, he ventured to change his position, for his long ordeal was beginning to induce cramp. The faint creaking of the metal bunk seemed, in the dead stillness and to his highly-tensed senses, like the rattling of castanets.

For ten minutes he lay in his new position; then moved slightly again and waited for fully three-quarters of an hour. Nothing happened, and he now determined to proceed with his inquiries.

Sitting upon the edge of the bunk, he looked about him, first directing his attention to that portion of the wall immediately above. So cunningly was the trap contrived that he could find no trace of its existence. Carefully balancing himself upon the rails on either side of the bunk, he stood up, and peered closely about that part of the wall from which the sound had seemed to come. He even ran his fingers lightly over the paper, up as high as he could reach; but not the slightest crevice was perceptible. He began to doubt the evidence of his own senses.

Unless his accursed imagination had been playing him tricks, a trap of some kind had been opened above his head and someone had looked in at him; yet — and his fingers were trained to such work — he was prepared to swear that the surface of the Chinese paper covering the wall was perfectly continuous. He drummed upon it lightly with his finger-tips, here and there over the surface above the bed. And in this fashion he became enlightened.

A portion, roughly a foot in height and two feet long, yielded a slightly different note to his drumming; whereby he knew that that part of the paper was not ATTACHED to the wall. He perceived the truth. The trap, when closed, fitted flush with the back of the wall-paper, and this paper (although when pasted upon the walls it showed no evidence of the fact) must be TRANSPARENT.

From some dark place beyond, it was possible to peer in THROUGH the rectangular patch of paper as through a window, at the occupant of the bunk below, upon whom the shaded lamp directly poured its rays!

He examined more closely a lower part of the wall, which did not fall within the shadow of the purple lamp-shade; for he was thinking of the draught which had followed the opening of the trap. By this examination he learnt two things: The explanation of the draught, and that of a peculiar property possessed by the mural decorations. These (as Soames had observed before him) assumed a new form if one stared at them closely; other figures, figures human and animal, seemed to take shape and to peer out from BEHIND the more obvious designs which were perceptible at a glance. The longer and the closer one studied these singular walls, the more evident the UNDER design became, until it usurped the field of vision entirely. It was a bewildering delusion; but M. Max had solved the mystery.

There were TWO designs; the first, an intricate Chinese pattern, was painted or printed upon material like the finest gauze. This was attached over a second and vividly colored pattern upon thick parchment-like paper — as he learnt by the application of the point of his pocket-knife.

The observation trap was covered with this paper, and fitted so nicely in the opening that his fingers had failed to detect, through the superimposed gauze, the slightest irregularity there. But, the trap opened, a perfectly clear view of the room could be obtained through the gauze, which, by reason of its texture, also admitted a current of air.

This matter settled, M. Max proceeded carefully to examine the entire room foot by foot. Opening the door in one corner, he entered the bathroom, in which, as in the outer apartment, an electric light was burning. No window was discoverable, and not even an opening for ventilation purposes. The latter fact he might have deduced from the stagnation of the atmosphere.

Half an hour or more he spent in this fashion, without having discovered anything beyond the secret of the observation trap. Again he took out his pocket-knife, which was a large one with a handsome mother-o'-pearl handle. Although Mr. Ho-Pin had examined this carefully, he had solved only half of its secrets. M. Max extracted a little pair of tweezers from the slot in which they were lodged — as Ho-Pin had not neglected to do; but Ho-Pin, having looked at the tweezers, had returned them to their place: M. Max did not do so. He opened the entire knife as though it had been a box, and revealed within it a tiny set of appliances designed principally for the desecration of locks!

Selecting one of these, he took up his watch from the table upon which it lay, and approached the door. It possessed a lever handle of the Continental pattern, and M. Max silently prayed that this might not be a snare and a delusion, but that the lock below might be of the same manufacture.

In order to settle the point, he held the face of his watch close to the keyhole, wound its knob in the wrong direction, and lo! it became an electric lamp!

One glance he cast into the tiny cavity, then dropped back upon the bunk, twisting his mobile mouth in that half smile at once humorous and despairful.

"Nom d'un p'tit bonhomme! — a Yale!" he muttered. "To open that without noise is impossible! Damn!"

M. Max threw himself back upon the pillow, and for an hour afterward lay deep in silent reflection.

He had cigarettes in his case and should have liked to smoke, but feared to take the risk of scenting the air with a perfume so unorthodox.

He had gained something by his exploit, but not all that he had hoped for; clearly his part now was to await what the morning should bring.

XXXII
BLUE BLINDS

Morning brought the silent opening of the door, and the entrance of Said, the Egyptian, bearing a tiny Chinese tea service upon a lacquered tray.

But M. Max lay in a seemingly deathly stupor, and from this the impassive Oriental had great difficulty in arousing him. Said, having shaken some symptoms of life into the limp form of M. Max, filled the little cup with fragrant China tea, and, supporting the dazed man, held the beverage to his lips. With his eyes but slightly opened, and with all his weight resting upon the arm of the Egyptian, he gulped the hot tea, and noted that it was of exquisite quality.

THEINE is an antidote to opium, and M. Max accordingly became somewhat restored, and lay staring at the Oriental, and blinking his eyes foolishly.

Said, leaving the tea service upon the little table, glided from the room. Something else the Egyptian had left upon the tray in addition to the dainty vessels of porcelain; it was a steel ring containing a dozen or more keys. Most of these keys lay fanwise and bunched together, but one lay isolated and pointing in an opposite direction. It was a Yale key — the key of the door!

Silently as a shadow, M. Max glided into the bathroom, and silently, swiftly, returned, carrying a cake of soap. Three clear, sharp impressions, he secured of the Yale, the soap leaving no trace of the operation upon the metal. He dropped the precious soap tablet into his open bag.

In a state of semi-torpor, M. Max sprawled upon the bed for ten minutes or more, during which time, as he noted, the door remained ajar. Then there entered a figure which seemed wildly out of place in the establishment of Ho-Pin. It was that of a butler, most accurately dressed and most deferential in all his highly-trained movements. His dark hair was neatly brushed, and his face, which had a pinched appearance, was composed in that "if-it-is-entirely-agreeable-to-you-Sir" expression, typical of his class.

The unhealthy, yellow skin of the new arrival, which harmonized so ill with the clear whites of his little furtive eyes, interested M. Max extraordinarily. M. Max was blinking like a week-old kitten, and one could have sworn that he was but hazily conscious of his surroundings; whereas in reality he was memorizing the cranial peculiarities of the new arrival, the shape of his nose, the disposition of his ears; the exact hue of his eyes; the presence of a discolored tooth in his lower jaw, which a fish-like, nervous trick of opening and closing the mouth periodically revealed.

"Good morning, sir!" said the valet, gently rubbing his palms together and bending over the bed.

M. Max inhaled deeply, stared in glassy fashion, but in no way indicated that he had heard the words.

The valet shook him gently by the shoulder.

"Good morning, sir. Shall I prepare your bath?"

"She is a serpent!" muttered M. Max, tossing one arm weakly above his head..."all yellow....
But roses are growing in the mud ... of the river!"

"If you will take your bath, sir," insisted the man in black, "I shall be ready to shave you
when you return."

"Bath... shave me!"

M. Max began to rub his eyes and to stare uncomprehendingly at the speaker.

"Yes, sir; good morning, sir," — there was another bow and more rubbing of palms.

"Ah! — of course! Morbleu! This is Paris...."

"No, sir, excuse me, sir, London. Bath hot or cold, sir?"

"Cold," replied M. Max, struggling upright with apparent difficulty; "yes, — cold."

"Very good, sir. Have you brought your own razor, sir?"

"Yes, yes," muttered Max — "in the bag — in that bag."

"I will fill the bath, sir."

The bath being duly filled, M. Max, throwing about his shoulders a magnificent silk kimono
which he found upon the armchair, steered a zigzag course to the bathroom. His tooth-brush
had been put in place by the attentive valet; there was an abundance of clean towels, soaps,
bath salts, with other necessities and luxuries of the toilet. M. Max, following his bath, saw fit
to evidence a return to mental clarity; and whilst he was being shaved he sought to enter into
conversation with the valet. But the latter was singularly reticent, and again M. Max changed
his tactics. He perceived here a golden opportunity which he must not allow to slip through
his fingers.

"Would you like to earn a hundred pounds?" he demanded abruptly, gazing into the beady
eyes of the man bending over him.

Soames almost dropped the razor. His state of alarm was truly pitiable; he glanced to the
right, he glanced to the left, he glanced over his shoulder, up at the ceiling and down at the floor.

"Excuse me, sir," he said, nervously; "I don't think I quite understand you, sir?"

"It is quite simple," replied M. Max. "I asked you if you had some use for a hundred pounds.
Because if you have, I will meet you at any place you like to mention and bring with me cash
to that amount!"

"Hush, sir! — for God's sake, hush, sir!" whispered Soames.

A dew of perspiration was glistening upon his forehead, and it was fortunate that he had
finished shaving M. Max, for his hand was trembling furiously. He made a pretense of hurrying
with towels, bay rum, and powder spray, but the beady eyes were ever glancing to right and left
and all about.

M. Max, who throughout this time had been reflecting, made a second move.

"Another fifty, or possibly another hundred, could be earned as easily," he said, with assumed
carelessness. "I may add that this will not be offered again, and... that you will shortly be out
of employment, with worse to follow."

Soames began to exhibit signs of collapse.

"Oh, my God!" he muttered, "what shall I do? I can't promise — I can't promise; but I
might — I MIGHT look in at the 'Three Nuns' on Friday evening about nine o'clock."...

He hastily scooped up M. Max's belongings, thrust them into the handbag and closed it. M.
Max was now fully dressed and ready to depart. He placed a sovereign in the valet's ready palm.

"That's an appointment," he said softly.

Said entered and stood bowing in the doorway.

"Good morning, sir, good morning," muttered Soames, and covertly he wiped the perspiration from his brow with the corner of a towel — "good morning, and thank you very much."

M. Max, buttoning his light overcoat in order to conceal the fact that he wore evening dress,
entered the corridor, and followed the Egyptian into the cave of the golden dragon. Ho-Pin,
sleek and smiling, received him there. Ho-Pin was smoking the inevitable cigarette in the long
tube, and, opening the door, he silently led the way up the steps into the covered courtyard,
Said following with the hand bag. The limousine stood there, dimly visible in the darkness.

Said placed the handbag upon the seat inside, and Ho-Pin assisted M. Max to enter, closing the door upon him, but leaning through the open window to shake his hand. The Chinaman's hand was icily cold and limp.

"Au wrevoir, my dear fwriend," he said in his metallic voice. "I hope to have the pleasure of gwreeting you again vewry shortly."

With that he pulled up the window from the outside, and the occupant of the limousine found himself in impenetrable darkness; for dark blue blinds covered all the windows. He lay back, endeavoring to determine what should be his next move. The car started with a perfect action, and without the slightest jolt or jar. By reason of the light which suddenly shone in through the chinks of the blinds, he knew that he was outside the covered courtyard; then he became aware that a sharp turning had been taken to the left, followed almost immediately, by one to the right.

He directed his attention to the blinds.

"Ah! nom d'un nom! they are clever — these!"

The blinds worked in little vertical grooves and had each a tiny lock. The blinds covering the glass doors on either side were attached to the adjustable windows; so that when Ho-Pin had raised the window, he had also closed the blind! And these windows operated automatically, and defied all M. Max's efforts to open them!

He was effectively boxed in and unable to form the slightest impression of his surroundings. He threw himself back upon the soft cushions with a muttered curse of vexation; but the mobile mouth was twisted into that wryly humorous smile. Always, M. Max was a philosopher.

At the end of a drive of some twenty-five minutes or less, the car stopped — the door was opened, and the radiant Gianapolis extended both hands to the occupant.

"My dear M. Gaston!" he cried, "how glad I am to see you looking so well! Hand me your bag, I beg of you!"

M. Max placed the bag in the extended hand of Gianapolis, and leapt out upon the pavement.

"This way, my dear friend!" cried the Greek, grasping him warmly by the arm.

The Frenchman found himself being led along toward the head of the car; and, at the same moment, Said reversed the gear and backed away. M. Max was foiled in his hopes of learning the number of the limousine.

He glanced about him wonderingly.

"You are in Temple Gardens, M. Gaston," explained the Greek, "and here, unless I am greatly mistaken, comes a disengaged taxi-cab. You will drive to your hotel?"

"Yes, to my hotel," replied M. Max.

"And whenever you wish to avail yourself of your privilege, and pay a second visit to the establishment presided over by Mr. Ho-Pin, you remember the number?"

"I remember the number," replied M. Max.

The cab hailed by Gianapolis drew up beside the two, and M. Max entered it.

"Good morning, M. Gaston."

"Good morning, Mr. Gianapolis."

XXXIII
LOGIC VS. INTUITION

And now, Henry Leroux, Denise Ryland and Helen Cumberly were speeding along the Richmond Road beneath a sky which smiled upon Leroux's convalescence; for this was a perfect autumn morning which ordinarily had gladdened him, but which saddened him to-day.

The sun shone and the sky was blue; a pleasant breeze played upon his cheeks; whilst Mira, his wife, was...

He knew that he had come perilously near to the borderland beyond which are gibbering, moving things: that he had stood upon the frontier of insanity; and realizing the futility of such reflections, he struggled to banish them from his mind, for his mind was not yet healed — and he must be whole, be sane, if he would take part in the work, which, now, strangers were doing, whilst he — whilst he was a useless hulk.

Denise Ryland had been very voluble at the commencement of the drive, but, as it progressed, had grown gradually silent, and now sat with her brows working up and down and with a little network of wrinkles alternately appearing and disappearing above the bridge of her nose. A self-reliant woman, it was irksome to her to know herself outside the circle of activity revolving around the mysterious Mr. King. She had had one interview with Inspector Dunbar, merely in order that she might give personal testimony to the fact that Mira Leroux had not visited her that year in Paris. Of the shrewd Scotsman she had formed the poorest opinion; and indeed she never had been known to express admiration for, or even the slightest confidence in, any man breathing. The amiable M. Gaston possessed virtues which appealed to her, but whilst she admitted that his conversation was entertaining and his general behavior good, she always spoke with the utmost contempt of his sartorial splendor.

Now, with the days and the weeks slipping by, and with the spectacle before her of poor Leroux, a mere shadow of his former self, with the case, so far as she could perceive, at a standstill, and with the police (she firmly believed) doing "absolutely... nothing... whatever" — Denise Ryland recognized that what was lacking in the investigation was that intuition and wit which only a clever woman could bring to bear upon it, and of which she, in particular, possessed an unlimited reserve.

The car sped on toward the purer atmosphere of the riverside, and even the clouds of dust, which periodically enveloped them, with the passing of each motor-'bus, and which at the commencement of the drive had inspired her to several notable and syncopated outbursts, now left her unmoved.

She thought that at last she perceived the secret working of that Providence which ever dances attendance at the elbow of accomplished womankind. Following the lead set by "H. C." in the Planet ("H. C." was Helen Cumberly's nom de plume) and by Crocket in the Daily Monitor, the London Press had taken Olaf van Noord to its bosom; and his exhibition in the Little Gallery was an established financial success, whilst "Our Lady of the Poppies" (which had, of course, been rejected by the Royal Academy) promised to be the picture of the year.

Mentally, Denise Ryland was again surveying that remarkable composition; mentally she was surveying Olaf van Noord's model, also. Into the scheme slowly forming in her brain, the yellow-wrapped cigarette containing "a small percentage of opium" fitted likewise. Finally, but not last in importance, the Greek gentleman, Mr. Gianapolis, formed a unit of the whole.

Denise Ryland had always despised those detective creations which abound in French literature; perceiving in their marvelous deductions a tortured logic incompatible with the classic models. She prided herself upon her logic, possibly because it was a quality which she lacked, and probably because she confused it with intuition, of which, to do her justice, she possessed an unusual share. Now, this intuition was at work, at work well and truly; and the result which this mental contortionist ascribed to pure reason was nearer to the truth than a real logician could well have hoped to attain by confining himself to legitimate data. In short, she had determined to her own satisfaction that Mr. Gianapolis was the clue to the mystery; that Mr. Gianapolis was not (as she had once supposed) enacting the part of an amiable liar when he declared that there were, in London, such apartments as that represented by Olaf van Noord; that Mr. Gianapolis was acquainted with the present whereabouts of Mrs. Leroux; that Mr. Gianapolis knew who murdered Iris Vernon; and that Scotland Yard was a benevolent institution for the support of those of enfeebled intellect.

These results achieved, she broke her long silence at the moment that the car was turning into Richmond High Street.

"My dear!" she exclaimed, clutching Helen's arm, "I see it all!"

"Oh!" cried the girl, "how you startled me! I thought you were ill or that you had seen something frightful."...

"I HAVE...seen something...frightful," declared Denise Ryland. She glared across at the haggard Leroux. "Harry...Leroux," she continued, "it is very fortunate...that I came to London...very fortunate."

"I am sincerely glad that you did," answered the novelist, with one of his kindly, weary smiles.

"My dear," said Denise Ryland, turning again to Helen Cumberly, "you say you met that...cross-eyed...being...Gianapolis, again?"

"Good Heavens!" cried Helen; "I thought I should never get rid of him; a most loathsome man!"

"My dear...child" — Denise squeezed her tightly by the arm, and peered into her face, intently — "cul-tivate...DELIBERATELY cul-tivate that man's acquaintance!"

Helen stared at her friend as though she suspected the latter's sanity.

"I am afraid I do not understand at all," she said, breathlessly.

"I am positive that I do not," declared Leroux, who was as much surprised as Helen. "In the first place I am not acquainted with this cross-eyed being."

"You are...out of this!" cried Denise Ryland with a sweeping movement of the left hand; "entirely...out of it! This is no MAN'S...business."...

"But my dear Denise!" exclaimed Helen....

"I beseech you; I entreat you;...I ORDER...you to cultivate...that...execrable...being."

"Perhaps," said Helen, with eyes widely opened, "you will condescend to give me some slight reason why I should do anything so extraordinary and undesirable?"

"Undesirable!" cried Denise. "On the contrary;...it is MOST ...desirable! It is essential. The wretched...cross-eyed ...creature has presumed to fall in love...with you."...

"Oh!" cried Helen, flushing, and glancing rapidly at Leroux, who now was thoroughly interested, "please do not talk nonsense!"

"It is no...nonsense. It is the finger...of Providence. Do you know where you can find...him?"

"Not exactly; but I have a shrewd suspicion," again she glanced in an embarrassed way at Leroux, "that he will know where to find ME."

"Who is this presumptuous person?" inquired the novelist, leaning forward, his dark blue eyes aglow with interest.

"Never mind," replied Denise Ryland, "you will know...soon enough. In the meantime...as I am simply...starving, suppose we see about...lunch?"

Moved by some unaccountable impulse, Helen extended her hand to Leroux, who took it quietly in his own and held it, looking down at the slim fingers as though he derived strength and healing from their touch.

"Poor boy," she said softly.

XXXIV
M. MAX REPORTS PROGRESS

Detective-Sergeant Sowerby was seated in Dunbar's room at New Scotland Yard. Some days had elapsed since that critical moment when, all unaware of the fact, they had stood within three yards of the much-wanted Soames, in the fauteuils of the east-end music-hall. Every clue thus far investigated had proved a cul-de-sac. Dunbar, who had literally been working night and day, now began to show evidence of his giant toils. The tawny eyes were as keen as ever, and the whole man as forceful as of old, but in the intervals of conversation, his lids would droop wearily; he would only arouse himself by a perceptible effort.

Sowerby, whose bowler hat lay upon Dunbar's table, was clad in the familiar raincoat, and his ruddy cheerfulness had abated not one whit.

"Have you ever read 'The Adventures of Martin Zeda'?" he asked suddenly, breaking a silence of some minutes' duration.

Dunbar looked up with a start, as...

"Never!" he replied; "I'm not wasting my time with magazine trash."

"It's not trash," said Sowerby, assuming that unnatural air of reflection which sat upon him so ill. "I've looked up the volumes of the Ludgate Magazine in our local library, and I've read all the series with much interest."

Dunbar leaned forward, watching him frowningly.

"I should have thought," he replied, "that you had enough to do without wasting your time in that way!"

"IS it a waste of time?" inquired Sowerby, raising his eyebrows in a manner which lent him a marked resemblance to a famous comedian. "I tell you that the man who can work out plots like those might be a second Jack-the-Ripper and not a soul the wiser!"...

"Ah!"

"I've never met a more innocent LOOKING man, I'll allow; but if you'll read the 'Adventures of Martin Zeda,' you'll know that"...

"Tosh!" snapped Dunbar, irritably; "your ideas of psychology would make a Manx cat laugh! I suppose, on the same analogy, you think the leader-writers of the dailies could run the Government better than the Cabinet does it?"

"I think it very likely"...

"Tosh! Is there anybody in London knows more about the inside workings of crime than the Commissioner? You will admit there isn't; very good. Accordingly to your ideas, the Commissioner must be the biggest blackguard in the Metropolis! I have said it twice before, and I'll be saying it again, Sowerby: TOSH!"

"Well," said Sowerby with an offended air, "has anybody ever seen Mr. King?"

"What are you driving at?"

"I am driving at this: somebody known in certain circles as Mr. King is at the bottom of this mystery. It is highly probable that Mr. King himself murdered Mrs. Vernon. On the evidence of your own notes, nobody left Palace Mansions between the time of the crime and the arrival of witnesses. Therefore, ONE of your witnesses must be a liar; and the liar is Mr. King!"

Inspector Dunbar glared at his subordinate. But the latter continued undaunted: —

"You won't believe it's Leroux; therefore it must be either Mr. Exel, Dr. Cumberly, or Miss Cumberly."...

Inspector Dunbar stood up very suddenly, thrusting his chair from him with much violence.

"Do you recollect the matter of Soames leaving Palace Mansions?" he snapped.

Sowerby's air of serio-comic defiance began to leave him. He scratched his head reflectively.

"Soames got away like that because no one was expecting him to do it. In the same way, neither Leroux, Exel, nor Dr. Cumberly knew that there was any one else IN the flat at the very time when the murderer was making his escape. The cases are identical. They were not looking for a fugitive. He had gone before the search commenced. A clever man could have slipped out in a hundred different ways unobserved. Sowerby, you are..."

What Sowerby was, did not come to light at the moment; for, the door quietly opened and in walked M. Gaston Max arrayed in his inimitable traveling coat, and holding his hat of velour in his gloved hand. He bowed politely.

"Good morning, gentlemen," he said.

"Good morning," said Dunbar and Sowerby together.

Sowerby hastened to place a chair for the distinguished visitor. M. Max, thanking him with a bow, took his seat, and from an inside pocket extracted a notebook.

"There are some little points," he said with a deprecating wave of the hand, "which I should like to confirm." He opened the book, sought the wanted page, and continued: "Do either of you know a person answering to the following description: Height, about four feet eight-and-a-half inches, medium build and carries himself with a nervous stoop. Has a habit of rubbing his palms together when addressing anyone. Has plump hands with rather tapering fingers, and a growth of reddish down upon the backs thereof, indicating that he has red or reddish hair. His chin recedes slightly and is pointed, with a slight cleft parallel with the mouth and situated equidistant from the base of the chin and the lower lip. A nervous mannerism of the latter periodically reveals the lower teeth, one of which, that immediately below the left canine, is much discolored. He is clean-shaven, but may at some time have worn whiskers. His eyes are small and ferret-like, set very closely together and of a ruddy brown color. His nose is wide at the bridge, but narrows to an unusual point at the end. In profile it is irregular, or may have been broken at some time. He has scanty eyebrows set very high, and a low forehead with two faint, vertical wrinkles starting from the inner points of the eyebrows. His natural complexion is probably sallow, and his hair (as hitherto mentioned) either red or of sandy color. His ears are set far back, and the lobes are thin and pointed. His hair is perfectly straight and sparse, and there is a depression of the cheeks where one would expect to find a prominence: that is — at the cheekbone. The cranial development is unusual. The skull slopes back from the crown at a remarkable angle, there being no protuberance at the back, but instead a straight slope to the spine, sometimes seen in the Teutonic races, and in this case much exaggerated. Viewed from the front the skull is narrow, the temples depressed, and the crown bulging over the ears, and receding to a ridge on top. In profile the forehead is almost apelike in size and contour...."

"SOAMES!" exclaimed Inspector Dunbar, leaping to his feet, and bringing both his palms with a simultaneous bang upon the table before him — "Soames, by God!"

M. Max, shrugging and smiling slightly, returned his notebook to his pocket, and, taking out a cigar-case, placed it, open, upon the table, inviting both his confreres, with a gesture, to avail themselves of its contents.

"I thought so," he said simply. "I am glad."

Sowerby selected a cigar in a dazed manner, but Dunbar, ignoring the presence of the cigar-case, leant forward across the table, his eyes blazing, and his small, even, lower teeth revealed in a sort of grim smile.

"M. Max," he said tensely — "you are a clever man! Where have you got him?"

"I have not got him," replied the Frenchman, selecting and lighting one of his own cigars. "He is much too useful to be locked up"...

"But"...

"But yes, my dear Inspector — he is safe; oh! he is quite safe. And on Tuesday night he is going to introduce us to Mr. King!"

"MR. KING!" roared Dunbar; and in three strides of the long legs he was around the table and standing before the Frenchman.

In passing he swept Sowerby's hat on to the floor, and Sowerby, picking it up, began mechanically to brush it with his left sleeve, smoking furiously the while.

"Soames," continued M. Max, quietly — "he is now known as Lucas, by the way — is a man of very remarkable character; a fact indicated by his quite unusual skull. He has no more will than this cigar" — he held the cigar up between his fingers, illustratively — "but of stupid pig obstinacy, that canaille — saligaud! — has enough for all the cattle in Europe! He is like a man who knows that he stands upon a sinking ship, yet, who whilst promising to take the plunge every moment, hesitates and will continue to hesitate until someone pushes him in. Pardieu! I push! Because of his pig obstinacy I am compelled to take risks most unnecessary. He will not consent, that Soames, to open the door for us..."

"What door?" snapped Dunbar.

"The door of the establishment of Mr. King," explained Max, blandly.

"But where is it?"

"It is somewhere between Limehouse Causeway — is it not called so? — and the riverside. But although I have been there, myself, I can tell you no more...."

"What! you have been there yourself?"

"But yes — most decidedly. I was there some nights ago. But they are ingenious, ah! they are so ingenious! — so Chinese! I should not have known even the little I do know if it were not for the inquiries which I made last week. I knew that the letters to Mr. Leroux which were supposed to come from Paris were handed by Soames to some one who posted them to Paris from Bow, East. You remember how I found the impression of the postmark?"

Dunbar nodded, his eyes glistening; for that discovery of the Frenchman's had filled him with a sort of envious admiration.

"Well, then," continued Max, "I knew that the inquiry would lead me to your east-end, and I suspected that I was dealing with Chinamen; therefore, suitably attired, of course, I wandered about in those interesting slums on more than one occasion; and I concluded that the only district in which a Chinaman could live without exciting curiosity was that which lies off the West India Dock Road."...

Dunbar nodded significantly at Sowerby, as who should say: "What did I tell you about this man?"

"On one of these visits," continued the Frenchman, and a smile struggled for expression upon his mobile lips, "I met you two gentlemen with a Mr. — I think he is called Stringer — "...

"You met US!" exclaimed Sowerby.

"My sense of humor quite overcoming me," replied M. Max, "I even tried to swindle you. I think I did the trick very badly!"

Dunbar and Sowerby were staring at one another amazedly.

"It was in the corner of a public house billiard-room," added the Frenchman, with twinkling eyes; "I adopted the ill-used name of Levinsky on that occasion."...

Dunbar began to punch his left palm and to stride up and down the floor; whilst Sowerby, his blue eyes opened quite roundly, watched M. Max as a schoolboy watches an illusionist.

"Therefore," continued M. Max, "I shall ask you to have a party ready on Tuesday night in Limehouse Causeway — suitably concealed, of course; and as I am almost sure that the haunt of Mr. King is actually upon the riverside (I heard one little river sound as I was coming away) a launch party might cooperate with you in affecting the raid."

"The raid!" said Dunbar, turning from a point by the window, and looking back at the Frenchman. "Do you seriously tell me that we are going to raid Mr. King's on Tuesday night?"

"Most certainly," was the confident reply. "I had hoped to form one of the raiding party; but nom d'un nom!" — he shrugged, in his graceful fashion — "I must be one of the rescued!"

"Of the rescued!"

"You see I visited that establishment as a smoker of opium"...

"You took that risk?"

"It was no greater risk than is run by quite a number of people socially well known in London, my dear Inspector Dunbar! I was introduced by an habitue and a member of the best society; and since nobody knows that Gaston Max is in London — that Gaston Max has any business in hand likely to bring him to London — pardieu, what danger did I incur? But, excepting the lobby — the cave of the dragon (a stranger apartment even than that in the Rue St. Claude) and the Chinese cubiculum where I spent the night — mon dieu! what a night! — I saw nothing of the establishment"...

"But you must know where it is!" cried Dunbar.

"I was driven there in a closed limousine, and driven away in the same vehicle"...

"You got the number?"

"It was impossible. These are clever people! But it must be a simple matter, Inspector, to trace a fine car like that which regularly appears in those east-end streets?"

"Every constable in the division must be acquainted with it," replied Dunbar, confidently. "I'll know all about that car inside the next hour!"

"If on Tuesday night you could arrange to have it followed," continued M. Max, "it would simplify matters. What I have done is this: I have bought the man, Soames — up to a point. But so deadly is his fear of the mysterious Mr. King that although he has agreed to assist me in my plans, he will not consent to divulge an atom of information until the raid is successfully performed."

"Then for heaven's sake what IS he going to do?"

"Visitors to the establishment (it is managed by a certain Mr. Ho-Pin; make a note of him, that Ho-Pin) having received the necessary dose of opium are locked in for the night. On Tuesday, Soames, who acts as valet to poor fools using the place, has agreed — for a price — to unlock the door of the room in which I shall be"...

"What!" cried Dunbar, "you are going to risk yourself alone in that place AGAIN?"

"I have paid a very heavy fee," replied the Frenchman with his odd smile, "and it entitles me to a second visit; I shall pay that second visit on Tuesday night, and my danger will be no greater than on the first occasion."

"But Soames may betray you!"

"Fear nothing; I have measured my Soames, not only anthropologically, but otherwise. I fear only his folly, not his knavery. He will not betray me. Morbleu! he is too much a frightened man. I do not know what has taken place; but I could see that, assured of escaping the police for complicity in the murder, he would turn King's evidence immediately"...

"And you gave him that assurance?"

"At first I did not reveal myself. I weighed up my man very carefully; I measured that Soames-pig. I had several stories in readiness, but his character indicated which I should use. Therefore, suddenly I arrested him!"

"Arrested him?"

"Pardieu! I arrested him very quietly in a corner of the bar of 'Three Nuns' public house. My course was justified. He saw that the reign of his mysterious Mr. King was nearing its close, and that I was his only hope"...

"But still he refused"...

"His refusal to reveal anything whatever under those circumstances impressed me more than all. It showed me that in Mr. King I had to deal with a really wonderful and powerful man; a man who ruled by means of FEAR; a man of gigantic force. I had taken the pattern of the key fitting the Yale lock of the door of my room, and I secured a duplicate immediately. Soames has not access to the keys, you understand. I must rely upon my diplomacy to secure the same room again — all turns upon that; and at an hour after midnight, or later if advisable, Soames has agreed to let me out. Beyond this, I could induce him to do nothing — nothing whatever. Cochon! Therefore, having got out of the locked room, I must rely upon my own wits — and the Browning pistol which I have presented to Soames together with the duplicate key"...

"Why not go armed?" asked Dunbar.

"One's clothes are searched, my dear Inspector, by an expert! I have given the key, the pistol, and the implements of the house-breaker (a very neat set which fits easily into the breast-pocket) to Soames, to conceal in his private room at the establishment until Tuesday night. All turns upon my securing the same apartment. If I am unable to do so, the arrangements for the raid will have to be postponed. Opium smokers are faddists essentially, however, and I think I can manage to pretend that I have formed a strange penchant for this particular cubiculum"...

"By whom were you introduced to the place?" asked Dunbar, leaning back against the table and facing the Frenchman.

"That I cannot in honor divulge," was the reply; "but the representative of Mr. King who actually admitted me to the establishment is one Gianapolis; address unknown, but telephone number 18642 East. Make a note of him, that Gianapolis."

"I'll arrest him in the morning," said Sowerby, writing furiously in his notebook.

"Nom d'un p'tit bonhomme! M. Sowerby, you will do nothing of that foolish description, my dear friend," said Max; and Dunbar glared at the unfortunate sergeant. "Nothing whatever must be done to arouse suspicion between now and the moment of the raid. You must be circumspect — ah, morbleu! so circumspect. By all means trace this Mr. Gianapolis; yes. But do not let him SUSPECT that he is being traced"...

XXXV

TRACKER TRACKED

Helen Cumberly and Denise Ryland peered from the window of the former's room into the dusk of the Square, until their eyes ached with the strain of an exercise so unnatural.

"I tell you," said Denise with emphasis, "that... sooner or later... he will come prowling... around. The mere fact that he did not appear... last night... counts for nothing. His own crooked... plans no doubt detain him... very often... at night."

Helen sighed wearily. Denise Ryland's scheme was extremely distasteful to her, but whenever she thought of the pathetic eyes of Leroux she found new determination. Several times she had essayed to analyze the motives which actuated her; always she feared to pursue such inquiries beyond a certain point. Now that she was beginning to share her friend's views upon the matter, all social plans sank into insignificance, and she lived only in the hope of again meeting Gianapolis, of tracing out the opium group, and of finding Mrs. Leroux. In what state did she hope and expect to find her? This was a double question which kept her wakeful through the dreary watches of the night....

"Look!"

Denise Ryland grasped her by the arm, pointing out into the darkened Square. A furtive figure crossed from the northeast corner into the shade of some trees and might be vaguely detected coming nearer and nearer.

"There he is!" whispered Denise Ryland, excitedly; "I told you he couldn't... keep away. I know that kind of brute. There is nobody at home, so listen: I will watch... from the drawing-room, and you... light up here and move about... as if preparing to go out."

Helen, aware that she was flushed with excitement, fell in with the proposal readily; and having switched on the lights in her room and put on her hat so that her moving shadow was thrown upon the casement curtain, she turned out the light again and ran to rejoin her friend. She found the latter peering eagerly from the window of the drawing-room.

"He thinks you are coming out!" gasped Denise. "He has slipped... around the corner. He will pretend to be... passing... this way... the cross-eyed... hypocrite. Do you feel capable ... of the task?"

"Quite," Helen declared, her cheeks flushed and her eyes sparkling. "You will follow us as arranged; for heaven's sake, don't lose us!"

"If the doctor knew of this," breathed Denise, "he would never... forgive me. But no woman... no true woman... could refuse to undertake... so palpable... a duty"...

Helen Cumberly, wearing a warm, golfing jersey over her dress, with a woolen cap to match, ran lightly down the stairs and out into the Square, carrying a letter. She walked along to the pillar-box, and having examined the address upon the envelope with great care, by the light of an adjacent lamp, posted the letter, turned — and there, radiant and bowing, stood Mr. Gianapolis!

"Kismet is really most kind to me!" he cried. "My friend, who lives, as I think I mentioned once before, in Peer's Chambers, evidently radiates good luck. I last had the good fortune to meet you when on my way to see him, and I now meet you again within five minutes of leaving him! My dear Miss Cumberly, I trust you are quite well?"

"Quite," said Helen, holding out her hand. "I am awfully glad to see you again, Mr. Gianapolis!"

He was distinctly encouraged by her tone. He bent forward confidentially.

"The night is young," he said; and his smile was radiant. "May I hope that your expedition does not terminate at this post-box?"

Helen glanced at him doubtfully, and then down at her jersey. Gianapolis was unfeignedly delighted with her naivete.

"Surely you don't want to be seen with me in this extraordinary costume!" she challenged.

"My dear Miss Cumberly, it is simply enchanting! A girl with such a figure as yours never looks better than when she dresses sportily!"

The latent vulgarity of the man was escaping from the bondage in which ordinarily he confined it. A real passion had him in its grip, and the real Gianapolis was speaking. Helen hesitated for one fateful moment; it was going to be even worse than she had anticipated. She glanced up at Palace Mansions.

Across a curtained window moved a shadow, that of a man wearing a long gown and having his hands clasped behind him, whose head showed as an indistinct blur because the hair was wildly disordered. This shadow passed from side to side of the window and was lost from view. It was the shadow of Henry Leroux.

"I am afraid I have a lot of work to do," said Helen, with a little catch in her voice.

"My dear Miss Cumberly," cried Gianapolis, eagerly, placing his hand upon her arm, "it is precisely of your work that I wish to speak to you! Your work is familiar to me — I never miss a line of it; and knowing how you delight in the outre and how inimitably you can describe scenes of Bohemian life, I had hoped, since it was my privilege to meet you, that you would accept my services as cicerone to some of the lesser-known resorts of Bohemian London. Your article, 'Dinner in Soho,' was a delightful piece of observation, and the third — I think it was the third — of the same series: 'Curiosities of the Cafe Royal,' was equally good. But your powers of observation would be given greater play in any one of the three establishments to which I should be honored to escort you."

Helen Cumberly, though perfectly self-reliant, as only the modern girl journalist can be, was fully aware that, not being of the flat-haired, bespectacled type, she was called upon to exercise rather more care in her selection of companions for copy-hunting expeditions than was necessary in the case of certain fellow-members of the Scribes' Club. No power on earth could have induced her to accept such an invitation from such a man, under ordinary circumstances; even now, with so definite and important an object in view, she hesitated. The scheme might lead to nothing; Denise Ryland (horrible thought!) might lose the track; the track might lead to no place of importance, so far as her real inquiry was concerned.

In this hour of emergency, new and wiser ideas were flooding her brain. For instance, they might have admitted Inspector Dunbar to the plot. With Inspector Dunbar dogging her steps, she should have felt perfectly safe; but Denise — she had every respect for Denise's reasoning powers, and force of character — yet Denise nevertheless might fail her.

She glanced into the crooked eyes of Gianapolis, then up again at Palace Mansions.

The shadow of Henry Leroux recrossed the cream-curtained window.

"So early in the evening," pursued the Greek, rapidly, "the more interesting types will hardly have arrived; nevertheless, at the Memphis Cafe"...

"Memphis Cafe!" muttered Helen, glancing at him rapidly; "what an odd name."

"Ah! my dear Miss Cumberly!" cried Gianapolis, with triumph — "I knew that you had never heard of the true haunts of Bohemia! The Memphis Cafe — it is actually a club — was founded by Olaf van Noord two years ago, and at present has a membership including some of the most famous artistic folk of London; not only painters, but authors, composers, actors, actresses. I may add that the peerage, male and female, is represented."

"It is actually a gaming-house, I suppose?" said Helen, shrewdly.

"A gaming-house? Not at all! If what you wish to see is play for high stakes, it is not to the Memphis Cafe you must go. I can show you Society losing its money in thousands, if the spectacle would amuse you. I only await your orders"...

"You certainly interest me," said Helen; and indeed this half-glimpse into phases of London life hidden from the world — even from the greater part of the ever-peering journalistic world — was not lacking in fascination.

The planning of a scheme in its entirety constitutes a mental effort which not infrequently blinds us to the shortcomings of certain essential details. Denise's plan, a good one in many respects, had the fault of being over-elaborate. Now, when it was too late to advise her friend of any amendment, Helen perceived that there was no occasion for her to suffer the society of Gianapolis.

To bid him good evening, and then to follow him, herself, was a plan much superior to that of keeping him company whilst Denise followed both!

Moreover, he would then be much more likely to go home, or to some address which it would be useful to know. What a VERY womanish scheme theirs had been, after all; Helen told herself that the most stupid man imaginable could have placed his finger upon its weak spot immediately.

But her mind was made up. If it were possible, she would warn Denise of the change of plan; if it were not, then she must rely upon her friend to see through the ruse which she was about to practise upon the Greek.

"Good night, Mr. Gianapolis!" she said abruptly, and held out her hand to the smiling man. His smile faded. "I should love to join you, but really you must know that it's impossible. I will arrange to make up a party, with pleasure, if you will let me know where I can 'phone you?"

"But," he began...

"Many thanks, it's really impossible; there are limits even to the escapades allowed under the cloak of 'Copy'! Where can I communicate with you?"

"Oh! how disappointed I am! But I must permit you to know your own wishes better than I can hope to know them, Miss Cumberly. Therefore" — Helen was persistently holding out her hand — "good night! Might I venture to telephone to YOU in the morning? We could then come to some arrangement, no doubt"...

"You might not find me at home"...

"But at nine o'clock!"

"It allows me no time to make up my party!"

"But such a party must not exceed three: yourself and two others"...

"Nevertheless, it has to be arranged."

"I shall ring up to-morrow evening, and if you are not at home, your maid will tell me when you are expected to return."

Helen quite clearly perceived that no address and no telephone number were forthcoming.

"You are committing yourself to endless and unnecessary trouble, Mr. Gianapolis, but if you really wish to do as you suggest, let it be so. Good night!"

She barely touched his extended hand, turned, and ran fleetly back toward the door of Palace Mansions. Ere reaching the entrance, however, she dropped a handkerchief, stooped to recover it, and glanced back rapidly.

Gianapolis was just turning the corner.

Helen perceived the unmistakable form of Denise Ryland lurking in the Palace Mansions doorway, and, waving frantically to her friend, who was nonplussed at this change of tactics, she hurried back again to the corner and peeped cautiously after the retreating Greek.

There was a cab rank some fifty paces beyond, with three taxis stationed there. If Gianapolis chartered a cab, and she were compelled to follow in another, would Denise come upon the scene in time to take up the prearranged role of sleuth-hound?

Gianapolis hesitated only for a few seconds; then, shrugging his shoulders, he stepped out into the road and into the first cab on the rank. The man cranked his engine, leapt into his seat and drove off. Helen Cumberly, ignoring the curious stares of the two remaining taxi-men, ran out from the shelter of the corner and jumped into the next cab, crying breathlessly:

"Follow that cab! Don't let the man in it suspect, but follow, and don't lose sight of it!"

They were off!

Helen glanced ahead quickly, and was just in time to see Gianapolis' cab disappear; then, leaning out of the window, she indulged in an extravagant pantomime for the benefit of Denise Ryland, who was hurrying after her.

"Take the next cab and follow ME!" she cried, whilst her friend raised her hand to her ear the better to detect the words. "I cannot wait for you or the track will be lost"...

Helen's cab swung around the corner — and she was not by any means certain that Denise Ryland had understood her; but to have delayed would have been fatal, and she must rely upon her friend's powers of penetration to form a third in this singular procession.

Whilst these thoughts were passing in the pursuer's mind, Gianapolis, lighting a cigarette, had thrown himself back in a corner of the cab and was mentally reviewing the events of the evening — that is, those events which were associated with Helen Cumberly. He was disappointed but hopeful: at any rate he had suffered no definite repulse. Without doubt, his reflections had been less roseate had he known that he was followed, not only by two, but by THREE trackers.

He had suspected for some time now, and the suspicion had made him uneasy, that his movements were being watched. Police surveillance he did not fear; his arrangements were too complete, he believed, to occasion him any ground for anxiety even though half the Criminal Investigation Department were engaged in dogging his every movement. He understood police methods very thoroughly, and all his experience told him that this elusive shadow which latterly had joined him unbidden, and of whose presence he was specially conscious whenever his steps led toward Palace Mansions, was no police officer.

He had two theories respecting the shadow — or, more properly, one theory which was divisible into two parts; and neither part was conducive to peace of mind. Many years, crowded with many happenings, some of which he would fain forget, had passed since the day when he had entered the service of Mr. King, in Pekin. The enterprises of Mr. King were always of a secret nature, and he well remembered the fate of a certain Burmese gentleman of Rangoon who had attempted to throw the light of publicity into the dark places of these affairs.

From a confidant of the doomed man, Gianapolias had learned, fully a month before a mysterious end had come to the Burman, how the latter (by profession a money-lender) had complained of being shadowed night and day by someone or something, of whom or of which he could never succeed in obtaining so much as a glimpse.

Gianapolis shuddered. These were morbid reflections, for, since he had no thought of betraying Mr. King, he had no occasion to apprehend a fate similar to that of the unfortunate money-lender of Rangoon. It was a very profitable service, that of Mr. King, yet there were times when the fear of his employer struck a chill to his heart; there were times when almost he wished to be done with it all...

By Whitechapel Station he discharged the cab, and, standing on the pavement, lighted a new cigarette from the glowing stump of the old one. A fair amount of traffic passed along the Whitechapel Road, for the night was yet young; therefore Gianapolis attached no importance to the fact that almost at the moment when his own cab turned and was driven away, a second cab swung around the corner of Mount Street and disappeared.

But, could he have seen the big limousine drawn up to the pavement some fifty yards west of London Hospital, his reflections must have been terrible, indeed.

Fate willed that he should know nothing of this matter, and, his thoughts automatically reverting again to Helen Cumberly, he enjoyed that imaginary companionship throughout the remainder of his walk, which led him along Cambridge Road, and from thence, by a devious route, to the northern end of Globe Road.

It may be enlightening to leave Gianapolis for a moment and to return to Mount Street.

Helen Cumberly's cabman, seeing the cab ahead pull up outside the railway station, turned around the nearest corner on the right (as has already appeared), and there stopped. Helen, who also had observed the maneuver of the taxi ahead, hastily descended, and giving the man half-a-sovereign, said rapidly:

"I must follow on foot now, I am afraid! but as I don't know this district at all, could you bring the cab along without attracting attention, and manage to keep me in sight?"

"I'll try, miss," replied the man, with alacrity; "but it won't be an easy job."

"Do your best," cried Helen, and ran off rapidly around the corner, and into Whitechapel Road.

She was just in time to see Gianapolis throw away the stump of his first cigarette and stroll off, smoking a second. She rejoiced that she was inconspicuously dressed, but, simple as was her attire, it did not fail to attract coarse comment from some whom she jostled on her way. She ignored all this, however, and, at a discreet distance followed the Greek, never losing sight of him for more than a moment.

When, leaving Cambridge Road — a considerable thoroughfare — he plunged into a turning, crooked and uninviting, which ran roughly at right angles with the former, she hesitated, but only for an instant. Not another pedestrian was visible in the street, which was very narrow and ill-lighted, but she plainly saw Gianapolis passing under a street-lamp some thirty yards along. Glancing back in quest of the cabman, but failing to perceive him, she resumed the pursuit.

She was nearly come to the end of the street (Gianapolis already had disappeared into an even narrower turning on the left) when a bright light suddenly swept from behind and cast her shadow far out in front of her upon the muddy road. She heard the faint thudding of a motor, but did not look back, for she was confident that this was the taxi-man following. She crept to the corner and peered around it; Gianapolis had disappeared.

The light grew brighter — brighter yet; and, with the engine running very silently, the car came up almost beside her. She considered this unwise on the man's part, yet welcomed his presence, for in this place not a soul was visible, and for the first time she began to feel afraid...

A shawl, or some kind of silken wrap, was suddenly thrown over her head!

She shrieked frenziedly, but the arm of her captor was now clasped tightly about her mouth and head. She felt herself to be suffocating. The silken thing which enveloped her was redolent of the perfume of roses; it was stifling her. She fought furiously, but her arms were now seized in an irresistible grasp, and she felt herself lifted — and placed upon a cushioned seat.

Instantly there was a forward movement of the vehicle which she had mistaken for a taxi-cab, and she knew that she was speeding through those unknown east-end streets — God! to what destination?

She could not cry out, for she was fighting for air — she seemed to be encircled by a swirling cloud of purplish mist. On — and on — and on, she was borne; she knew that she must have been drugged in some way, for consciousness was slipping — slipping...

Helpless as a child in that embrace which never faltered, she was lifted again and carried down many steps. Insensibility was very near now, but with all the will that was hers she struggled to fend it off. She felt herself laid down upon soft cushions...

A guttural voice was speaking, from a vast distance away:

"What is this that you bwring us, Mahara?"

Answered a sweet, silvery voice:

"Does it matter to you what I bringing? It is one I hate — hate — HATE! There will be TWO cases of 'ginger' to go away some day instead of ONE — that is all! Said, yalla!"

"Your pwrimitive passions will wruin us"...

The silvery voice grew even more silvery:

"Do you quarrel with me, Ho-Pin, my friend?"

"This is England, not Burma! Gianapolis"...

"Ah! Whisper — WHISPER it to HIM, and"...

Oblivion closed in upon Helen Cumberly; she seemed to be sinking into the heart of a giant rose.

XXXVI

IN DUNBAR'S ROOM

Dr. Cumberly, his face unusually pale, stood over by the window of Inspector Dunbar's room, his hands locked behind him. In the chair nearest to the window sat Henry Leroux, so muffled up in a fur-collared motor-coat that little of his face was visible; but his eyes were tragic as he leant forward resting his elbows upon his knees and twirling his cap between his thin fingers. He was watching Inspector Dunbar intently; only glancing from the gaunt face of the detective occasionally to look at Denise Ryland, who sat close to the table. At such times his gaze was pathetically reproachful, but always rather sorrowful than angry.

As for Miss Ryland, her habitual self-confidence seemed somewhat to have deserted her, and it was almost with respectful interest that she followed Dunbar's examination of a cabman who, standing cap in hand, completed the party so strangely come together at that late hour.

"This is what you have said," declared Dunbar, taking up an official form, and, with a movement of his hand warning the taxi-man to pay attention: "'I, Frederick Dean, motor-cab driver, was standing on the rank in Little Abbey Street to-night at about a quarter to nine. My cab was the second on the rank. A young lady who wore, I remember, a woolen cap and jersey, with a blue serge skirt, ran out from the corner of the Square and directed me to follow the cab in front of me, which had just been chartered by a dark man wearing a black overcoat and silk hat. She ordered me to keep him in sight; and as I drove off I heard her calling from the window of my cab to another lady who seemed to be following her. I was unable to see this other lady, but my fare addressed her as 'Denise.' I followed the first cab to Whitechapel Station; and as I saw it stop there, I swung into Mount Street. The lady gave me half-a-sovereign, and told me that she proposed to follow the man on foot. She asked me if I could manage to keep her in sight, without letting my cab be seen by the man she was following. I said I would try, and I crept along at some distance behind her, going as slowly as possible until she went into a turning branching off to the right of Cambridge Road; I don't know the name of this street. She was some distance ahead of me, for I had had trouble in crossing Whitechapel Road.

"'A big limousine had passed me a moment before, but as an electric tram was just going by on my off-side, between me and the limousine, I don't know where the limousine went. When I was clear of the tram I could not see it, and it may have gone down Cambridge Road and then down the same turning as the lady. I pulled up at the end of this turning, and could not see a sign of any one. It was quite deserted right to the end, and although I drove down, bore around to the right and finally came out near the top of Globe Road, I did not pass anyone. I waited about the district for over a quarter-of-an-hour and then drove straight to the police station, and they sent me on here to Scotland Yard to report what had occurred.'

"Have you anything to add to that?" said Dunbar, fixing his tawny eyes upon the cabman.

"Nothing at all," replied the man — a very spruce and intelligent specimen of his class and one who, although he had moved with the times, yet retained a slightly horsey appearance, which indicated that he had not always been a mechanical Jehu.

"It is quite satisfactory as far as it goes," muttered Dunbar. "I'll get you to sign it now and we need not detain you any longer."

"There is not the slightest doubt," said Dr. Cumberly, stepping forward and speaking in an unusually harsh voice, "that Helen endeavored to track this man Gianapolis, and was abducted by him or his associates. The limousine was the car of which we have heard so much"...

"If my cabman had not been such a...fool," broke in Denise Ryland, clasping her hands, "we should have had a different...tale to tell."

"I have no wish to reproach anybody," said Dunbar, sternly; "but I feel called upon to remark, madam, that you ought to have known better than to interfere in a case like this; a case in which we are dealing with a desperate and clever gang."

For once in her life Denise Ryland found herself unable to retort suitably. The mildly reproachful gaze of Leroux she could not meet; and although Dr. Cumberly had spoken no word of complaint against her, from his pale face she persistently turned away her eyes.

The cabman having departed, the door almost immediately reopened, and Sergeant Sowerby came in.

"Ah! there you are, Sowerby!" cried Dunbar, standing up and leaning eagerly across the table. "You have the particulars respecting the limousine?"

Sergeant Sowerby, removing his hat and carefully placing it upon the only vacant chair in the room, extracted a bulging notebook from a pocket concealed beneath his raincoat, cleared his throat, and reported as follows:

"There is only one car known to members of that division which answers to the description of the one wanted. This is a high-power, French car which seems to have been registered first in Paris, where it was made, then in Cairo, and lastly in London. It is the property of the gentleman whose telephone number is 18642 East — Mr. I. Gianapolis; and the reason of its frequent presence in the neighborhood of the West India Dock Road, is this: it is kept in a garage in Wharf-End Lane, off Limehouse Causeway. I have interviewed two constables at present on that beat, and they tell me that there is nothing mysterious about the car except that the chauffeur is a foreigner who speaks no English. He is often to be seen cleaning the car in the garage, and both the men are in the habit of exchanging good evening with him when passing the end of the lane. They rarely go that far, however, as it leads nowhere."

"But if you have the telephone number of this man, Gianapolis," cried Dr. Cumberly, "you must also have his address"...

"We obtained both from the Eastern Exchange," interrupted Inspector Dunbar. "The instrument, number 18642 East, is installed in an office in Globe Road. The office, which is situated in a converted private dwelling, bears a brass plate simply inscribed, 'I. Gianapolis, London and Smyrna.'"

"What is the man's reputed business?" jerked Cumberly.

"We have not quite got to the bottom of that, yet," replied Sowerby; "but he is an agent of some kind, and evidently in a large way of business, as he runs a very fine car, and seems to live principally in different hotels. I am told that he is an importer of Turkish cigarettes and"...

"He is an importer and exporter of hashish!" snapped Dunbar irritably. "If I could clap my eyes upon him I should know him at once! I tell you, Sowerby, he is the man who was convicted last year of exporting hashish to Egypt in faked packing cases which contained pottery ware, ostensibly, but had false bottoms filled with cakes of hashish"...

"But," began Dr. Cumberly...

"But because he came before a silly bench," snapped Dunbar, his eyes flashing angrily, "he got off with a fine — a heavy one, certainly, but he could well afford to pay it. It is that kind of judicial folly which ties the hands of Scotland Yard!"

"What makes you so confident that this is the man?" asked the physician.

"He was convicted under the name of G. Ionagis," replied the detective; "which I believe to be either his real name or his real name transposed. Do you follow me? I. Gianapolis is Ionagis Gianapolis, and G. Ionagis is Gianapolis Ionagis. I was not associated with the hashish case; he stored the stuff in a china warehouse within the city precincts, and at that time he did not come within my sphere. But I looked into it privately, and I could see that the prosecution was merely skimming the surface; we are only beginning to get down to the depths NOW."

Dr. Cumberly raised his hand to his head in a distracted manner.

"Surely," he said, and he was evidently exercising a great restraint upon himself — "surely we're wasting time. The office in Globe Road should be raided without delay. No stone should be left unturned to effect the immediate arrest of this man Gianapolis or Ionagis. Why, God almighty! while we are talking here, my daughter"...

"Morbleu! who talks of arresting Gianapolis?" inquired the voice of a man who silently had entered the room.

All turned their heads; and there in the doorway stood M. Gaston Max.

"Thank God you've come!" said Dunbar with sincerity. He dropped back into his chair, a strong man exhausted. "This case is getting beyond me!"

Denise Ryland was staring at the Frenchman as if fascinated. He, for his part, having glanced around the room, seemed called upon to give her some explanation of his presence.

"Madame," he said, bowing in his courtly way, "only because of very great interests did I dare to conceal my true identity. My name is Gaston, that is true, but only so far as it goes. My real name is Gaston Max, and you who live in Paris will perhaps have heard it."

"Gaston Max!" cried Denise Ryland, springing upright as though galvanized; "you are M. Gaston Max! But you are not the least bit in the world like"...

"Myself?" said the Frenchman, smiling. "Madame, it is only a man fortunate enough to possess no enemies who can dare to be like himself."

He bowed to her in an oddly conclusive manner, and turned again to Inspector Dunbar.

"I am summoned in haste," he said; "tell me quickly of this new development."

Sowerby snatched his hat from the vacant chair, and politely placed the chair for M. Max to sit upon. The Frenchman, always courteous, gently forced Sergeant Sowerby himself to occupy the chair, silencing his muttered protests with upraised hand. The matter settled, he lowered his hand, and, resting it fraternally upon the sergeant's shoulder, listened to Inspector Dunbar's account of what had occurred that night. No one interrupted the Inspector until he was come to the end of his narrative.

"Mille tonnerres!" then exclaimed M. Max; and, holding a finger of his glove between his teeth, he tugged so sharply that a long rent appeared in the suede.

His eyes were on fire; the whole man quivered with electric force.

In silence that group watched the celebrated Frenchman; instinctively they looked to him for aid. It is at such times that personality proclaims itself. Here was the last court of appeal, to which came Dr. Cumberly and Inspector Dunbar alike; whose pronouncement they awaited, not questioning that it would be final.

"To-morrow night," began Max, speaking in a very low voice, "we raid the headquarters of Ho-Pin. This disappearance of your daughter, Dr. Cumberly, is frightful; it could not have been foreseen or it should have been prevented. But the least mistake now, and" — he looked at Dr. Cumberly as if apologizing for his barbed words — "she may never return!"

"My God!" groaned the physician, and momentarily dropped his face into his hands.

But almost immediately he recovered himself and with his mouth drawn into a grim straight line, looked again at M. Max, who continued:

"I do not think that this abduction was planned by the group; I think it was an accident and that they were forced, in self-protection, to detain your daughter, who unwisely — morbleu! how unwisely! — forced herself into their secrets. To arrest Gianapolis (even if that were possible) would be to close their doors to us permanently; and as we do not even know the situation of those doors, that would be to ruin everything. Whether Miss Cumberly is confined in the establishment of Ho-Pin or somewhere else, I cannot say; whether she is a captive of Gianapolis or of Mr. King, I do not know. But I know that the usual conduct of the establishment is not being interrupted at present; for only half-an-hour ago I telephoned to Mr. Gianapolis!"

"At Globe Road?" snapped Dunbar, with a flash of the tawny eyes.

"At Globe Road — yes (oh! they would not detain her there!). Mr. Gianapolis was present to speak to me. He met me very agreeably in the matter of occupying my old room in the delightful Chinese hotel of Mr. Ho-Pin. Therefore" — he swept his left hand around forensically, as if to include the whole of the company — "to-morrow night at eleven o'clock I shall be meeting Mr. Gianapolis at Piccadilly Circus, and later we shall join the limousine and be driven to the establishment of Ho-Pin." He turned to Inspector Dunbar. "Your arrangements for watching all the approaches to the suspected area are no doubt complete?"

"Not a stray cat," said Dunbar with emphasis, "can approach Limehouse Causeway or Pennyfields, or any of the environs of the place, to-morrow night after ten o'clock, without the fact being reported to me! You will know at the moment that you step from the limousine that a cyclist scout, carefully concealed, is close at your heels with a whole troup to follow; and if, as you suspect, the den adjoins the river bank, a police cutter will be lying at the nearest available point."

"Eh bien!" said M. Max; then, turning to Denise Ryland and Dr. Cumberly, and shrugging his shoulders: "you see, frightful as your suspense must be, to make any foolish arrests to-night, to move in this matter at all to-night — would be a case of more haste and less speed"...

"But," groaned Cumberly, "is Helen to lie in that foul, unspeakable den until the small hours of to-morrow morning? Good God! they may"...

"There is one little point," interrupted M. Max with upraised hand, "which makes it impossible that we should move to-night — quite apart from the advisability of such a movement. We do not know exactly where this place is situated. What can we do?"

He shrugged his shoulders, and, with raised eyebrows, stared at Dr. Cumberly.

"It is fairly evident," replied the other slowly, and with a repetition of the weary upraising of his hand to his head, "it is fairly evident that the garage used by the man Gianapolis must be very near to — most probably adjoining — the entrance to this place of which you speak."

"Quite true," agreed the Frenchman. "But these are clever, these people of Mr. King. They are Chinese, remember, and the Chinese — ah, I know it! — are the most mysterious and most cunning people in the world. The entrance to the cave of black and gold will not be as wide as a cathedral door. A thousand men might search this garage, which, as Detective Sowerby" (he clapped the latter on the shoulder) "informed me this afternoon, is situated in Wharf-End Lane — all day and all night, and become none the wiser. To-morrow evening" — he lowered his voice — "I myself, shall be not outside, but inside that secret place; I shall be the concierge for one night — Eh bien, that concierge will admit the policeman!"

A groan issued from Dr. Cumberly's lips; and M. Max, with ready sympathy, crossed the room and placed his hands upon the physician's shoulders, looking steadfastly into his eyes.

"I understand, Dr. Cumberly," he said, and his voice was caressing as a woman's. "Pardieu! I understand. To wait is agony; but you, who are a physician, know that to wait sometimes is necessary. Have courage, my friend, have courage!"

XXXVII
THE WHISTLE

Luke Soames, buttoning up his black coat, stood in the darkness, listening.

His constitutional distaste for leaping blindfolded had been over-ridden by circumstance. He felt himself to be a puppet of Fate, and he drifted with the tide because he lacked the strength to swim against it. That will-o'-the-wisp sense of security which had cheered him when first he had realized how much he owed to the protective wings of Mr. King had been rudely extinguished upon the very day of its birth; he had learnt that Mr. King was a sinister protector; and almost hourly he lived again through the events of that night when, all unwittingly, he had become a witness of strange happenings in the catacombs.

Soames had counted himself a lost man that night; the only point which he had considered debatable was whether he should be strangled or poisoned. That his employers were determined upon his death, he was assured; yet he had lived through the night, had learnt from his watch that the morning was arrived... and had seen the flecks at the roots of his dyed hair, blanched by the terrors of that vigil — of that watching, from moment to moment, for the second coming of Ho-Pin.

Yes, the morning had dawned, and with it a faint courage. He had shaved and prepared himself for his singular duties, and Said had brought him his breakfast as usual. The day had passed uneventfully, and once, meeting Ho-Pin, he had found himself greeted with the same mirthless smile but with no menace. Perhaps they had believed his story, or had disbelieved it but realized that he was too closely bound to them to be dangerous.

Then his mind had reverted to the conversation overheard in the music-hall. Should he seek to curry favor with his employers by acquainting them with the fact that, contrary to Gianapolis' assertion, an important clue had fallen into the hands of the police? Did they know this already?

So profound was his belief in the omniscience of the invisible Mr. King that he could not believe that Power ignorant of anything appertaining to himself.

Yet it was possible that those in the catacombs were unaware how Scotland Yard, night and day, quested for Mr. King. The papers made no mention of it; but then the papers made no mention of another fact — the absence of Mrs. Leroux. Now that he was no longer panic-ridden, he could mentally reconstruct that scene of horror, could hear again, imaginatively, the shrieks of the maltreated woman. Perhaps this same active imagination of his was playing him tricks, but, her voice... Always he preferred to dismiss these ideas.

He feared Ho-Pin in the same way that an average man fears a tarantula, and he was only too happy to avoid the ever smiling Chinaman; so that the days passed on, and, finding himself unmolested and the affairs of the catacombs proceeding apparently as usual, he kept his information to himself, uncertain if he shared it with his employers or otherwise, but hesitating to put the matter to the test — always fearful to approach Ho-Pin, the beetlesque.

But this could not continue indefinitely; at least he must speak to Ho-Pin in order to obtain leave of absence. For, since that unforgettable night, he had lived the life of a cave-man indeed, and now began to pine for the wider vault of heaven. Meeting the impassive Chinaman in the corridor one morning, on his way to valet one of the living dead, Soames ventured to stop him.

"Excuse me, sir," he said, confusedly, "but would there be any objection to my going out on Friday evening for an hour?"

"Not at all, Soames," replied Ho-Pin, with his mirthless smile: "you may go at six, wreturn at ten."

Ho-Pin passed on.

Soames heaved a gentle sigh of relief. The painful incident was forgotten, then. He hurried into the room, the door of which Said was holding open, quite eager for his unsavory work.

In crossing its threshold, he crossed out of his new peace into a mental turmoil greater in its complexities than any he yet had known; he met M. Gaston Max, and his vague doubts respecting the omniscience of Mr. King were suddenly reinforced.

Soames' perturbation was so great on that occasion that he feared it must unfailingly be noticed. He realized that now he was definitely in communication with the enemies of Mr. King! Ah; but Mr. King did not know how formidable was the armament of those enemies! He (Soames) had overrated Mr. King; and because that invisible being could inspire Fear in an inconceivable degree, he had thought him all-powerful. Now, he realized that Mr. King was unaware of the existence of at least one clue held by the police; was unaware that his name was associated with the Palace Mansions murder.

The catacombs of Ho-Pin were a sinking ship, and Soames was first of the rats to leave.

He kept his appointment at the "Three Nuns" as has appeared; he accepted the blood-money that was offered him, and he returned to the garage adjoining Kan-Suh Concessions, that night, hugging in his bosom a leather case containing implements by means whereof his new accomplice designed to admit the police to the cave of the golden dragon.

Also, in the pocket of his overcoat, he had a neat Browning pistol; and when the door at the back of the garage was opened for him by Said, he found that the touch of this little weapon sent a thrill of assurance through him, and he began to conceive a sentiment for the unknown investigator to whom he was bound, akin to that which formerly he had cherished for Mr. King!

Now the time was come.

The people of the catacombs acquired a super-sensitive power of hearing, and Soames was able at this time to detect, as he sat or lay in his own room, the movements of persons in the corridor outside and even in the cave of the golden dragon. That mysterious trap in the wall gave him many qualms, and to-night he had glanced at it a thousand times. He held the pistol in his hand, and buttoned up within his coat was the leather case. Only remained the opening of his door in order to learn if the lights were extinguished in the corridor.

He did not anticipate any serious difficulty, provided he could overcome his constitutional nervousness. In his waistcoat pocket was a brand new Yale key which, his latest employer had assured him, fitted the lock of the end door of Block A. The door between the cave of the dragon and Block A was never locked, so far as Soames was aware, nor was that opening from the corridor in which his own room was situated. Therefore, only a few moments — fearful moments, certainly — need intervene, ere he should have a companion; and within a few minutes of that time, the police — his friends! — would be there to protect him! He recognized that the law, after all, was omnipotent, and of all masters was the master to be served.

There was no light in the corridor. Leaving his door ajar, he tiptoed cautiously along toward the cave. Assuring himself once again that the pistol lay in his pocket, he fumbled for the lever which opened the door, found it, depressed it, and stepped quietly forward in his slippered feet.

The unmistakable odor of the place assailed his nostrils. All was in darkness, and absolute silence prevailed. He had a rough idea of the positions of the various little tables, and he stepped cautiously in order to skirt them; but evidently he had made a miscalculation. Something caught his foot, and with a muffled thud he sprawled upon the floor, barely missing one of the tables which he had been at such pains to avoid.

Trembling like a man with an ague, he lay there, breathing in short, staccato breaths, and clutching the pistol in his pocket. Certainly he had made no great noise, but...

Nothing stirred.

Soames summoned up courage to rise and to approach again the door of Block A. Without further mishap he reached it, opened it, and entered the blackness of the corridor. He could make no mistake in regard to the door, for it was the end one. He stole quietly along, his fingers touching the matting, until he came in contact with the corner angle; then, feeling along from the wall until he touched the strip of bamboo which marked the end of the door, he probed about gently with the key; for he knew to within an inch or so where the keyhole was situated.

Ah! he had it! His hand trembling slightly, he sought to insert the key in the lock. It defied his efforts. He felt it gently with the fingers of his left hand, thinking that he might have been endeavoring to insert the key with the irregular edge downward, and not uppermost; but no — such was not the case.

Again he tried, and with no better result. His nerves were threatening to overcome him, now; he had not counted upon any such hitch as this: but fear sharpened his wits. He recollected the fall which he had sustained, and how he had been precipitated upon the polished floor, outside.

Could he have mistaken his direction? Was it not possible that owing to his momentary panic, he had arisen, facing not the door at the foot of the steps, as he had supposed, but that by which a moment earlier he had entered the cave of the golden dragon?

Desperation was with him now; he was gone too far to draw back. Trailing his fingers along the matting covering of the wall, he retraced his steps, came to the open door, and reentered the apartment of the dragon. He complimented himself, fearfully, upon his own address, for he was inspired with an idea whereby he might determine his position. Picking his way among the little tables and the silken ottomans, he groped about with his hands in the impenetrable darkness for the pedestal supporting the dragon. At last his fingers touched the ivory. He slid them downward, feeling for the great vase of poppies which always stood before the golden image....

The vase was on the LEFT and not on the RIGHT of the pedestal. His theory was correct; he had been groping in the mysterious precincts of that Block B which he had never entered, which he had never seen any one else enter, and from whence he had never known any one to emerge! It was the fall that had confused him; now, he took his bearings anew, bent down to feel for any tables that might lie in his path, and crept across the apartment toward the door which he sought.

Ah! this time there could be no mistake! He depressed the lever handle, and, as the door swung open before him, crept furtively into the corridor.

Repeating the process whereby he had determined the position of the end door, he fumbled once again for the keyhole. He found it with even less difficulty than he had experienced in the wrong corridor, inserted the key in the lock, and with intense satisfaction felt it slip into place.

He inhaled a long breath of the lifeless air, turned the key, and threw the door open. One step forward he took...

A whistle (God! he knew it!) a low, minor whistle, wavered through the stillness. He was enveloped, mantled, choked, by the perfume of ROSES!

The door, which, although it had opened easily, had seemed to be a remarkably heavy one, swung to behind him; he heard the click of the lock. Like a trapped animal, he turned, leaped back, and found his quivering hands in contact with books — books — books...

A lamp lighted up in the center of the room.

Soames turned and stood pressed closely against the book-shelves, against the book-shelves which magically had grown up in front of the door by which he had entered. He was in the place of books and roses — in the haunt of MR. KING!

A great clarity of mind came to him, as it comes to a drowning man; he knew that those endless passages, through which once he had been led in darkness, did not exist, that he had been deceived, had been guided along the same corridor again and again; he knew that this room of roses did not lie at the heart of a labyrinth, but almost adjoined the cave of the golden dragon.

He knew that he was a poor, blind fool; that his plotting had been known to those whom he had thought to betray; that the new key which had opened a way into this place of dread was not the key which his accomplice had given him. He knew that that upon which he had tripped at the outset of his journey had been set in his path by cunning design, in order that the fall might confuse his sense of direction. He knew that the great vase of poppies had been moved, that night....

God! his brain became a seething furnace.

There, before him, upstood the sandalwood screen, with one corner of the table projecting beyond it. Nothing of life was visible in the perfumed place, where deathly silence prevailed....

No lion has greater courage than a cornered rat. Soames plucked the pistol from his pocket and fired at the screen — ONCE! — TWICE!

He heard the muffled report, saw the flash of the little weapon, saw the two holes in the carven woodwork, and gained a greater, hysterical courage — the courage of a coward's desperation.

Immediately before him was a little ebony table, bearing a silver bowl, laden to the brim with sulphur-colored roses. He overturned the table with his foot, laughing wildly. In three strides he leapt across the room, grasped the sandalwood screen, and hurled it to the floor....

In the instant of its fall, he became as Lot's wife. The pistol dropped from his nerveless grasp, thudding gently on the carpet, and, with his fingers crooked paralytically, he stood swaying... and looking into the face of MR. KING!

Soames' body already was as rigid as it would be in death; his mind was numbed — useless. But his outraged soul forced utterance from the lips of the man.

A scream, a scream to have made the angels shudder, to have inspired pity in the devils of Hell, burst from him. Two yellow hands leaped at his throat....

XXXVIII
THE SECRET TRAPS

Gaston Max, from his silken bed in the catacombs of Ho-Pin, watched the hand of his watch which lay upon the little table beside him. Already it was past two o'clock, and no sign had come from Soames; a hundred times his imagination had almost tricked him into believing that the door was opening; but always the idea had been illusory and due to the purple shadow of the lamp-shade which overcast that side of the room and the door.

He had experienced no difficulty in arranging with Gianapolis to occupy the same room as formerly; and, close student of human nature though he was, he had been unable to detect in the Greek's manner, when they had met that night, the slightest restraint, the slightest evidence of uneasiness. His reception by Ho-Pin had varied scarce one iota from that accorded him on his first visit to the cave of the golden dragon. The immobile Egyptian had brought him the opium, and had departed silently as before. On this occasion, the trap above the bed had not been opened. But hour after hour had passed, uneventfully, silently, in that still, suffocating room....

A key in the lock! — yes, a key was being inserted in the lock! He must take no unnecessary risks; it might be another than Soames. He waited — the faint sound of fumbling ceased. Still, he waited, listening intently.

Half-past-two. If it had been Soames, why had he withdrawn? M. Max arose noiselessly and looked about him. He was undecided what to do, when...

Two shots, followed by a most appalling shriek — the more frightful because it was muffled; the shriek of a man in extremis, of one who stands upon the brink of Eternity, brought him up rigid, tense, with fists clenched, with eyes glaring; wrought within this fearless investigator an emotion akin to terror.

Just that one gruesome cry there was and silence again.

What did it mean?

M. Max began hastily to dress. He discovered, in endeavoring to fasten his collar, that his skin was wet with cold perspiration.

"Pardieu!" he said, twisting his mouth into that wry smile, "I know, now, the meaning of fright!"

He was ever glancing toward the door, not hopefully as hitherto, but apprehensively, fearfully.

That shriek in the night might portend merely the delirium of some other occupant of the catacombs; but the shots...

"It was SOAMES!" he whispered aloud; "I have risked too much; I am fast in the rat-trap!"

He looked about him for a possible weapon. The time for inactivity was past. It would be horrible to die in that reeking place, whilst outside, it might be, immediately above his head, Dunbar and the others waited and watched.

The construction of the metal bunk attracted his attention. As in the case of steamer bunks one of the rails — that nearer to the door — was detachable in order to facilitate the making of the bed. Rapidly, nervously, he unscrewed it; but the hinges were riveted to the main structure, and after a brief examination he shrugged his shoulders despairingly. Then, he recollected that in the adjoining bathroom there was a metal towel rail, nickeled, and with a heavy knock at either end, attached by two brackets to the wall.

He ran into the inner room and eagerly examined these fastenings. They were attached by small steel screws. In an instant he was at work with the blade of his pocket-knife. Six screws in all there were to be dealt with, three at either end. The fifth snapped the blade and he uttered an exclamation of dismay. But the shortened implement proved to be an even better screw-driver than the original blade, and half a minute later he found himself in possession of a club such as would have delighted the soul of Hercules.

He managed to unscrew one of the knobs, and thus to slide off from the bar the bracket attachments; then, replacing the knob, he weighed the bar in his hand, appreciatively. His mind now was wholly composed, and his course determined. He crossed the little room and rapped loudly upon the door.

The rapping sounded muffled and dim in that sound-proof place. Nothing happened, and thrice he repeated the rapping with like negative results. But he had learnt something: the door was a very heavy one.

He made a note of the circumstance, although it did not interfere with the plan which he had in mind. Wheeling the armchair up beside the bed, he mounted upon its two arms and, ONCE — TWICE — THRICE — crashed the knob of the iron bar against that part of the wall which concealed the trap.

Here the result was immediate. At every blow of the bar the trap behind yielded. A fourth blow sent the knob crashing through the gauze material, and far out into some dark place beyond. There was a sound as of a number of books falling.

He had burst the trap.

Up on the back of the chair he mounted, resting his bar against the wall, and began in feverish haste to tear away the gauze concealing the rectangular opening.

An almost overpowering perfume of roses was wafted into his face. In front of him was blackness.

Having torn away all the gauze, he learned that the opening was some two feet long by one foot high. Resting the bar across the ledge he extended his head and shoulders forward through this opening into the rose-scented place beyond, and without any great effort drew himself up with his hands, so that, provided he could find some support upon the other side, it would be a simple matter to draw himself through entirely.

He felt about with his fingers, right and left, and in doing so disturbed another row of books, which fell upon the floor beneath him. He had apparently come out in the middle of a large book-shelf. To the left of him projected the paper-covered door of the trap, at right angles; above and below were book-laden shelves, and on the right there had been other books, until his questing fingers had disturbed them.

M. Max, despite his weight, was an agile man. Clutching the shelf beneath, he worked his way along to the right, gradually creeping further and further into the darkened room, until at last he could draw his feet through the opening and crouch sideways upon the shelf.

He lowered his left foot, sought for and found another shelf beneath, and descended as by a ladder to the thickly carpeted floor. Grasping the end of the bar, he pulled that weapon down; then he twisted the button which converted his timepiece into an electric lantern, and, holding the bar in one tensely quivering hand, looked rapidly about him.

This was a library; a small library, with bowls of roses set upon tables, shelves, in gaps between the books, and one lying overturned upon the floor. Although it was almost drowned by their overpowering perfume, he detected a faint smell of powder. In one corner stood a large writing-table with papers strewn carelessly upon it. Its appointments were markedly Chinese in character, from the singular, gold inkwell to the jade paperweight; markedly Chinese — and — FEMININE. A very handsome screen lay upon the floor in front of this table, and the rich carpet he noted to be disordered as if a struggle had taken place upon it. But, most singular circumstance of all, and most disturbing... there was no door to this room!

For a moment he failed to appreciate the entire significance of this. A secret room difficult to enter he could comprehend, but a secret room difficult to QUIT passed his comprehension completely. Moreover, he was no better off for his exploit.

Three minutes sufficed him in which to examine the shelves covering the four walls of the room from floor to ceiling. None of the books were dummies, and slowly the fact began to dawn upon his mind that what at first he had assumed to be a rather simple device, was, in truth, almost incomprehensible.

For how, in the name of Sanity, did the occupant of this room — and obviously it was occupied at times — enter and leave it?

"Ah!" he muttered, shining the light upon a row of yellow-bound volumes from which he had commenced his tour of inspection and to which that tour had now led him back, "it is uncanny — this!"

He glanced back at the rectangular patch of light which marked the trap whereby he had entered this supernormal room. It was situated close to one corner of the library, and, acting upon an idea which came to him (any idea was better than none) he proceeded to throw down the books occupying the corresponding position at the other end of the shelf.

A second trap was revealed, identical with that through which he had entered!

It was fastened with a neat brass bolt; and, standing upon one of the little Persian tables — from which he removed a silver bowl of roses — he opened this trap and looked into the lighted room beyond. He saw an apartment almost identical with that which he himself recently had quitted; but in one particular it differed. It was occupied... AND BY A WOMAN!

Arrayed in a gossamer nightrobe she lay in the bed, beneath the trap, her sunken face matching the silken whiteness. Her thin arms drooped listlessly over the rails of the bunk, and upon her left hand M. Max perceived a wedding ring. Her hair, flaxen in the electric light, was spread about in wildest disorder upon the pillow, and a breath of fetid air assailed his nostrils as he pressed his face close to the gauze masking the opening in order to peer closely at this victim of the catacombs.

He watched the silken covering of her bosom, intently, but failed to detect the slightest movement.

"Morbleu!" he muttered, "is she dead?"

He rent the gauze with a sweep of his left hand, and standing upon the bottom shelf of the case, craned forward into the room, looking all about him. A purple shaded lamp burnt above the bed as in the adjoining apartment which he himself had occupied. There were dainty feminine trifles littered in the big armchair, and a motor-coat hung upon the hook of the bathroom door. A small cabin-trunk in one corner of the room bore the initials: "M. L."

Max dropped back into the incredible library with a stifled gasp.

"Pardieu!" he said. "It is Mrs. Leroux that I have found!"

A moment he stood looking from trap to trap; then turned and surveyed again the impassable walls, the rows of works, few of which were European, some of them bound in vellum, some in pigskin, and one row of huge volumes, ten in number, on the bottom shelf, in crocodile hide.

"It is weird, this!" he muttered, "nightmare!" — turning the light from row to row. "How is this lamp lighted that swings here?"

He began to search for the switch, and, even before he found it, had made up his mind that, once discovered, it would not only enable him more fully to illuminate the library, but would constitute a valuable clue.

At last he found it, situated at the back of one of the shelves, and set above a row of four small books, so that it could readily be reached by inserting the hand.

He flooded the place with light; and perceived at a glance that a length of white flex crossing the ceiling enabled anyone seated at the table to ignite the lamp from there also. Then, replacing his torch in his pocket, and assuring himself that the iron bar lay within easy reach, he began deliberately to remove all of the books from the shelves covering that side of the room upon which the switch was situated. His theory was a sound one; he argued that the natural and proper place for such a switch in such a room would be immediately inside the door, so that one entering could ignite the lamp without having to grope in the darkness. He was encouraged, furthermore, by the fact that at a point some four feet to the left of this switch there was a gap in the bookcases, running from floor to ceiling; a gap no more than four inches across.

Having removed every book from its position, save three, which occupied a shelf on a level with his shoulder and adjoining the gap, he desisted wearily, for many of the volumes were weighty, and the heat of the room was almost insufferable. He dropped with a sigh upon a silk ottoman close beside him....

A short, staccato, muffled report split the heavy silence...and a little round hole appeared in the woodwork of the book-shelf before which, an instant earlier, M. Max had been standing — in the woodwork of that shelf, which had been upon a level with his head.

In one giant leap he hurled himself across the room — ...as a second bullet pierced the yellow silk of the ottoman.

Close under the trap he crouched, staring up, fearful-eyed....

A yellow hand and arm — a hand and arm of great nervous strength and of the hue of old ivory, directed a pistol through the opening above him. As he leaped, the hand was depressed with a lightning movement, but, lunging suddenly upward, Max seized the barrel of the pistol, and with a powerful wrench, twisted it from the grasp of the yellow hand. It was his own Browning!

At the time — in that moment of intense nervous excitement — he ascribed his sensations to his swift bout with Death — with Death who almost had conquered; but later, even now, as he wrenched the weapon into his grasp, he wondered if physical fear could wholly account for the sickening revulsion which held him back from that rectangular opening in the bookcase.

He thought that he recognized in this a kindred horror — as distinct from terror — to that which had come to him with the odor of roses through this very trap, upon the night of his first visit to the catacombs of Ho-Pin.

It was not as the fear which one has of a dangerous wild beast, but as the loathing which is inspired by a thing diseased, leprous, contagious....

A mighty effort of will was called for, but he managed to achieve it. He drew himself upright, breathing very rapidly, and looked through into the room — the room which he had occupied, and from which a moment ago the murderous yellow hand had protruded.

That room was empty... empty as he had left it!

"Mille tonnerres! he has escaped me!" he cried aloud, and the words did not seem of his own choosing.

WHO had escaped? Someone — man or woman; rather some THING, which, yellow handed, had sought to murder him!

Max ran across to the second trap and looked down at the woman whom he knew, beyond doubt, to be Mrs. Leroux. She lay in her death-like trance, unmoved.

Strung up to uttermost tension, he looked down at her and listened — listened, intently.

Above the fumes of the apartment in which the woman lay, a stifling odor of roses was clearly perceptible. The whole place was tropically hot. Not a sound, save the creaking of the shelf beneath him, broke the heavy stillness.

XXXIX
THE LABYRINTH

Feverishly, Max clutched at the last three books upon the shelf adjoining the gap. Of these, the center volume, a work bound in yellow calf and bearing no title, proved to be irremovable; right and left it could be inclined, but not moved outward. It masked the lever handle of the door!

But that door was locked.

Max, with upraised arms, swept the perspiration from his brows and eyes; he leant dizzily up against the door which defied him; his mind was working with febrile rapidity. He placed the pistol in his pocket, and, recrossing the room, mounted up again upon the shelves, and crept through into the apartment beyond, from which the yellow hand had protruded. He dropped, panting, upon the bed, then, eagerly leaping to the door, grasped the handle.

"Pardieu!" he muttered, "it is unlocked!"

Though the light was still burning in this room, the corridor outside was in darkness. He pressed the button of the ingenious lamp which was also a watch, and made for the door communicating with the cave of the dragon. It was readily to be detected by reason of its visible handle; the other doors being externally indistinguishable from the rest of the matting-covered wall.

The cave of the dragon proved to be empty, and in darkness. He ran across its polished floor and opened at random the door immediately facing him. A corridor similar to the one which he had just quitted was revealed. Another door was visible at one end, and to this he ran, pulled it open, stepped through the opening, and found himself back in the cave of the dragon!

"Morbleu!" he muttered, "it is bewildering — this!"

Yet another door, this time one of ebony, he opened; and yet another matting-lined corridor presented itself to his gaze. He swept it with the ray of the little lamp, detected a door, opened it, and entered a similar suite to those with which he already was familiar. It was empty, but, unlike the one which he himself had tenanted, this suite possessed two doors, the second opening out of the bathroom. To this he ran; it was unlocked; he opened it, stepped ahead...and was back again in the cave of the dragon.

"Mon dieu!" he cried, "this is Chinese — quite Chinese!"

He stood looking about him, flashing the ray of light upon doors which were opened and upon openings in the walls where properly there should have been no doors.

"I am too late!" he muttered; "they had information of this and they have 'unloaded.' That they intend to fly the country is proven by their leaving Mrs. Leroux behind. Ah, nom d'un nom, the good God grant that they have left also."...

Coincident with his thoughts of her, the voice of Helen Cumberly reached his ears! He stood there quivering in every nerve, as: "Help! Help!" followed by a choking, inarticulate cry, came, muffled, from somewhere — he could not determine where.

But the voice was the voice of Helen Cumberly. He raised his left fist and beat his brow as if to urge his brain to super-activity. Then, leaping, he was off.

Door after door he threw open, crying, "Miss Cumberly! Miss Cumberly! Where are you? Have courage! Help is here!"

But the silence remained unbroken — and always his wild search brought him back to the accursed cave of the golden dragon. He began to grow dizzy; he felt that his brain was bursting. For somewhere — somewhere but a few yards removed from him — a woman was in extreme peril!

Clutching dizzily at the pedestal of the dragon, he cried at the top of his voice: —

"Miss Cumberly! For the good God's sake answer me! Where are you?"

"Here, M. Max!" he was answered; "the door on your right... and then to your right again — quick! QUICK! Saints! she has killed me!"

It was Gianapolis who spoke!

Max hurled himself through the doorway indicated, falling up against the matting wall by reason of the impetus of his leap. He turned, leaped on, and one of the panels was slightly ajar; it was a masked door. Within was darkness out of which came the sounds of a great turmoil, as of wild beasts in conflict.

Max kicked the door fully open and flashed the ray of the torch into the room. It poured its cold light upon a group which, like some masterpiece of classic statuary, was to remain etched indelibly upon his mind.

Helen Cumberly lay, her head and shoulders pressed back upon the silken pillows of the bed, with both hands clutching the wrist of the Eurasian and striving to wrench the latter's fingers from her throat, in the white skin of which they were bloodily embedded. With his left arm about the face and head of the devilish half-caste, and grasping with his right hand her slender right wrist — putting forth all his strength to hold it back — was Gianapolis!

His face was of a grayish pallor and clammy with sweat; his crooked eyes had the glare of madness. The lithe body of the Eurasian writhing in his grasp seemed to possess the strength of two strong men; for palpably the Greek was weakening. His left sleeve was torn to shreds — to bloody shreds beneath the teeth of the wild thing with which he fought; and lower, lower, always nearer to the throat of the victim, the slender, yellow arm forced itself, forced the tiny hand clutching a poniard no larger than a hatpin but sharp as an adder's tooth.

"Hold her!" whispered Gianapolis in a voice barely audible, as Max burst into the room. "She came back for this and... I followed her. She has the strength of... a tigress!"

Max hurled himself into the melee, grasping the wrist of the Eurasian below where it was clutched by Gianapolis. Nodding to the Greek to release his hold, he twisted it smartly upward.

The dagger fell upon the floor, and with an animal shriek of rage, the Eurasian tottered back. Max caught her about the waist and tossed her unceremoniously into a corner of the room.

Helen Cumberly slipped from the bed, and lay very white and still upon the garish carpet, with four tiny red streams trickling from the nail punctures in her throat. Max stooped and raised her shoulders; he glanced at the Greek, who, quivering in all his limbs, and on the verge of collapse, only kept himself upright by dint of clutching at the side of the doorway. Max realized that Gianapolis was past aiding him; his own resources were nearly exhausted, but, stooping, he managed to lift the girl and to carry her out into the corridor.

"Follow me!" he gasped, glancing back at Gianapolis; "Morbleu, make an effort! The keys — the keys!"

Laying Helen Cumberly upon one of the raised divans, with her head resting upon a silken cushion, Max, teeth tightly clenched and dreadfully conscious that his strength was failing him, waited for Gianapolis. Out from the corridor the Greek came staggering, and Max now perceived that he was bleeding profusely from a wound in the breast.

"She came back," whispered Gianapolis, clutching at the Frenchman for support…"the hell-cat!…I did not know…that…Miss Cumberly was here. As God is my witness I did not know! But I followed…HER — Mahara…thank God I did! She has finished me, I think, but" — he lowered the crooked eyes to the form of Helen Cumberly — "never mind…Saints!"

He reeled and sank upon his knees. He clutched at the edge of his coat and raised it to his lips, wherefrom blood was gushing forth. Max stooped eagerly, for as the Greek had collapsed upon the floor, he had heard the rattle of keys.

"She had…the keys," whispered Gianapolis. "They have…tabs…upon them…Mrs. Leroux… number 3 B. The door to the stair" — very, very slowly, he inclined his head toward the ebony door near which Max was standing — "is marked X. The door…at the top — into garage…B."

"Tell me," said Max, his arm about the dying man's shoulders — "try to tell me: who killed Mrs. Vernon and why?"

"MR. KING!" came in a rattling voice. "Because of the…carelessness of someone…Mrs. Vernon wandered into the room …of Mrs. Leroux. She seems to have had a fit of remorse…or something like it. She begged Mrs. Leroux to pull up…before…too late. Ho-Pin arrived just as she was crying to …Mrs. Leroux…and asking if she could ever forgive her …for bringing her here….It was Mrs. Vernon who…introduced Mrs….Leroux. Ho-Pin heard her…say that she …would tell…Leroux the truth…as the only means"…

"Yes, yes, morbleu! I understand! And then?"

"Ho-Pin knows…women…like a book. He thought Mrs. Vernon would…shirk the scandal. We used to send our women …to Nurse Proctor's, then…to steady up a bit…We let Mrs. Vernon go…as usual. The scene with…Mrs. Leroux had shaken…her and she fainted…in the car… Victoria Street….I was with her. Nurse Proctor had…God! I am dying!…a time with her;…she got so hysterical that they had to…detain her…and three days later…her husband died; Proctor, the…fool…somehow left a paper containing the news in Mrs. Vernon's room….They had had to administer an injection that afternoon…and they thought she was…sleeping."…

"Morbleu! Yes, yes! — a supreme effort, my friend!"

"Directly Ho-Pin heard of Vernon's death, he knew that his hold …on Mrs. Vernon…was lost….He…and Mahara…and…MR. KING…drove straight to…Gillingham…Street…to…arrange….Ah!…she rushed like a mad woman into the street, a moment before…they arrived. A cab was passing, and"…

"I know this! I know this! What happened at Palace Mansions?"

The Greek's voice grew fainter.

"Mr. King followed…her…upstairs. Too late;…but whilst Leroux was in…Cumberly's flat… leaving door open …Mr. King went…in…Mahara…was watching…gave signal…whistle…of someone's approach. It was thought…Mr. King…had secured ALL the message…Mrs. Vernon…was…writing….Mr. King opened the door of …the lift-shaft…lift not working…climbed down that way…and out by door on…ground floor…when Mr….the Member of Parliament… went upstairs."…

"Ah! pardieu! one last word! WHO IS MR. KING?"

Gianapolis lurched forward, his eyes glazing, half raised his arm — pointing back into the cave of the dragon — and dropped, face downward, on the floor, with a crimson pool forming slowly about his head.

An unfamiliar sound had begun to disturb the silence of the catacombs. Max glanced at the white face of Helen Cumberly, then directed the ray of the little lamp toward the further end of the apartment. A steady stream of dirty water was pouring into the cave of the dragon through the open door ahead of him.

Into the disc of light, leaped, fantastic, the witch figure of the Eurasian. She turned and faced him, threw up both her arms, and laughed shrilly, insanely. Then she turned and ran like a hare, her yellow silk dress gleaming in the moving ray. Inhaling sibilantly, Max leaped after her. In three strides he found his foot splashing in water. An instant he hesitated. Through the corridor ahead of him sped the yellow figure, and right to the end. The seemingly solid wall opened before her; it was another masked door.

Max crossed the threshold hard upon her heels. Three descending steps were ahead of him, and then a long brick tunnel in which swirled fully three feet of water, which, slowly rising, was gradually flooding the cave of the dragon.

On went the Eurasian, up to her waist in the flood, with Max gaining upon her, now, at every stride. There was a damp freshness in the air of the passage, and a sort of mist seemed to float above the water. This mist had a familiar smell....

They were approaching the river, and there was a fog to-night!

Even as he realized the fact, the quarry vanished, and the ray of light from Max's lamp impinged upon the opening in an iron sluice gate. The Eurasian had passed it, but Max realized that he must lower his head if he would follow. He ducked rapidly, almost touching the muddy water with his face. A bank of yellow fog instantly enveloped him, and he pulled up short, for, instinctively, he knew that another step might precipitate him into the Thames.

He strove to peer about him, but the feeble ray of the lamp was incapable of penetrating the fog. He groped with his fingers, right and left, and presently found slimy wooden steps. He drew himself closely to these, and directed the light upon them. They led upward. He mounted cautiously, and was clear of the oily water, now, and upon a sort of gangway above which lowered a green and rotting wooden roof.

Obviously, the tide was rising; and, after seeking vainly to peer through the fog ahead, he turned and descended the steps again, finding himself now nearly up to his armpits in water. He just managed to get in under the sluice gate without actually submerging his head, and to regain the brick tunnel.

He paused for a moment, hoping to be able to lower the gate, but the apparatus was out of his reach, and he had nothing to stand upon to aid him in manipulating it.

Three or four inches of water now flooded the cave of the golden dragon. Max pulled the keys from his pocket, and unlocked the door at the foot of the steps. He turned, resting the electric lamp upon one of the little ebony tables, and lifting Helen Cumberly, carried her half-way up the steps, depositing her there with her back to the wall. He staggered down again; his remarkable physical resources were at an end; it must be another's work to rescue Mrs. Leroux. He stooped over Gianapolis, and turned his head. The crooked eyes glared up at him deathly.

"May the good God forgive you," he whispered. "You tried to make your peace with Him."

The sound of muffled blows began to be audible from the head of the steps. Max staggered out of the cave of the golden dragon. A slight freshness and dampness was visible in its atmosphere, and the gentle gurgling of water broke its heavy stillness. There was a new quality come into it, and, strangely, an old quality gone out from it. As he lifted the lamp from the table — now standing in slowly moving water — the place seemed no longer to be the cave of the golden dragon he had known....

He mounted the steps again, with difficulty, resting his shaking hands upon the walls. Shattering blows were being delivered upon the door, above.

"Dunbar!" he cried feebly, stepping aside to avoid Helen Cumberly, where she lay. "Dunbar!"...

XL

The river police seemed to be floating, suspended in the fog, which now was so dense that the water beneath was invisible. Inspector Rogers, who was in charge, fastened up his coat collar about his neck and turned to Stringer, the Scotland Yard man, who sat beside him in the stern of the cutter gloomily silent.

"Time's wearing on," said Rogers, and his voice was muffled by the fog as though he were speaking from inside a box. "There must be some hitch."

"Work it out for yourself," said the C. I. D. man gruffly. "We know that the office in Globe Road belongs to Gianapolis, and according to the Eastern Exchange he was constantly ringing up East 39951; that's the warehouse of Kan-Suh Concessions. He garages his car next door to the said warehouse, and to-night our scouts follow Gianapolis and Max from Piccadilly Circus to Waterloo Station, where they discharge the taxi and pick up Gianapolis' limousine. Still followed, they drive — where? Straight to the garage at the back of that wharf yonder! Neither Gianapolis, Max, nor the chauffeur come out of the garage. I said, and I still say, that we should have broken in at once, but Dunbar was always pigheaded, and he thinks Max is a tin god."...

"Well, there's no sign from Max," said Rogers; "and as we aren't ten yards above the wharf, we cannot fail to hear the signal. For my part I never noticed anything suspicious, and never had anything reported, about this ginger firm, and where the swell dope-shop I've heard about can be situated, beats me. It can't very well be UNDER the place, or it would be below the level of the blessed river!"

"This waiting makes me sick!" growled Stringer. "If I understand aright — and I'm not sure that I do — there are two women tucked away there somewhere in that place" — he jerked his thumb aimlessly into the fog; "and here we are hanging about with enough men in yards, in doorways, behind walls, and freezing on the river, to raid the Houses of Parliament!"

"It's a pity we didn't get the word from the hospitals before Max was actually inside," said Rogers. "For three wealthy ladies to be driven to three public hospitals in a sort of semi-conscious condition, with symptoms of opium, on the same evening isn't natural. It points to the fact that the boss of the den has UNLOADED! He's been thoughtful where his lady clients were concerned, but probably the men have simply been kicked out and left to shift for themselves. If we only knew one of them it might be confirmed."

"It's not worth worrying about, now," growled Stringer. "Let's have a look at the time."

He fumbled inside his overcoat and tugged out his watch.

"Here's a light," said Rogers, and shone the ray of an electric torch upon the watch-face.

"A quarter-to-three," grumbled Stringer. "There may be murder going on, and here we are."...

A sudden clamor arose upon the shore, near by; a sound as of sledge-hammers at work. But above this pierced shrilly the call of a police whistle.

"What's that?" snapped Rogers, leaping up. "Stand by there!"

The sound of the whistle grew near and nearer; then came a voice — that of Sergeant Sowerby — hailing them through the fog.

"DUNBAR'S IN! But the gang have escaped! They've got to a motor launch twenty yards down, on the end of the creek"...

But already the police boat was away.

"Let her go!" shouted Rogers — "close inshore! Keep a sharp lookout for a cutter, boys!"

Stringer, aroused now to excitement, went blundering forward through the fog, joining the men in the bows. Four pairs of eyes were peering through the mist, the damnable, yellow mist that veiled all things.

"Curse the fog!" said Stringer; "it's just our damn luck!"

"Cutter 'hoy!" bawled a man at his side suddenly, one of the river police more used to the mists of the Thames. "Cutter on the port bow, sir!"

"Keep her in sight," shouted Rogers from the stern; "don't lose her for your lives!"

Stringer, at imminent peril of precipitating himself into the water, was craning out over the bows and staring until his eyes smarted.

"Don't you see her?" said one of the men on the lookout. "She carries no lights, of course, but you can just make out the streak of her wake."

Harder, harder stared Stringer, and now a faint, lighter smudge in the blackness, ahead and below, proclaimed itself the wake of some rapidly traveling craft.

"I can hear her motor!" said another voice.

Stringer began, now, also to listen.

Muffled sirens were hooting dismally all about Limehouse Reach, and he knew that this random dash through the night was fraught with extreme danger, since this was a narrow and congested part of the great highway. But, listen as he might, he could not detect the sounds referred to.

The brazen roar of a big steamer's siren rose up before them. Rogers turned the head of the cutter sharply to starboard but did not slacken speed. The continuous roar grew deeper, grew louder.

"Sharp lookout there!" cried the inspector from the stern.

Suddenly over their bows uprose a black mass.

"My God!" cried Stringer, and fell back with upraised arms as if hoping to fend off that giant menace.

He lurched, as the cutter was again diverted sharply from its course, and must have fallen under the very bows of the oncoming liner, had not one of the lookouts caught him by the collar and jerked him sharply back into the boat.

A blaze of light burst out over them, and there were conflicting voices raised one in opposition to another. Above them all, even above the beating of the twin screws and the churning of the inky water, arose that of an officer from the bridge of the steamer.

"Where the flaming hell are YOU going?" inquired this stentorian voice; "haven't you got any blasted eyes and ears"...

High on the wash of the liner rode the police boat; down she plunged again, and began to roll perilously; up again — swimming it seemed upon frothing milk.

The clangor of bells, of voices, and of churning screws died, remote, astern.

"Damn close shave!" cried Rogers. "It must be clear ahead; they've just run into it."

One of the men on the lookout in the bows, who had never departed from his duty for an instant throughout this frightful commotion, now reported:

"Cutter crossing our bow, sir! Getting back to her course."

"Keep her in view," roared Rogers.

"Port, sir!"

"How's that?"

"Starboard, easy!"

"Keep her in view!"

"As she is, sir!"

Again they settled down to the pursuit, and it began to dawn upon Stringer's mind that the boat ahead must be engined identically with that of the police; for whilst they certainly gained nothing upon her, neither did they lose.

"Try a hail," cried Rogers from the stern. "We may be chasing the wrong boat!"

"Cutter 'hoy!" bellowed the man beside Stringer, using his hands in lieu of a megaphone — "heave to!"

"Give 'em 'in the King's name!'" directed Rogers again.

"Cutter 'hoy," roared the man through his trumpeted hands, — "heave to — in the King's name!"

Stringer glared through the fog, clutching at the shoulder of the shouter almost convulsively.

"Take no notice, sir," reported the man.

"Then it's the gang!" cried Rogers from the stern; "and we haven't made a mistake. Where the blazes are we?"

"Well on the way to Blackwall Reach, sir," answered someone. "Fog lifting ahead."

"It's the rain that's doing it," said the man beside Stringer.

Even as he spoke, a drop of rain fell upon the back of Stringer's hand. This was the prelude; then, with ever-increasing force, down came the rain in torrents, smearing out the fog from the atmosphere, as a painter, with a sponge, might wipe a color from his canvas. Long tails of yellow vapor, twining — twining — but always coiling downward, floated like snakes about them; and the oily waters of the Thames became pock-marked in the growing light.

Stringer now quite clearly discerned the quarry — a very rakish-looking motor cutter, painted black, and speeding seaward ahead of them. He quivered with excitement.

"Do you know the boat?" cried Rogers, addressing his crew in general.

"No, sir," reported his second-in-command; "she's a stranger to me. They must have kept her hidden somewhere." He turned and looked back into the group of faces, all directed toward the strange craft. "Do any of you know her?" he demanded.

A general shaking of heads proclaimed the negative.

"But she can shift," said one of the men. "They must have been going slow through the fog; she's creeping up to ten or twelve knots now, I should reckon."

"Your reckoning's a trifle out!" snapped Rogers, irritably, from the stern; "but she's certainly showing us her heels. Can't we put somebody ashore and have her cut off lower down?"

"While we're doing that," cried Stringer, excitedly, "she would land somewhere and we should lose the gang!"

"That's right," reluctantly agreed Rogers. "Can you see any of her people?"

Through the sheets of rain all peered eagerly.

"She seems to be pretty well loaded," reported the man beside Stringer, "but I can't make her out very well."

"Are we doing our damnedest?" inquired Rogers.

"We are, sir," reported the engineer; "she hasn't got another oat in her!"

Rogers muttered something beneath his breath, and sat there glaring ahead at the boat ever gaining upon her pursuer.

"So long as we keep her in sight," said Stringer, "our purpose is served. She can't land anybody."

"At her present rate," replied the man upon whose shoulders he was leaning, "she'll be out of sight by the time we get to Tilbury or she'll have hit a barge and gone to the bottom!"

"I'll eat my hat if I lose her!" declared Rogers angrily. "How the blazes they slipped away from the wharf beats me!"

"They didn't slip away from the wharf," cried Stringer over his shoulder. "You heard what Sowerby said; they lay in the creek below the wharf, and there was some passageway underneath."

"But damn it all, man!" cried Rogers, "it's high tide; they must be a gang of bally mermaids. Why, we were almost level with the wharf when we left, and if they came from BELOW that, as you say, they must have been below water!"

"There they are, anyway," growled Stringer.

Mile after mile that singular chase continued through the night. With every revolution of the screw, the banks to right and left seemed to recede, as the Thames grew wider and wider. A faint saltiness was perceptible in the air; and Stringer, moistening his dry lips, noted the saline taste.

The shipping grew more scattered. Whereas, at first, when the fog had begun to lift, they had passed wondering faces peering at them from lighters and small steamers, tow boats and larger anchored craft, now they raced, pigmy and remote, upon open waters, and through the raindrift gray hulls showed, distant, and the banks were a faint blur. It seemed absurd that, with all those vessels about, they nevertheless could take no steps to seek assistance in cutting off the boat which they were pursuing, but must drive on through the rain, ever losing, ever dropping behind that black speck ahead.

A faint swell began to be perceptible. Stringer, who throughout the whole pursuit thus far had retained his hold upon the man in the bows, discovered that his fingers were cramped. He had much difficulty in releasing that convulsive grip.

"Thank you!" said the man, smiling, when at last the detective released his grip. "I'll admit I'd scarcely noticed it myself, but now I come to think of it, you've been fastened onto me like a vise for over two hours!"

"Two hours!" cried Stringer; and, crouching down to steady himself, for the cutter was beginning to roll heavily, he pulled out his watch, and in the gray light inspected the dial.

It was true! They had been racing seaward for some hours!

"Good God!" he muttered.

He stood up again, unsteadily, feet wide apart, and peered ahead through the grayness.

The banks he could not see. Far away on the port bow a long gray shape lay — a moored vessel. To starboard were faint blurs, indistinguishable, insignificant; ahead, a black dot with a faint comet-like tail — the pursued cutter — and ahead of that, again, a streak across the blackness, with another dot slightly to the left of the quarry...

He turned and looked along the police boat, noting that whereas, upon the former occasion of his looking, forms and faces had been but dimly visible, now he could distinguish them all quite clearly. The dawn was breaking.

"Where are we?" he inquired hoarsely.

"We're about one mile northeast of Sheerness and two miles southwest of the Nore Light!" announced Rogers — and he laughed, but not in a particularly mirthful manner.

Stringer temporarily found himself without words.

"Cutter heading for the open sea, sir," announced a man in the bows, unnecessarily.

"Quite so," snapped Rogers. "So are you!"

"We have got them beaten," said Stringer, a faint note of triumph in his voice. "We've given them no chance to land."

"If this breeze freshens much," replied Rogers, with sardonic humor, "they'll be giving US a fine chance to sink!"

Indeed, although Stringer's excitement had prevented him from heeding the circumstance, an ever-freshening breeze was blowing in his face, and he noted now that, quite mechanically, he had removed his bowler hat at some time earlier in the pursuit and had placed it in the bottom of the boat. His hair was blown in the wind, which sang merrily in his ears, and the cutter, as her course was slightly altered by Rogers, ceased to roll and began to pitch in a manner very disconcerting to the lands-man.

"It'll be rather fresh outside, sir," said one of the men, doubtfully. "We're miles and miles below our proper patrol"...

"Once we're clear of the bank it'll be more than fresh," replied Rogers; "but if they're bound for France, or Sweden, or Denmark, that's OUR destination, too!"...

On — and on — and on they drove. The Nore Light lay astern; they were drenched with spray. Now green water began to spout over the nose of the laboring craft.

"I've only enough juice to run us back to Tilbury, sir, if we put about now!" came the shouted report.

"It's easy to TALK!" roared Rogers. "If one of these big 'uns gets us broadside on, our number's up!"...

"Cutter putting over for Sheppey coast, sir!" bellowed the man in the bows.

Stringer raised himself, weakly, and sought to peer through the driving spray and rain-mist.

"By God! THEY'VE TURNED — TURTLE!"...

"Stand by with belts!" bellowed Rogers.

Rapidly life belts were unlashed; and, ahead, to port, to starboard, brine-stung eyes glared out from the reeling craft. Gray in the nascent dawn stretched the tossing sea about them; and lonely they rode upon its billows.

"PORT! PORT! HARD A-PORT!" screamed the lookout.

But Rogers, grimly watching the oncoming billows, knew that to essay the maneuver at that moment meant swamping the cutter. Straight ahead they drove. A wave, higher than any they yet had had to ride, came boiling down upon them... and twisting, writhing, upcasting imploring arms to the elements — the implacable elements — a girl, a dark girl, entwined, imprisoned in silken garments, swept upon its crest!

Out shot a cork belt into the boiling sea... and fell beyond her reach. She was swept past the cutter. A second belt was hurled from the stern...

The Eurasian, uttering a wailing cry like that of a seabird, strove to grasp it...

Close beside her, out of the wave, uprose a yellow hand, grasping — seeking — clutching. It fastened itself into the meshes of her floating hair...

"Here goes!" roared Rogers.

They plunged down into an oily trough; they turned; a second wave grew up above them, threateningly, built its terrible wall higher and higher over their side. Round they swung, and round, and round...

Down swept the eager wave... down — down — down... It lapped over the stern of the cutter; the tiny craft staggered, and paused, tremulous — dragged back by that iron grip of old Neptune — then leaped on — away — headed back into the Thames estuary, triumphant.

"God's mercy!" whispered Stringer — "that was touch-and-go!"

No living thing moved upon the waters.

XLI
WESTMINSTER — MIDNIGHT

Detective-Sergeant Sowerby reported himself in Inspector Dunbar's room at New Scotland Yard.

"I have completed my inquiries in Wharf-end Lane," he said; and pulling out his bulging pocketbook, he consulted it gravely.

Inspector Dunbar looked up.

"Anything important?" he asked.

"We cannot trace the makers of the sanitary fittings, and so forth, but they are all of American pattern. There's nothing in the nature of a trademark to be found from end to end of the place; even the iron sluice-gate at the bottom of the brick tunnel has had the makers' name chipped off, apparently with a cold chisel. So you see they were prepared for all emergencies!"

"Evidently," said Dunbar, resting his chin on the palms of his hands and his elbows upon the table.

"The office and warehouse staff of the ginger importing concern are innocent enough, as you know already. Kan-Suh Concessions was conducted merely as a blind, of course, but it enabled the Chinaman, Ho-Pin, to appear in Wharf-end Lane at all times of the day and night without exciting suspicion. He was supposed to be the manager, of course. The presence of the wharf is sufficient to explain how they managed to build the place without exciting suspicion. They probably had all the material landed there labeled as preserved ginger, and they would take it down below at night, long after the office and warehouse staff of Concessions had gone home. The workmen probably came and went by way of the river, also, commencing work after nightfall and going away before business commenced in the morning."

"It beats me," said Dunbar, reflectively, "how masons, plumbers, decorators, and all the other artisans necessary for a job of that description, could have been kept quiet."

"Foreigners!" said Sowerby triumphantly. "I'll undertake to say there wasn't an Englishman on the job. The whole of the gang was probably imported from abroad somewhere, boarded and lodged during the day-time in the neighborhood of Limehouse, and watched by Mr. Ho-Pin or somebody else until the job was finished; then shipped back home again. It's easily done if money is no object."

"That's right enough," agreed Dunbar; "I have no doubt you've hit upon the truth. But now that the place has been dismantled, what does it look like? I haven't had time to come down myself, but I intend to do so before it's closed up."

"Well," said Sowerby, turning over a page of his notebook, "it looks like a series of vaults, and the Rev. Mr. Firmingham, a local vicar whom I got to inspect it this morning, assures me, positively, that it's a crypt."

"A crypt!" exclaimed Dunbar, fixing his eyes upon his subordinate.

"A crypt — exactly. A firm dealing in grease occupied the warehouse before Kan-Suh Concessions rented it, and they never seem to have suspected that the place possessed any cellars. The actual owner of the property, Sir James Crozel, an ex-Lord Mayor, who is also ground landlord of the big works on the other side of the lane, had no more idea than the man in the moon that there were any cellars beneath the place. You see the vaults are below the present level of the Thames at high tide; that's why nobody ever suspected their existence. Also, an examination of the bare walls — now stripped — shows that they were pretty well filled up to the top with ancient debris, to within a few years ago, at any rate."

"You mean that our Chinese friends excavated them?"

"No doubt about it. They were every bit of twenty feet below the present street level, and, being right on the bank of the Thames, nobody would have thought of looking for them unless he knew they were there."

"What do you mean exactly, Sowerby?" said Dunbar, taking out his fountain-pen and tapping his teeth with it.

"I mean," said Sowerby, "that someone connected with the gang must have located the site of these vaults from some very old map or book."

"I think you said that the Reverend Somebody-or-Other avers that they were a crypt?"

"He does; and when he pointed out to me the way the pillars were placed, as if to support the nave of a church, I felt disposed to agree with him. The place where the golden dragon used to stand (it isn't really gold, by the way!) would be under the central aisle, as it were; then there's a kind of side aisle on the right and left and a large space at top and bottom. The pillars are stone and of very early Norman pattern, and the last three or four steps leading down to the place appear to belong to the original structure. I tell you it's the crypt of some old forgotten Norman church or monastery chapel."

"Most extraordinary!" muttered Dunbar.

"But I suppose it is possible enough. Probably the church was burnt or destroyed in some other way; deposits of river mud would gradually cover up the remaining ruins; then in later times, when the banks of the Thames were properly attended to, the site of the place would be entirely forgotten, of course. Most extraordinary!"

"That's the reverend gentleman's view, at any rate," said Sowerby, "and he's written three books on the subject of early Norman churches! He even goes so far as to say that he has heard — as a sort of legend — of the existence of a very large Carmelite monastery, accommodating over two hundred brothers, which stood somewhere adjoining the Thames within the area now covered by Limehouse Causeway and Pennyfields. There is a little turning not far from the wharf, known locally — it does not appear upon any map — as Prickler's Lane; and my friend, the vicar, tells me that he has held the theory for a long time" — Sowerby referred to his notebook with great solemnity — "that this is a corruption of Pre-aux-Clerce Lane."

"H'm!" said Dunbar; "very ingenious, at any rate. Anything else?"

"Nothing much," said Sowerby, scanning his notes, "that you don't know already. There was some very good stuff in the place — Oriental ware and so on, a library of books which I'm told is unique, and a tremendous stock of opium and hashish. It's a perfect maze of doors and observation-traps. There's a small kitchen at the end, near the head of the tunnel — which, by the way, could be used as a means of entrance and exit at low tide. All the electric power came through the meter of Kan-Suh Concessions."

"I see," said Dunbar, reflectively, glancing at his watch; "in a word, we know everything except"...

"What's that?" said Sowerby, looking up.

"The identity of Mr. King!" replied the inspector, reaching for his hat which lay upon the table.

Sowerby replaced his book in his pocket.

"I wonder if any of the bodies will ever come ashore?" he said.

"God knows!" rapped Dunbar; "we can't even guess how many were aboard. You might as well come along, Sowerby, I've just heard from Dr. Cumberly. Mrs. Leroux"...

"Dead?"

"Dying," replied the inspector; "expected to go at any moment. But the doctor tells me that she may — it's just possible — recover consciousness before the end; and there's a bare chance"...

"I see," said Sowerby eagerly; "of course she must know!"

The two hastened to Palace Mansions. Despite the lateness of the hour, Whitehall was thronged with vehicles, and all the glitter and noise of midnight London surrounded them.

"It only seems like yesterday evening," said Dunbar, as they mounted the stair of Palace Mansions, "that I came here to take charge of the case. Damme! it's been the most exciting I've ever handled, and it's certainly the most disappointing."

"It is indeed," said Sowerby, gloomily, pressing the bell-button at the side of Henry Leroux's door.

The door was opened by Garnham; and these two, fresh from the noise and bustle of London's streets, stepped into the hushed atmosphere of the flat where already a Visitant, unseen but potent, was arrived, and now was beckoning, shadowlike, to Mira Leroux.

"Will you please sit down and wait," said Garnham, placing chairs for the two Scotland Yard men in the dining-room.

"Who's inside?" whispered Dunbar, with that note of awe in his voice which such a scene always produces; and he nodded in the direction of the lobby.

"Mr. Leroux, sir," replied the man, "the nurse, Miss Cumberly, Dr. Cumberly and Miss Ryland"...

"No one else?" asked the detective sharply.

"And Mr. Gaston Max," added the man. "You'll find whisky and cigars upon the table there, sir."

He left the room. Dunbar glanced across at Sowerby, his tufted brows raised, and a wry smile upon his face.

"In at the death, Sowerby!" he said grimly, and lifted the stopper from the cut-glass decanter.

In the room where Mira Leroux lay, so near to the Borderland that her always ethereal appearance was now positively appalling, a hushed group stood about the bed.

"I think she is awake, doctor," whispered the nurse softly, peering into the emaciated face of the patient.

Mira Leroux opened her eyes and smiled at Dr. Cumberly, who was bending over her. The poor faded eyes turned from the face of the physician to that of Denise Ryland, then to M. Max, wonderingly; next to Helen, whereupon an indescribable expression crept into them; and finally to Henry Leroux, who, with bowed head, sat in the chair beside her. She feebly extended her thin hand and laid it upon his hair. He looked up, taking the hand in his own. The eyes of the dying woman filled with tears as she turned them from the face of Leroux to Helen Cumberly — who was weeping silently.

"Look after... him," whispered Mira Leroux.

Her hand dropped and she closed her eyes again. Cumberly bent forward suddenly, glancing back at M. Max who stood in a remote corner of the room watching this scene.

Big Ben commenced to chime the hour of midnight. That frightful coincidence so startled Leroux that he looked up and almost rose from his chair in his agitation. Indeed it startled Cumberly, also, but did not divert him from his purpose.

"It is now or never!" he whispered.

He took the seemingly lifeless hand in his own, and bending over Mira Leroux, spoke softly in her ear:

"Mrs. Leroux," he said, "there is something which we all would ask you to tell us; we ask it for a reason — believe me."

Throughout the latter part of this scene the big clock had been chiming the hour, and now was beating out the twelve strokes of midnight; had struck six of them and was about to strike the seventh.

SEVEN! boomed the clock.

Mira Leroux opened her eyes and looked up into the face of the physician.

EIGHT!...

"Who," whispered Dr. Cumberly, "is he?"

NINE!

In the silence following the clock-stroke, Mira Leroux spoke almost inaudibly.

"You mean...MR. KING?"

TEN!

"Yes, yes! Did you ever SEE him?"...

Every head in the room was craned forward; every spectator tensed up to the highest ultimate point.

"Yes," said Mira Leroux quite clearly; "I saw him, Dr. Cumberly...He is"...

ELEVEN!

Mira Leroux moved her head and smiled at Helen Cumberly; then seemed to sink deeper into the downy billows of the bed. Dr. Cumberly stood up very slowly, and turned, looking from face to face.

"It is finished," he said — "we shall never know!"

But Henry Leroux and Helen Cumberly, their glances meeting across the bed of the dead Mira, knew that for them it was not finished, but that Mr. King, the invisible, invisibly had linked them.

TWELVE!...

The Golden Scorpion

Part I
THE COWLED MAN

CHAPTER I
THE SHADOW OF A COWL

Keppel Stuart, M.D., F. R. S., awoke with a start and discovered himself to be bathed in cold perspiration. The moonlight shone in at his window, but did not touch the bed, therefore his awakening could not be due to this cause. He lay for some time listening for any unfamiliar noise which might account for the sudden disturbance of his usually sound slumbers. In the house below nothing stirred. His windows were widely open and he could detect that vague drumming which is characteristic of midnight London; sometimes, too, the clashing of buffers upon some siding of the Brighton railway where shunting was in progress and occasional siren notes from the Thames. Otherwise — nothing.

He glanced at the luminous disk of his watch. The hour was half-past two. Dawn was not far off. The night seemed to have become almost intolerably hot, and to this heat Stuart felt disposed to ascribe both his awakening and also a feeling of uncomfortable tension of which he now became aware. He continued to listen, and, listening and hearing nothing, recognized with anger that he was frightened. A sense of some presence oppressed him. Someone or something evil was near him — perhaps in the room, veiled by the shadows. This uncanny sensation grew more and more marked.

Stuart sat up in bed, slowly and cautiously, looking all about him. He remembered to have awakened once thus in India — and to have found a great cobra coiled at his feet. His inspection revealed the presence of nothing unfamiliar, and he stepped out on to the floor.

A faint clicking sound reached his ears. He stood quite still. The clicking was repeated.

"There is someone downstairs in my study!" muttered Stuart.

He became aware that the fear which held him was such that unless he acted and acted swiftly he should become incapable of action, but he remembered that whereas the moonlight poured into the bedroom, the staircase would be in complete darkness. He walked barefooted across to the dressing-table and took up an electric torch which lay there. He had not used it for some time, and he pressed the button to learn if the torch was charged. A beam of white light shone out across the room, and at the same instant came another sound.

If it came from below or above, from the adjoining room or from

Outside in the road, Stuart knew not. But following hard upon the mysterious disturbance which had aroused him it seemed to pour ice into his veins, it added the complementary touch to his panic. For it was a kind of low wail — a ghostly minor wail in falling cadences — unlike any sound he had heard. It was so excessively horrible that it produced a curious effect.

Discovering from the dancing of the torch-ray that his hand was trembling, Stuart concluded that he had awakened from a nightmare and that this fiendish wailing was no more than an unusually delayed aftermath of the imaginary horrors which had bathed him in cold perspiration.

He walked resolutely to the door, threw it open and cast the beam of light on to the staircase. Softly he began to descend. Before the study door he paused. There was no sound. He threw open the door, directing the torch-ray into the room.

Cutting a white lane through the blackness, it shone fully upon his writing-table, which was a rather fine Jacobean piece having a sort of quaint bureau superstructure containing cabinets and drawers. He could detect nothing unusual in the appearance of the littered table. A tobacco jar stood there, a pipe resting in the lid. Papers and books were scattered untidily as he had left them, surrounding a tray full of pipe and cigarette ash. Then, suddenly, he saw something else.

One of the bureau drawers was half opened.

Stuart stood quite still, staring at the table. There was no sound in the room. He crossed slowly, moving the light from right to left. His papers had been overhauled methodically. The drawers had been replaced, but he felt assured that all had been examined. The light switch was immediately beside the outer door, and Stuart walked over to it and switched on both lamps. Turning, he surveyed the brilliantly illuminated room. Save for himself, it was empty. He looked out into the hallway again. There was no one there. No sound broke the stillness. But that consciousness of some near presence asserted itself persistently and uncannily.

"My nerves are out of order!" he muttered. "No one has touched my papers. I must have left the drawer open myself."

He switched off the light and walked across to the door. He had actually passed out intending to return to his room, when he became aware of a slight draught. He stopped.

Someone or something, evil and watchful, seemed to be very near again. Stuart turned and found himself gazing fearfully in the direction of the open study door. He became persuaded anew that someone was hiding there, and snatching up an ash stick which lay upon a chair in the hall he returned to the door. One step into the room he took and paused — palsied with a sudden fear which exceeded anything he had known.

A white casement curtain was drawn across the French windows… and outlined upon this moon-bright screen he saw a tall figure. It was that of a *cowled man*!

Such an apparition would have been sufficiently alarming had the cowl been that of a monk, but the outline of this phantom being suggested that of one of the Misericordia brethren or the costume worn of old by the familiars of the Inquisition!

His heart leapt wildly, and seemed to grow still. He sought to cry out in his terror, but only emitted a dry gasping sound.

The psychology of panic is obscure and has been but imperfectly explored. The presence of the terrible cowled figure afforded a confirmation of Stuart's theory that he was the victim of a species of waking nightmare.

Even as he looked, the shadow of the cowled man moved — and was gone.

Stuart ran across the room, jerked open the curtains and stared out across the moon-bathed lawn, its prospect terminated by high privet hedges. One of the French windows was wide open. There was no one on the lawn; there was no sound.

"Mrs. M'Gregor swears that I always forget to shut these windows at night!" he muttered.

He closed and bolted the window, stood for a moment looking out across the empty lawn, then turned and went out of the room.

CHAPTER II
THE PIBROCH OF THE M'GREGORS

Dr. Stuart awoke in the morning and tried to recall what had occurred during the night. He consulted his watch and found the hour to be six a. m. No one was stirring in the house, and he rose and put on a bath robe. He felt perfectly well and could detect no symptoms of nervous disorder. Bright sunlight was streaming into the room, and he went out on to the landing, fastening the cord of his gown as he descended the stairs.

His study door was locked, with the key outside. He remembered having locked it. Opening it, he entered and looked about him. He was vaguely disappointed. Save for the untidy litter of papers upon the table, the study was as he had left it on retiring. If he could believe the evidence of his senses, nothing had been disturbed.

Not content with a casual inspection, he particularly examined those papers which, in his dream adventure, he had believed to have been submitted to mysterious inspection. They showed no signs of having been touched. The casement curtains were drawn across the recess formed by the French windows, and sunlight streamed in where, silhouetted against the pallid illumination of the moon, he had seen the man in the cowl. Drawing back the curtains, he examined the window fastenings. They were secure. If the window had really been open in the night, he must have left it so himself.

"Well," muttered Stuart — "of all the amazing nightmares!"

He determined, immediately he had bathed and completed his toilet, to write an account of the dream for the Psychical Research Society, in whose work he was interested. Half an hour later, as the movements of an awakened household began to proclaim themselves, he sat down at his writing-table and commenced to write.

Keppel Stuart was a dark, good-looking man of about thirty-two, an easy-going bachelor who, whilst not over ambitious, was nevertheless a brilliant physician. He had worked for the Liverpool School of Tropical Medicine and had spent several years in India studying snake poisons. His purchase of this humdrum suburban practice had been dictated by a desire to make a home for a girl who at the eleventh hour had declined to share it. Two years had elapsed since then, but the shadow still lay upon Stuart's life, its influence being revealed in a certain apathy, almost indifference, which characterised his professional conduct.

His account of the dream completed, he put the paper into a pigeon-hole and forgot all about the matter. That day seemed to be more than usually dull and the hours to drag wearily on. He was conscious of a sort of suspense. He was waiting for something, or for someone. He did not choose to analyse this mental condition. Had he done so, the explanation was simple — and one that he dared not face.

At about ten o'clock that night, having been called out to a case, he returned to his house, walking straight into the study as was his custom and casting a light Burberry with a soft hat upon the sofa beside his stick and bag. The lamps were lighted, and the book-lined room, indicative of a studious and not over-wealthy bachelor, looked cheerful enough with the firelight dancing on the furniture.

Mrs. M'Gregor, a grey-haired Scotch lady, attired with scrupulous neatness, was tending the fire at the moment, and hearing Stuart come in she turned and glanced at him.

"A fire is rather superfluous to-night, Mrs. M'Gregor," he said. "I found it unpleasantly warm walking."

"May is a fearsome treacherous month, Mr. Keppel," replied the old housekeeper, who from long association with the struggling practitioner had come to regard him as a son. "An' a wheen o' dry logs is worth a barrel o' pheesic. To which I would add that if ye're hintin' it's time ye shed ye're woolsies for ye're summer wear, all I have to reply is that I hope sincerely ye're patients are more prudent than yoursel'."

She placed his slippers in the fender and took up the hat, stick and coat from the sofa. Stuart laughed.

"Most of the neighbors exhibit their wisdom by refraining from becoming patients of mine, Mrs. M'Gregor."

"That's no weesdom; it's just preejudice."

"Prejudice!" cried Stuart, dropping down upon the sofa.

"Aye," replied Mrs. M'Gregor firmly — "preejudice! They're no' that daft but they're well aware o' who's the cleverest physeecian in the deestrict, an' they come to nane other than Dr. Keppel Stuart when they're sair sick and think they're dying; but ye'll never establish the practice you desairve, Mr. Keppel — never — until —"

"Until when, Mrs. M'Gregor?"

"Until ye take heed of an auld wife's advice and find a new housekeeper."

"Mrs. M'Gregor!" exclaimed Stuart with concern. "You don't mean that you want to desert me? After — let me see — how many years is it, Mrs. M'Gregor?"

"Thirty years come last Shrove Tuesday; I dandled ye on my knee, and eh! but ye were bonny! God forbid, but I'd like to see ye thriving as ye desairve, and that ye'll never do whilst ye're a bachelor."

"Oh!" cried Stuart, laughing again — "oh, that's it, is it? So you would like me to find some poor inoffensive girl to share my struggles?"

Mrs. M'Gregor nodded wisely. "She'd have nane so many to share. I know ye think I'm old-fashioned, Mr. Keppel and it may be I am; but I do assure you I would be sair harassed, if stricken to my bed — which, please God, I won't be — to receive the veesits of a pairsonable young bachelor —"

"Er — Mrs. M'Gregor!" interrupted Stuart, coughing in mock rebuke — "quite so! I fancy we have discussed this point before, and as you say your ideas are a wee bit, just a wee bit, behind the times. On this particular point I mean. But I am very grateful to you, very sincerely grateful, for your disinterested kindness; and if ever I should follow your advice —— "

Mrs. M'Gregor interrupted him, pointing to his boots. "Ye're no' that daft as to sit in wet boots?"

"Really they are perfectly dry. Except for a light shower this evening, there has been no rain for several days. However, I may as well, since I shall not be going out again."

He began to unlace his boots as Mrs. M'Gregor pulled the white casement curtains across the windows and then prepared to retire. Her hand upon the door knob, she turned again to Stuart.

"The foreign lady called half an hour since, Mr. Keppel."

Stuart desisted from unlacing his boots and looked up with lively interest. "Mlle. Dorian! Did she leave any message?"

"She obsairved that she might repeat her veesit later," replied Mrs. M'Gregor, and, after a moment's hesitation; "she awaited ye're return with exemplary patience."

"Really, I am sorry I was detained," declared Stuart, replacing his boot. "How long has she been gone, then?"

"Just the now. No more than two or three minutes. I trust she is no worse."

"Worse!"

"The lass seemed o'er anxious to see you."

"Well, you know, Mrs. M'Gregor, she comes a considerable distance."

"So I am given to understand, Mr. Keppel," replied the old lady; "and in a grand luxurious car."

Stuart assumed an expression of perplexity to hide his embarrassment. "Mrs. M'Gregor," he said rather ruefully, "you watch over me as tenderly as my own mother would have done. I have observed a certain restraint in your manner whenever you have had occasion to refer to Mlle. Dorian. In what way does she differ from my other lady patients?" And even as he spoke the words he knew in his heart that she differed from every other woman in the world.

Mrs. M'Gregor sniffed. "Do your other lady patients wear furs that your airnings for six months could never pay for, Mr. Keppel?" she inquired.

"No, unfortunately they pin their faith, for the most part, to gaily coloured shawls. All the more reason why I should bless the accident which led Mlle. Dorian to my door."

Mrs. M'Gregor, betraying, in her interest, real suspicion, murmured *sotto voce*: "Then she *is* a patient?"

"What's that?" asked Stuart, regarding her surprisedly. "A patient? Certainly. She suffers from insomnia."

"I'm no' surprised to hear it."

"What do you mean, Mrs. M'Gregor?"

"Now, Mr. Keppel, laddie, ye're angry with me, and like enough I am a meddlesome auld woman. But I know what a man will do for shining een and a winsome face — nane better to my sorrow — and twa times have I heard the Warning."

Stuart stood up in real perplexity. "Pardon my density, Mrs. M'Gregor, but — er — the Warning? To what 'warning' do you refer?"

Seating herself in the chair before the writing-table, Mrs. M'Gregor shook her head pensively. "What would it be," she said softly, "but the Pibroch o' the M'Gregors?"

Stuart came across and leaned upon a corner of the table. "The Pibroch of the M'Gregors?" he repeated.

"Nane other. 'Tis said to be Rob Roy's ain piper that gives warning when danger threatens ane o' the M'Gregors or any they love."

Stuart restrained a smile, and, "A well-meaning but melancholy retainer!" he commented.

"As well as I hear you now, laddie, I heard the pibroch on the day a certain woman first crossed my threshold, nigh thirty years ago, in Inverary. And as plainly as I heard it wailing then, I heard it the first evening that Miss Dorian came to this house!"

Torn between good-humoured amusement and real interest, "If I remember rightly," said Stuart, "Mlle. Dorian first called here just a week ago, and immediately before I returned from an Infirmary case?"

"Your memory is guid, Mr. Keppel."

"And when, exactly, did you hear this Warning?"

"Twa minutes before you entered the house; and I heard it again the now."

"What! you heard it to-night?"

"I heard it again just the now and I lookit out the window."

"Did you obtain a glimpse of Rob Roy's piper?"

"Ye're laughing at an old wife, laddie. No, but I saw Miss Dorian away in her car and twa minutes later I saw yourself coming round the corner."

"If she had only waited another two minutes," murmured Stuart. "No matter; she may return. And are these the only occasions upon which you have heard this mysterious sound, Mrs. M'Gregor?"

"No, Master Keppel, they are not. I assure ye something threatens. It wakened me up in the wee sma' hours last night — the piping — an' I lay awake shaking for long eno'."

"How extraordinary. Are you sure your imagination is not playing you tricks?"

"Ah, you're no' takin' me seriously, laddie."

"Mrs. M'Gregor" — he leaned across the table and rested his hands upon her shoulders — "you are a second mother to me, your care makes me feel like a boy again; and in these grey days it's good to feel like a boy again. You think I am laughing at you, but I'm not. The strange tradition of your family is associated with a tragedy in your life; therefore I respect it. But have no fear with regard to Mlle. Dorian. In the first place she is a patient; in the second — I am merely a penniless suburban practitioner. Good-night, Mrs. M'Gregor. Don't think of waiting up. Tell Mary to show Mademoiselle in here directly she arrives — that is if she really returns."

Mrs. M'Gregor stood up and walked slowly to the door. "I'll show Mademoiselle in mysel', Mr. Keppel," she said, — "and show her out."

She closed the door very quietly.

CHAPTER III
THE SCORPION'S TAIL

Seating himself at the writing-table, Stuart began mechanically to arrange his papers. Then from the tobacco jar he loaded his pipe, but his manner remained abstracted. Yet he was not thinking of the phantom piper but of Mlle. Dorian.

Until he had met this bewilderingly pretty woman he had thought that his heart was for evermore proof against the glances of bright eyes. Mademoiselle had disillusioned him. She was the most fragrantly lovely creature he had ever met, and never for one waking moment since her first visit, had he succeeded in driving her bewitching image from his mind. He had tried to laugh at his own folly, then had grown angry with himself, but finally had settled down to a dismayed acceptance of a wild infatuation.

He had no idea who Mlle. Dorian was; he did not even know her exact nationality, but he strongly suspected there was a strain of Eastern blood in her veins. Although she was quite young, apparently little more than twenty years of age, she dressed like a woman of unlimited means, and although all her visits had been at night he had had glimpses of the big car which had aroused Mrs. M'Gregor's displeasure.

Yes — so ran his musings, as, pipe in mouth, he rested his chin in his hands and stared grimly into the fire — she had always come at night and always alone. He had supposed her to be a Frenchwoman, but an unmarried French girl of good family does not make late calls, even upon a medical man, unattended. Had he perchance unwittingly made himself a party to the escapade of some unruly member of a noble family? From the first he had shrewdly suspected the ailments of Mlle. Dorian to be imaginary — Mlle. Dorian? It was an odd name.

"I shall be imagining she is a disguised princess if I wonder about her any more!" he muttered angrily.

Detecting himself in the act of heaving a weary sigh, he coughed in self-reproval and reached into a pigeon-hole for the MS. of his unfinished paper on "Snake Poisons and Their Antidotes." By chance he pulled out the brief account, written the same morning, of his uncanny experience during the night. He read it through reflectively.

It was incomplete. A certain mental haziness which he had noted upon awakening had in some way obscured the facts. His memory of the dream had been imperfect. Even now, whilst recognizing that some feature of the experience was missing from his written account, he could not identify the omission. But one memory arose starkly before him — that of the cowled man who had stood behind the curtains. It had power to chill him yet. The old incredulity returned and methodically he re-examined the contents of some of the table drawers. Ere long, however, he desisted impatiently.

"What the devil could a penniless doctor have hidden in his desk that was worth stealing!" he said aloud. "I must avoid cold salmon and cucumber in future."

He tossed the statement aside and turned to his scientific paper.

There came knock at the door.

"Come in!" snapped Stuart irritably; but the next moment he had turned, eager-eyed to the servant who had entered.

"Inspector Dunbar has called, sir."

"Oh, all right," said Stuart, repressing another sigh. "Show him in here."

There entered, shortly, a man of unusual height, a man gaunt and square both of figure and of face. He wore his clothes and his hair untidily. He was iron grey and a grim mouth was ill concealed by the wiry moustache. The most notable features of a striking face were the tawny leonine eyes, which could be fierce, which could be pensive and which were often kindly.

"Good evening, doctor," he said — and his voice was pleasant and unexpectedly light in tome. "Hope I don't intrude."

"Not at all, Inspector," Stuart assured him.

"Make yourself comfortable in the armchair and fill your pipe."

"Thanks," said Dunbar. "I will." He took out his pipe and reached out a long arm for the tobacco jar. "I came to see if you could give me a tip on a matter that has cropped up."

"Something in my line?" asked Stuart, a keen professional look coming momentarily into his eyes.

"It's supposed to be a poison case, although I can't see it myself," answered the detective — to whom Keppel Stuart's unusual knowledge of poisons had been of service in the past; "but if what I suspect is true, it's a very big case all the same."

Laying down his pipe, which he had filled but not lighted, Inspector Dunbar pulled out from the inside pocket of his tweed coat a bulging note-book and extracted therefrom some small object wrapped up in tissue paper. Unwrapping this object, he laid it upon the table.

"Tell me what that is, doctor," he said, "and I shall be obliged."

Stuart peered closely at that which lay before him. It was a piece of curiously shaped gold, cunningly engraved in a most unusual way. Rather less than an inch in length, it formed a crescent made up of six oval segments joined one to another, the sixth terminating in a curled point. The first and largest segment ended jaggedly where it had evidently been snapped off from the rest of the ornament — if the thing had formed part of an ornament. Stuart looked up, frowning in a puzzled way.

"It is a most curious fragment of jewellery — possibly of Indian origin," he said.

Inspector Dunbar lighted his pipe and tossed the match-end into the fire. "But what does it represent?" he asked.

"Oh, as to that — I said a *curious* fragment advisedly, because I cannot imagine any woman wearing such a beastly thing. It is the *tail of a scorpion.*"

"Ah!" cried Dunbar, the tawny eyes glittering with excitement. "The tail of a scorpion! I thought so! And Sowerby would have it that it represented the stem of a Cactus or Prickly Pear!"

"Not so bad a guess," replied Stuart. "There *are* resemblances — not in the originals but in such a miniature reproduction as this. He was wrong, however. May I ask where you obtained the fragment?"

"I'm here to tell you, doctor, for now that I know it's a scorpion's tail I know that I'm out of my depth as well. You've travelled in the East and lived in the East — two very different things. Now, while you were out there, in India, China, Burma, and so on, did you ever come across a religion or a cult that worshipped scorpions?"

Stuart frowned thoughtfully, rubbing his chin with the mouthpiece of his pipe. Dunbar watched him expectantly.

"Help yourself to whiskey-and-soda, Inspector," said Stuart absently.

"You'll find everything on the side-table yonder. I'm thinking."

Inspector Dunbar nodded, stood up and crossed the room, where he busied himself with syphon and decanter. Presently he returned, carrying two full glasses, one of which he set before Stuart. "What's the answer, doctor?" he asked.

"The answer is *no.* I am not acquainted with any sect of scorpion-worshippers, Inspector. But I once met with a curious experience at Su-Chow in China, which I have never been able to explain, but which may interest you. It wanted but a few minutes to sunset, and I was anxious to get back to my quarters before dusk fell. Therefore I hurried up my boy, who was drawing the rickshaw, telling him to cross the Canal by the Wu-men Bridge. He ran fleetly in that direction, and we were actually come to the steep acclivity of the bridge, when suddenly the boy dropped the shafts and fell down on his knees, hiding his face in his hands.

"'Shut your eyes tightly, master!' he whispered. 'The Scorpion is coming!'

"I stared down at him in amazement, as was natural, and not a little angrily; for his sudden action had almost pitched me on my head. But there he crouched, immovable, and staring up the slope I say that it was entirely deserted except for one strange figure at that moment crossing the crown of the bridge and approaching. It was the figure of a tall and dignified Chinaman, or of one who wore the dress of a Chinaman. For the extra-ordinary thing about the stranger's appearance was this; he also wore a thick green veil!"

"Covering his face?"

"So as to cover his face completely. I was staring at him in wonder, when the boy, seeming to divine the other's approach, whispered, 'Turn your head away! Turn your head away!'"

"He was referring to the man with the veil?"

"Undoubtedly. Of course I did nothing of the kind, but it was impossible to discern the stranger's features through the thick gauze, although he passed quite close to me. He had not proceeded another three paces, I should think, before my boy had snatched up the shafts and darted across the bridge as though all hell were after him! Here's the odd thing, though; I could never induce him to speak a word on the subject afterwards! I bullied him and bribed him, but all to no purpose. And although I must have asked more than a hundred Chinamen in every station of society from mandarin to mendicant, 'Who or what is *The Scorpion?*' one and all looked stupid, blandly assuring me that they did not know what I meant."

"H'm!" said Dunbar, "it's a queer yarn, certainly. How long ago would that be, doctor?"

"Roughly — five years."

"It sounds as though it might belong to the case. Some months back, early in the winter, we received instructions at the Yard to look out everywhere in the press, in buffets, theatres, but particularly in criminal quarters, for any reference (of any kind whatever) to a scorpion. I was so puzzled that I saw the Commissioner about it, and he could tell me next to nothing. He said the word had come through from Paris, but that Paris seemed to know no more about it than we did. It was associated in some way with the sudden deaths of several notable public men about that time; but as there was no evidence of foul play in any of the cases, I couldn't see what it meant at all. Then, six weeks ago, Sir Frank Narcombe, the surgeon, fell dead in the foyer of a West-End theatre — you remember?"

CHAPTER IV
MADEMOISELLE DORIAN

The telephone bell rang.

Stuart reached across for the instrument and raised the receiver. "Yes," he said — "Dr. Stuart speaking. Inspector Dunbar is here. Hold on."

He passed the instrument to Dunbar, who had stood up on hearing his name mentioned. "Sergeant Sowerby at Scotland Yard wishes to speak to you, Inspector."

"Hullo," said Dunbar — "that you, Sowerby. Yes — but I arrived here only a short time ago. What's that? — Max? Good God! what does it all mean! Are you sure of the number — 49685? Poor chap — he should have worked with us instead of going off alone like that. But he was always given to that sort of thing. Wait for me. I'll be with you in a few minutes. I can get a taxi. And, Sowerby — listen! It's 'The Scorpion' case right enough. That bit of gold found on the dead man is not a cactus stem; it's a scorpion's tail!"

He put down the telephone and turned to Stuart, who had been listening to the words with growing concern. Dunbar struck his open palm down on to the table with a violent gesture.

"We have been asleep!" he exclaimed. "Gaston Max of the Paris Service has been at work in London for a month, and we didn't know it!"

"Gaston Max!" cried Start — "then it must be a big case indeed."

As a student of criminology the name of the celebrated Frenchman was familiar to him as that of the foremost criminal investigator in Europe, and he found himself staring at the fragment of gold with a new and keener interest.

"Poor chap," continued Dunbar — "it was his last. The body brought in from Hanover Hole has been identified as his."

"What! it is the body of Gaston Max!"

"Paris has just wired that Max's reports ceased over a week ago. He was working on the case of Sir Frank Narcombe, it seems, and I never knew! But I predicted a long time ago that Max would play the lone-hand game once too often. They sent particulars. The identification disk is his. Oh! there's no doubt about it, unfortunately. The dead man's face is unrecognizable, but it's not likely there are two disks of that sort bearing the initials G.M. and the number 49685. I'm going along now. Should you care to come, doctor?"

"I am expecting a patient, Inspector," replied Stuart — "er — a special case. But I hope you will keep me in touch with this affair?"

"Well, I shouldn't have suggested your coming to the Yard if I hadn't wanted to do that. As a matter of fact, this scorpion job seems to resolve itself into a case of elaborate assassination by means of some unknown poison; and although I should have come to see you in any event, because you have helped me more than once, I came to-night at the suggestion of the Commissioner. He instructed me to retain your services if they were available."

"I am honoured," replied Stuart. "But after all, Inspector, I am merely an ordinary suburban practitioner. My reputation has yet to be made. What's the matter with Halesowen of Upper Wimpole Street? He's the big man."

"And if Sir Frank Narcombe was really poisoned — as Paris seems to think he was — he's also a big fool." retorted Dunbar bluntly. "He agreed that death was due to heart trouble."

"I know he did; unsuspected ulcerative endocarditis. Perhaps he was right."

"If he was right," said Dunbar, taking up the piece of gold from the table, "what was Gaston Max doing with this thing in his possession?"

"There may be no earthly connection between Max's inquiries and the death of Sir Frank."

"On the other hand — there may! Leaving Dr. Halesowen out of the question, are you open to act as expert adviser in this case?"

"Certainly; delighted."

"Your fee is your own affair, doctor. I will communicate with you later, if you wish, or call again in the morning."

Dunbar wrapped up the scorpion's tail in the piece of tissue paper and was about to replace it in his note-case. Then:

"I'll leave this with you, doctor," he said. "I know it will be safe enough, and you might like to examine it at greater leisure."

"Very well," replied Stuart. "Some of the engraving is very minute. I will have a look at it through a glass later."

He took the fragment from Dunbar, who had again unwrapped it, and, opening a drawer of the writing-table in which he kept his cheque-book and some few other personal valuables, he placed the curious piece of gold-work within and relocked the drawer.

"I will walk as far as the cab-rank with you," he said, finding himself to be possessed of a spirit of unrest. Whereupon the two went out of the room, Stuart extinguishing the lamps as he came to the door.

They had not left the study for more than two minutes ere a car drew up outside the house, and Mrs. M'Gregor ushered a lady into the room but lately quitted by Stuart and Dunbar, turning up the lights as she entered.

"The doctor has gone out but just now, Miss Dorian," she said stiffly. "I am sorry that ye are so unfortunate in your veesits. But I know he'll be no more than a few minutes."

The girl addressed was of a type fully to account for the misgivings of the shrewd old Scotswoman. She had the slim beauty of the East allied to the elegance of the West. Her features, whilst cast in a charming European mould, at the same time suggested in some subtle way the Oriental. She had the long, almond-shaped eyes of the Egyptian, and her hair, which she wore unconventionally in a picturesque fashion reminiscent of the *harem*, was inclined to be "fuzzy," but gleamed with coppery tints where the light touched its waves.

She wore a cloak of purple velvet having a hooded collar of white fox fur; it fastened with golden cords. Beneath it was a white and gold robe, cut with classic simplicity of line and confined at the waist by an ornate Eastern girdle. White stockings and dull gold shoes exhibited to advantage her charming little feet and slim ankles, and she carried a handbag of Indian beadwork. Mlle. Dorian was a figure calculated to fire the imagination of any man and to linger long and sweetly in the memory.

Mrs. M'Gregor, palpably ill at ease, conducted her to an armchair.

"You are very good," said the visitor, speaking with a certain hesitancy and with a slight accent most musical and fascinating. "I wait a while if I may."

"Dear, dear," muttered Mrs. M'Gregor, beginning to poke the fire, "he has let the fire down, of course! Is it out? No...I see a wee sparkie!"

She set the poker upright before the nearly extinguished fire and turned triumphantly to Mlle. Dorian, who was watching her with a slight smile.

"That will be a comforting blaze in a few minutes, Miss Dorian," she said, and went towards the door.

"If you please," called the girl, detaining her — "do you permit me to speak on the telephone a moment? As Dr. Stuart is not at home, I must explain that I wait for him."

"Certainly, Miss Dorian," replied Mrs. M'Gregor; "use the telephone by all means. But I think the doctor will be back any moment now."

"Thank you so much."

Mrs. M'Gregor went out, not without a final backward glance at the elegant figure in the armchair. Mlle. Dorian was seated, her chin resting in her hand and her elbow upon the arm of the chair, gazing into the smoke arising from the nearly extinguished ember of the fire. The door closed, and Mrs. M'Gregor's footsteps could be heard receding along the corridor.

Mlle. Dorian sprang from the chair and took out of her handbag a number of small keys attached to a ring. Furtively she crossed the room, all the time listening intently, and cast her cloak over the back of the chair which was placed before the writing-table. Her robe of white and gold clung to her shapely figure as she bent over the table and tried three of the keys in the lock of the drawer which contained Stuart's cheque-book and in which he had recently placed the mysterious gold ornament. The third key fitted the lock, and Mlle. Dorian pulled open the drawer. She discovered first the cheque-book and next a private account-book; then from under the latter she drew out a foolscap envelope sealed with red wax and bearing, in Stuart's handwriting, the address:

> Lost Property Office,
> Metropolitan Police,
> New Scotland Yard, S. W. I.

She uttered a subdued exclamation; then, as a spark of light gleamed within the open drawer, she gazed as if stupefied at the little ornament which she had suddenly perceived lying near the cheque-book. She picked it up and stared at it aghast. A moment she hesitated; then, laying down the fragment of gold and also the long envelope upon the table, she took up the telephone. Keeping her eyes fixed upon the closed door of the study, she asked for the number East 89512, and whilst she waited for the connection continued that nervous watching and listening. Suddenly she began to speak, in a low voice.

"Yes!...Miska speaks. Listen! One of the new keys — it fits. I have the envelope. But, also in the same drawer, I find a part of a broken gold *'agrab* (scorpion). Yes, it is broken. It must be they find it, on him." Her manner grew more and more agitated. "Shall I bring it? The envelope it is very large. I do not know if ——"

From somewhere outside the house came a low, wailing cry — a cry which Stuart, if he had heard it, must have recognized to be identical with that which he had heard in the night — but which he had forgotten to record in his written account.

"Ah!" whispered the girl — "there is the signal! It is the doctor who returns." She listened eagerly, fearfully, to the voice which spoke over the wires. "Yes — yes!"

Always glancing toward the door, she put down the instrument, took up the long envelope and paused for a moment, thinking that she had heard the sound of approaching footsteps. She exhibited signs of nervous indecision, tried to thrust the envelope into her little bag and realized that even folded it would not fit so as to escape observation. She ran across to the grate and dropped the envelope upon the smouldering fire. As she did so, the nicely balanced poker fell with a clatter upon the tiled hearth.

She started wildly, ran back to the table, took up the broken ornament and was about to thrust it into the open drawer, when the study door was flung open and Stuart came in.

CHAPTER V
THE SEALED ENVELOPE

"MADEMOISELLE DORIAN!" cried Stuart joyously, advancing with outstretched hand. She leaned back against the table watching him — and suddenly he perceived the open drawer. He stopped. His expression changed to one of surprise and anger, and the girl's slim fingers convulsively clutched the table edge as she confronted him. Her exquisite colour fled and left her pallid, dark-eyed and dismayed.

"So," he said bitterly —"I returned none too soon, Mlle. — *Dorian*"

"Oh! she whispered, and shrank from him as he approached nearer.

"Your object in selecting an obscure practitioner for your medical adviser becomes painfully evident to me. Diagnosis of your case would have been much more easy if I had associated your symptoms with the presence in my table drawer of" — he hesitated — "of something which you have taken out. Give me whatever you have stolen and compose yourself to await the arrival of the police."

He was cruel in his disillusionment. Here lay the explanation of his romance; here was his disguised princess — a common thief! She stared at him wildly.

"I take nothing!" she cried. "Oh, let me go! Please, please let me go!"

"Pleading is useless. What have you stolen?"

"Nothing — see." She cast the little gold ornament on the table. "I look at this, but I do not mean to steal it."

She raised her beautiful eyes to his face again, and he found himself wavering. That she had made his acquaintance in order to steal the fragment of the golden scorpion was impossible, for he had not possessed it at the time of her first visit. He was hopelessly mystified and utterly miserable.

"How did you open the drawer?" he asked sternly.

She took up the bunch of keys which lay upon the table and naively exhibited that which fitted the lock of the drawer. Her hands were shaking.

"Where did you obtain this key; and why?"

She watched him intently, her lips trembling and her eyes wells of sorrow into which he could not gaze unmoved.

"If I tell you — will you let me go?"

"I shall make no promises, for I can believe nothing that you may tell me. You gained my confidence by a lie — and now, by another lie, you seem to think that you can induce me to overlook a deliberate attempt at burglary — common burglary." He clenched his hands. "Heavens! I could never have believed it of you!"

She flinched as though from a blow and regarded him pitifully as he stood, head averted.

"Oh, please listen to me," she whispered. "At first I tell you a lie, yes."

"And now?"

"Now — I tell you the truth."

"That you are a petty thief?"

"Ah! you are cruel — you have no pity! You judge me as you judge — one of your English-women. Perhaps I cannot help what I do. In the East a woman is a chattel and has no will of her own."

"A chattel!" cried Stuart scornfully. "Your resemblance to the 'chattels' of the East is a remote one. There is Eastern blood in your veins, no doubt, but you are educated, you are a linguist, you know the world. Right and wrong are recognizable to the lowest savage."

"And if they recognize, but are helpless?"

Stuart made a gesture of impatience.

"You are simply seeking to enlist my sympathy," he said bitterly. "But you have said nothing which inclines me to listen to you any longer. Apart from the shock of finding you to be — what you are, I am utterly mystified as to your object. I am a poor man. The entire contents of my house would fetch only a few hundred pounds if sold to-morrow. Yet you risk your liberty to rifle my bureau. For the last time — what have you taken from that drawer?"

She leaned back against the table, toying with the broken piece of gold and glancing down at it as she did so. Her long lashes cast shadows below her eyes, and a hint of colour was returning to her cheeks. Stuart studied her attentively — even delightedly, for all her shortcomings, and knew in his heart that he could never give her in charge of the police. More and more the wonder of it all grew upon him, and now he suddenly found himself thinking of the unexplained incident of the previous night.

"You do not answer," he said. "I will ask you another question: have you attempted to open that drawer prior to this evening?"

Mlle. Dorian looked up rapidly, and her cheeks, which had been pale, now flushed rosily.

"I try twice before," she confessed, "and cannot open it."

"Ah! And — has *someone else* tried also?"

Instantly her colour fled again, and she stared at him wide-eyed, fearful.

"Someone else?" she whispered.

"Yes — someone else. A man…wearing a sort of cowl — —"

"Oh?" she cried and threw out her hands in entreaty. "Do not ask me of *him*! I dare not answer — I dare not!"

"You have answered," said Stuart, in a voice unlike his own; for a horrified amazement was creeping upon him and supplanting the contemptuous anger which the discovery of this beautiful girl engaged in pilfering his poor belongings had at first aroused.

The mystery of her operations was explained — explained by a deeper and a darker mystery. The horror of the night had been no dream but an almost incredible reality. He now saw before him an agent of the man in the cowl; he perceived that he was in some way entangled in an affair vastly more complex and sinister than a case of petty larceny.

"Has the golden scorpion anything to do with the matter?" he demanded abruptly.

And in the eyes of his beautiful captive he read the answer. She flinched again as she had done when he had taunted her with being a thief; but he pressed his advantage remorselessly.

"So you were concerned in the death of Sir Frank Narcombe!" he said.

"I was not!" she cried at him fiercely, and her widely opened eyes were magnificent. "Sir Frank Narcombe is — —"

She faltered — and ceased speaking, biting her lip which had become tremulous again.

"Sir Frank Narcombe is?" prompted Stuart, feeling himself to stand upon the brink of a revelation.

"I know nothing of him — this Sir Frank Narcombe."

Stuart laughed unmirthfully.

"Am I, by any chance, in danger of sharing the fate of that distinguished surgeon?" he asked.

His question produced an unforeseen effect. Mlle. Dorian suddenly rested her jewelled hands upon his shoulders, and he found himself looking hungrily into those wonderful Eastern eyes.

"If I swear that I speak the truth, will you believe me?" she whispered, and her fingers closed convulsively upon his shoulders.

He was shaken. Her near presence was intoxicating. "Perhaps," he said unsteadily.

"Listen, then. *Now* you are in danger, yes. Before, you were not, but now you must be very careful. Oh! indeed, indeed, I tell you true! I tell you for your own sake. Do with me what you please. I do not care. It does not matter. You ask me why I come here. I tell you that also. I come for what is in the long envelope — look, I cannot hide it. It is on the fire!"

Stuart turned and glanced toward the grate. A faint wisp of brown smoke was arising from a long white envelope which lay there. Had the fire been actually burning, it must long ago have been destroyed. More than ever mystified, for the significance of the envelope was not evident to him, he ran to the grate and plucked the smouldering paper from the embers.

As he did so, the girl, with one quick glance in his direction, snatched her cloak, keys and bag and ran from the room. Stuart heard the door close, and racing back to the table he placed the slightly charred envelope there beside the fragment of gold and leapt to the door.

"Damn!" he said.

His escaped prisoner had turned the key on the outside. He was locked in his own study!

Momentarily nonplussed, he stood looking at the closed door. The sound of a restarted motor from outside the house spurred him to action. He switched off the lamps, crossed the darkened room and drew back the curtain, throwing open the French windows. Brilliant moonlight bathed the little lawn with its bordering of high privet hedges. Stuart ran out as the sound of the receding car reached his ears. By the time that he had reached the front of the house the street was vacant from end to end. He walked up the steps to the front door, which he unfastened with his latch-key. As he entered the hall, Mrs. M'Gregor appeared from her room.

"I did no' hear ye go out with Miss Dorian," she said.

"That's quite possible, Mrs. M'Gregor, but she has gone, you see."

"Now tell me, Mr. Keppel, did ye or did ye no' hear the wail o' the pibroch the night?

"No —I am afraid I cannot say that I did, Mrs. M'Gregor," replied Stuart patiently. "I feel sure you must be very tired and you can justifiably turn in now. I am expecting no other visitor. Good-night."

Palpably dissatisfied and ill at ease, Mrs. M'Gregor turned away.

"Good-night, Mr. Keppel," she said.

Stuart, no longer able to control his impatience, hurried to the study door, unlocked it and entered. Turning on the light, he crossed and hastily drew the curtains over the window recess, but without troubling to close the window which he had opened. Then he returned to the writing-table and took up the sealed envelope whose presence in his bureau was clearly responsible for the singular visitation of the cowled man and for the coming of the lovely Mlle. Dorian.

The "pibroch of the M'Gregors": He remembered something — something which, unaccountably, he hitherto had failed to recall: that fearful wailing in the night — which had heralded the coming of the cowled man! — or had it been a *signal* of some kind?

He stared at the envelope blankly, then laid it down and stood looking for some time at the golden scorpion's tail. Finally, his hands resting upon the table, he found that almost unconsciously he had been listening — listening to the dim night sounds of London and to the vague stirrings within the house.

"*Now*, you are in danger. Before, you were not...."

Could he believe her? If in naught else, in this at least surely she had been sincere? Stuart started — then laughed grimly.

A clock on the mantel-piece had chimed the half-hour.

CHAPTER VI
THE ASSISTANT COMMISSIONER

Detective-Inspector Dunbar arrived at New Scotland Yard in a veritable fever of excitement. Jumping out of the cab he ran into the building and without troubling the man in charge of the lift went straight on upstairs to his room. He found it to be in darkness and switched on the green-shaded lamp which was suspended above the table. Its light revealed a bare apartment having distempered walls severely decorated by an etching of a former and unbeautiful Commissioner. The blinds were drawn. A plain, heavy deal table (bearing a blotting-pad, a pewter ink-pot, several pens and a telephone), together with three uncomfortable chairs, alone broke the expanse of highly polished floor. Dunbar glanced at the table and then stood undecided in the middle of the bare room, tapping his small, widely separated teeth with a pencil which he had absently drawn from his waistcoat pocket. He rang the bell.

A constable came in almost immediately and stood waiting just inside the door.

"When did Sergeant Sowerby leave?" asked Dunbar.

"About three hours ago, sir."

"What!" cried Dunbar. "Three hours ago! But I have been here myself within that time — in the Commissioner's office."

"Sergeant Sowerby left before then. I saw him go."

"But, my good fellow, he has been back again. He spoke to me on the telephone less than a quarter of an hour ago."

"Not from here, sir."

"But I say it *was* from here!" shouted Dunbar fiercely; "and I told him to wait for me."

"Very good, sir. Shall I make inquiries?"

"Yes. Wait a minute. Is the Commissioner here?"

"Yes, sir, I believe so. At least I have not seen him go."

"Find Sergeant Sowerby and tell him to wait here for me," snapped Dunbar.

He walked out into the bare corridor and along to the room of the Assistant Commissioner. Knocking upon the door, he opened it immediately, and entered an apartment which afforded a striking contrast to his own. For whereas the room of Inspector Dunbar was practically unfurnished, that of his superior was so filled with tables, cupboards, desks, bureaux, files, telephones, bookshelves and stacks of documents that one only discovered the Assistant Commissioner sunk deep in a padded armchair and a cloud of tobacco smoke by dint of close scrutiny. The Assistant Commissioner was small, sallow and satanic. His black moustache was very black and his eyes were of so dark a brown as to appear black also. When he smiled he revealed a row of very large white teeth, and his smile was correctly Mephistophelean. He smoked a hundred and twenty Egyptian cigarettes per diem, and the first and second fingers of either hand were coffee-coloured.

"Good-evening, Inspector," he said courteously. "You come at an opportune moment." He lighted a fresh cigarette. "I was detained here unusually late to-night or this news would not have reached us till the morning." He laid his finger upon a yellow form. "There is an unpleasant development in 'The Scorpion' case."

"So I gather, sir. That is what brought me back to the Yard."

The Assistant Commissioner glanced up sharply.

"What brought you back to the Yard?" he asked.

"The news about Max."

The assistant Commissioner leaned back in his chair. "Might I ask, Inspector," he said, "what news you have learned and how you have learned it?"

Dunbar stared uncomprehendingly.

"Sowerby 'phoned me about half an hour ago, sir. Did he do so without your instructions?"

"Most decidedly. What was his message?"

"He told me," replied Dunbar, in ever-growing amazement, "that the body brought in by the River Police last night had been identified as that of Gaston Max."

The Assistant Commissioner handed a pencilled slip to Dunbar. It read as follows: —

"Gaston Max in London. Scorpion, Narcombe. No report since 30th ult.
Fear trouble. Identity-disk G. M. 49685."

"But, sir," said Dunbar — "this is exactly what Sowerby told me!"

"Quite so. That is the really extraordinary feature of the affair. Because, you see, Inspector, I only finished decoding this message at the very moment that you knocked at my door!"

"But ——"

"There is no room for a 'but,' Inspector. This confidential message from Paris reached me ten minutes ago. You know as well as I know that there is no possibility of leakage. No one has entered my room in the interval, yet you tell me that Sergeant Sowerby communicated this information to you, by telephone, half an hour ago."

Dunbar was tapping his teeth with the pencil. His amazement was too great for words.

"Had the message been a false one," continued the Commissioner, "the matter would have been resolved into a meaningless hoax, but the message having been what it was, we find ourselves face to face with no ordinary problem. Remember, Inspector, that voices on the telephone are deceptive. Sergeant Sowerby has marked vocal mannerisms ——"

"Which would be fairly easy to imitate? Yes, sir — that's so."

"But it brings us no nearer to the real problems; viz., first, the sender of the message; and, second, his purpose."

There was a dull purring sound and the Assistant Commissioner raised the telephone.

"Yes. Who is it that wishes to speak to him? Dr. Keppel Stuart? Connect with my office."

He turned again to Dunbar.

"Dr. Stuart has a matter of the utmost urgency to communicate, Inspector. It was at the house of Dr. Stuart, I take it, that you received the unexplained message?"

"It was —yes."

"Did you submit to Dr. Stuart the broken gold ornament?"

"Yes. It's a scorpion's tail."

"Ah!" The Assistant Commissioner smiled satanically and lighted a fresh cigarette. "And is Dr. Stuart agreeable to placing his unusual knowledge at our disposal for the purposes of this case?"

"He is, sir."

The purring sound was repeated.

"You are through to Dr. Stuart," said the Assistant Commissioner.

"Hullo" cried Dunbar, taking up the receiver — "is that Dr. Stuart? Dunbar speaking."

He stood silent for a while, listening to the voice over the wires. Then: "You want me to come around now, doctor? Very well. I'll be with you in less than half an hour."

He put down the instrument.

"Something extraordinary seems to have taken place at Dr. Stuart's house a few minutes after I left, sir," he said. "I'm going back there, now, for particulars. It sounds as though the 'phone message might have been intended to get me away." He stared down at the pencilled slip which the Assistant Commissioner had handed him, but stared vacantly, and: "Do you mind if I call someone up, sir?" he asked. "It should be done at once."

"Call by all means, Inspector."

Dunbar again took up the telephone.

"Battersea 0996," he said, and stood waiting. Then:

"Is that Battersea 0996?" he asked. "Is Dr. Stuart there? He is speaking? Oh, this is Inspector Dunbar. You called me up here at the Yard a few moments ago, did you not? Correct, doctor; that's all I wanted to know. I am coming now."

"Good," said the Assistant Commissioner, nodding his approval. "You will have to check 'phone messages in that way until you have run your mimic to earth, Inspector. I don't believe for a moment that it was Sergeant Sowerby who rang you up at Dr. Stuart's."

"Neither do I," said Dunbar grimly. "But I begin to have a glimmer of a notion who it was. I'll be saying good-night, sir. Dr. Stuart seems to have something very important to tell me."

As a mere matter of form he waited for the report of the constable who had gone in quest of Sowerby, but it merely confirmed the fact that Sowerby had left Scotland Yard over three hours earlier. Dunbar summoned a taxicab and proceeded to the house of Dr. Stuart.

CHAPTER VII
CONTENTS OF THE SEALED ENVELOPE

Stuart personally admitted Dunbar, and once more the Inspector found himself in the armchair in the study. The fire was almost out and the room seemed to be chilly. Stuart was labouring under the influence of suppressed excitement and was pacing restlessly up and down the floor.

"Inspector," he began, "I find it difficult to tell you the facts which have recently come to my knowledge bearing upon this most mysterious 'Scorpion' case. I clearly perceive, now, that without being aware of the fact I have nevertheless been concerned in the case for at least a week."

Dunbar stared surprisedly, but offered no comment.

"A fortnight ago," Stuart continued, "I found myself in the neighbourhood of the West India Docks. I had been spending the evening with a very old friend, chief officer of a liner in dock. I had intended to leave the ship at about ten o'clock and to walk to the railway station, but, as it fell out, the party did not break up until after midnight. Declining the offer of a berth on board,

I came ashore determined to make my way home by tram and afoot. I should probably have done so and have been spared — much; but rain began to fall suddenly and I found myself, foolishly unprovided with a top-coat, in those grey East End streets without hope of getting a lift.

"It was just as I was crossing Limehouse Causeway that I observed, to my astonishment, the head-lamps of a cab or car shining out from a dark and forbidding thoroughfare which led down to the river. The sight was so utterly unexpected that I paused, looking through the rainy mist in the direction of the stationary vehicle. I was still unable to make out if it were a cab or a car, and accordingly I walked along to where it stood and found that it was a taxicab and apparently for hire.

"'Are you disengaged?' I said to the man. "Well, sir, I suppose I am,' was his curious reply. 'Where do you want to go?'

"I gave him this address and he drove me home. On arriving, so grateful did I feel that I took pity upon the man, for it had settled down into a brute of a night, and asked him to come in and take a glass of grog. He was only too glad to do so. He turned out to be quite an intelligent sort of fellow, and we chatted together for ten minutes or so.

"I had forgotten all about him when, I believe on the following night, he reappeared in the character of a patient. He had a badly damaged skull, and I gathered that he had had an accident with his cab and had been pitched out into the road.

"When I had fixed him up, he asked me to do him a small favour. From inside his tunic he pulled out a long stiff envelope, bearing no address but the number 30 in big red letters. It was secured at both ends with black wax bearing the imprint of a curious and complicated seal.

"A gentleman left this behind in the cab today, sir,' said the man — 'perhaps the one who was with me when I had the spill, and I've got no means of tracing him; but he may be able to trace *me* if he happened to notice my number, or he may advertise. It evidently contains something valuable.'

"Then why not take it to Scotland Yard?' I asked. 'Isn't that the proper course?'

"It is,' he admitted; 'but here's the point: if the owner reclaims it from Scotland Yard he's less likely to dub up handsome than if he gets it direct from me!'

"I laughed at that, for the soundness of the argument was beyond dispute. 'But what on earth do you want to leave it with *me* for?' I asked."

"Self-protection,' was the reply. 'They can't say I meant to pinch it! Whereas, directly there's any inquiry I can come and collect it and get the reward; and your word will back me up if any questions are asked; that's if you don't mind, sir.'

"I told him I didn't mind in the least, and accordingly I sealed the envelope in a yet larger one which I addressed to the Lost Property Office and put into a private drawer of my bureau. 'You will have no objection,' I said, 'to this being posted if it isn't reclaimed within a reasonable time?'

"He said that would be all right and departed — since which moment I have not set eyes upon him. I now come to the sequel, or what I have just recognized to be the sequel."

Stuart's agitation grew more marked and it was only by dint of a palpable effort that he forced himself to resume.

"On the evening of the following day a lady called professionally. She was young, pretty, and dressed with extraordinary elegance. My housekeeper admitted her, as I was out at the time but momentarily expected. She awaited my return here, in this room. She came again two days later. The name she gave was an odd one: Mademoiselle Dorian. There is her card," — Stuart opened a drawer and laid a visiting-card before Dunbar — "no initials and no address. She travelled in a large and handsome car. That is to say, according to my housekeeper's account it is a large and handsome car. I personally, have had but an imperfect glimpse of it. It does not await her in front of the house, for some reason, but just around the corner in the side turning. Beyond wondering why Mademoiselle Dorian had selected me as her medical advisor I had detected nothing suspicious in her behaviour up to the time of which I am about to speak.

"Last night there was a singular development, and to-night matters came to a head."

Thereupon Stuart related as briefly as possible the mysterious episode of the cowled man, and finally gave an account of the last visit of Mlle. Dorian. Inspector Dunbar did not interrupt him, but listened attentively to the singular story.

"And there," concluded Stuart, "on the blotting-pad, lies the sealed envelope!"

Dunbar took it up eagerly. A small hole had been burned in one end of the envelope and much of the surrounding paper was charred. The wax with which Stuart had sealed it had lain uppermost, and although it had been partly melted, the mark of his signet-ring was still discernible upon it. Dunbar stood staring at it.

"In the circumstances, Inspector, I think you would be justified in opening both envelopes," said Stuart.

"I am inclined to agree. But let me just be clear on one or two points." He took out the bulging note-book and also a fountain-pen with which he prepared to make entries. "About this cabman, now. You didn't by any chance note the number of his cab?"

"I did not."

"What build of man was he?"

"Over medium height and muscular. Somewhat inclined to flesh and past his youth, but active all the same."

"Dark or fair?"

"Dark and streaked with grey. I noted this particularly in dressing his skull. He wore his hair cropped close to the scalp. He had a short beard and moustache and heavily marked eyebrows. He seemed to be very short-sighted and kept his eyes so screwed up that it was impossible to detect their colour, by night at any rate."

"What sort of wound had he on his skull?"

"A short ugly gash. He had caught his head on the footboard in falling. I may add that on the occasion of his professional visit his breath smelled strongly of spirits, and I rather suspected that his accident might have been traceable to his condition."

"But he wasn't actually drunk?"

"By no means. He was perfectly sober, but he had recently been drinking — possibly because his fall had shaken him, of course."

"His hands?"

"Small and very muscular. Quite steady. Also very dirty."

"What part of the country should you say he hailed from?"

"London. He had a marked cockney accent."

"What make of cab was it?"

"I couldn't say."

"An old cab?"

"Yes. The fittings were dilapidated, I remember, and the cab had a very musty smell."

"Ah," said Dunbar, making several notes. "And now — the lady: about what would be her age?"

"Difficult to say, Inspector. She had Eastern blood and may have been much younger than she appeared to be. Judged from a European standpoint and from her appearance and manner of dress, she might be about twenty-three or twenty-four."

"Complexion?"

"Wonderful. Fresh as a flower."

"Eyes?"

"Dark. They looked black at night."

"Hair?"

"Brown and 'fuzzy' with copper tints."

"Tall?"

"No; slight but beautifully shaped."

"Now — from her accent what should you judge her nationality to be?"

Stuart paced up and down the room, his head lowered in reflection, then:

"She pronounced both English and French words with an intonation which suggested familiarity with Arabic."

"Arabic? That still leaves a fairly wide field."

"It does, Inspector, but I had no means of learning more. She had certainly lived for a long time somewhere in the Near East."

"Her jewellery?"

"Some of it was European and some of it Oriental, but not characteristic of any particular country of the Orient."

"Did she use perfume?"

"Yes, but it was scarcely discernible. Jasmine — probably the Eastern preparation."

"Her ailment was imaginary?"

"I fear so."

"H'm — and now you say that Mrs. M'Gregor saw the car?"

"Yes, but she has retired."

"Her evidence will do to-morrow. We come to the man in the hood. Can you give me any kind of a description of him?"

"He appeared to be tall, but a shadow is deceptive, and his extraordinary costume would produce that effect, too. I can tell you absolutely nothing further about him. Remember, I thought I was dreaming. I could not credit my senses."

Inspector Dunbar glanced over the notes which he had made, then returning the note-book and pen to his pocket, he took up the long smoke-discoloured envelope and with a paper-knife which lay upon the table slit one end open. Inserting two fingers, he drew out the second envelope which the first enclosed. It was an ordinary commercial envelope only notable by reason of the number, 30, appearing in large red figures upon it and because it was sealed with black wax bearing a weird-looking device:

Stuart bent over him intently as he slit this envelope in turn. Again, he inserted two fingers — and brought forth the sole contents...a plain piece of cardboard, roughly rectangular and obviously cut in haste from the lid of a common cardboard box!

CHAPTER VIII
THE ASSISTANT COMMISSIONER'S THEORY

On the following morning Inspector Dunbar, having questioned Mrs. M'Gregor respecting the car in which Mlle. Dorian had visited the house and having elicited no other evidence than that it was "a fine luxurious concern," the Inspector and Dr. Stuart prepared to set out upon gruesome business. Mrs. M'Gregor was very favourably impressed with the Inspector. "A grand, pairsonable body," she confided to Stuart. "He'd look bonny in the kilt."

To an East-End mortuary the cab bore them, and they were led by a constable in attendance to a stone-paved, ill-lighted apartment in which a swathed form lay upon a long deal table. The spectacle presented, when the covering was removed, was one to have shocked less hardened nerves than those of Stuart and Dunbar; but the duties of a police officer, like those of a medical man, not infrequently necessitate such inspections. The two bent over the tragic flotsam of the Thames unmoved and critical.

"H'm," said Stuart — "he's about the build, certainly. Hair iron-grey and close cropped and he seems to have worn a beard. Now, let us see."

He bent, making a close inspection of the skull; then turned and shook his head.

"No, Inspector," he said definitely. "This is not the cabman. There is no wound corresponding to the one which I dressed."

"Right," answered Dunbar, covering up the ghastly face. "That's settled."

"You were wrong, Inspector. It was not Gaston Max who left the envelope with me."

"No," mused Dunbar, "so it seems."

"Your theory that Max, jealously working alone, had left particulars of his inquiries, and clues, in my hands, knowing that they would reach Scotland Yard in the event of his death, surely collapsed when the envelope proved to contain nothing but a bit of cardboard?"

"Yes — I suppose it did. But it sounded so much like Max's round-about methods. Anyway I wanted to make sure that the dead man from Hanover Hole and your mysterious cabman were not one and the same."

Stuart entertained a lively suspicion that Inspector Dunbar was keeping something up his sleeve, but with this very proper reticence he had no quarrel, and followed by the constable, who relocked the mortuary behind them, they came out into the yard where the cab waited which was to take them to Scotland Yard. Dunbar, standing with one foot upon the step of the cab, turned to the constable.

"Has anyone else viewed the body?" he asked.

"No sir."

"No one is to be allowed to do so — you understand? — *no one*, unless he has written permission from the Commissioner."

"Very good, sir."

Half an hour later they arrived at New Scotland Yard and went up to Dunbar's room. A thick-set, florid man of genial appearance, having a dark moustache, a breezy manner and a head of hair resembling a very hard-worked blacking-brush, awaited them. This was Detective-Sargeant Sowerby with whom Stuart was already acquainted.

"Good-morning, Sergeant Sowerby," he said.

"Good-morning, sir. I hear that someone was pulling your leg last night."

"What do you mean exactly, Sowerby?" inquired Dunbar, fixing his fierce eyes upon his subordinate.

Sergeant Sowerby exhibited confusion.

"I mean nothing offensive, Inspector. I was referring to the joker who gave so good an imitation of my voice that even *you* were deceived."

"Ah," replied Dunbar — "I see. Yes — he did it well. He spoke just like you. I could hardly make out a word he said."

With this Caledonian shaft and a side-glance at Stuart, Inspector Dunbar sat down at the table.

"Here's Dr. Stuart's description of the missing cabman," he continued, taking out his note-book. "Dr. Stuart has viewed the body and it is not the man. You had better take a proper copy of this."

"Then the cabman wasn't Max?" cried Sowerby eagerly. "I thought not."

"I believe you told me so before," said Dunbar sourly. "I also seem to recall that you thought a scorpion's tail was a Prickly Pear. However — here, on the page numbered twenty-six, is a description of the woman known as Mlle. Dorian. It should be a fairly easy matter to trace the car through the usual channels, and she ought to be easy to find, too."

He glanced at his watch. Stuart was standing by the lofty window looking out across the Embankment.

"Ten o'clock," said Dunbar. "The Commissioner will be expecting us."

"I am ready," responded Stuart.

Leaving Sergeant Sowerby seated at the table studying the note-book, Stuart and Dunbar proceeded to the smoke-laden room of the Assistant Commissioner. The great man, suavely satanic, greeted Stuart with that polished courtesy for which he was notable.

"You have been of inestimable assistance to us in the past, Dr. Stuart," he said, "and I feel happy to know that we are to enjoy the aid of your special knowledge in the present case. Will you smoke one of my cigarettes? They are some which a friend is kind enough to supply to me direct from Cairo, and are really quite good."

"Thanks," replied Stuart. "May I ask in what direction my services are likely to prove available?"

The Commissioner lighted a fresh cigarette. Then from a heap of correspondence he selected a long report typed upon blue foolscap.

"I have here," he said, "confirmation of the telegraphic report received last night. The name of M. Gaston Max will no doubt be familiar to you?"

Stuart nodded.

"Well," continued the Commissioner, "it appears that he has been engaged in England for the past month endeavouring to trace the connection which he claims to exist between the sudden deaths of various notable people, recently — a list is appended — and some person or organisation represented by, or associated with, a scorpion. His personal theory not being available — poor fellow, you have heard of his tragic death — I have this morning consulted such particulars as I could obtain respecting these cases. If they were really cases of assassination, some obscure poison was the only mode of death that could possibly have been employed. Do you follow me?"

"Perfectly."

"Now, the death of Gaston Max under circumstances not yet explained, would seem to indicate that his theory was a sound one. In other words, I am disposed to believe that he himself represents the most recent outrage of what we will call 'The Scorpion.' Even at the time that the body of the man found by the River Police had not been identified, the presence upon his person of a fragment of gold strongly resembling the tail of a scorpion prompted me to instruct Inspector Dunbar to consult you. I had determined upon a certain course. The identification of the dead man with Gaston Max merely strengthens my determination and enhances the likelihood of my idea being a sound one."

He flicked the ash from his cigarette and resumed:

"Without mentioning names, the experts consulted in the other cases which — according to the late Gaston Max — were victims of 'The Scorpion,' do not seem to have justified their titles. I am arranging that you shall be present at the autopsy upon the body of Gaston Max. And now, permit me to ask you a question: are you acquainted with any poison which would produce the symptoms noted in the case of Sir Frank Narcombe, for instance?"

Stuart shook his head slowly.

"All that I know of the case," he said, "is that he was taken suddenly ill in the foyer of a West-End theatre, immediately removed to his house in Half Moon Street, and died shortly afterward. Can you give me copies of the specialists' reports and other particulars? I may then be able to form an opinion."

"I will get them for you," replied the Commissioner, the exact nature of whose theory was by no means evident to Stuart. He opened a drawer. "I have here," he continued, "the piece of cardboard and the envelope left with you by the missing cab-man. Do you think there is any possibility of invisible writing?"

"None," said Stuart confidently. "I have tested in three or four places as you will see by the spots, but my experiments will in no way interfere with those which no doubt your own people will want to make. I have also submitted both surfaces to a microscopic examination. I am prepared to state definitely that there is no writing upon the cardboard, and except for the number, 30, none upon the envelope."

"It is only reasonable to suppose," continued the Commissioner, "that the telephone message which led Inspector Dunbar to leave your house last night was originated by that unseen intelligence against which we find ourselves pitted. In the first place, no one in London, myself and, presumably, 'The Scorpion' excepted, knew at that time that M. Gaston Max was in England or that M. Gaston Max was dead. I say, presumably 'The Scorpion' because it is fair to assume that the person whom Max pursued was responsible for his death.

"Of course" — the Commissioner reached for the box of cigarettes — "were it not for the telephone message, we should be unjustified in assuming that Mlle. Dorian and this" — he laid his finger upon the piece of cardboard — "had any connection with the case of M. Max. But the message was so obviously designed to facilitate the purloining of the sealed envelope and so obviously emanated from one already aware of the murder of M. Max, that the sender is identified at once with — 'The Scorpion.'"

The Assistant Commissioner complacently lighted a fresh cigarette.

"Finally," he said, "the mode of death in the case of M. Max may not have been the same as in the other cases. Therefore, Dr. Stuart" — he paused impressively — "if you fail to detect anything suspicious at the post mortem examination I propose to apply to the Home Secretary for power to exhume the body of the late Sir Frank Narcombe!"

Deep in reflection, Stuart walked alone along the Embankment. The full facts contained in the report from Paris the Commissioner had not divulged, but Stuart concluded that this sudden activity was directly due, not to the death of M. Max, but to the fact that he (Max) had left behind him some more or less tangible clue. Stuart fully recognized that the Commissioner had accorded him an opportunity to establish his reputation — or to wreck it.

Yet, upon closer consideration, it became apparent that it was to Fate and not to the Commissioner that he was indebted. Strictly speaking, his association with the matter dated from the night of his meeting with the mysterious cabman in West India Dock road. Or had the curtain first been lifted upon this occult drama that evening, five years ago, as the setting sun reddened the waters of the Imperial Canal and a veiled figure passed him on the Wu-Men Bridge?

"Shut your eyes tightly, master — the Scorpion is coming!"

He seemed to hear the boy's words now, as he passed along the Embankment; he seemed to see again the tall figure. And suddenly he stopped, stood still and stared with unseeing eyes across the muddy waters of the Thames. He was thinking of the cowled man who had stood behind the curtains in his study — of that figure so wildly bizarre that even now he could scarcely believe that he had ever actually seen it. He walked on.

Automatically his reflections led him to Mlle. Dorian, and he remembered that even as he paced along there beside the river the wonderful mechanism of New Scotland Yard was in motion, its many tentacles seeking — seeking tirelessly — for the girl, whose dark eyes haunted his sleeping and waking hours. *He* was responsible, and if she were arrested *he* would be called upon to identify her. He condemned himself bitterly.

After all, what crime had she committed? She had tried to purloin a letter — which did not belong to Stuart in the first place. And she had failed. Now — the police were looking for her. His reflections took a new form.

What of Gaston Max, foremost criminologist in Europe, who now lay dead and mutilated in an East-End mortuary? The telephone message which had summoned Dunbar away had been too opportune to be regarded as a mere coincidence. Mlle. Dorian was, therefore, an accomplice of a murderer.

Stuart sighed. He would have given much — more than he was prepared to admit to himself — to have known her to be guiltless.

The identity of the missing cabman now engaged his mind. It was quite possible, of course, that the man had actually found the envelope in his cab a was in no other way concerned in the matter. But how had Mlle. Dorian, or the person instructing her, traced the envelope to his study? And why, if they could establish a claim to it, had they preferred to attempt to steal it? Finally, why all this disturbance about a blank piece of cardboard?

A mental picture of the envelope arose before him, the number, 30, written upon it and the two black seals securing the lapels. He paused again in his walk. His reflections had led him to a second definite point and he fumbled in his waistcoat pocket for a time, seeking a certain brass coin about the size of a halfpenny, having a square hole in the middle and peculiar characters engraved around the square, one on each of the four sides.

He failed to find the coin in his pocket, however, but he walked briskly up a side street until he came to the entrance to a tube station. Entering a public telephone call-box, he asked for the number, City 400. Being put through and having deposited the necessary fee in the box:

"Is that the Commissioner's Office, New Scotland Yard?" he asked. "Yes! My name is Dr. Keppel Stuart. If Inspector Dunbar is there, would you kindly allow me to speak to him."

There was a short interval, then:

"Hullo!" came — "is that Dr. Stuart?"

"Yes. That you, Inspector? I have just remembered something which I should have observed in the first place if I had been really wide-awake. The envelope — you know the one I mean? — the one bearing the number, 30, has been sealed with a Chinese coin, known as *cash*. I have just recognized the fact and thought it wise to let you know at once."

"Are you sure?" asked Dunbar.

"Certain. If you care to call at my place later to-day I can show you some *cash*. Bring the envelope with you and you will see that the coins correspond to the impression in the wax. The inscriptions vary in different provinces, but the form of all *cash* is the same."

"Very good. Thanks for letting me know at once. It seems to establish a link with China, don't you think?"

"It does, but it merely adds to the mystery."

Coming out of the call-box, Stuart proceeded home, but made one or two professional visits before he actually returned to the house. He now remembered having left his particular *cash* piece (which he usually carried) in his dispensary, which satisfactorily accounted for his failure to find the coin in his waistcoat pocket. He had broken the cork of a flask, and in the absence of another of correct size had manufactured a temporary stopper with a small cork to the top of which he had fixed the Chinese coin with a drawing-pin. His purpose served he had left the extemporised stopper lying somewhere in the dispensary.

Stuart's dispensary was merely a curtained recess at one end of the waiting-room and shortly after entering the house he had occasion to visit it. Lying upon a shelf among flasks and bottles was the Chinese coin with the cork still attached. He took it up in order to study the inscription. Then:

"Have I cultivated somnambulism!" he muttered.

Fragments of black sealing-wax adhered to the coin!

Incredulous and half fearful he peered at it closely. He remembered that the impression upon the wax sealing the mysterious envelope had had a circular depression in the centre. It had been made by the head of the drawing-pin!

He found himself staring at the shelf immediately above that upon which the coin had lain. A stick of black sealing-wax used for sealing medicine was thrust in beside a bundle of long envelopes in which he was accustomed to post his Infirmary reports!

One hand raised to his head, Stuart stood endeavouring to marshal his ideas into some sane order. Then, knowing what he should find, he raised the green baize curtain hanging from the lower shelf, which concealed a sort of cupboard containing miscellaneous stores and not a little rubbish, including a number of empty cardboard boxes.

A rectangular strip had been roughly cut from the lid of the topmost box!

The mysterious envelope and its contents, the wax and the seal — all had come from his own dispensary!

CHAPTER IX
THE CHINESE COIN

Deep in reflection, Stuart walked alone along the Embankment. The full facts contained in the report form Paris the Commissioner had not divulged, but Stuart concluded that this sudden activity was directly due, not to the death of M. Max, but to the fact that he (Max) had left behind him some more or less tangible clue. Stuart fully recognized that the Commissioner had accorded him an opportunity to establish his reputation — or to wreck it.

Yet, upon closer consideration, it became apparent that it was to Fate and not to the Commissioner that he was indebted. Strictly speaking, his association with the matter dated from the night of his meeting with the mysterious cabman in West India Dock Road. Or had the curtain first been lifted upon this occult drama that evening, five years ago, as the setting sun reddened the waters of the Imperial Canal and a veiled figure passed him on the Wu-Men Bridge?

"Shut your eyes tightly, master — the Scorpion is coming!"

He seemed to hear the boy's words now, as he passed along the Embankment; he seemed to see again the tall figure. And suddenly he stopped, stood still and stared with unseeing eyes across the muddy waters of the Thames. He was thinking of the cowled man who had stood behind the curtains in his study — of that figure so wildly bizarre that even now he could scarcely believe that he had ever actually seen it. He walked on.

Automatically his reflections led him to Mlle. Dorian, and he remembered that even as he paced along there beside the river the wonderful mechanism of New Scotland Yard was in motion, its many tentacles seeking — seeking tirelessly — for the girl, whose dark eyes haunted his sleeping and waking hours. *He* was responsible, and if she were arrested *he* would be called upon to identify her. He condemned himself bitterly.

After all, what crime had she committed? She had tried to purloin a letter — which did not belong to Stuart in the first place. And she had failed. Now — the police were looking for her. His reflections took a new form.

What of Gaston Max, foremost criminologist in Europe, who now lay dead and mutilated in an East-End mortuary? The telephone message which had summoned Dunbar away had been too opportune to be regarded as a mere coincidence. Mlle. Dorian was, therefore, an accomplice of a murderer.

Stuart sighed. He would have given much — more than he was prepared to admit to himself — to have known her to be guiltless.

The identity of the missing cabman now engaged his mind. It was quite possible, of course, that the man had actually found the envelope in his cab and was in no other way concerned in the matter. But how had Mlle. Dorian, or the person instructing her, traced the envelope to his study? And why, if they could establish a claim to it, had they preferred to attempt to steal it? Finally, why all this disturbance about a blank pieced of cardboard?

A mental picture of the envelope arose before him, the number, 30, written upon it and the two black seals securing the lapels. He paused again in his walk. His reflections had led him to a second definite point and he fumbled in his waistcoat pocket for a time, seeking a certain brass coin about the size of a halfpenny, having a square hole in the middle and peculiar characters engraved around the square, one on each of the four sides.

He failed to find the coin in his pocket, however, but he walked briskly up a side street until he came to the entrance to a tube station. Entering a public telephone call-box, he asked for the number, City 400. Being put through and having deposited the necessary fee in the box:

"Is that the Commissioner's Office, New Scotland Yard?" he asked. "Yes! My name is Dr. Keppel Stuart. If Inspector Dunbar is there, would you kindly allow me to speak to him."

There was a short interval, then:

"Hullo!" came — "is that Dr. Stuart?"

"Yes. That you, Inspector? I have just remembered something which I should have observed in the first place if I had been really wide-awake. The envelope — you know the one I mean? — the one bearing the number, 30, has been sealed with a Chinese coin, known as *cash*. I have just recognized the fact and thought it wise to let you know at once."

"Are you sure?" asked Dunbar.

"Certain. If you care to call at my place later to-day I can show you some *cash*. Bring the envelope with you and you will see that the coins correspond to the impression in the wax. The inscriptions vary in different provinces, but the form of all *cash* is the same."

"Very good. Thanks for letting me know at once. It seems to establish a link with China, don't you think?"

"It does, but it merely adds to the mystery."

Coming out of the call-box, Stuart proceeded home, but made one or two professional visits before he actually returned to the house. He now remembered having left this particular *cash* piece (which he usually carried) in his dispensary, which satisfactorily accounted fro his failure to find the coin in his waistcoat pocket. He had broken the cork of a flask, and in the absence of another of correct size had manufactured a temporary stopper with a small cork to the top of which he had fixed the Chinese coin with a drawing-pin. His purpose served he had left the extemporized stopper somewhere in the dispensary.

Stuart's dispensary was merely a curtained recess at one end of the waiting-room and shortly after entering the house he had occasion to visit it. Lying upon a shelf among flasks and bottles was the Chinese coin with the cork still attached. He took it up in order to study the inscription. Then:

"Have I cultivated somnambulism!" he muttered.

Fragments of black sealing-wax adhered to the coin!

Incredulous and half fearful he peered at it closely. He remembered that the impression upon the wax sealing the mysterious envelope had had a circular depression in the centre. It had been made by the head of the drawing-pin!

He found himself at the shelf immediately above that upon which the coin had lain. A stick of black sealing wax used for sealing medicine was thrust in beside a bundle of long envelopes in which he was accustomed to post his Infirmary reports!

One hand raised to his head, Stuart stood endeavouring to marshal his ideas into some sane order. Then, knowing what he should find, he raised the green baize curtain hanging from the lower shelf, which concealed a sort of cupboard containing miscellaneous stores and not a little rubbish, including a number of empty cardboard boxes.

A rectangular strip had been roughly cut from the lid of the topmost box!

The mysterious envelope and its contents, the wax and the seal — all had come from his own dispensary!

CHAPTER X
"CLOSE YOUR SHUTTERS AT NIGHT"

Inspector Dunbar stood in the little dispensary tapping his teeth with the end of a fountain-pen.

"The last time he visited you, doctor — the time when he gave you the envelope — did the cabman wait here in the waiting-room?"

"He did — yes. He came after my ordinary consulting hours and I was at supper, I remember, as I am compelled to dine early."

"He would be in here alone?"

"Yes. No one else was in the room."

"Would he have had time to find the box, cut out the piece of cardboard from the lid, put it in the envelope and seal it?"

"Ample time. But what could be his object? And why mark the envelope 30?"

"It was in your consulting-room that he asked you to take charge of the envelope?"

"Yes."

"Might I take a peep at the consulting room?"

"Certainly, Inspector."

From the waiting-room they went up a short flight of stairs into the small apartment in which Stuart saw his patients. Dunbar looked slowly about him, standing in the middle of the room, then crossed and stared out of the window into the narrow lane below.

"Where were you when he gave you the envelope?" he snapped suddenly.

"At the table," replied Stuart with surprise.

"Was the table-lamp alight?"

"Yes. I always light it when seeing patients."

"Did you take the letter into the study to seal it in the other envelope?"

"I did, and he came along and witnessed me do it."

"Ah," said Dunbar, and scribbled busily in his note-book. "We are badly tied at Scotland Yard, doctor, and this case looks like being another for which somebody else will reap the credit. I am going to make a request that will surprise you."

He tore a leaf out of the book and folded it carefully.

"I am going to ask you to seal up something and lock it away! But I don't think you'll be troubled by cowled burglars or beautiful women because of it. On this piece of paper I have written — *a*" — he ticked off the points on his fingers: "what I believe to be the name of the man who cut out the cardboard and sealed it in an envelope; *b*: the name of the cabman; and, *c*: the name of the man who rang me up here last night and gave me information which had only just reached the Commissioner. I'll ask you to lock it away until it's wanted, doctor."

"Certainly, if you wish it," replied Stuart. "Come into the study and you shall see me do as you direct. I may add that the object to be served is not apparent to me."

Entering the study, he took an envelope, enclosed the piece of paper, sealed the lapel and locked the envelope in the same drawer of the bureau which once had contained that marked 30.

"Mlle. Dorian has a duplicate key to this drawer." he said. "Are you prepared to take the chance?"

"Quite," replied Dunbar, smiling; "although my information is worth more than that which she risked so much to steal."

"It's most astounding. At every step the darkness increases. Why should *anyone* have asked me to lock up a blank piece of cardboard?"

"Why, indeed," murmured Dunbar. "Well, I may as well get back. I am expecting a report from Sowerby. Look after yourself, sir. I'm inclined to think your pretty patient was talking square when she told you there might be danger."

Stuart met the glance of the tawny eyes.

"What d'you mean, Inspector? Why should *I* be in danger?"

"Because," replied Inspector Dunbar, "if 'The Scorpion' is a poisoner, as the chief seems to think, there's really only one man in England he has to fear, and that man is Dr. Keppel Stuart."

When the Inspector had taken his departure Stuart stood for a long time staring out of the study window at the little lawn with its bordering of high neatly-trimmed privet above which at intervals arose the mop crowns of dwarf acacias. A spell of warm weather seemed at last to have begun, and clouds of gnats floated over the grass, their minute wings glittering in the sunshine. Despite the nearness of teeming streets, this was a backwater of London's stream.

He sighed and returned to some work which the visit of the Scotland Yard man had interrupted.

Later in the afternoon he had occasion to visit the institution to which he had recently been appointed as medical officer, and in contemplation of the squalor through which his steps led him he sought forgetfulness of the Scorpion problem — and of the dark eyes of Mlle. Dorian. He was not entirely successful, and returning by a different route he lost himself in memories which were sweetly mournful.

A taxicab passed him, moving slowly very close to the pavement. He scarcely noted it until it had proceeded some distance ahead of him. Then its slow progress so near to the pavement at last attracted his attention, and he stared vacantly towards the closed vehicle.

Mlle. Dorian was leaning out of the window and looking back at him!

Stuart's heart leapt high. For an instant he paused, then began to walk rapidly after the retreating vehicle. Perceiving that she had attracted his attention, the girl extended a white-gloved hand from the window and dropped a note upon the edge of the pavement. Immediately she withdrew into the vehicle — which moved away at accelerated speed, swung around the next corner and was gone.

Stuart ran forward and picked up the note. Without pausing to read it, he pressed on to the corner. The cab was already two hundred yards away, and he recognized pursuit to be out of the question. The streets were almost deserted at the moment, and no one apparently had witnessed the episode. He unfolded the sheet of plain note-paper, faintly perfumed with jasmine, and read the following, written in an uneven feminine hand:

"Close your shutters at night. Do not think too bad of me."

CHAPTER XI
THE BLUE RAY

Dusk found Stuart in a singular frame of mind. He was torn between duty — or what he conceived to be his duty — to the community, and…something else. A messenger from New Scotland Yard had brought him a bundle of documents relating to the case of Sir Frank Narcombe, and a smaller packet touching upon the sudden end of Henrik Ericksen, the Norwegian electrician, and the equally unexpected death of the Grand Duke Ivan. There were medical certificates, proceedings of coroners, reports of detectives, evidence of specialists and statements of friends, relatives and servants of the deceased. A proper examination of all the documents represented many hours of close study.

Stuart was flattered by the opinion held of his ability by the Assistant Commissioner, but dubious of his chance of detecting any flaw in the evidence which had escaped the scrutiny of so many highly trained observers.

He paced the study restlessly. Although more than six hours had elapsed, he had not communicated to Scotland Yard the fact of his having seen Mlle. Dorian that afternoon. A hundred times he had read the message, although he knew it by heart, knew the form of every letter, the odd crossing of the _t'_s and the splashy dotting of the *i*'s.

If only he could have taken counsel with someone — with someone not bound to act upon such information — it would have relieved his mental stress. His ideas were so chaotic that he felt himself to be incapable of approaching the task presented by the pile of papers lying upon his table.

The night was pleasantly warm and the sky cloudless. Often enough he found himself glancing toward the opened French windows, and once he had peered closely across into the belt of shadow below the hedge, thinking that he had detected something which moved there. Stepping to the window, the slinking shape had emerged into the moonlight — and had proclaimed itself to be that of a black cat!

Yet he had been sorely tempted to act upon the advice so strangely offered. He refrained from doing so, however, reflecting that to spend his evenings with closed and barred shutters now that a spell of hot weather seemed to be imminent would be insufferable. Up and down the room he paced tirelessly, always confronted by the eternal problem.

Forcing himself at last to begin work if only as a sedative, he filled and lighted his pipe, turned off the centre lamp and lighted the reading lamp upon his table. He sat down to consider the papers bearing upon the death of Eriksen. For half an hour he read on steadily and made a number of pencil notes. Then he desisted and sat staring straight before him.

What possible motive could there be in assassinating these people? The case of the Grand Duke might be susceptible of explanation, but those of Henrik Ericksen and Sir Frank Narcombe were not. Furthermore he could perceive no links connecting the three, and no reason why they should have engaged the attention of a common enemy. Such crimes would seem to be purposeless. Assuming that "The Scorpion" was an individual, that individual apparently was a dangerous homicidal maniac.

But, throughout the documents, he could discover no clue pointing to the existence of such an entity. "The Scorpion" might be an invention of the fertile brain of M. Gaston Max; for it had become more and more evident, as he had read, that the attempt to trace these deaths to an identical source had originated at the Service de Surete, and it was from Paris that the name "The Scorpion" had come. The fate of Max was significant, of course. The chances of his death proving to have been due to accident were almost negligible and the fact that a fragment of a golden scorpion had actually been found upon his body was certainly curious.

"Close your shutters at night...."

How the words haunted him and how hotly he despised himself for a growing apprehension which refused to be ignored. It was more mental than physical, this dread which grew with the approach of midnight, and it resembled that which had robbed him of individuality and all but stricken him inert when he had seen upon the moon-bright screen of the curtains the shadow of a cowled man.

Dark forces seemed to be stirring, and some unseen menace crept near to him out of the darkness.

The house was of early Victorian fashion and massive folding shutters were provided to close the French windows. He never used them, as a matter of fact, but now he tested the fastenings which kept them in place against the inner wall and even moved them in order to learn if they were still serviceable.

Of all the mysteries which baffled him, that of the piece of cardboard in the envelope sealed with a Chinese coin was the most irritating. It seemed like the purposeless trick of a child, yet it had led to the presence of the cowled man — and to the presence of Mlle. Dorian. Why?

He sat down at his table again.

"Damn the whole business!" he said. "It is sending me crazy."

Selecting from the heap of documents a large sheet of note-paper bearing a blue diagram of a human bust, marked with figures and marginal notes, he began to read the report to which it was appended — that of Dr. Halesowen. It stated that the late Sir Frank Narcombe had a "horizontal" heart, slightly misplaced and dilatated, with other details which really threw no light whatever upon the cause of his death.

"*I* have a horizontal heart," growled Stuart — "and considering my consumption of tobacco it is certainly dilatated. But I don't expect to drop dead in a theatre nevertheless."

He read on, striving to escape from that shadowy apprehension, but as he read he was listening to the night sounds of London, to the whirring of distant motors, the whistling of engines upon the railway and dim hooting of sirens from the Thames. A slight breeze had arisen and it rustled in the feathery foliage of the acacias and made a whispering sound as it stirred the leaves of the privet hedge.

The drone of an approaching car reached his ears. Pencil in hand, he sat listening. The sound grew louder, then ceased. Either the car had passed or had stopped somewhere near the house. Came a rap on the door.

"Yes," called Stuart and stood up, conscious of excitement.

Mrs. M'Gregor came in.

"There is nothing further you'll be wanting to-night?" she asked.

"No," said Stuart, strangely disappointed, but smiling at the old lady cheerfully. "I shall turn in very shortly."

"A keen east wind has arisen," she continued, severely eyeing the opened windows, "and even for a medical man you are strangely imprudent. Shall I shut the windows?"

"No, don't trouble, Mrs. M'Gregor. The room gets very stuffy with tobacco smoke, and really it is quite a warm night. I shall close them before I retire, of course."

"Ah well," sighed Mrs. M'Gregor, preparing to depart. "Good-night, Mr. Keppel."

"Good-night, Mrs. M'Gregor."

She retired, and Stuart sat staring out into the darkness. He was not prone to superstition, but it seemed like tempting providence to remain there with the windows open any longer. Yet paradoxically, he lacked the moral courage to close them — to admit to himself that he was afraid!

The telephone bell rang, and he started back in his chair as though to avoid a blow.

By doing so he avoided destruction.

At the very instant that the bell rang out sharply in the silence — so exact is the time-table of Kismet — a needle-like ray of blue light shot across the lawn from beyond and above the hedge and — but for that nervous start — must have struck fully upon the back of Stuart's skull. Instead, it shone past his head, which it missed only by inches, and he experienced a sensation as though some one had buffeted him upon the cheek furiously. He pitched out of his chair and on to the carpet.

The first object which the ray touched was the telephone; and next, beyond it, a medical dictionary; beyond that again, the grate, in which a fire was laid.

"My God!" groaned Stuart — "what is it!"

An intense crackling sound deafened him, and the air of the room seemed to have become hot as that of an oven. There came a series of dull reports — an uncanny wailing… and the needle-ray vanished. A monstrous shadow, moon-cast, which had lain across the carpet of the lawn — the shadow of a cowled man — vanished also.

Clutching the side of his head, which throbbed and tingled as though from the blow of an open hand, Stuart struggled to his feet. There was smoke in the room, a smell of burning and of fusing metal. He glared at the table madly.

The mouthpiece of the telephone had vanished!

"My God!" he groaned again, and clutched at the back of the chair.

His dictionary was smouldering slowly. It had a neat round hole some three inches in diameter, bored completely through, cover to cover! The fire in the grate was flaring up the chimney!

He heard the purr of a motor in the lane beside the house. The room was laden with suffocating fumes. Stuart stood clutching the chair and striving to retain composure — sanity. The car moved out of the lane.

Someone was running towards the back gate of the house… was scrambling over the hedge… was racing across the lawn!

A man burst into the study. He was a man of somewhat heavy build, clean-shaven and inclined to pallor. The hirsute blue tinge about his lips and jaw lent added vigour to a flexible but masterful mouth. His dark hair was tinged with grey, his dark eyes were brilliant with excitement. He was very smartly dressed and wore light tan gloves. He reeled suddenly, clutching at a chair for support.

"Quick! quick!" he cried — "the telephone!… Ah!"

Just inside the window he stood, swaying and breathing rapidly, his gaze upon the instrument.

"Mon Dieu!" he cried — "what has happened, then!"

Stuart stared at the new-comer dazedly.

"Hell has been in my room!" he replied. "That's all!"

"Ah!" said the stranger — "again he eludes me! The telephone was the only chance. *Pas d'blaque!* we are finished!"

He dropped into a chair, removed his light grey hat and began to dry his moist brow with a fine silk handkerchief. Stuart stared at him like a man who is stupefied. The room was still laden with strange fumes.

"Blimey!" remarked the new-comer, and his Whitechapel was as perfect as his Montmatre. He was looking at the decapitated telephone. "This is a knock-out!"

"Might I ask," said Stuart, endeavouring to collect his scattered senses, "where you came from?"

"From up a tree!" was the astonishing reply. "It was the only way to get over!"

"Up a tree!"

"Exactly. Yes, I was foolish. I am too heavy. But what could I do! We must begin all over again."

Stuart began to doubt his sanity. This was no ordinary man.

"Might I ask," he said, "who you are and what you are doing in my house?"

"Ah!" The stranger laughed merrily. "You wonder about me — I can see it. Permit me to present myself — Gaston Max, at your service!"

"Gaston Max!" Stuart glared at the speaker incredulously. "Gaston Max! Why, I conduct a *post mortem* examination upon Gaston Max tomorrow, in order to learn if he was poisoned!"

"Do not trouble, doctor. That poor fellow is not Gaston Max and he was not poisoned. You may accept my word for it. I had the misfortune to strangle him."

PART II
STATEMENT OF GASTON MAX

THE DANCER OF MONTMARTRE

CHAPTER I
RA EL-KHALA

The following statement which I, Gaston Max, am drawing up in duplicate for the guidance of whoever may inherit the task of tracing "The Scorpion" — a task which I have begun — will be lodged — one copy at the Service de Surete in Paris, and the other copy with the Commissioner of Police, New Scotland Yard. As I apprehend that I may be assassinated at any time, I propose to put upon record all that I have learned concerning the series of murders which I believe to be traceable to a certain person. In the event of my death, my French colleagues will open the sealed packet containing this statement and the English Assistant Commissioner of the Special Branch responsible for international affairs will receive instructions to open that which I shall have lodged at Scotland Yard.

This matter properly commenced, then, with the visit to Paris, incognito, of the Grand Duke Ivan, that famous soldier of whom so much was expected, and because I had made myself responsible for his safety during the time that he remained in the French capital, I (also incognito be it understood) struck up a friendship with one Casimir, the Grand Duke's valet. Nothing is sacred to a valet, and from Casimir I counted upon learning the real reason which had led this nobleman to visit Paris at so troublous a time. Knowing the Grand Duke to be a man of gallantry, I anticipated finding a woman in the case — and I was not wrong.

Yes, there was a woman, and _nom d'nom!_she was beautiful. Now in Paris we have many beautiful women, and in times of international strife it is true that we have had to shoot some of them. For my own part I say with joy that I have never been instrumental in bringing a woman to such an end. Perhaps I am sentimental; it is a French weakness; but on those few occasions when I have found a guilty woman in my power — and she has been pretty — *morbleu!* — she has escaped! It may be that I have seen to it that she was kept out of further mischief, but nevertheless she has never met a firing-party because of me. Very well.

From the good fellow Casimir I learned that a certain dancer appearing at one of our Montmartre theatres had written to the Grand Duke craving the honour of his autograph — and enclosing her photograph.

Pf! it was enough. One week later the autograph arrived — attached to an invitation to dine with the Grand Duke at his hotel in Paris. Yes — he had come to Paris. I have said that he was susceptible and I have said that she was beautiful. I address myself to men of the world, and I shall not be in error if I assume that they will say, "A wealthy fool and a designing woman. It is an old story." Let us see.

The confidences of Casimir interested me in more ways than one. In the first place I had particular reasons for suspecting anyone who sought to obtain access to the Grand Duke. These were diplomatic. And in the second place I had suspicions of Zara el-Khala. These were personal.

Yes — so she called herself — Zara el-Khala, which in Arabic is "Flower of the Desert." She professed to be an Egyptian, and certainly she had the long, almond-shaped eyes of the East, but her white skin betrayed her, and I knew that whilst she might possess Eastern blood, she was more nearly allied to Europe than to Africa. It is my business to note unusual matters, you understand, and I noticed that this beautiful and accomplished woman of whom all Paris was beginning to speak rapturously remained for many weeks at a small Montmartre theatre. Her performance, which was unusually decorous for the type of establishment at which she appeared, had not apparently led to an engagement elsewhere.

This aroused the suspicions to which I have referred. In the character of a vaudeville agent I called at the Montmartre theatre and was informed by the management that Zara-el-Khala received no visitors, professional or otherwise. A small but expensive car awaited her at the stage door. My suspicions increased. I went away, but returned on the following night, otherwise attired, and from a hiding-place which I had selected on the previous evening I watched the dancer depart.

She came out so enveloped in furs and veils as to be unrecognizable, and a Hindu wearing a chauffeur's uniform opened the door of the car for her, and then, having arranged the rugs to her satisfaction, mounted to the wheel and drove away.

I traced the car. It had been hired for the purpose of taking Zara el-Khala from her hotel — to the theatre and home nightly. I sent a man to call upon her at the hotel — in order to obtain press material, ostensibly. She declined to see him. I became really interested. I sent her a choice bouquet, having the card of a nobleman attached to it, together with a message of respectful admiration. It was returned. I prevailed upon one of the most handsome and gallant cavalry officers in Paris to endeavour to make her acquaintance. He was rebuffed.

Eh bien! I knew then that Mlle. Zara of the Desert was unusual.

You will at once perceive that when I heard from the worthy Casimir how this unapproachable lady had actually written to the Grand Duke Ivan and had gone so far as to send him her photograph, I became excited. It appeared to me that I found myself upon the brink of an important discovery. I set six of my first-class men at work: three being detailed to watch the hotel of the Grand Duke Ivan and three to watch Zara el-Khala. Two more were employed in watching the Hindu servant and one in watching my good friend Casimir. Thus, nine clever men and myself were immediately engaged upon the case.

Why do I speak of a "case" when thus far nothing of apparent importance had occurred? I will explain. Although the Grand Duke travelled incognito, his Government knew of the journey and wished to learn with what object it had been undertaken.

At the time that I made the acquaintance of Casimir the Grand Duke had been in Paris for three days, and he was — according to my informant — "like a raging lion." The charming dancer had vouchsafed no reply to his invitation and he had met with the same reception, on presenting himself in person, which had been accorded to myself and to those others who had sought to obtain an interview with Zara el-Khala!

My state of mystification grew more and more profound. I studied the reports of my nine assistants.

It appeared that the girl had been in Paris for a period of two months. She occupied a suite of rooms in which all her meals were served. Except the Hindu who drove the hired car, she had no servant. She never appeared in the public part of the hotel unless veiled, and then merely in order to pass out to the car or in from it on returning. She drove out every day. She had been followed, of course, but her proceedings were unexceptionable. Leaving the car at a point in the Bois De Boulogne, she would take a short walk, if the day was fine enough, never proceeding out of sight of the Hindu, who followed with the automobile, and would then drive back to her hotel. She never received visits and never met any one during these daily excursions.

I turned to the report dealing with the Hindu. He had hired a room high up under the roof of an apartment house where foreign waiters and others had their abodes. He bought and cooked his own food, which apparently consisted solely of rice, lentils and fruit. He went every morning to the garage and attended to the car, called for his mistress, and having returned remained until evening in his own apartment. At night, after returning from the theatre, he sometimes went out, and my agent had failed to keep track of him on every occasion that he had attempted pursuit. I detached the man who was watching Casimir and whose excellent reports revealed the fact that Casimir was an honest fellow — as valets go — and instructed him to assist in tracing the movements of the Hindu.

Two nights later they tracked him to a riverside cafe kept by a gigantic quadroon from Dominique and patronized by that type which forms a link between the lowest commercial and the criminal classes: itinerant vendors of Eastern rugs, street performers and Turkish cigarette makers.

At last I began to have hopes. The Grand Duke at this time was speaking of leaving Paris, but as he had found temporary consolation in the smiles of a lady engaged at the "Folies" I did not anticipate that he would depart for several days at any rate. Also he was the kind of man who is stimulated by obstacles.

The Hindu remained for an hour in the cafe, smoking and drinking some kind of syrup, and one of my fellows watched him. Presently the proprietor called him into a little room behind the counter and closed the door. The Hindu and the quadroon remained there for a few minutes, then the Hindu came out and left the cafe, returning to his abode. There was a telephone in this inner room, and my agent was of opinion that the Indian had entered either to make or to receive a call. I caused the line to be tapped.

On the following night the Hindu came back to the cafe, followed by one of my men. I posted myself at a selected point and listened for any message that might pass over the line to or from the cafe. At about the same hour as before — according to the report — someone called up the establishment, asking for "Miguel." This was the quadroon, and I heard his thick voice replying. The other voice — which had first spoken — was curiously sibilant but very distinct. Yet it did not sound like the voice of a Frenchman or of any European. This was the conversation:

"Miguel."

"Miguel speaks."

"*Scorpion.* A message for Chunda Lal."

"Very good."

Almost holding my breath, so intense was my excitement, I waited whilst Miguel went to bring the Hindu. Suddenly a new voice spoke — that of the Hindu.

"Chunda Lal speaks," it said.

I clenched by teeth; I knew that I must not miss a syllable.

"Scorpion" replied... in voluble *Hindustani* — a language of which I know less than a dozen words!

CHAPTER II
CONCERNING THE GRAND DUKE

Although I had met with an unforeseen check, I had nevertheless learned three things. I had learned that Miguel the quadroon was possibly in league with the Hindu; that the Hindu was called Chunda Lal; and that Chunda Lal received messages, probably instructions, from a third party who announced his presence by the word *"Scorpion."*

One of my fellows, of course, had been in the cafe all the evening, and from him I obtained confirmation of the fact that it had been the Hindu who had been summoned to the telephone and whom I had heard speaking. Instant upon the man at the cafe replacing the telephone and disconnecting, I called up the exchange. They had been warned and were in readiness.

"From what subscriber did that call come?" I demanded.

Alas! another check awaited me. It had originated in a public call office, and "Scorpion" was untraceable by this means!

Despair is not permitted by the traditions of the Service de Surete. Therefore I returned to my flat and recorded the facts of the matter thus far established. I perceived that I had to deal, not with a designing woman, but with some shadowy being of whom she was an instrument. The anomaly of her life was in a measure explained. She sojourned in Paris for a purpose — a mysterious purpose which was concerned (I could not doubt it) with the Grand Duke Ivan. This was not an amorous but a political intrigue.

I communicated, at a late hour, with the senior of the three men watching the Grand Duke. The Grand Duke that evening had sent a handsome piece of jewellery purchased in Rue de la Paix to the dancer. It had been returned.

In the morning I met with the good Casimir at his favorite cafe. He had just discovered that Zara el-Khala drove daily to the Bois de Boulogne, alone, and that afternoon the Grand Duke had determined to accost her during her solitary walk. I prepared myself for this event. Arrayed in a workman's blouse and having a modest luncheon and a small bottle of wine in a basket, I concealed myself in that part of the Bois which was the favourite recreation ground of the dancer, and awaited her appearance.

The Grand Duke appeared first upon the scene, accompanied by Casimir. The latter pointed out to him a path through the trees along which Zara el-Khala habitually strolled and showed him the point at which she usually rejoined the Hindu who followed along the road with the car. They retired. I seated myself beneath a tree from whence I could watch the path and the road and began to partake of the repast which I had brought with me.

At about three o'clock the dancer's car appeared, and the girl, veiled as usual, stepped out, and having exchanged a few words with the Indian, began to walk slowly towards me, sometimes pausing to watch a bird in the boughs above her and sometimes to examine some wild plant growing beside the way. I ate cheese from the point of a clasp-knife and drank wine out of the bottle.

Suddenly she saw me.

She had cast her veil aside in order to enjoy the cool and fragrant air, and as she stopped and regarded me doubtfully where I sat, I saw her beautiful face, undefiled, now, by make-up and unspoiled by the presence of garish Eastern ornaments. *Nom d'un nom!* but she was truly a lovely woman! My heart went out in sympathy to the poor Grand Duke. Had I received such a mark of favour from her as he had received, and had I then been scorned as now she scorned him, I should have been desperate indeed.

Coming around a bend in the path, then, she stood only a few paces away, looking at me. I touched the peak of my cap.

"Good-day, mademoiselle," I said. "The weather is very beautiful."

"Good-day," she replied.

I continued to eat cheese, and reassured she walked on past me. Twenty yards beyond, the Grand Duke was waiting. As I laid down my knife upon the paper which had been wrapped around the bread and cheese, and raised the bottle to my lips, the enamoured nobleman stepped out from the trees and bowed low before Zara el-Khala.

She started back from him — a movement of inimitable grace, like that of a startled gazelle. And even before I had time to get upon my feet she had raised a little silver whistle to her lips and blown a short shrill note.

The Grand Duke, endeavouring to seize her hand, was pouring out voluble expressions of adoration in execrable French, and Zara el-Khala was retreating step by step. She had quickly thrown the veil about her again. I heard the pad of swiftly running feet. If I was to intervene before the arrival of the Hindu, I must act rapidly. I raced along the path and thrust myself between the Grand Duke and the girl.

"Mademoiselle," I said, "is this gentleman annoying you?"

"How dare you, low pig!" cried the Grand Duke, and with a sweep of his powerful arm he hurled me aside.

"Thank you," replied Zara el-Khala with great composure. "But my servant is here."

As I turned, Chunda Lal hurled himself upon the Grand Duke from behind. I had never seen an expression in a man's eyes like that in the eyes of the Hindu at this moment. They blazed like the eyes of a tiger, and his teeth were bared in a savage grin which I cannot hope to describe. His lean body seemed to shoot through the air, and he descended upon his burly adversary as a jungle beast falls upon its prey. Those long brown fingers clasping his neck, the Grand Duke fell forward upon his face.

"Chunda Lal!" said the dancer.

Kneeling, his right knee thrust between the shoulder blades of the prostrate man, the Hindu looked up — and I read murder in those glaring eyes. That he was an accomplished wrestler — or perhaps a strangler — I divined from the helplessness of the Grand Duke, who lay inert, robbed of every power except that of his tongue. He was swearing savagely.

"Chunda Lal!" said Zara el-Khala again. The Hindu shifted his grip from the neck to the arms of the Grand Duke. He pinioned him as is done in *jiu-jitsu* and forced him to stand upright. It was a curious spectacle — the impotency of this burly nobleman in the hands of his slight adversary. As they swayed to their feet, I thought I saw the glint of metal in the right hand of the Indian, but I could not be sure, for my attention was diverted. At this moment Casimir appeared upon the scene, looking very frightened.

Suddenly releasing his hold altogether, the Hindu glaring into the empurpled face of the Grand Duke, shot out one arm and pointed with a quivering finger along the path.

"Go!" he said.

The Grand Duke clenched his fists, looked from face to face as if calculating his chances, then shrugged his shoulders, very deliberately wiped his neck and wrists, where the Indian had held him, with a large silk handkerchief and threw the handkerchief on the ground. I saw a speck of blood upon the silk. Without another glance he walked away, Casimir following sheepishly. It is needless, perhaps, to add that Casimir had not recognized me.

I turned to the dancer, touching the peak of my cap.

"Can I be of any assistance to mademoiselle?" I asked.

"Thank you — no," she replied.

She placed five francs in my hand and set off rapidly through the trees in the direction of the road, her bloodthirsty but faithful attendant at her heels!

I stood scratching my head and looking after her.

That afternoon I posted a man acquainted with Hindustani to tap any message which might be sent to or from the cafe used by Chunda Lal. I learned that the Grand Duke had taken a stage box at the Montmartre theatre at which the dancer was appearing, and I decided that I would be present also.

A great surprise was in store for me.

Zara el-Khala had at this time established a reputation which extended beyond those circles from which the regular patrons of this establishment were exclusively drawn and which had begun to penetrate to all parts of Paris. You will remember that it was the extraordinary circumstance of her remaining at this obscure place of entertainment so long which had first interested me in the lady. I had learned that she had rejected a number of professional offers, and, as I have already stated, I had assured myself of this unusual attitude by presenting the card of a well-known Paris agency — and being refused admittance.

Now, as I leaned upon the rail at the back of the auditorium and the time for the dancer's appearance grew near, I could not fail to observe that there was a sprinkling of evening-dress in the stalls and that the two boxes already occupied boasted the presence of parties of well-known men of fashion. Then the Grand Duke entered as a troupe of acrobats finished their performance. Zara el-Khala was next upon the programme. I glanced at the Grand Duke and thought that he looked pale and unwell.

The tableau curtain fell and the manager appeared behind the footlights.

He, also, seemed to be much perturbed.

"Ladies and gentlemen," he said, "I greatly regret to announce that Mlle. Zara el-Kahla is indisposed and unable to appear. We have succeeded in obtaining the services — —"

Of whom he had succeeded in obtaining the services I never heard, for the rougher section of the audience rose at him like a menacing wave! They had come to see the Egyptian dancer and they would have their money back! It was a swindle; they would smash the theatre!

If one had doubted the great and growing popularity of Zara el-Kahla, this demonstration must have proved convincing. Over the heads of the excited audience, I saw the Grand Duke rise as if to retire. The other box parties were also standing up and talking angrily.

"Why was it not announced outside the theatre?" someone shouted. "We did not know until twenty minutes ago!" cried the manager in accents of despair.

I hurried from the theatre and took a taxicab to the hotel of the dancer. Running into the hall, I thrust a card in the hand of a concierge who stood there.

"Announce to Mlle. Zara el-Khala that I must see her at once," I said.

The man smiled and returned the card to me.

"Mlle. Zara el-Khala left Paris at seven o'clock, monsieur!"

"What! I cried — left Paris!"

"But certainly. Her baskets were taken to the Gare du Nord an hour earlier by her servant and she went off by the seven-fifty rapid for Calais. The theatre people were here asking for her an hour ago."

I hurried to my office to obtain the latest reports of my men, I had lost touch with them, you understand, during the latter part of the afternoon and evening. I found there the utmost confusion. They had been seeking me all over Paris to inform me that Zara el-Khala had left. Two men had followed her and had telephoned from Calais for instructions. She had crossed by the night mail for Dover. It was already too late to instruct the English police.

For a few hours I had relaxed my usual vigilance — and this was the result. What could I do? Zara el-Khala had committed no crime, but her sudden flight — for it looked like flight you will agree — was highly suspicious. And as I sat there in my office filled with all sorts of misgivings, in ran one of the men engaged in watching the Grand Duke.

The Grand Duke had been seized with illness as he left his box in the Montmartre theatre and had died before his car could reach the hotel!

CHAPTER III
A STRANGE QUESTION

A conviction burst upon my mind that a frightful crime had been committed. By whom and for what purpose I knew not. I hastened to the hotel of the Grand Duke. Tremendous excitement prevailed there, of course. There is no more certain way for a great personage to court publicity than to travel incognito. Everywhere that "M. de Stahler" had appeared all Paris had cried, "There goes the Grand Duke Ivan!" And now as I entered the hotel, press, police and public were demanding: "Is it true that the Grand Duke is dead?" Just emerging from the lift I saw Casimir. *In propria persona* — as M. Max — he failed to recognize me.

"My good man," I said — "are you a member of the suite of the late Grand Duke?"

"I am, or was, the valet of M. de Stahler, monsieur," he replied.

I showed him my card.

"To me 'M. de Stahler' is the Grand Duke Ivan. What other servants had he with him?" I asked, although I knew very well.

"None, monsieur."

"Where and when was he taken ill?"

"At the Theatre Coquerico. Montmartre, at about a quarter past ten o'clock to-night."

"Who was with him?"

"No one, monsieur. His Highness was alone in a box. I had instructions to call with the car at eleven o'clock."

"Well?"

"The theatre management telephoned at a quarter past ten to say that His Highness had been taken ill and that a physician had been sent for. I went in the car at once and found him lying in one of the dressing-rooms to which he had been carried. A medical man was in attendance. The Grand Duke was unconscious. We moved him to the car ———"

"We?"

"The doctor, the theatre manager, and myself. The Grand Duke was then alive, the physician declared, although he seemed to me to be already dead. But just before we reached the hotel, the physician, who was watching His Highness anxiously, cried, 'Ah,*mon Dieu!* It is finished. What a catastrophe!'"

"He was dead?"

"He was dead, monsieur."

"Who has seen him?"

"They have telephoned for half the doctors in Paris, monsieur, but it is too late."

He was affected, the good Casimir. Tears welled up in his eyes. I mounted in the lift to the apartment in which the Grand Duke lay. Three doctors were there, one of them being he of whom Casimir had spoken. Consternation was written on every face.

"It was his heart," I was assured by the doctor who had been summoned to the theatre. "We shall find that he suffered from heart trouble."

They were all agreed upon the point.

"He must have sustained a great emotional shock," said another.

"You are convinced that there was no foul play, gentlemen?" I asked.

They were quite unanimous on the point.

"Did the Grand Duke make any statement at the time of the seizure which would confirm the theory of a heart attack?"

No. He had fallen down unconscious outside the door of his box, and from this unconsciousness he had never recovered. (Depositions of witnesses, medical evidence and other documents are available for the guidance of whoever may care to see them, but, as is well known, the death of the Grand Duke was ascribed to natural causes and it seemed as though my trouble would after all prove to be in vain.) Let us see what happened.

Leaving the hotel, on the night of the Grand Duke's death, I joined the man who was watching the cafe telephone.

There had been a message during the course of the evening, but it had been for a Greek cigarette-maker and it referred to the theft of several bales of Turkish tobacco — useful information, of minor kind, but of little interest to me. I knew that it would be useless to question the man Miguel, although I strongly suspected him of being a member of "The Scorpion's" organization. Any patron of the establishment enjoyed the privilege of receiving private telephone calls at the cafe on payment of a small fee.

A man of less experience in obscure criminology might now have assumed that he had been misled by a series of striking coincidences. Remember, there was not a shadow of doubt in the minds of the medical experts that the Grand Duke had died from syncope. His own professional advisor had sent written testimony to show that there was hereditary heart trouble, although not of a character calculated to lead to a fatal termination except under extraordinary circumstances. His own Government, which had every reason to suspect that the Grand Duke's assassination might be attempted, was satisfied. *Eh bien!* I was not.

I cross-examined the manager of the Theatre Coquerico. He admitted that Mlle. Zara el-Khala had been a mystery throughout her engagement. Neither he nor anyone else connected with the house had ever entered her dressing-room or held any conversation with her, whatever, except the stage-manager and the musical director. These had spoken to her about her music and about lighting and other stage effects. She spoke perfect French.

Such a state of affairs was almost incredible, but was explained by the fact that the dancer, at a most modest salary, had doubled the takings of the theatre in a few days and had attracted capacity business throughout the remainder of her engagement. She had written from Marseilles, enclosing press notices and other usual matter and had been booked direct for one week. She had remained for two months, and might have remained for ever, the poor manager assured me, at five times the salary!

A curious fact now came to light. In all her photographs Zara el-Khala appeared veiled, in the Eastern manner; that is to say, she wore a white silk *yashmak* which concealed all her face except her magnificent eyes! On the stage the veil was discarded; in the photographs it was always present.

And the famous picture which she had sent to the Grand Duke? He had destroyed it, in a fit of passion, on returning from the Bois de Boulogne after his encounter with Chunda Lal!

It is Fate after all — Kismet — and not the wit of man which leads to the apprehension of really great criminals — a tireless Fate which dogs their footsteps, a remorseless Fate from which they fly in vain. Long after the funeral of the Grand Duke, and at a time when I had almost forgotten Zara el-Khala, I found myself one evening at the opera with a distinguished French scientist and he chanced to refer to the premature death (which had occurred a few months earlier) of Henrik Ericksen, the Norwegian.

"A very great loss to the century, M. Max," he said. "Ericksen was as eminent in electrical science as the Grand Duke Ivan was eminent in the science of war. Both were stricken down in the prime of life — and under almost identical circumstances."

"That is true," I said thoughtfully.

"It would almost seem," he continued, "as if Nature had determined to foil any further attempts to rifle her secrets and Heaven to check mankind in the making of future wars. Only three months after the Grand Duke's death, the American admiral, Mackney, died at sea — you will remember? Now, following Ericksen, Van Rembold, undoubtedly the greatest mining engineer of the century and the only man who has ever produced radium in workable quantities, is seized with illness at a friend's house and expires even before medical aid can be summoned."

"It is very strange.'

"It is uncanny."

"Were you personally acquainted with the late Van Rembold?" I asked.

"I knew him intimately — a man of unusual charm, M. Max; and I have particular reason to remember his death, for I actually met him and spoke to him less than an hour before he died. We only exchanged a few words — we met on the street; but I shall never forget the subject of our chat."

"How is that?" I asked.

"Well, I presume Van Rembold's question was prompted by his knowledge of the fact that I had studied such subjects at one time; but he asked me if I knew of any race or sect in Africa or Asia who worshipped scorpions."

"*Scorpions!*" I cried. "*Ah, mon Dieu!* monsieur say it again — *scorpions?*"

"But yes, certainly. Does it surprise you?"

"Did it not surprise *you?*"

"Undoubtedly. I could not imagine what had occurred to account for his asking so strange a question. I replied that I knew of no such sect, and Van Rembold immediately changed the subject, nor did he revert to it. So that I never learned why he had made that singular inquiry."

You can imagine that this conversation afforded me much food for reflection. Whilst I could think of no reason why anyone should plot to assassinate Grand Dukes, admirals and mining engineers, the circumstances of the several cases were undoubtedly similar in a number of respects. But it was the remarkable question asked by Van Rembold which particularly aroused my interest.

Of course it might prove to be nothing more than a coincidence, but when one comes to consider how rarely the word "scorpion" is used, outside those in which these insects abound, it appears to be something more. Van Rembold, then, had had some occasion to feel curious about the scorpions; the name "Scorpion" was associated with the Hindu follower of Zara el-Khala; and she was who had brought the Grand Duke to Paris, where he had died.

Oh! it was a very fragile thread, but by following such a thread as this we are sometimes led to the heart of a labyrinth.

Beyond wondering if some sinister chain bound together this series of apparently natural deaths I might have made no move in the matter, but something occurred which spurred me to action. Sir Frank Narcombe, the great English surgeon, collapsed in the foyer of a London theatre and died shortly afterwards. Here again I perceived a case of a notable man succumbing unexpectedly in a public place — a case parallel to that of the Grand Duke, of Ericksen, of Van Rembold! it seemed as though some strange epidemic had attacked men of science — yes! they were all men of science, even including the Grand Duke, who was said to be the most scientific soldier in Europe, and the admiral, who had perfected the science of submarine warfare.

"The Scorpion!"...that name haunted me persistently. So much so that at last I determined to find out for myself if Sir Frank Narcombe had ever spoken about a scorpion or if there was any evidence to show that he had been interested in the subject.

I could not fail to remember, too, that Zara el-Khala had last been reported as crossing to England.

CHAPTER IV
THE FIGHT IN THE CAFE

New Scotland Yard had been advised that any reference to a scorpion, in whatever form it occurred, should be noted and followed up, but nothing had resulted and as a matter of fact I was not surprised in the least. All that I had learned — and this was little enough — I had learned more or less by accident. But I came to the conclusion that a visit to London might be advisable.

I had caused a watch to be kept upon the man Miguel, whose establishment seemed to be a recognized resort of shady characters. I had no absolute proof, remember, that he knew anything of the private affairs of the Hindu, and no further reference to a scorpion had been made by anyone using the cafe telephone. Nevertheless I determined to give him a courtesy call before leaving for London...and to this determination I cannot doubt that once again I was led by providence.

Attired in a manner calculated to enable me to pass unnoticed among the patrons of the establishment, I entered the place and ordered cognac. Miguel having placed it before me, I lighted a cigarette and surveyed my surroundings.

Eight or nine men were in the cafe, and two women. Four of the men were playing cards at a corner table, and the others were distributed about the place, drinking and smoking. The women, who were flashily dressed but who belonged to that order of society which breeds the Apache, were deep in conversation with a handsome Algerian. I recognized only one face in the cafe — that of a dangerous character, Jean Sach, who had narrowly escaped the electric chair in the United States and who was well known to the Bureau. He was smiling at one of the two women — the woman to whom the Algerian seemed to be more particularly addressing himself.

Another there was in the cafe who interested me as a student of physiognomy — a dark, bearded man, one of the card-players. His face was disfigured by a purple scar extending from his brow to the left corner of his mouth, which it had drawn up into a permanent snarl, so that he resembled an enraged and dangerous wild animal. Mentally I classified this person as "Le Balafre."

I had just made up my mind to depart when the man Sach arose, crossed the cafe and seated himself insolently between the Algerian and the woman to whom the latter was talking. Turning his back upon the brown man, he addressed some remark to the woman, at the same time leering in her face.

Women of this class are difficult, you understand? Sach received from the lady a violent blow upon the face which rolled him on the floor! As he fell, the Algerian sprang up and drew a knife. Sach rolled away from him and also reached for the knife which he carried in a hip-pocket.

Before he could draw it, Miguel, the quadroon proprietor, threw himself upon him and tried to pitch him into the street. But Sach, although a small man, was both agile and ferocious. He twisted out of the grasp of the huge quadroon and turned, raising the knife. As he did so, the Algerian deftly kicked it from his grasp and left Sach to face Miguel unarmed. Screaming with rage, he sprang at Miguel's throat, and the tow fell writhing upon the floor.

There could only be one end to such a struggle, of course, as the Algerian recognized by replacing his knife in his pocket and resuming his seat. Miguel obtained a firm hold upon Sacah and raised him bodily above his head, as one has seen a professional weight-lifter raise a heavy dumb-bell. Thus he carried him, kicking and foaming at the mouth with passion, to the open door. From the step he threw him into the middle of the street.

At this moment I observed something glittering upon the floor close to the chair occupied by the Algerian. Standing up — for I had determined to depart — I crossed in that direction, stooped and picked up this object which glittered. As my fingers touched it, so did my heart give a great leap.

The object was a *golden scorpion!*

Forgetful of my dangerous surroundings I stood looking at the golden ornament in my hand…when suddenly and violently it was snatched from me! The Algerian, his brown face convulsed with rage, confronted me.

"Where did you find that charm?" he cried. "It belongs to me."

"Very well," I replied — "you have it."

He glared at me with a ferocity which the incident scarcely seemed to merit and exchanged a significant glance with someone who had approached and who now stood behind me. Turning, I met a second black gaze — that of the quadroon who having restored order had returned from the cafe door and now stood regarding me. "Did you find it on the floor?" asked Miguel suspiciously.

"I did."

He turned to the Algerian.

"It fell when you kicked the knife from the hand of that pig," he said. "You should be more careful."

Again they exchanged significant glances, but the Algerian resumed his seat and Miguel went behind the counter. I left the cafe conscious of the fact that black looks pursued me.

The night was very dark, and as I came out on to the pavement someone touched me on the arm. I turned in a flash.

"Walk on, friend," said the voice of Jean Sach. "What was it that you picked up from the floor?"

"A golden scorpion," I answered quickly.

"Ah!" he whispered — "I thought so! It is enough. They shall pay for what they have done to me — those two. Hurry, friend, as I do."

Before I could say another word or strive to detain him, he turned and ran off along a narrow courtway which at this point branched from the street.

I stood for a moment, nonplussed, staring after him. By good fortune I had learned more in ten minutes than by the exercise of all my ingenuity and the resources of the Service I could have learned in ten months! *Par al barbe du prophete* the Kismet which dogs the footsteps of malefactors assisted me!

Recollecting the advice of Jean Sach, I set off at a brisk pace along the street, which was dark and deserted and which passed through a district marked red on the Paris crimes-map. Arriving at the corner, above which projected a lamp, I paused and glanced back into the darkness. I could see no one, but I thought I could detect the sound of stealthy footsteps following me.

The suspicion was enough. I quickened my pace, anxious to reach the crowded boulevard upon which this second street opened. I reached it unmolested, but intending to throw any pursuer off the track, I dodged and doubled repeatedly on the way to my flat and arrived there about midnight, convinced that I had eluded pursuit — if indeed I had been pursued.

All my arrangements were made for leaving Paris, and now I telephoned to the assistant on duty in my office, instructing him to take certain steps in regard to the proprietor of the cafe and the Algerian and to find the hiding-place of the man Jean-Sach. I counted it more than ever important that I should go to London at once.

In this belief I was confirmed at the very moment that I boarded the Channel steamer at Boulogne: for as I stepped upon the deck I found myself face to face with a man who was leaning upon the rail and apparently watching the passengers coming on board. He was a man of heavy build, dark and bearded, and his face was strangely familiar.

Turning, as I lighted a cigarette, I glanced back at him in order to obtain a view of his profile. I knew him instantly — for now the scar was visible. It was "Le Balafre" who had been playing cards in Miguel's cafe on the previous night!

I have sometimes been criticised, especially by my English confreres, for my faith in disguise. I have been told that no disguise is impenetrable to the trained eye. I reply that there are many disguises but few trained eyes! To my faith in disguise I owed the knowledge that a golden scorpion was the token of some sort of gang, society, or criminal group, and to this same faith which an English inspector of police once assured me to be a misplaced one I owed, on boarding the steamer, my escape from detection by this big bearded fellow who was possibly looking out for me!

Yet, I began to wonder if after all I had escaped the shadowy pursuer whose presence I had suspected in the dark street outside the cafe or if he had tracked me and learned my real identity. In any event, the roles were about to be reversed! "Le Balafre" at Folkestone took a seat in a third-class carriage of the London train. I took one in the next compartment.

Arrived at Charing Cross, he stood for a time in the booking-hall, glanced at his watch, and then took up the handbag which he carried and walked out into the station yard. I walked out also.

"Le Balafre" accosted a cabman; and as he did so I passed close behind him and overheard a part of the conversation.

"...Bow Road Station East! It's too far. What?"

I glanced back. The bearded man was holding up a note — a pound note apparently. I saw the cabman nod. Without an instant's delay I rushed up to another cabman who had just discharged a passenger.

"To Bow Road Station East!" I said to the man. "Double fare if you are quick!"

It would be a close race. But I counted on the aid of that Fate which dogs the steps of wrong-doers! My cab was off first and the driver had every reason for hurrying. From the moment that we turned out into the Strand until we arrived at our destination I saw no more of "Le Balafre." My extensive baggage I must hope to recover later.

At Bow Road Station I discovered a telephone box in a dark corner which commanded a view of the street. I entered this box and waited. It was important that I should remain invisible. Unless my bearded friend had been unusually fortunate he could not well have arrived before me.

As it chanced I had nearly six minutes to wait. Then, not ten yards away, I saw "Le Balafre" arrive and dismiss the cabman outside the station.

There was nothing furtive in his manner; he was evidently satisfied that no one pursued him; and he stood in the station entrance almost outside my box and lighted a cigar!

Placing his bag upon the floor, he lingered, looking to left and right, when suddenly a big closed car painted dull yellow drew up beside the pavement. It was driven by a brown-faced chauffeur whose nationality I found difficulty in placing, for he wore large goggles. But before I could determine upon my plan of action, "Le Balafre" crossed the pavement and entered the car — and the car glided smoothly away, going East. A passing lorry obstructed my view and I even failed to obtain a glimpse of the number on the plate.

But I had seen something which had repaid me for my trouble. As the man of the scar had walked up to the car, had exhibited to the brown-skinned chauffeur some object which he held in the palm of his hand...an object which glittered like gold!

II
"LE BALAFRE"

CHAPTER I
I BECOME CHARLES MALET

Behold me established in rooms in Battersea and living retired during the day while I permitted my beard to grow. I had recognized that my mystery of "The Scorpion" was the biggest case which had ever engaged the attention of the Service de Surete, and I was prepared, if necessary, to devote my whole time for twelve months to its solution. I had placed myself in touch with Paris, and had had certain papers and licenses forwarded to me. A daily bulletin reached me, and one of these bulletins was sensational.

The body of Jean Sach had been recovered from the Seine. The man had been stabbed to the heart. Surveillance of Miguel and his associates continued unceasingly, but I had directed that no raids or arrests were to be made without direct orders from me.

I was now possessed of a French motor license and also that of a Paris taxi-driver, together with all the other documents necessary to establish the identity of one Charles Malet. Everything was in order. I presented myself — now handsomely bearded — at New Scotland Yard and applied for a license. The "knowledge of London" and other tests I passed successfully and emerged a fully-fledged cabman!

Already I had opened negotiations for the purchase of a dilapidated but seviceable cab which belonged to a small proprietor who had obtained a car of more up-to-date pattern to replace this obsolete one. I completed these negotiations by paying down a certain sum and arranged to garage my cab in the disused stable of a house near my rooms in Battersea.

Thus I now found myself in a position to appear anywhere at any time without exciting suspicion, enabled swiftly to proceed from point to point and to pursue anyone either walking or driving whom it might please me to pursue. It was a *modus operandi* which had served me well in Paris and which had led to one of my biggest successes (the capture of the French desperado known as "Mr. Q.") in New York.

I had obtained, *via* Paris, particulars of the recent death of Sir Frank Narcombe, and the circumstances attendant upon his end were so similar to those which had characterized the fate of the Grand Duke, of Van Rembold and the others, that I could not for a moment believe them to be due to mere coincidence. Acting upon my advice Paris advised Scotland Yard to press for a *post mortem* examination of the body, but the influence of Sir Frank's family was exercised to prevent this being carried out — and exercised successfully.

Meanwhile, I hovered around the houses, flats, clubs and offices of everyone who had been associated with the late surgeon, noting to what addresses they directed me to drive and who lived at those address. In this way I obtained evidence sufficient to secure three judicial separations, but not a single clue leading to "The Scorpion"! No matter.

At every available opportunity I haunted the East-End streets, hoping for a glimpse of the big car and the brown-skinned chauffeur or of my scarred man from Paris. I frequented all sorts of public bars and eating-houses used by foreign and Asiatics. By day and by night I roamed about the dismal thoroughfares of that depressing district, usually with my flag down to imply that I was engaged.

Such diligence never goes long unrewarded. One evening, having discharged a passenger, a mercantile officer, at the East India Docks, as I was drifting, watchfully, back through Limehouse, I saw a large car pull up just ahead of me in the dark. A man got out and the car was driven off.

Two courses presented themselves. I was not sure that this was the car for which I sought, but it strangely resembled it. Should I follow the car or the man? A rapid decision was called for. I followed the man.

That I had not been mistaken in the identity of the car shortly appeared. The man took out a cigar and standing on the corner opposite the Town Hall, lighted it. I was close to him at the time, and by the light of the match, which he sheltered with his hands, I saw the scarred and bearded face! *Triomphe!* it was he!

Having lighted his cigar, he crossed the road and entered the saloon of a neighbourhood public-house. Locking my cab I, also, entered that saloon. I ordered a glass of bitter beer and glanced around at the object of my interest. He had obtained a glass of brandy and was contorting his hideous face as he sipped the beverage. I laughed.

"Have they tried to poison you, mister!" I said.

"Ah,*pardieu!* poison — yes!" he replied.

"You want to have it out of a bottle," I continued confidentially —

"Martell's Three Stars."

He stared at me uncomprehendingly.

"I don't know," he said haltingly. "I have very little English."

"Oh, that's it!" I cried, speaking French with a barbarous accent.

"You only speak French?"

"Yes, yes," he replied eagerly. "It is so difficult to make oneself understood. This spirit is not cognac, it is some kind of petrol!"

Finishing my bitter, I ordered two glasses of good brandy and placed one before "Le Balafre."

"Try that," I said, continuing to speak in French, "You will find it is better."

He sipped from his glass and agreed that I was right. We chatted together for ten minutes and had another drink, after which my dangerous-looking acquaintance wished me good-night and went out. The car had come from the West, and I strongly suspected that my man either lived in the neighbourhood or had come there to keep an appointment. Leaving my cab outside the public-house, I followed him on foot, down Three Colt Street to Ropemaker Street, where he turned into a narrow alley leading to the riverside. It was straight and deserted, and I dared not follow further until he had reached the corner. I heard his footsteps pass right to the end. Then the sound died away. I ran to the corner. The back of a wharf building — a high blank wall — faced a row of ramshackle tenements, some of them built of wood; but not a soul was in sight.

I reluctantly returned to the spot at which I had left the cab — and found a constable there who wanted to know what I meant by leaving a vehicle in the street unattended. I managed to enlist his sympathy by telling him that I had been in pursuit of a "fare" who had swindled me with a bad half-crown. The ruse succeeded.

"Which street did he go down, mate?" asked the constable.

I described the street and described the scarred man. The constable shook his head.

"Sounds like one o' them foreign sailormen," he said. "But I don't know what he can have gone down there for. It's nearly all Chinese, that part."

His words came as a revelation; they changed the whole complexion of the case. It dawned upon me even as he spoke the word "Chinese" that the golden scorpion which I had seen in the Paris cafe was of Chinese workmanship! I started my engine and drove slowly to that street in which I had lost the track of "Le Balafre." I turned the cab so that I should be ready to drive off at a moment's notice, and sat there wondering what my next move should be. How long I had been there I cannot say, when suddenly it began to rain in torrents.

What I might have done or what I had hoped to do is of no importance; for as I sat there staring out at the dismal rain-swept street, a man came along, saw the head-lamps of the cab and stopped, peering in my direction. Evidently perceiving that I drove a cab and not a private car, he came towards me.

"Are you disengaged?" he asked.

Whether it was that I sympathized with him — he had no topcoat or umbrella — or whether I was guided by Fate I know not, but as he spoke I determined to give up my dreary vigil for that night. *Pardieu!* but certainly it was Fate again!

"Well, I suppose I am, sir," I said, and asked him where he wanted to go.

He gave an address not five hundred yards from my own rooms! I thought this so curious that I hesitated no longer.

"Jump in," I said; and still seeking in my mind for a link between the scorpion case and China, I drove off, and in less than half an hour, for the streets were nearly empty, arrived at my destination.

The passenger, whose name was Dr. Keppel Stuart, very kindly suggested a glass of hot grog, and I did not refuse his proferred hospitality. When I came out of his house again, the rain had almost ceased, and just as I stooped to crank the car I thought I saw a shadowy figure moving near the end of a lane which led to the tradesmen's entrance of Dr. Stuart's house. A sudden suspicion laid hold upon me — a horrible doubt.

Having driven some twenty yards along the road, I leaned from my seat and looked back. A big man wearing a black waterproof overall was standing looking after me!

Remembering how cleverly I had been trailed from Miguel's cafe to my flat, in Paris (for I no longer doubted that someone had followed me on that occasion), I now perceived that I might again be the object of the same expert's attention. Stopping my engine half-way along the next road, I jumped out and ran back, hiding in the bushes which grew beside the gate of a large empty house. I had only a few seconds to wait.

A big closed car, running almost silently, passed before me...and "Le Balafre" was leaning out of the window!

At last I saw my chance of finding the headquarters of "The Scorpion." Alas! The man of the scar was as swift to recognize that possibility as I. A moment after he had passed my stationary cab, and found it to be deserted, his big car was off like the wind, and even before I could step out from the bushes the roar of the powerful engine was growing dim in the distance!

I was detected. I had to deal with dangerously clever people.

CHAPTER II
BAITING THE TRAP

The following morning I spent at home, in my modest rooms, reviewing my position and endeavouring to adjust my plans in accordance with the latest development. "The Scorpion" had scored a point. What had aroused the suspicions "Le Balafre," I knew not; but I was inclined to think that he had been looking from some window or peep-hole in the narrow street with the wooden houses when I had, injudiciously, followed him there.

On the other hand, the leakage might be in Paris — or in my correspondence system. The man of the scar might have been looking for me as I was looking for him. That he was looking for someone on the cross-channel boat I had not doubted.

He was aware, then that Charles Malet, cabman, was watching him. But was he aware that Charles Malet was Gaston Max? And did he know where I lived? Also — did he perchance think that my meeting with Dr. Stuart in Limehouse had been prearranged? Clearly he had seen Dr. Stuart enter my cab, for he had pursued us to Battersea.

This course of reflection presently led me to a plan. It was a dangerous plan, but I doubted if I should ever find myself in greater danger than I was already. *Nom d'un nom!* I had not forgotten the poor Jean Sach!

That night, well knowing that I carried my life in my hands, I drove again to Limehouse Town Hall, and again leaving my cab outside went into the bar where I had preciously me "Le Balafre." If I had doubted that my movements were watched I must now have had such doubts dispelled; for two minutes later the man with the scar came in and greeted me affably!

I had learned something else. He did not know that I had recognized him as the person who had tracked me to Dr. Stuart's house!

He invited me to drink with him, and I did so. As we raised our glasses I made a move. Looking all about me suspiciously:

"Am I right in supposing that you have business in this part of London?" I asked.

"Yes," he replied "My affairs bring me here sometimes."

"You are well acquainted with the neighbourhood?"

"Fairly well. But actually of course I am a stranger to London."

I tapped him confidentially upon the breast.

"Take my advice, as a friend," I said, "and visit these parts as rarely as possible."

"Why do you say that?"

"It is dangerous. From the friendly manner in which you entered into conversation with me, I perceived that you were of a genial and unsuspicious nature. Very well. I warn you. Last night I was followed from a certain street not far from here to the house of a medical man who is a specialist in certain kinds of criminology, you understand."

He stared at me very hard, his teeth bared by that fearful snarl. "You are a strange cabman."

"Perhaps I am. No matter. Take my advice. I have things written here" — I tapped the breast of my tunic — "which will astonish all the world shortly. I tell you, my friend, my fortune is made."

I finished my drink and ordered another for myself and one for my acquaintance. He was watching me doubtfully. Taking up my replenished glass, I emptied it at a draught and ordered a third. I leaned over towards the scarred man, resting my hand heavily upon his shoulder.

"Five thousand pounds," I whispered thickly, "has been offered for the information which I have here in my pocket. It is not yet complete, you understand, and because they may murder me before I obtain the rest of the facts, do you know what I am going to do with this?"

Again I tapped my tunic pocket. "Le Balafre" frowned perplexedly.

"I don't even know what you are talking about, my friend," he replied.

"*I* know what I am talking about," I assured him, speaking more and more huskily. "Listen, then: I am going to take all my notes to my friend, the doctor, and leave them with him, sealed — sealed, you follow me? If I do not come back for them, In a week, shall we say? — he sends them to the police. *I* do not profit, you think? No.*morbleu!* but there are some who hang!"

Emptying my third glass, I ordered a fourth and one for my companion.

He checked me.

"No more for me, thank you," he said. "I have — business to attend to. I will wish you good-night."

"Good-night!" I cried boisterously — "good-night, friend! take heed of my good advice!"

As he went out, the barman brought me my fourth glass of cognac, staring at me doubtfully. Our conversation had been conducted in French, but the tone of my voice had attracted attention.

"Had about enough, ain't you, mate?" he said. "Your ugly pal jibbed!"

"Quite enough!" I replied, in English now of course. "But I've had a stroke of luck to-night and I feel happy. Have one with me. This is a final."

On going out into the street I looked cautiously about me, for I did not expect to reach the house of Dr. Stuart unmolested. I credited "Le Balafre" with sufficient acumen to distrust the genuineness of my intoxication, even if he was unaware of my real identity. I never make the mistake of underestimating an opponent's wit, and whilst acting on the assumption that the scarred man knew me to be forcing his hand, I recognized that whether he believed me to be drunk or sober, Gaston Mas or another, his line of conduct must be the same. He must take it for granted that I actually designed to lodge my notes with Dr. Stuart and endeavour to prevent me doing so.

I could detect no evidence of surveillance whatever and cranking the engine I mounted and drove off. More than once, as I passed along Commercial Road, I stopped and looked back. But so far as I could make out no one was following me. The greater part of my route lay along populous thoroughfares, and of this I was not sorry; but I did not relish the prospect of Thames Street, along which presently my course led me.

Leaving the city behind me, I turned into that thoroughfare, which at night is almost quite deserted, and there I pulled up. *Pardieu!* I was disappointed! It seemed as though my scheme had miscarried. It could not understand why I had been permitted to go unmolested, and

I intended to walk back to the corner for a final survey before continuing my journey. This survey was never made.

As I stopped the cab and prepared to descend, a faint — a very faint — sound almost in my ear, set me keenly on the alert. Just in the nick of time I ducked... as the blade of a long knife flashed past my head, ripping its way through my cloth cap!

Yes! That movement had saved my life, for otherwise the knife must have entered my shoulder — and pierced to my heart!

Someone was hidden in the cab!

He had quietly opened one of the front windows and had awaited a suitable opportunity to stab me. Now, recognizing failure, he leapt out on the near side as I lurched and stumbled from my seat, and ran off like the wind. I never so much as glimpsed him.

"Mon Dieu!" I muttered, raising my hand to my head, from which blood was trickling down my face, "the plan succeeds!"

I bound a handkerchief as tightly as possible around the wound in my scalp and put my cap on to keep the bandage in place. The wound was only a superficial one, and except for the bleeding I suffered no inconvenience from it. But I had now a legitimate reason for visiting Dr. Stuart, and as I drove on towards Battersea I was modifying my original plan in accordance with the unforeseen conditions.

It was long past Dr. Stuart's hours of consultation when I arrived at his house, and the servant showed me into a waiting-room, informing me that the doctor would join me in a few minutes. Directly she had gone out I took from the pocket of my tunic the sealed envelope which I had intended to lodge with the doctor. Pah! it was stained with blood which had trickled down from the wound in my scalp!

Actually, you will say, there was no reason why I should place a letter in the hand of Dr. Stuart; my purpose would equally well be served by *pretending* that I had done so. Ah, but I knew that I had to deal with clever people — with artists in crime — and it behooved me to be an artist also. I had good reason to know that their system of espionage was efficient; and the slipshod way is ever the wrong way.

The unpleasantly sticky letter I returned to my pocket, looking around me for some means of making up any kind of packet which could do duty as a substitute. Beyond a certain draped over a recess at one end of the waiting-room I saw a row of boxes, a box of lint and other medical paraphernalia. It was the doctor's dispensary. Perhaps I might find there an envelope.

I crossed the room and looked. Immediately around the corner, on a level with my eyes, was a packet of foolscap envelopes and a stick of black sealing-wax! *Bien!* all that I now required was a stout sheet of paper to enclose in one of those envelopes. But not a scrap of paper could I find, except the blood-stained letter in my pocket — towards which I had formed a strong antipathy. I had not even a newspaper in my possession. I thought of folding three or four envelopes, but there were only six in all, and the absence of so many might be noted.

Drawing aside a baize curtain which hung from the bottom shelf, I discovered a number of old card-board boxes. It was sufficient. With a pair of surgical scissors I cut a piece from the lid of one and thrust it into an envelope, gumming down the lapel. At a little gas jet intended for the purpose I closed both ends with wax and — singular coincidence! — finding a Chinese coin fastened to a cork lying on the shelf, my sense of humour prompted me to use it as a seal! Finally, to add to the verisimilitude of the affair I borrowed a pen which rested in a bottle of red ink and wrote upon the envelope the number: 30, that day being the thirtieth day of the month.

It was well that the artist within me had dictated this careful elaboration, as became evident a few minutes later when the doctor appeared at the head of a short flight of stairs and requested me to step up to his consulting-room. It was a small room, so that the window, over which a linen blind was drawn, occupied nearly the whole of one wall. As Dr. Stuart, having examined the cut on my scalp, descended to the dispensary for lint, the habits of a lifetime asserted themselves.

I quickly switched off the light and peeped out of the window around the edge of the blind, which I drew slightly aside. In the shadow of the wall upon the opposite side of the narrow lane a man was standing! I turned on the light again. The watcher should not be disappointed!

My skull being dressed, I broached the subject of the letter, which I said I had found in my cab after the accident which had caused the injury.

"Someone left this behind to-day, sir," I said; "perhaps the gentleman who was with me when I had the accident; and I've got no means of tracing him. He may be able to trace *me*, though, or he may advertise. It evidently contains something valuable. I wonder if you would do me a small favour? Would you mind taking charge of it for a week or so, until it is claimed?"

He asked me why I did not take it to Scotland Yard.

"Because," said I, "if the owner claims it from Scotland Yard he is less likely to be generous than if he gets it direct from me!"

"But what is the point," asked Dr. Stuart, "in leaving it here?"

I explained that if *I* kept the letter I might be suspected of an intention of stealing it, whereas directly there was any inquiry, he could certify that I had left it in his charge. He seemed to be satisfied and asked me to come into his study for a moment. The man in the lane was probably satisfied, too. I had stood three paces from the table-lamp all the time, waving the letter about as I talked, and casting a bold shadow on the linen blind!

The first thing that struck me as I entered the doctor's study was that the French windows, which opened on a sheltered lawn, were open. I acted accordingly.

"You see," said Dr. Stuart, "I am enclosing your letter in this big envelope which I am sealing."

"Yes, sir," I replied, standing at some distance from him, so that he had to speak loudly. "And would you mind addressing it to the Lost Property Office."

"Not at all," said he, and did as I suggested. "If not reclaimed within a reasonable time, it will be sent to Scotland Yard."

I edged nearer to the open window.

"If it is not reclaimed," I said loudly, "it goes to Scotland Yard — yes."

"Meanwhile," concluded the doctor, "I am locking it in this private drawer in my bureau."

"It is locked in your bureau. Very good."

CHAPTER III
DISAPPEARANCE OF CHARLES MALET

Knowing, and I knew it well, that people of "The Scorpion" were watching, I do not pretend that I felt at my ease as I drove around to the empty house in which I garaged my cab. My inquiry had entered upon another stage, and Charles Malet was about to disappear from the case. I was well aware that if he failed in his vigilance for a single moment he might well disappear from the world!

The path which led to the stables was overgrown with weeds and flanked by ragged bushes; weeds and grass sprouted between the stones paving the little yard, also, although they were withered to a great extent by the petrol recently spilled there. Having run the cab into the yard, I alighted and looked around the deserted grounds, mysterious in the moonlight. Company would have been welcome, but excepting a constable who had stopped and chatted with me on one or two evenings I always had the stables to myself at night.

I determined to run the cab into the stable and lock it up without delay, for it was palpably dangerous in the circumstances to remain longer than necessary in that lonely spot. Hurriedly I began to put out the lamps. I unlocked the stable doors and stood looking all about me again. I was dreading the ordeal of driving the cab those last ten yards into the garage, for whilst I had my back to the wilderness of bushes it would be an easy matter for anyone in hiding there to come up behind me.

Nevertheless, it had to be done. Seating myself at the wheel I drove into the narrow building, stopped the engine and peered cautiously around toward the bright square formed by the open doors. Nothing was to be seen. No shadow moved.

A magazine pistol held in my hand, I crept, step by step, along the wall until I stood just within the opening. There I stopped.

I could hear a sound of quick breathing! There was someone waiting outside!

Dropping quietly down upon the pavement, I slowly protruded my head around the angle of the brick wall at a point not four inches above the ground. I knew that whoever waited would have his eyes fixed upon the doorway at the level of a man's head.

Close to the wall, a pistol in his left hand and an upraised stand-bag in his right, stood "Le Balafre!" His eyes gleamed savagely in the light of the moon and his teeth were bared in that fearful animal snarl. But he had not seen me.

Inch by inch I thrust my pistol forward, the barrel raised sharply. I could not be sure of my aim, of course, nor had I time to judge it carefully.

I fired.

The bullet was meant for his right wrist, but it struck him in the fleshy part of his arm. Uttering a ferocious cry he leapt back, dropped his pistol — and perceiving me as I sprang to my feet, lashed at my head with the sand-bag. I raised my left arm to guard my skull and sustained the full force of the blow upon it.

I staggered back against the wall, and my own pistol was knocked from my grasp. My left arm was temporarily useless and the man of the scar was deprived of the use of his right. *Pardieu!* I had the better chance!

He hurled himself upon me.

Instantly he recovered the advantage, for he grasped me by the throat with his left hand — and, *nom d'un nom!* what a grip he had! Flat against the wall he held me, and began, his teeth bared in that fearful grin, to crush the life from me.

To such an attack there was only one counter. I kicked him savagely — and that death-grip relaxed. I writhed, twisted — and was free! As I regained my freedom I struck up at him, and by great good fortune caught him upon the point of the jaw. He staggered. I struck him over the heart, and he fell I pounced upon him, exulting, for he had sought my life and I knew no pity.

Yet I had not thought so strong a man would choke so easily, and for some moments I stood looking down at him, believing that he sought to trick me. But it was not so. His affair was finished.

I listened. The situation in which I found myself was full of difficulty. An owl screeched somewhere in the trees, but nothing else stirred. The sound of the shot had not attracted attention, apparently. I stooped and examined the garments of the man who lay at my feet.

He carried a travel coupon to Paris bearing that day's date, together with some other papers, but, although I searched all his pockets, I could find nothing of real interest, until in an inside pocket of his coat I felt some hard, irregularly shaped object. I withdrew it, and in the moonlight it lay glittering in my palm…a *golden scorpion!*

It had apparently been broken in the struggle. The tail was missing, nor could I find it: but I must confess that I did not prolong the search.

Some chance effect produced by the shadow of the moonlight, and the presence of that recently purchased ticket, gave me the idea upon which without delay I proceeded to act. Satisfying myself that there was no mark upon any of his garments by which the man could be identified, I unlocked from my wrist an identification disk which I habitually wore there, and locked it upon the wrist of the man with the scar!

Clearly, I argued, he had been detailed to dispatch me and then to leave at once for France. I would make it appear that he had succeeded.

Behold me, ten minutes later, driving slowly along a part of the Thames Embankment which I chanced to remember, a gruesome passenger riding behind me in the cab. I was reflecting as

I kept a sharp look-out for a spot which I had noted one day during my travels, how easily one could commit murder in London, when a constable ran out and intercepted me!

Mon Deiu! how my heart leapt!

"I'll trouble you for your name and number, my lad," he said.

"What for?" I asked, and remembering a rare fragment of idiom: "What's up with you?" I added.

"Your lamp's out!" he cried, "that's what's up with me!"

"Oh," said I, climbing from my seat — "very well. I'm sorry. I didn't know. But here is my license."

I handed him the little booklet and began to light my lamps, cursing myself for a dreadful artist because I had forgotten to do so.

"All right," he replied, and handed it back to me. "But how the devil you've managed to get *all* your lamps out, I can't imagine!"

"This is my first job since dusk," I explained hurrying around to the tail-light. "And *he* don't say much!" remarked the constable.

I replaced my matches in my pocket and returned to the front of the cab, making a gesture as of one raising a glass to his lips and jerking my thumb across my shoulder in the direction of my unseen fare.

"Oh, that's it!" said the constable, and moved off.

Never in my whole career have I been so glad to see the back of any man!

I drove on slowly. The point for which I was making was only some three hundred yards further along, but I had noted that the constable had walked off in the opposite direction. Therefore, arriving at my destination — a vacant wharf open to the road — I pulled up and listened.

Only the wash of the tide upon the piles of the wharf was audible, for the night was now far advanced.

I opened the door of the cab and dragged out "Le Balafre." Right and left I peered, truly like a stage villain, and then hauled my unpleasant burden along the irregularly paved path and on to the little wharf. Out in mid-stream a Thames Police patrol was passing, and I stood for a moment until the creak of the oars grew dim.

Then: there was a dull splash far below…and silence again.

Gaston Max had been consigned to a watery grave!

Returning again to the garage, I wondered very much who he had been, this one, "Le Balafre." Could it be that he was "The Scorpion"? I could not tell, but I had hopes very shortly of finding out. I had settled up my affairs with my landlady and had removed from my apartments all papers and other effects. In the garage I had placed a good suit of clothes and other necessities, and by telephone I had secured a room at a West-End hotel.

The cab returned to the stable, I locked the door, and by the light of one of the lamps, shaved off my beard and moustache. My uniform and cap I hung up on the hook where I usually left them after working hours, and changed into the suit which I had placed there in readiness. I next destroyed all evidences of identity and left the place in a neat condition. I extinguished the lamp, went out and locked the door behind me, and carrying a travelling-grip and a cane I set off for my new hotel.

Charles Malet had disappeared!

CHAPTER IV
I MEET AN OLD ACQUAINTANCE

On the corner opposite Dr. Stuart's establishment stood a house which was "to be let or sold." From the estate-agent whose name appeared upon the notice-board I obtained the keys — and had a duplicate made of that which opened the front door. It was a simple matter, and the locksmith returned both keys to me within an hour. I informed the agent that the house would not suit me.

Nevertheless, having bolted the door, in order that prospective purchasers might not surprise me, I "camped out" in an upper room all day, watching from behind the screen of trees all who came to the house of Dr. Stuart. Dusk found me still at my post, armed with a pair of good binoculars. Every patient who presented himself I scrutinized carefully, and finding as the darkness grew that it became increasingly difficult to discern the features of visitors, I descended to the front garden and resumed my watch from the lower branches of a tree which stood some twenty feet from the roadway.

At selected intervals I crept from my post and surveyed the lane upon which the window of the consulting-room opened and also the path leading to the tradesmen's entrance, from which one might look across the lawn and in at the open study windows. It was during one of these tours of inspection and whilst I was actually peering through a gap in the hedge, that I heard the telephone bell. Dr. Stuart was in the study and I heard him speaking.

I gathered that his services were required immediately at some institution in the neighbourhood. I saw him take his hat, stick and bag from the sofa and go out of the room. Then I returned to the front garden of my vacant house.

No one appeared for some time. A policeman walked slowly up the road, and flashed his lantern in at the gate of the house I had commandeered. His footsteps died away. Then, faintly, I heard the hum of a powerful motor. I held my breath. The approaching car turned into the road at a point above me to the right, came nearer... and stopped before Dr. Stuart's door.

I focussed my binoculars upon the chauffeur.

It was the brown-skinned man! *Nom d'un nom!* a *woman* was descending form the car. She was enveloped in furs and I could not see her face. She walked up the steps to the door and was admitted.

The chauffeur backed the car into the lane beside the house.

My heart beating rapidly with excitement, I crept out by the further gate of the drive, crossed the road at a point fifty yards above the house and walking very quietly came back to the tradesmen's entrance. Into its enveloping darkness I glided and on until I could peep across the lawn.

The elegant visitor, as I hoped, had been shown, not into the ordinary waiting-room but into the doctor's study. She was seated with her back to the window, talking to a grey-haired old lady — probably the doctor's housekeeper. Impatiently I waited for this old lady to depart, and the moment that she did so, the visitor stood up, turned and... it was *Zara el-Khala!*

It was only with difficulty that I restrained the cry of triumph which arose to my lips. On the instant that the study door closed, Zara el-Khala began to try a number of keys which she took from her handbag upon the various drawers of the bureau!

"So!" I said — "they are uncertain of the drawer!"

Suddenly she desisted, looking nervously at the open windows; then, crossing the room, she drew the curtains. I crept out into the road again and by the same roundabout route came back to the empty house. Feeling my way in the darkness of the shrubbery, I found the motor bicycle which I had hidden there and I wheeled it down to the further gate of the drive and waited.

I could see the doctor's door, and I saw him returning along the road. As he appeared, from somewhere — -I could not determine from where — came a strange and uncanny wailing sound, a sound that chilled me like an evil omen.

Even as it died away, and before Dr. Stuart had reached his door I knew what it portended — that horrible wail. Some one hidden I knew not where, had warned Zara el-Khala that the doctor returned! But stay! Perhaps that some one was the dark-skinned chauffeur!

How I congratulated myself upon the precautions which I had taken to escape observation. Evidently the watcher had placed himself somewhere where he could command a view of the front door and the road.

Five minutes later the girl came out, the old housekeeper accompanying her to the door, the car emerged from the lane, Zara el-Khala entered it and was driven away. I could see no one seated beside the chauffeur. I started my "Indian" and leapt in pursuit.

As I had anticipated, the route was Eastward, and I found myself traversing familiar ground. From the south-west to the east of London whirled the big car of mystery — and I was ever close behind it. Sometimes, in the crowded streets, I lost sight of my quarry for a time, but always I caught up again, and at last I found myself whirling along Commercial Road and not fifty yards behind the car.

Just by the canal bridge a drunken sailor lurched out in front of my wheel, and only by twisting perilously right into a turning called, I believe, Salmon Lane, did I avoid running him down.

Sacre nom! how I cursed him! The lane was too narrow for me to turn and I was compelled to dismount and to wheel my "Indian" back to the highroad. The yellow car had vanished, of course, but I took it for granted that it had followed the main road. At a dangerous speed, pursued by execrations from the sailor and all his friends, I set off east once more turning to the right down West India Dock Road.

Arriving at the dock, and seeing nothing ahead of me but desolation and ships' masts, I knew that that inebriated pig had spoiled everything! I could have sat down upon the dirty pavement and wept, so mortified was I! For if Zara el-Khala had secured the envelope I had missed my only chance.

However, *pardieu!* I have said that despair is not permitted by the Bureau. I rode home to my hotel, deep in reflection. Whether the girl had the envelope or not, at least she had escaped detection by the doctor; therefore if she had failed she would try again. I could sleep in peace until the morrow.

Of the following day, which I spent as I had spent the preceding one, I have nothing to record. At about the same time in the evening the yellow car again rolled into view, and on this occasion I devoted all my attention to the dark-skinned chauffeur, upon whom I directed my glasses.

As the girl alighted and spoke to him for a moment, he raised the goggles which habitually he wore and I saw his face. A theory which I had formed on the previous night proved correct. The chauffeur was the Hindu, Chunda Lal! As Zara el-Khala walked up the steps he backed the car into the narrow lane and I watched him constantly. Yet, watch as closely as I might, I could not see where he concealed himself in order to command a view of the road.

On this occasion, as I know, Dr. Stuart was at home. Nevertheless, the girl stayed for close upon half an hour, and I began to wonder if some new move had been planned. Suddenly the door opened and she came out.

I crept through the bushes to my bicycle and wheeled it on to the drive. I saw the car start; but Madame Fortune being in playful mood, my own engine refused to start at all, and when ten minutes later I at last aroused a spark of life in the torpid machine I knew that pursuit would be futile.

Since this record is intended for the guidance of those who take up the quest of "The Scorpion" either in co-operation with myself or, in the event of my failure, alone, it would be profitless for me to record my disasters. Very well, I had one success. One night I pursued the yellow car from Dr. Stuart's house to the end of Limehouse Causeway without once losing sight of it.

A string of lorries form the docks, drawn by a traction engine, checked me at the corner for a time, although the yellow car passed. But I raced furiously on and by great good luck overtook it near the Dock Station. From thence onward pursuing a strangely tortuous route, I kept it in sight to Canning Town, when it turned into a public garage. I followed — to purchase petrol.

Chunda Lal was talking to the man in charge; he had not yet left his seat. But the car was empty!

At first I was stupid with astonishment. *Par la barbe du prophete!* I was astounded. Then I saw that I had really made a great discovery. The street into which I had injudiciously followed "Le Balafre" lay between Limehouse Causeway and Ropemaker Street, and it was at no great distance from this point that I had lost sight of the yellow car. In that street, which according to my friend the policeman was "nearly all Chinese," Zara el-Khala had descended; in that street was "The Scorpion's" lair!

CHAPTER V
CONCLUSION OF STATEMENT

I come now to the conclusion of this statement and to the strange occurrence which led to my proclaiming myself. The fear of imminent assassination which first had prompted me to record what I knew of "The Scorpion" had left me since I had ceased to be Charles Malet. And that the disappearance of "Le Balafre" had been accepted by his unknown chief as evidence of his success in removing *me*, I did not doubt. Therefore I breathed more freely… and more freely still when my body was recovered!

Yes, my body was recovered from Hanover Hole; I read of it — a very short paragraph, but it is the short paragraphs that matter — in my morning paper. I knew then that I should very shortly be dead indeed — officially dead. I had counted on this happening before, you understand, for I more than ever suspected that "The Scorpion" knew me to be in England and I feared that he would "lie low" as the English say. However, since a fortunate thing happens better late than never, I say in this paragraph two things: (1) that the enemy would cease to count upon Gaston Max; (2) that the Scotland Yard Commissioner would be authorised to open Part First of this Statement which had been lodged at his office two days after I landed in England — the portion dealing with my inquiries in Paris and with my tracking of "Le Balafre" to Bow Road Station and observing that he showed a golden scorpion to the chauffeur of the yellow car.

This would happen because Paris would wire that the identification disk found on the dead man was that of Gaston Max. Why would Paris do so? Because my reports had been discounted since I had ceased to be Charles Malet and Paris would be seeking evidence of my whereabouts. My reports had discontinued because I had learned that I had to do with a criminal organization of whose ramifications I knew nothing. Therefore I took no more chances. I died.

I return to the night when Inspector Dunbar, the grim Dunbar of Scotland Yard, came to Dr. Stuart's house. His appearance there puzzled me. I could not fail to recognize him, for as dusk had fully come I had descended from my top window and was posted among the bushes of the empty house from whence I commanded a perfect view of the doctor's door. The night was unusually chilly — there had been some rain — and when I crept around to the lane bordering the lawn, hoping to see or hear something of what was taking place in the study, I found that the windows were closed and the blinds drawn.

Luck seemed to have turned against me; for that night, at dusk, when I had gone to a local garage where I kept my motor bicycle, I had discovered the back tire to be perfectly flat and had been forced to contain my soul in patience whilst the man repaired a serious puncture. The result was of course that for more than half an hour I had not had Dr. Stuart's house under observation. And a hundred and one things can happen in half an hour.

Had Dr. Stuart sent for the Inspector? If so, I feared that the envelope was missing, or at any rate that he had detected Zara el-Khala in the act of stealing it and had determined to place the matter in the hands of the police. It was a maddening reflection. Again — I shrewdly suspected that I was not the only watcher of Dr. Stuart's house. The frequency with which the big yellow car drew up at the door a few moments after the doctor had gone out could not be due to accident. Yet I had been unable to detect the presence of this other watcher, nor had I any idea of the spot where the car remained hidden — if my theory was a correct one. Nevertheless I did not expect to see it come along whilst the Inspector remained at the house — always supposing that Zara el-Khala had not yet succeeded. I wheeled out the "Indian" and rode to a certain tobacconist's shop at which I had sometimes purchased cigarettes.

He had a telephone in a room at the rear which customers were allowed to use on payment of a fee, and a public call-box would not serve my purpose, since the operator usually announces to a subscriber the fact that a call emanated from such an office. The shop was closed, but I rang the bell at the side door and obtained permission to use the telephone upon pleading urgency. I had assiduously cultivated a natural gift for mimicry, having found it of inestimable service in the practice of my profession. It served me now. I had worked in the past with Inspector Dunbar and his subordinate Sergeant Sowerby, and I determined to trust to my memory of the latter's mode of speech.

I rang up Dr. Stuart and asked for the Inspector, saying Sergeant Sowerby spoke from Scotland Yard. "Hullo!" he cried, "is that you, Sowerby?"

"Yes," I replied in Sowerby's voice. "I thought I should find you there. About the body of Max.."

"Eh!" said Dunbar — "what's that? Max?"

I knew immediately that Paris had not yet wired, therefore I told him that Paris *had* done so, and that the disk numbered 49685 was that of Gaston Max. He was inexpressibly shocked, deploring the rashness of Max in working alone.

"Come to Scotland Yard," I said, anxious to get him away from the house.

He said he would be with me in a few minutes, and I was racking my brains for some means of learning what business had taken him to Dr. Stuart when he gave me the desired information spontaneously.

"Sowerby, listen," said he: "It's 'The Scorpion' case right enough! That bit of gold found on the dead man is not a cactus stem; it's a scorpion's tail!"

So! they had found what I had failed to find! It must have been attached, I concluded, to some inner part of "Le Balafre's" clothing. There had been no mention of Zara el-Khala; therefore, as I rode back to my post I permitted myself to assume that she would come again, since presumably she had thus far failed. I was right.

Morbleu! quick as I was the car was there before me! But I had not overlooked this possibility and I had dismounted at a good distance from the house and had left the "Indian" in someone's front garden. As I had turned out of the main road I had seen Dr. Stuart and Inspector Dunbar approaching a rank upon which two or three cabs usually stood.

I watched *la Bell* Zara enter the house, a beautiful woman most elegantly attired, and then, even before Chunda Lal had backed the car into the lane I was off... to the spot at which I had abandoned my motor bicycle. In little more than half an hour I had traversed London, and was standing in the shadow of that high, blank wall to which I have referred as facing a row of wooden houses in a certain street adjoining Limehouse Causeway.

You perceive my plan? I was practically sure of the street; all I had to learn was which house sheltered "The Scorpion"!

I had already suspected that this night was to be for me an unlucky night. *Nom d'un p'tit bon-homme!* it was so. Until an hour before dawn I crouched under that wall and saw no living thing except a very old Chinaman who came out of one of the houses and walked slowly away. The other houses appeared to be empty. No vehicle of any kind passed that way all night.

Turning over in my mind the details of this most perplexing case, it became evident to me that the advantages of working alone were now outweighed by the disadvantages. The affair had reached a stage at which ordinary police methods should be put into operation. I had collected some of the threads; the next thing was for Scotland Yard to weave these together whilst I sought for more.

I determined to remain dead. It would afford me greater freedom of action. The disappearance of "Le Balafre" which must by this time have been noted by his associates, might possibly lead to a suspicion that the dead man was *not* Gaston Max; but providing no member of "The Scorpion" group obtained access to the body I failed to see how this suspicion could be confirmed. I reviewed my position.

The sealed letter had achieved its purpose in part. Although I had failed to locate the house from which these people operated, I could draw a circle on the map within which I knew it to be; and I had learned that Zara el-Khala and the Hindu were in London. What it all meant — to what end "The Scorpion" was working I did not know. But having learned so much, be sure I did not despair of learning more.

It was now imperative that I should find out exactly what had occurred at Dr. Stuart's house. Accordingly I determined to call upon the Inspector at Scotland Yard. I presented myself towards evening of the day following my vigil in Limehouse, sending up the card of a Bureau confrere, for I did not intend to let it be generally known that I was alive.

Presently I was shown up to that bare and shining room which I remembered having visited in the past. I stood just within the doorway, smiling. Inspector Dunbar rose, as the constable went out, and stood looking across at me.

I had counted on striking him dumb with astonishment. He was Scottishly unmoved.

"Well," he said, coming forward with outstretched hand, "I'm glad to see you. I knew you would have come to us sooner or later!"

I felt that my eyes sparkled. There was no resentment within my heart.

I rejoiced.

"Look," he continued, taking a slip of paper from his note-book. "This is a copy of a note I left with Dr. Stuart some time ago. Read it."

I did so, and this is what I read:

"A: the name of the man who cut out the lid of the cardboard box and sealed it in the envelope — Gaston Max!

"B: the name of the missing cabman — Gaston Max!

"C: the name of the man who rang me up at Dr. Stuart's and told me that Gaston Max was dead — Gaston Max!"

I returned the slip to Inspector Dunbar. I bowed.

"It is a pleasure and a privilege to work with you, Inspector," I said....

This statement is nearly concluded. The whole of the evening I spent in the room of the Assistant Commissioner discussing the matters herein set forth and comparing notes with Inspector Dunbar. One important thing I learned: that I had abandoned my nightly watches too early. For one morning just before dawn someone who was *not* Zara had paid a visit to the house of Dr. Stuart! I determined to call upon the doctor.

As it chanced I was delayed and did not actually arrive until so late an hour that I had almost decided not to present myself...when a big yellow car flashed past the taxicab in which I was driving!

Nom d'un nom! I could not mistake it! This was within a few hundred yards of the house of Dr. Stuart, you understand, and I instantly dismissed my cabman and proceeded to advance cautiously on foot. I could no longer hear the engine of the car which had passed ahead of me, but then I knew that it could run almost noiselessly. As I crept along in that friendly shadow cast by a high hedge which had served me so well before, I saw the yellow car. It was standing on the opposite side of the road. I reached the tradesman's entrance.

From my left, in the direction of the back lawn of the house, came a sudden singular crackling noise and I discerned a flash of blue flame resembling faint "summer lightning." A series of muffled explosions followed...and in the darkness I tripped over something which lay along the ground at my feet — a length of cable it seemed to be.

Stumbling, I uttered a slight exclamation...and instantly received a blow on the head that knocked me flat upon the ground! Everything was swimming around me, but I realized that someone — Chunda Lal probably — had been hiding in the very passage which I had entered! I heard again that uncanny wailing, close beside me.

Vaguely I discerned an incredible figure — like that of a tall cowled monk, towering over me. I struggled to retain consciousness — there was a rush of feet...the throb of a motor.

It stimulated me — that sound! I must get to the telephone and cause the yellow car to be intercepted.

I staggered to my feet and groped my way along the hedge to where I had observed a tree by means of which one might climb over. I was dizzy as a drunken man; but I half climbed and half fell on to the lawn. The windows were open. I rushed into the study of Dr. Stuart.

Pah! it was full of fumes. I looked around me. *Mon Dieu!* I staggered. For I knew that in this fume-laden room a thing more horrible and more strange than any within my experience had taken place that night.

Part III
AT THE HOUSE OF AH-FANG-FU

CHAPTER I
BRAIN-THIEVES

The Assistant Commissioner lighted a cigarette. "It would appear, then," he said, "that whilst some minor difficulties have been smoothed away, we remain face to face with the major problem: who is 'The Scorpion' and to what end are his activities directed?"

Gaston Max shrugged his shoulders and smiled at Dr. Stuart.

"Let us see," he suggested, "what we really know about this 'Scorpion'. Let us make a brief survey of our position in the matter. Let us take first what we have learned of him — if it is a 'him' with whom we have to deal — from the strange experiences of Dr. Stuart. Without attaching too much importance to that episode five years ago on the Wu-Men Bridge; perhaps he is not. We will talk about this one again presently.

"We come to the arrival on the scene of Zara el-Khala, also called Mlle. Dorian. She comes because of what *I* have told to the scarred man from Paris, she comes to obtain that dangerous information which is to be sent to Scotland Yard, she comes, in a word, from 'The Scorpion.' We have two links binding the poor one 'Le Balafre' to 'The Scorpion': (1) his intimacy with Miguel and those others with whom 'Scorpion' communicated by telephone; (2) his possession of the golden ornament which lies there upon the table and which I took from his pocket. What can we gather from the statement made to Dr. Stuart by Mlle. Dorian? Let us study this point for a moment.

"In the first place we can only accept her words with a certain skepticism. Her story may be nothing but a fabrication. However, it is interesting because she claims to be the unwilling servant of a dreaded master. She lays stress upon the fact that she is an Oriental and does not enjoy the same freedom as a European woman. This is possible, up to a point. On the other hand she seems to enjoy not only freedom but every luxury. Therefore it may equally well be a lie. Some slight colour is lent to her story by the extraordinary mode of life which she followed in Paris. In the midst of Bohemianism she remained secluded as an odalisque in some harem garden of Stambul, whether by her own will or by will of another we do not know. One little point her existence seems to strengthen: that we are dealing with Easterns; for Zara el-Khala is partly of Eastern blood and her follower Chunda Lal is a Hindu. *Eh bien.*

"Consider the cowled man whose shadow Dr. Stuart has seen on two occasions: once behind the curtain of his window and once cast by the moonlight across the lawn of his house. The man himself he has never seen. Now this hooded man cannot have been 'Le Balafre', for 'Le Balafre' was already dead at the time of his first appearance. He may be 'The Scorpion'!"

Max paused impressively, looking around at those in the Commissioner's room.

"For a moment I return to the man of the Wu Men Bridge. The man of the Wu-Men Bridge was veiled and this one is hooded! The man of the Wu-Men Bridge was known as 'The Scorpion,' and this one also is associated with a scorpion. We will return yet again to this point in a moment.

"Is there something else which we may learn from the experiences of Dr. Stuart? Yes! We learn that 'The Scorpion' suddenly decides that Dr. Stuart is dangerous, either because of his special knowledge (which would be interesting) or because the 'Scorpion' believes that he has become acquainted with the contents of the sealed envelope — which is not so interesting although equally dangerous for Dr. Stuart. 'The Scorpion' acts. He pays a second visit, again accompanied by Chunda Lal, who seems to be a kind of watch-dog who not only guards the person of Zara el-Kahla but who also howls when danger threatens the cowled man!

"And what is the weapon which the cowled man (who may be 'The Scorpion') uses to remove Dr. Stuart? It is a frightful weapon, my friends; it is a novel and deadly weapon. It is a weapon of which science knows nothing — a blue ray of the colour produced by a Mercury Vapour Lamp, according to Dr. Stuart who has seen it, and producing an odour like that of a blast furnace according to myself, who smelled it! Or this odour might have been caused by the fusing of the telephone; for the blue ray destroys such fragile things as telephones as easily as it destroys wood and paper! There is even a large round hole burned through the clay at the back of the study grate and through the brick wall behind it! Very well. 'The Scorpion' is a scientist and he is also the greatest menace to the world which the world has ever been called upon to deal with. You agree with me?"

Inspector Dunbar heaved a great sigh, Stuart silently accepted a cigarette from the Assistant Commissioner's box and the Assistant Commissioner spoke, slowly.

"I entirely agree with you, M. Max. Respecting this ray, as well as some one or two other *minutiae*, I have made a short note which we will discuss when you have completed your admirably lucid survey of the case."

"These are the things, then, which we learn from the terrible experiences of Dr. Stuart. Placing these experiences side by side with my own in Paris and in London — which we have already discussed in detail — we find that we have to deal with an organisation — the object of which is unknown — comprising among its members both Europeans ('Le Balafre' was a Frenchman, I believe), cross-breeds such as Miguel and Zara el-Khala" (Stuart winced), "one Algerian and a Hindu. It is then an organisation having ramifications throughout Europe, the East and, *mon Dieu!* where not? To continue. This little image" — he took up from the Commissioner's table the golden scorpion, and the broken fragment of tail — "is now definitely recognized by Dr. Stuart — who is familiar with the work of Oriental goldsmiths — to be of *Chinese* craftsmanship!"

"It may possibly be Tibetan," interrupted Stuart; "but it comes to the same thing."

"Very well," continued Max. "It is Chinese. We hope, very shortly, to identify a house situated somewhere within this red ink circle" — he placed his finger on a map of London which lay open on the table — "and which I know to be used as a meeting-place by members of this mysterious group. That circle, my friends, surrounds what is now known as 'Chinatown'! For the third time I return to the man of the Wu-Men Bridge; for the man of the Wu-Men Bridge was, apparently, a *Chinaman!* Do I make myself clear?"

"Remarkably so," declared the Assistant Commissioner, taking a fresh cigarette. "Pray continue, M. Max."

"I will do so. One of my most important investigations, in which I had the honour and the pleasure to be associated with Inspector Dunbar, led to the discovery of a dangerous group controlled by a certain 'Mr. King' ——"

"Ah!" cried Dunbar, his tawny eyes sparkling with excitement, "I was waiting for that!"

"I knew you would be waiting for it, Inspector. Your powers of deductive reasoning more and more are earning my respect. You recall that singular case? The elaborate network extending from London to Buenos Ayres, from Peking to Petrograd? Ah! a wonderful system. It was an opium syndicate, you understand," — turning again to the Assistant Commissioner.

"I recall the case," replied the Commissioner, "although I did not hold my present appointment at the time. I believe there were unsatisfactory features?"

"There were," agreed Max. "We never solved the mystery of the identity of 'Mr. King,' and although we succeeded in destroying the enterprise I have since thought that we acted with undue precipitation."

"Yes," said Dunbar rapidly; "but there was that poor girl to be rescued, you will remember? We couldn't waste time."

"I agree entirely, Inspector. Our hands were forced. Yet, I repeat, I have since thought that we acted with undue precipitation. I will tell you why. Do you recall the loss — not explained to this day — of the plans of the Haley torpedo?"

"Perfectly," replied the Commissioner; and Dunbar also nodded affirmatively.

"Very well. A similar national loss was sustained about the same time by my own Government. I am not at liberty to divulge its exact nature, as in the latter case the loss never became known to the public. But the only member of the French Chamber who had seen this document to which I refer was a certain 'M. Blank,' shall we say? I believe also that I am correct in stating that the late Sir Brian Malpas was a member of the British Cabinet at the time that the Haley plans were lost?"

"That is correct," said the Assistant Commissioner, "but surely the honour of the late Sir Brian was above suspicion?"

"Quite," agreed Max; "so also was that of 'M. Blank.' But my point is this: Both 'M. Blank' and the late Sir Brian were clients of the opium syndicate!"

Dunbar nodded again eagerly.

"Hard work I had to hush it up," he said. "It would have finished his political career."

The Assistant Commissioner looked politely puzzled.

"It was generally supposed that Sir Brian Malpas was addicted to drugs," he remarked; "and I am not surprised to learn that he patronised this syndicate to which you refer. But —— " he paused, smiling satanically. "Ah!" he added — "I see! I see!"

"You perceive the drift of my argument?" cried Max. "You grasp what I mean when I say that we were too hasty? This syndicate existed for a more terrible purpose than the promulgating of a Chinese vice; it had in its clutches men entrusted with national secrets, men of genius but slaves of a horrible drug. Under the influence of that drug, my friends, how many of those secrets may they not have divulged?"

His words were received in hushed silence.

"What became of those stolen plans?" he continued, speaking now in a very low voice. "In the stress of recent years has the Haley torpedo made its appearance so that we might learn to which Government the plans had been taken? No! the same mystery surrounds the fate of the information filched from the drugged brain of 'M. Blank.' In a word" — he raised a finger dramatically — "someone is hoarding up those instruments of destruction! Who is it that collects such things and for what purpose does he collect them?"

Following another tense moment of silence:

"Let us have your own theory, M. Max," said the Assistant Commissioner.

Gaston Max shrugged his shoulders.

"It is not worthy of the name of a theory," he replied, "the surmise which I have made. But recently I found myself considering the fact that 'The Scorpion' might just conceivably be a Chinaman. Now, 'Mr. King,' we believe was a Chinaman, and 'Mr. King,' as I am now convinced, operated not for a personal but for a deeper, political purpose. He stole the brains of genius and *accumulated* that genius. Is it not possible that these contrary operations may be part of a common plan?"

CHAPTER II
THE RED CIRCLE

"You are not by any chance," suggested Stuart, smiling slightly, "hinting at that defunct bogey, the 'Yellow Peril'?"

"Ah!" cried Max, "but certainly I am not! Do not misunderstand me. This group with which we are dealing is shown to be not of a national but of an international character. The same applied to the organisation of 'Mr. King.' But a Chinaman directed the one, and I begin to suspect that a Chinaman directs the other. No, I speak of no ridiculous 'Yellow Peril,' my friends. John Chinaman, as I have known him, is the whitest man breathing; but can you not imagine" — he dropped his voice again in that impressive way which was yet so truly Gallic — "can you not imagine a kind of Oriental society which like a great, a formidable serpent, lies hidden somewhere below that deceptive jungle of the East? These are troubled times. It is a wise state to-day that knows its own leaders. Can you not imagine a dreadful sudden menace, not of men and guns but of *brains* and *capital*?"

"You mean," said Dunbar slowly, "that 'The Scorpion' may be getting people out of the way who might interfere with this rising or invasion or whatever it is?"

"Just as 'Mr. King' accumulated material for it," interjected the Assistant Commissioner. "It is a bold conception, M. Max, and it raises the case out of the ordinary category and invests it with enormous international importance."

All were silent for a time, Stuart, Dunbar and the Commissioner watching the famous Frenchman as he sat there, arrayed in the latest fashion of Saville Row, yet Gallic to his finger-tips and in every gesture. It was almost impossible at times to credit the fact that a Parisian was speaking, for the English of Gaston Max was flawless except that he spoke with a faint American accent. Then, suddenly, a gesture, an expletive, would betray the Frenchman.

But such betrayals never escaped him when, in one of his inimitable disguises, he penetrated to the purlieu of Whitechapel, to the dens of Limehouse. Then he was the perfect Hooligan, as, mingling with the dangerous thieves of Paris, he was the perfect Apache. It was an innate gift of mimicry which had made him the greatest investigator of his day. He could have studied Chinese social life for six months and thereupon have become a mandarin whom his own servants would never have suspected to be a "foreign barbarian." It was pure genius, as opposed to the brilliant efficiency of Dunbar.

But in the heart of the latter, as he studied Gaston Max and realized the gulf that separated them, there was nothing but generous admiration of a master; yet Dunbar was no novice, for by a process of fine deductive reasoning he had come to the conclusion, as has appeared, that Gaston Max had been masquerading as a cabman and that the sealed letter left with Dr. Stuart had been left as a lure. By one of those tricks of fate which sometimes perfect the plans of men but more often destroy them, the body of "Le Balafre" had been so disfigured during the time that it had been buffeted about in the Thames that it was utterly unrecognizable and indescribable. But even the disk had not deceived Dunbar. He had seen in it another ruse of his brilliant confrere, and his orders to the keeper of the mortuary to admit no one without a written permit had been dictated by the conviction that Max wished the body to be mistaken for his own. In Inspector Dunbar, Gaston Max immediately had recognized an able colleague as Mrs. M'Gregor had recognized "a grand figure of a man."

The Assistant Commissioner broke the silence.

"There have been other cases," he said reflectively, "now that one considers the matter, which seemed to point to the existence of such a group or society as you indicate, M. Max, notably one with which, if I remember rightly, Inspector" — turning his dark eyes towards Dunbar — "Inspector Weymouth, late of this Branch, was associated?"

"Quite right, sir. It was his big case, and it got him a fine billet as Superintendent in Cairo if you remember?"

"Yes," mused the Assistant Commissioner — "he transferred to Egypt — a very good appointment, as you say. That, again, was before my term of office, but there were a number of very ghastly crimes connected with the case and it was more or less definitely established, I believe, that some extensive secret society did actually exist throughout the East, governed, I fancy, by a Chinaman."

"And from China," added Dunbar.

"Yes, yes, from China as you say, Inspector." He turned to Gaston Max. "Can it really be, M. Max, that we have to deal with an upcrop of some deeply-seated evil which resides in the Far East? Are all these cases, not the work of individual criminal but manifestations of a more sinister, a darker force?"

Gaston Max met his glance and Max's mouth grew very grim.

"I honestly believe so." he answered. "I have believed it for nearly two years — ever since the Grand Duke died. And now, you said, I remember, that you had made a note the nature of which you would communicate."

"Yes," replied the Assistant Commissioner — "a small point, but one which may be worthy of attention. This ray, Dr. Stuart, which played such havoc in your study — do you know of anything approaching to it in more recent scientific devices?"

"Well," said Stuart, "it my be no more than a development of one of several systems, notably of that of the late Henrik Ericksen upon which he was at work at the time of his death."

"Exactly." The Assistant Commissioner smiled in his most Mephistophelean manner. "Of the late Henrik Ericksen, as you say."

He said no more for a moment and sat smoking and looking from face to face. Then:

"That is the subject of my note, gentlemen," he added. "The other *minutiae* are of no immediate importance."

"*Non d'un p'tit bonhomme!*" whispered Gaston Max. "I see! You think that Ericksen had completed his experiments before he died, but that he never lived to give them to the world?"

The Assistant Commissioner waved one hand in the air so that he discoloration of the first and second fingers was very noticeable.

"It is for you to ascertain these points, M. Max," he said — "I only suggest. But I begin to share your belief that a series of daring and unusual assassinations has been taking place under the eyes of the police authorities of Europe. It can only be poison — an unknown poison, perhaps. We shall be empowered to exhume the body of the late Sir Frank Narcombe in a few days' time, I hope. His case puzzles me hopelessly. What obstacle did a surgeon offer to this hypothetical Eastern movement? On the other hand, what can have been filched from him before his death? The death of an inventor, a statesman, a soldier, can be variously explained by your 'Yellow' hypothesis, M. Max, but what of the death of a surgeon?"

Gaston Max shrugged, and his mobile mouth softened in a quaint smile.

"We have learned a little," he said, "and guessed a lot. Let us hope to guess more — and learn everything!"

"May I suggest," added Dunbar, "that we hear Sowerby's report, sir?"

"Certainly," agreed the Assistant Commissioner — "call Sergeant Sowerby."

A moment later Sergeant Sowerby entered, his face very red and his hair bristling more persistently than usual.

"Anything to report, Sowerby?" asked Dunbar.

"Yes, Inspector," replied Sowerby, in his Police Court manner; — he faced the Assistant Commissioner, "with your permission, sir."

He took out a note-book which appeared to be the twin of Dunbar's and consulted it, assuming an expression of profound reflection.

"In the first place, sir," he began, never raising his eyes from the page, "I have traced the cab sold on the hire-purchase system to a certain Charles *Mallett*..."

"Ha, ha!" laughed Max breezily — "he calls me a hammer! It is not Mallett, Sergeant Sowerby — you have got too many *l*'s in that name; it is Malet and is called like one from the Malay States!"

"Oh," commented Sowerby, glancing up — "indeed. Very good, sir. The owner claims the balance of purchase money!"

Every one laughed at that, even the satanic Assistant Commissioner.

"Pay your debts, M. Max," he said. "You will bring the Service de Surete into bad repute! Carry on, Sergeant."

"This cab," continued Sowerby, when Dunbar interrupted him.

"Cut out the part about the cab, Sowerby," he said. "We've found that out from M. Max. Have you anything to report about the yellow car?"

"Yes," replied Sowerby, unperturbed, and turning over to the next page. "It was hired form Messrs. Wickers' garage, at Canning Town, by the week. The lady who hired it was a Miss Dorian, a French lady. She gave no reference, except that of the Savoy Hotel, where she was stopping. She paid a big deposit and had her own chauffeur, a colored man of some kind."

"Is it still in use by her?" snapped Dunbar eagerly.

"No, Inspector. She claimed her deposit this morning and said she was leaving London."

"The cheque?" cried Dunbar.

"Was cashed half an hour later."

"At what bank?"

"London County & Birmingham, Canning Town. Her own account at a Strand bank was closed yesterday. The details all concern milliners, jewellers, hotels and so forth. There's nothing there. I've been to the Savoy, of course."

"Yes!"

"A lady named Dorian has had rooms there for six weeks, has dined there on several occasions, but was more often away than in the hotel."

"Visitors?"

"Never had any."

"She used to dine alone, then?"

"Always."

"In the public dining-room?"

"No. In her own room."

"*Morbleu!*" muttered Max. "It is she beyond doubt. I recognize her sociable habits!"

"Has she left now?" asked Dunbar.

"She left a week ago."

Sowerby closed his note-book and returned it to his pocket.

"Is that all you have to report, Sergeant?" asked the Assistant Commissioner.

"That's all, sir."

"Very good."

Sergeant Sowerby retired.

"Now, sir," said Dunbar, "I've got Inspector Kelly here. He looks after the Chinese quarter. Shall I call him?"

"Yes, Inspector."

Presently there entered a burly Irishman, bluff and good-humoured, a very typical example of the intelligent superior police officer, looking keenly around him.

"Ah, Inspector," the Assistant Commissioner greeted him — "we want your assistance in a little matter concerning the Chinese residential quarter. You know this district?"

"Certainly, sir. I know it very well."

"On this map" — the Assistant Commissioner laid a discoloured forefinger upon the map of London — "you will perceive that we have drawn a circle."

Inspector Kelly bent over the table.

"Yes, sir."

"Within that circle, which is no larger in circumference that a shilling as you observe, lies a house used by a certain group of people. It has been suggested to me that these people may be Chinese or associates of Chinese."

"Well, sir," said Inspector Kelly, smiling broadly, "considering the patch inside the circle I think it more than likely! Seventy-five or it may be eighty per cent of the rooms and cellars and attics in those three streets are occupied by Chinese."

"For your guidance, Inspector, we believe these people to be a dangerous gang of international criminals. Do you know of any particular house, or houses, likely to be used as a meeting-place by such a gang?"

Inspector Kelly scratched his close-cropped head.

"A woman was murdered just there, sir," he said, taking up a pen from the table and touching a point near the corner of Three Colt Street, "about a twelve-month ago. We traced the man — a Chinese sailor — to a house lying just about here." Again he touched the map. "It's a sort of little junk-shop with a ramshackle house attached, all cellars and rabbit-hutches, as you might say, overhanging a disused cutting which is filled at high tide. Opium is to be had there and card-playing goes on, and I won't swear that you couldn't get liquor. But it's well conducted as such dives go."

"Why is it not closed?" inquired the Assistant Commissioner, seizing an opportunity to air his departmental ignorance.

"Well, sir," replied Inspector Kelly, his eyes twinkling — "if we shut up all these places we should never know where to look for some of our regular customers! As I mentioned, we found the wanted Chinaman, three parts drunk, in one of the rooms."

"It's a sort of lodging-house, then?"

"Exactly. There's a moderately big room just behind the shop, principally used by opium-smokers, and a whole nest of smaller rooms above and below. Mind you, sir, I don't say this is the place you're looking for, but it's the most likely inside your circle."

"Who is the proprietor?"

"A retired Chinese sailor called Ah-Fang-Fu, but better known as 'Pidgin.' His establishment is called locally 'The Pidgin House.'"

"Ah." The Commissioner lighted a cigarette. "And you know of no other house which might be selected for such a purpose as I have mentioned?"

"I can't say I do, sir. I know pretty well all the business affairs of that neighbourhood, and none of the houses inside your circle have changed hands during the past twelve months. Between ourselves, sir, nearly all the property in the district belongs to Ah-Fang-Fu, and anything that goes on in Chinatown *he* knows about!"

"Ah, I see. Then in any event he is the man we want to watch?"

"Well, sir, you ought to keep an eye on his visitors, I should say."

"I am obliged to you, Inspector," said the courteous Assistant Commissioner, "for your very exact information. If necessary I shall communicate with you again. Good-day."

"Good-day, sir," replied the Inspector. "Good-day, gentlemen."

He went out.

Gaston Max, who had diplomatically remained in the background throughout this interview, now spoke.

"*Pardieu!* but I have been thinking," he said. "Although 'The Scorpion,' as I hope, believes that that troublesome Charles Malet is dead, he may also wonder if Scotland Yard has secured from Dr. Stuart's fire any fragments of the information sealed in the envelope! What does it mean, this releasing of the yellow car, closing of the bank account and departure from the Savoy?"

"It means flight!" cried Dunbar, jumping violently to his feet. "By gad, sir!" he turned to the Assistant Commissioner — "the birds may have flown already!"

The Assistant Commissioner leaned back in his chair.

"I have sufficient confidence in M. Max," he said, "to believe that, having taken the responsibility of permitting this dangerous group to learn that they were under surveillance, he has good reason to suppose that they have not slipped through our fingers."

Gaston Max bowed.

"It is true," he replied, and from his pocket he took a slip of flimsy paper. "This code message reached me as I was about to leave my hotel. The quadroon, Miguel, left Paris last night and arrived in London this morning — —"

"He was followed?" cried Dunbar.

"But certainly. He was followed to Limehouse, and he was definitely seen to enter the establishment described to us by Inspector Kelly!"

"Gad!" said Dunbar — "then *someone* is still there?"

"Someone, as you say, is still there," replied Max. "But everything points to the imminent departure of this someone. Will you see to it, Inspector, that not a rat — *pardieu* not a little mouse — is allowed to slip out of our red circle to-day. For to-night we shall pay a friendly visit to the house of Ah-Fang-Fu, and I should wish all the company to be present."

CHAPTER III

Stuart returned to his house in a troubled frame of mind. He had refrained so long from betraying the circumstances of his last meeting with Mlle. Dorian to the police authorities that this meeting now constituted a sort of guilty secret, a link binding him to the beautiful accomplice of "The Scorpion" — to the dark-eyed servant of the uncanny cowled thing which had sought his life by strange means. He hugged this secret to his breast, and the pain of it afforded him a kind of savage joy.

In his study he found a Post Office workman engaged in fitting a new telephone. As Stuart entered the man turned.

"Good-afternoon, sir," he said, taking up the destroyed instrument from the litter of flux, pincers and screw drivers lying upon the table. "If it's not a rude question, how on earth did *this* happen?"

Stuart laughed uneasily.

"It got mixed up with an experiment which I was conducting," he replied evasively.

The man inspected the headless trunk of the instrument.

"It seems to be fused, as though the top of it had been in a blast furnace," he continued. "Experiments of that sort are a bit dangerous outside a proper laboratory, I should think."

"They are," agreed Stuart. "But I have no facilities here, you see, and I was — er — compelled to attempt the experiment. I don't intend to repeat it."

"That's lucky," murmured the man, dropping the instrument into a carpet-bag. "If you do, it will cost you a tidy penny for telephones!"

Walking out towards the dispensary, Stuart met Mrs. M'Gregor.

"A Post Office messenger brought this letter for you, Mr. Keppel, just the now," she said, handing Stuart a sealed envelope.

He took the envelope from her hand, and turned quickly away. He felt that he had changed colour. For it was addressed in the handwriting of...Mlle. Dorian!

"Thank you, Mrs. M'Gregor," he said and turned into the dining-room.

Mrs. M'Gregor proceeded about her household duties, and as her footsteps receded, Stuart feverishly tore open the envelope. That elusive scent of jasmine crept to his nostrils. In the envelope was a sheet of thick note-paper (having the top cut off evidently in order to remove the printed address), upon which the following singular message was written:

"Before I go away there is something I want to say to you. You do not trust me. It is not wonderful that you do not. But I swear that I only want to save you from a *great* danger. If you will promise not to tell the police anything of it, I will meet you at six o'clock by the Book Stall at Victoria Station — on the Brighton side. If you agree you will wear something white in your button-hole. If not you cannot find me there. Nobody ever sees me again."

There was no signature, but no signature was necessary.

Stuart laid the letter on the table, and began to pace up and down the room. His heart was beating ridiculously. His self-contempt was profound. But he could not mistake his sentiments.

His duty was plain enough. But he had failed in it once, and even as he strode up and down the room, already he knew that he must fail again. He knew that, rightly or wrongly, he was incapable of placing this note in the hands of the police...and he knew that he should be at Victoria Station at six o'clock.

He would never have believed himself capable of becoming accessory to a series of crimes — for this was what his conduct amounted to; he had thought that sentiment no longer held any meaning for him. Yet the only excuse which he could find wherewith to solace himself was that this girl had endeavoured to save him from assassination. Weighed against the undoubted fact that she was a member of a dangerous criminal group what was it worth? If the supposition of Gaston Max was correct, "The Scorpion" had at least six successful murders to his credit, in addition to the attempt upon his (Stuart's) life and that of "Le Balafre", upon the life of Gaston Max.

It was an accomplice of this nameless horror called "The Scorpion" with whom at six o'clock he had a tryst, whom he was protecting from justice, by the suppression of whose messages to himself he was adding difficulties to the already difficult task of the authorities!

Up and down he paced, restlessly, every now and again glancing at a clock upon the mantelpiece. His behavior he told himself was contemptible.

Yet, at a quarter to six, he went out — and seeing a little cluster of daisies growing amongst the grass bordering the path, he plucked one and set it in his button-hole!

A few minutes before the hour he entered the station and glanced sharply around at the many groups scattered about in the neighbourhood of the bookstall. There was no sign of Mlle. Dorian. He walked around the booking office without seeing her and glanced into the waiting-room. Then, looking up at the station clock, he saw that the hour had come, and as he stood there staring upward he felt a timid touch upon his shoulder.

He turned — and she was standing by his side!

She was Parisian from head to foot, simply but perfectly gowned. A veil hung from her hat and half concealed her face, but could not hide her wonderful eyes nor disguise the delightful curves of her red lips. Stuart automatically raised his hat, and even as he did so wondered what she should have said and done had she suddenly found Gaston Max standing at his elbow! He laughed shortly.

"You are angry with me," said Mlle. Dorian, and Stuart thought that her quaint accent was adorable. "Or are you angry with yourself for seeing me?"

"I am angry with myself," he replied, "for being so weak."

"Is it so weak," she said, rather tremulously, "not to judge a woman by what she seems to be and not to condemn her before you hear what she has to say? If that is weak, I am glad; I think it is how a man should be."

Her voice and her eyes completed the spell, and Stuart resigned himself without another struggle to this insane infatuation.

"We cannot very well talk here," he said. "Suppose we go into the hotel and have late tea, Mlle. Dorian."

"Yes. Very well. But please do not call me that. It is not my name."

Stuart was on the point of saying, "Zara el-Khala then," but checked himself in the nick of time. He might hold communication with the enemy, but at least he would give away no information.

"I am called Miska," she added. "Will you please call me Miska?"

"Of course, if you wish," said Stuart, looking down at her as she walked by his side and wondering what he would do when he had to stand up in Court, look at Miska in the felon's dock and speak words which would help to condemn her — perhaps to death, at least to penal servitude! He shuddered.

"Have I said something that displeases you?" she asked, resting a white-gloved hand on his arm. "I am sorry."

"No, no," he assured her. "But I was thinking — I cannot help thinking..."

"How wicked I am?" she whispered.

"How lovely you are!" he said hotly, "and how maddening it is to remember that you are an accomplice of criminals!"

"Oh," she said, and removed her hand, but not before he had felt how it trembled. They were about to enter the tea-room when she added: "Please don't say that until I have told you why I do what I do."

Obeying a sudden impulse, he took her hand and drew it close under his arm.

"No," he said; "I won't. I was a brute, Miska. Miska means 'musk', surely?"

"Yes." She glanced up at him timidly. "Do you think it a pretty name?"

"Very," he said, laughing.

Underlying the Western veneer was the fascinating naivete of the Eastern woman, and Miska had all the suave grace, too, which belongs to the women of the Orient, so that many admiring glances followed her charming figure as she crossed the room to a vacant table.

"Now," said Stuart, when he had given an order to the waiter, "what do you want to tell me? Whatever it may be, I am all anxiety to hear it. I promise that I will only act upon anything you may tell me in the event of my life, or that of another, being palpably endangered by my silence."

"Very well. I want to tell you," replied Miska, "why I stay with Fo-Hi."

"Who is Fo-Hi?"

"I do not know!"

"What!" said Stuart. "I am afraid I don't understand you."

"If I speak in French will you be able to follow what I say?"

"Certainly. Are you more at ease with French?"

"Yes," replied Miska, beginning to speak in the latter language. "My mother was French, you see, and although I can speak in English fairly well I cannot yet *think* in English. Do you understand?

"Perfectly. So perhaps you will now explain to whom you refer when you speak of Fo-Hi."

Miska glanced apprehensively around her, bending further forward over the table.

"Let me tell you from the beginning," she said in a low voice, "and then you will understand. It must not take me long. You see me as I am to-day because of a dreadful misfortune that befell me when I was fifteen years old."

"My father was *Wali* of Aleppo, and my mother, his third wife, was a Frenchwoman, a member of a theatrical company which had come to Cairo, where he had first seen her. She must have loved him, for she gave up the world, embraced Islam and entered his *harem* in the great house on the outskirts of Aleppo. Perhaps it was because he, too, was half French, that they were mutually attracted. My father's mother was a Frenchwoman also, you understand.

"Until I was fifteen years of age, I never left the *harem,* but my mother taught me French and also a little English; and she prevailed upon my father not to give me in marriage so early as is usual in the East. She taught me to understand the ways of European women, and we used to have Paris journals and many books come to us regularly. Then an awful pestilence visited Aleppo. People were dying in the mosques and in the streets, and my father decided to send my mother and myself and some others of the *harem* to his brother's house in Damaskus.

"Perhaps you will think that such things do not happen in these days, and particularly to members of the household of a chief magistrate, but I can only tell you what is true. On the second night of our journey a band of Arabs swept down upon the caravan, overpowered the guards, killing them all, and carried of everything of value which we had. Me, also, they carried off — me and one other, a little Syrian girl, my cousin. Oh!" she shuddered violently — "even now I can sometimes hear the shrieks of my mother...and I can hear, also, the way they suddenly ceased, those cries..."

Stuart looked up with a start to find a Swiss waiter placing tea upon the table. He felt like rubbing his eyes. He had been dragged rudely back from the Syrian desert to the prosaic realities of a London hotel.

"Perhaps," continued Miska, "you will think that we were ill-treated, but it was not so. No one molested us. We were given every comfort which desert life can provide, servant to wait upon us and plenty of good food. After several weeks' journeying we came to a large city, having many minarets and domes glimmering in the moonlight; for we entered at night. Indeed, we always travelled at night. At the time I had no idea of the name of this city but I learned afterwards that it was Mecca.

"As we proceeded through the streets, the Assyrian girl and I peeped out through the little windows of the *shibriyeh* — which is a kind of tent on the back of a camel — in which we travelled, hoping to see some familiar face or someone to whom we could appeal. But there seemed to be scarcely anyone visible in the streets, although lights shone out from many windows, and the few men we saw seemed to be anxious to avoid us. In fact, several ran down side turnings as the camels approached.

"We stopped before the gate of a large house which was presently opened, and the camels entered the courtyard. We descended, and I saw that a number of small apartments surrounded the courtyard in the manner of a *caravanserai*. Then, suddenly, I saw something else, and I knew why we had been treated with such consideration on the journey; I knew into what hand I had fallen — I knew that I was in the house of a *slave-dealer!*"

"Good heavens!" muttered Stuart — "this is almost incredible."

"I knew you would doubt what I had to tell you," declared Miska plaintively; "but I solemnly swear what I tell you is the truth. Yes, I was in the house of a slave-dealer, and on the very next day, because I was proficient in languages, in music and in dancing, and also because — according to their Eastern ideas — I was pretty, the dealer, Mohammed Abd-el-Bali...offered me for sale."

She stopped, lowering her eyes and flushing hotly, then continued with hesitancy.

"In a small room which I can never forget I was offered the only indignity which I had been called upon to suffer since my abduction. I was *exhibited* to prospective purchasers."

"As she spoke the words, Miska's eyes flashed passionately and her hand, which lay on the table, trembled. Stuart silently reached across and rested his own upon it.

"There were all kinds of girls," Miska continued, "black and brown and white, in the adjoining rooms, and some of them were singing and some dancing, whilst others wept. Four different visitors inspected me critically, two of them being agents for royal *harems* and the other two — how shall I say it? — wealthy connoisseurs. But the price asked by Mohammed Abd-el-Bali was beyond the purses of all except one of the agents. He had indeed settled the bargain, when the singing and dancing and shouting — every sound it seemed — ceased about me...and into the little room in which I crouched amongst perfumed cushions at the feet of the two men, walked Fo-Hi."

CHAPTER IV
MISKA'S STORY *(concluded)*

"Of course, I did not know that this was his name at the time; I only knew that a tall Chinaman had entered the room — and that his face was entirely covered by a green veil."

Stuart started, but did not interrupt Miska's story.

"This veil gave him in some way a frightfully malign and repellent appearance. As he stood in the doorway looking down I seemed to *feel* his gaze passing over me like a flame, although of course I could not see his eyes. For a moment he stood there looking at me; and much as his presence had affected me, its affect upon the slave-dealer and my purchaser was extraordinary. They seemed to be stricken dumb. Suddenly the Chinaman spoke, in perfect Arabic. 'Her price?' he said.

"Mohammed Abd-el-Bali, standing trembling before him, replied:

"'Miska is already sold, lord, but —— '

"'Her price?' repeated the Chinaman, in the same hard metallic voice and without the slightest change of intonation.

"The *harem* agent who had bought me now said, his voice shaking so that the words were barely audible:

"'I give her up, Mohammed — I give her up. Who am I to dispute with the Mandarin Fo-Hi;' and performing an abject obeisance he backed out of the room.

"At the same moment, Mohammed, whose knees were trembling so that they seemed no longer capable of supporting him, addressed the Chinaman.

"'Accept the maiden as an unworthy gift,' he began —

"'Her price?' repeated Fo-Hi.

"Mohammed, whose teeth had begun to chatter, asked him twice as much as he had agreed to accept from the other, Fo-Hi clapped his hands, and a fierce-eyed Hindu entered the room.

"Fo-Hi addressed him in a language which I did not understand, although I have since learned that it was Hindustani, and the Indian from a purse which he carried counted out the amount demanded by the dealer and placed the money upon a little inlaid table which stood in the room. Fo-Hi gave him some brief order, turned and walked out of the room. I did not see him again for four years — that is until my nineteenth birthday.

"I know that you are wondering about many things and I will try to make some of them clear to you. You are wondering, no doubt, how such a trade as I have described is carried on in the East to-day almost under the eyes of European Governments. Now I shall surprise you. When I was taken from the house of the slave-dealer, in charge of Chunda Lal — for this was the name of the Hindu — do you know where I was carried to? I will tell you: to *Cairo!*"

"Cairo!" cried Stuart — then, perceiving that he had attracted attention by speaking so loudly, he lowered his voice. "Do you mean to tell me that you were taken as a *slave* to Cairo?"

Miska smiled — and her smile was the taunting smile of the East, which is at once a caress and an invitation.

"You think, no doubt, that there are no slaves in Cairo!" she said. "So do most people, and so did I — once. I learned better. There are palaces in Cairo, I assure you, in which there are many slaves. I myself lived in such a palace for four years, and I was not the only slave there. What do British residents and French residents know of the inner domestic life of their Oriental neighbours? Are they ever admitted to the *harem?* And the slaves — are they ever admitted outside the walls of the palace? Sometimes, yes, but never alone!

"By slow stages, following the ancient caravan routes, and accompanied by an extensive retinue of servants in charge of Chunda Lal, we came to Cairo; and one night, approaching the city from the north-east and entering by the Bab en-Nasr, I was taken to the old palace which was to be my prison for four years. How I passed those four years has no bearing upon the matters which I have to tell you, but I lived the useless, luxurious life of some Arabian princess, my lightest wish anticipated and gratified; nothing was denied me, except freedom.

"Then, one day — it was actually my nineteenth birthday — Chunda Lal presented himself and told me that I was to have an interview with Fo-Hi. Hearing these words, I nearly swooned, for a hundred times during the years of my strange luxurious captivity I had awakened trembling in the night, thinking that the figure of the awful veiled Chinaman had entered the room.

"You must understand that having spent my childhood in a *harem,* the mode of life which I was compelled to follow in Cairo was not so insufferable as it must have been for a European woman. Neither was my captivity made unduly irksome. I often drove through the European quarters, always accompanied by Chunda Lal, and closely veiled, and I regularly went shopping in the bazaars — but never alone. The death of my mother — and later that of my father, of which Chunda Lal had told me — were griefs that time had dulled. But the horror of Fo-Hi was one which lived with me, day and night.

"To a wing of the palace kept closely locked, and which I had never seen opened, I was conducted by Chunda Lal. There, in a room of a kind with which was part library and part *mandarah,* part museum and part laboratory, I found the veiled man seated at a great littered table. As I stood trembling before him he raised a long yellow hand and waved to Chunda Lal to depart. When he obeyed and I heard the door close I could scarcely repress a shriek of terror.

"For what seemed an interminable time he sat watching me. I dared not look at him, but again I felt his gaze passing over me like a flame. Then he began to speak, in French, which he spoke without a trace of accent.

"He told me briefly that my life of idleness had ended and that a new life of activity in many parts of the world was about to commence. His manner was quite unemotional, neither harsh nor kindly, his metallic voice conveyed no more than the bare meaning of the words which he uttered. When, finally, he ceased speaking, he struck a gong which hung from a corner of the huge table, and Chunda Lal entered.

"Fo-Hi addressed a brief order to him in Hindustani — and a few moments later a second Chinaman walked slowly into the room."

Miska paused, as if to collect her ideas, but continued almost immediately.

"He wore a plain yellow robe and had a little black cap on his head.

His face, his wonderful evil face I can never forget, and his eyes — I fear you will think I exaggerate — but his eyes were green as emeralds!

He fixed them upon me.

"'This,' said Fo-Hi, 'is Miska.'

"The other Chinaman continued to regard me with those dreadful eyes; then:

"'You have chosen well.' he said, turned and slowly went out again.

"I thank God that I have never seen him since, for his dreadful face haunted my dreams for long afterwards. But I have learned of him, and I know that next to Fo-Hi he is the most dangerous being in the known world. He has invented horrible things — poisons and instruments, which I cannot describe because I have never seen them; but I have seen…some of their effects."

She paused, overcome with the horror of her memories.

"What is the name of this other man?" asked Stuart eagerly. Miska glanced at him rapidly.

"Oh, do not ask me questions, please!" she pleaded. "I will tell you all I can, all I dare; what I do not tell you I cannot tell you — and this is one of the things I dare not tell. He is a Chinese scientist and, I have heard, the greatest genius in the whole world, but I can say no more — yet."

"Is he still alive — this man?"

"I do not know that. If he is alive, he is in China — at some secret palace in the province of Ho-Nan, which is the headquarters of what is called the 'Sublime Order.' I have never been there, but there are Europeans there, as well as Orientals."

"What! in the company of these fiends!"

"It is useless to ask me — oh! indeed, I would tell you if I could, but I cannot! Let me go on from the time when I saw Fo-Hi in Cairo. He told me that I was a member of an organization dating back to remote antiquity which was destined to rule all the races of mankind — the Celestial age he called their coming triumph. Something which they had lacked in order to achieve success had been supplied by the dreadful man who had entered the room and expressed his approval of me.

"For many years they had been at work in Europe, secretly, as well as in the East. I understood that they had acquired a quantity of valuable information of some kind by means of a system of opium-houses situated in the principal capitals of the world and directed by Fo-Hi and a number of Chinese assistants. Fo-Hi had remained in China most of the time, but had paid occasional visits to Europe. The other man — the monster with the black skull cap — had been responsible for the conduct of the European enterprises."

"Throughout this interview," interrupted Stuart, forgetful of the fact that Miska had warned him of the futility of asking questions, "and during others which you must have had with Fo-Hi, did you never obtain a glimpse of his face?"

"Never! No one has ever seen his face! I know that his eyes are a brilliant and unnatural yellow colour, but otherwise I should not know him if I saw him unveiled, to-morrow. Except," she added, "by a sense of loathing which his presence inspires in me. But I must hurry. If you interrupt me, I shall not have time.

"From that day in Cairo — oh! how can I tell you! I began the life of an adventuress! I do not deny it. I came here to confess it to you. I went to New York, to London, to Paris, to Petrograd; I went all over the world. I had beautiful dresses, jewels, admiration — all that women live for! And in the midst of it all mine was the life of the cloister; no nun could be more secluded!

"I see the question in your eyes — why did I do it? Why did I lure men into the clutches of Fo-Hi? For this is what I did; and when I have failed, I have been punished."

Stuart shrank from her.

"You confess," he said hoarsely, "that you knowing lured men to *death?*"

"Ah, no!" she whispered, looking about her fearfully — "never! never! I swear it — never!"

"Then" — he stared at her blankly — "I do not understand you!"

"I dare not make it clearer — now: I dare not — dare not! But *believe* me! Oh, please, please," she pleaded, her soft voice dropping to a whisper — "believe me! If you know what I risked to tell you so much, you would be more merciful. A horror which cannot be described" — again she shuddered — "will fall upon me if *he* ever suspects! You think me young and full of life, with all the world before me. You do not know. I am, literally, *already dead!* Oh! I have followed a strange career. I have danced in a Paris theatre and I have sold flowers in Rome; I have had my box at the Opera and I have filled opium pipes in a den at San Francisco! But never, never have I lured a man to his death. And through it all, from first to last, no man has so much as kissed my finger-tips!

"At a word, at a sign, I have been compelled to go from Monte Carlo to Buenos Ayres; at another sign from there to Tokio! Chunda Lal has guarded me as only the women of the East are guarded. Yet, in his fierce way, he has always tried to befriend me, he has always been faithful. But ah! I shrink from him many times, in horror, because I know *what* he is! But I may not tell you. Look! Chunda Lal has never been out of sound of this whistle" — she drew a little silver whistle from her dress — "for a moment since that day when he came into the house of the slave-dealer in Mecca, except — —"

And now, suddenly, a wave of glorious colour flooded her beautiful face and swiftly she lowered her eyes, replacing the little whistle. Stuart's rebellious heart leapt madly, for whatever he might think of her almost incredible story, that sweet blush was no subterfuge, no product of acting.

"You almost drive me mad," he said in low voice, resembling the tones of repressed savagery. "You tell me so much, but withhold so much that I am more bewildered than ever. I can understand your helplessness in an Eastern household, but why should you obey the behests of this veiled monster in London, in New York, in Paris?"

She did not raise her eyes.

"I dare not tell you. But I dare not disobey him."

"Who is he!"

"No one knows, because no one has ever seen his face! Ah! you are laughing! But I swear before heaven I speak the truth! Indoors he wears a Chinese dress and a green veil. In passing from place to place, which he always does at night, he is attired in a kind of cowl which only exposes his eyes — —"

"But how *can* such a fantastic being travel?"

"By road, on land, and in a steam yacht, at sea. Why should *you* doubt my honesty?" She suddenly raises her glance to Stuart's face and he saw that she had grown pale. "I have risked what I cannot tell you, and more than once — for you! I tried to call you on the telephone on the night that he set out from the house near Hampton Court to kill you, but I could get no reply, and — —"

"Stop!" said Stuart, almost too exited to note at the time that she had betrayed a secret. "It was *you* who rang up that night?

"Yes. Why did you not answer?"

"Never mind. Your call saved my life. I shall not forget." He looked into her eyes. "But can you not tell me what it all means? What or whom is 'The Scorpion'?"

She flinched.

"The Scorpion is — a passport. See." From a little pocket in the coat of her costume she drew out a golden scorpion! "I have one." She replaced it hurriedly. "I dare not, dare not tell you more. But this much I had to tell you, because…I shall never see you again!"

"What!"

"A French detective, a very clever man, learned a lot about 'The Scorpion' and he followed one of the members to England. This man killed him. Oh, I know I belong to a horrible organization!" she cried bitterly. "But I tell you I am helpless and *I* have never aided in such a thing. You should know that! But all he found out he left with you — and I do not know if I succeeded in destroying it. I do not ask you. I do not care. But I leave England to-night. Good-bye."

She suddenly stood up. Stuart rose also. He was about to speak when Miska's expression changed. A look of terror crept over her face, and hastily lowering her veil she walked rapidly away from the table and out of the room!

Many curious glances followed the elegant figure to the door. Then those glances were directed upon Stuart.

Flushing with embarrassment, he quickly settled the bill and hurried out of the hotel. Gaining the street, he looked eagerly right and left.

But Miska had disappeared!

CHAPTER V
THE HEART OF CHUNDA LAL

Dusk had drawn a grey mantle over the East-End streets when Miska, discharging the cab in which she had come from Victoria, hurried furtively along a narrow alley tending Thamesward. Unconsciously she crossed a certain line — a line invisible except upon a map of London which lay upon the table of the Assistant Commissioner in New Scotland Yard — the line forming the "red circle" of M. Gaston Max. And, crossing this line, she became the focus upon which four pairs of watchful eyes were directed.

Arriving at the door of a mean house some little distance removed from that of Ah-Fang-Fu, Miska entered, for the door was open, and disappeared from the view of the four detectives who were watching the street. Her heart was beating rapidly. For she had thought, as she had stood up to leave the restaurant, that the fierce eyes of Chunda Lal had looked in through the glass panel of one of the doors.

This gloomy house seemed to swallow her up, and the men who watched wondered more and more what had become of the elegant figure, grotesque in such a setting, which had vanished into the narrow doorway — and which did not reappear. Even Inspector Kelly, who knew so much about Chinatown, did not know that the cellars of the three houses left and right of Ah-Fang-Fu's were connected by a series of doors planned and masked with Chinese cunning.

Half an hour after Miska had disappeared into the little house near the corner, the hidden door in the damp cellar below "The Pidgin House" opened and a bent old woman, a ragged, grey-haired and dirty figure, walked slowly up the rickety wooden stair and entered a bare room behind and below the shop and to the immediate left of the den of the opium-smoker. This room, which was windowless, was lighted by a tin paraffin lamp hung upon a nail in the dirty plaster wall. The floor presented a litter of straw, paper and broken packing-cases. Two steps led up to a second door, a square heavy door of great strength. The old woman, by means of a key which she carried, was about to open this door when it was opened from the other side.

Lowering his head as he came through, Chunda Lal descended. He wore European clothes and a white turban. Save for his ardent eyes and the handsome fanatical face of the man, he might have passed for a lascar. He turned and half closed the door. The woman shrank from him, but extending a lean brown hand he gripped her arm. His eyes glittered feverishly.

"So!" he said, "we are all leaving England? Five of the Chinese sail with the P. and O. boat to-night. Ali Khan goes to-morrow, and Rama Dass, with Miguel, and the *Andaman*. I meet them at Singapore. But you?"

The woman raised her finger to her lips, glancing fearfully towards the open door. But the Hindu, drawing her nearer, repeated with subdued fierceness:

"I ask it again — but *you*?"

"I do not know," muttered the woman, keeping her head lowered and moving in the direction of the steps.

But Chunda Lal intercepted her.

"Stop!" he said — "not yet are you going. There is something I have to speak to you."

"Ssh!" she whispered, half turning and pointing up toward the door.

"Those!" said the Hindu contemptuously — "the poor slaves of the black smoke! Ah! they are floating in their dream paradise; they have no ears to hear, no eyes to see!" He grasped her wrist again. "They contest for shadow smiles and dream kisses, but Chunda Lal have eyes to see and ears to hear. He dream, too but of lips more sweet than honey, of a voice like the Song of the Daood! *Inshalla!*"

Suddenly he clutched the grey hair of the bent old woman and with one angry jerk snatched it from her head — for it was a cunning wig. Disordered, hair gleaming like bronze waves in the dim lamplight was revealed and the great dark eyes of Miska looked out from the artificially haggard face — eyes wide open and fearful.

"Bend not that beautiful body so," whispered Chunda Lal, "that is straight and supple as the willow branch. O, Miska" — his voice trembled emotionally and he that had been but a moment since so fierce stood abashed before her — "for you I become as the meanest and the lowest; for you I die!"

Miska started back from him as a muffled outcry sounded in the room beyond the half-open door. Chunda Las started also, but almost immediately smiled — and his smile was tender as a woman's.

"It is the voice of the black smoke that speaks, Miska. We are alone. Those are dead men speaking from their tombs."

"Ah-Fang-Fu is in the shop," whispered Miska.

"And there he remain."

"But what of... *him!*"

Miska pointed toward the eastern wall of the room in which they stood.

Chunda Lal clenched his hands convulsively and turned his eyes in the same direction.

"It is of *him*," he replied in a voice of suppressed vehemence, "it is of *him* I would speak." He bent close to Miska's ear. "In the creek, below the house, is lying the motor-boat. I go to-day to bring it down for him. He goes to-night to the other house up the river. To-morrow I am gone. Only you remaining."

"Yes, yes. He also leaves England to-morrow."

"And you?"

"I go with him," she whispered.

Chunda Lal glanced apprehensively toward the door. Then:

"Do not go with him!" he said, and sought to draw Miska into his arms.

"O, light of my eyes, do not go with him!"

Miska repulsed him, but not harshly.

"No, no, it is no good, Chunda Lal. I cannot hear you."

"You think" — the Hindu's voice was hoarse with emotion — "that *he* will trace you — and kill you?"

"*Trace me!*" exclaimed Miska with sudden scorn. "Is it necessary for him to trace me? Am I not already dead except for *him!* Would I be his servant, his lure, his slave for one little hour, for one short minute, if my life was my own!"

Beads of perspiration gleamed upon the brown forehead of the Hindu, and his eyes turned from the door to the eastern wall and back again to Miska. He was torn by conflicting desires, but suddenly came resolution.

"Listen, then." His voice was barely audible. "If I tell you that your life *is* your own — if I reveal to you a secret which I learned in the house of Abdul Rozan in Cairo — —"

Miska watched him with eyes in which a new, a wild expression was dawning.

"If I tell you that life and not death awaits you, will you come away to-night, and we sail for India to-morrow! Ah! I have money! Perhaps I am rich as well as — someone; perhaps I can buy you the robes of a princess" — he drew her swiftly to him — "and cover those white arms with jewels."

Miska shrank from him.

"All this means nothing," she said. "How can the secret of Abdul Rozan help me to live! And you — you will be dead before I die! — yes! One little hour after *he* finds out that I go!"

"Listen again," hissed Chunda Lal intensely. "Promise me, and I will open for you a gate of life. For you, Miska, I will do it, and we shall be free. *He* will never find out. He shall not be living to find out!"

"No, no, Chunda Lal," she moaned. "You have been my only friend, and I have tried to forget..."

"I will forswear Kali forever," he said fervently, "and shed no blood for all my life! I will live for you alone and be your slave."

"It is no good. I cannot, Chunda Lal, I cannot."

"Miska!" he pleaded tenderly.

"No, no," she repeated, her voice quivering — "I cannot...Oh! do not ask it; I cannot!"

She picked up the hideous wig, moving towards the door. Chunda Lal watched her, clenching his hands; and his eyes, which had been so tender, grew fierce.

"Ah!" he cried — "and it may be I know a reason!"

She stopped, glancing back at him.

"It may be," he continued, and his repressed violence was terrible, "it may be that I, whose heart is never sleeping, have seen and heard! One night" — he crept towards her — "one night when I cry the warning that the Doctor Sahib returns to his house, you do not come! He goes in at the house and you remain. But at last you come, and I see in your eyes — — "

"Oh!" breathed Miska, watching him fearfully.

"Do I not see it in your eyes now! Never before have I thought so until you go to that house, never before have you escaped from my care as here in London. Twice again I have doubted, and because there was other work to do I have been helpless to find out. *To-night*" — he stood before her, glaring madly into her face — "I think so again — that you have gone to him...."

"Oh, Chunda Lal!" cried Miska piteously and extended her hands towards him. "No, no — do not say it!"

"So!" he whispered — "I understand! You risk so much for him — for me you risk nothing! If he — the Doctor Sahib — say to you: 'Come with me, Miska — — ' "

"No, no! Can I never have one friend in all the world! I hear you call, Chunda Lal, but I am burning the envelope and — Doctor Stuart — finds me. I am trapped. You know it is so.

"I know you say so. And because he — Fo-Hi — is not sure and because of the piece of the scorpion which you find there, we go to that house — *he* and I — and we fail in what we go for." Chunda Lal's hand dropped limply to his sides. "Ah! I cannot understand, Miska. If we are not sure then, are we sure *now?* It may be" — he bent towards her — "we are trapped!"

"Oh, what do you mean?"

"We do not know how much they read of what he had written. Why do we wait?"

"*He* has some plan, Chunda Lal," replied Miska wearily. "Does he ever fail?"

Her words rekindled the Hindu's ardour; his eyes lighted up anew.

"I tell you his plan," he whispered tensely. "Oh! you shall hear me! He watch you grow from a little lovely child, as he watch his death-spiders and his grey scorpions grow! He tend you and care for you and make you perfect, and he plan for you as he plan for this other creatures. Then, he see what I see, that you are not only his servant but also a woman and that you have a woman's heart. He learn — who think he knows all — that he, too, is not yet a spirit but only a man, and have a man's heart, a man's blood, a man's longings! It is because of the Doctor Sahib that he learn it — — "

He grasped Miska again, but she struggled to elude him. "Oh, let me go!" she pleaded. "It is madness you speak!"

"It is madness, yes — for *you!* Always I have watched, always I have waited; and I also have seen you bloom like a rose in the desert. To-night I am here — watching...and *he* knows it! Tomorrow I am gone! Do you stay, for — *him?*

"Oh," she whispered fearfully, "it cannot be."

"You say true when you say I have been your only friend, Miska. To-morrow *he* plan that you have no friend."

He released her, and slowly, from the sleeve of his coat, slipped into view the curved blade of a native knife.

"*Ali Khan Bhai Salam!*" he muttered — by which formula he proclaimed himself a *Thug!*

Rolling his eyes in the direction of the eastern wall, he concealed the knife.

"Chunda Lal!" Miska spoke wildly. "I am frightened! Please let me go, and tomorrow — — "

"To-morrow!" Chunda Lal raised his eyes, which were alight with the awful light of fanaticism. "For me there may be no tomorrow! *Jey Bhowani! Yah Allah!*"

"Oh, *he* may hear you!" whispered Miska pitifully. "Please go now. I shall know that you are near me, if — — "

"And then?"

"I will ask your aid."

Her voice was very low.

"And if it is written that I succeed?"

Miska averted her head.

"Oh, Chunda Lal…I cannot."

She hid her face in her hands.

Chunda Lal stood watching her for a moment in silence, then he turned toward the cellar door, and then again to Miska. Suddenly he dropped upon one knee before her, took her hand and kissed it, gently.

"I am your slave," he said, his voice shaken with emotion. "For myself I ask nothing — only your pity."

He rose, opened the door by which Miska had entered the room and went down into the cellars. She watched him silently, half fearfully, yet her eyes were filled with compassionate tears. Then, readjusting the hideous grey wig, she went up the steps and passed through the doorway into the den of the opium smokers.

CHAPTER VI
THE MAN WITH THE SCAR

Stuart read through a paper, consisting of six closely written pages, then he pinned the sheets together, folded them and placed them in one of those long envelopes associated in his memory with the opening phase of "The Scorpion" mystery. Smiling grimly, he descended to his dispensary and returned with the Chinese coin attached to the cork. With this he sealed the envelope.

He had volunteered that night for onerous service, and his offer had been accepted. Gaston Max's knowledge of Eastern languages was slight, whilst Stuart's was sound and extensive, and the Frenchman had cordially welcomed the doctor's proposal that he should accompany him to the house of Ah-Fang-Fu. Reviewing the facts gleaned from Miska during the earlier part of the evening, Stuart perceived that, apart from the additional light which they shed upon her own relations with the group, they could be of slight assistance to the immediate success of the inquiry — unless the raid failed. Therefore he had determined upon the course which now he was adopting.

As he completed the sealing of the envelope and laid it down upon the table, he heard a cab drawn up in front of the house, and presently Mrs. M'Gregor knocked and entered the study.

"Inspector Dunbar to see you, Mr. Keppel," she said — "and he has with him an awful-looking body, all cuts and bandages. A patient, no doubt."

Stuart stood up, wondering what this could mean.

"Will you please show them up, Mrs. M'Gregor," he replied.

A few moments later Dunbar entered, accompanied by a bearded man whose head was bandaged so as to partly cover one eye and who had an evil-looking scar running from his cheekbone, apparently — or at any rate from the edge of the bandage — to the corner of his mouth, so that the lip was drawn up in a fierce and permanent snarl.

At this person Stuart stared blankly, until Dunbar began to laugh.

"It's a wonderful make-up, isn't it?" he said. "I used to say that disguises were out of date, but M. Max has taught me I was wrong."

"Max!" cried Stuart.

"At your service," replied the apparition, "but for this evening only I am 'Le Belafre.' Yes, *pardieu!* I am a real dead man!"

The airy indifference which he proclaimed himself to represent one whose awful body had but that day been removed from a mortuary, and one whom in his own words he had "had the misfortune to strangle," was rather ghastly and at the same time admirable. For "Le Balafre" had deliberately tried to murder him, and false sentiment should form no part of the complement of a criminal investigator.

"It is a daring idea," said Stuart, "and relies for its success upon the chance that 'The Scorpion' remains ignorant of the fate of his agent and continues to believe that the body found off Hanover Hole was yours."

"The admirable precautions of my clever colleague," replied Max, laying his hand upon Dunbar's shoulder, "in closing the mortuary and publishing particulars of the identification disk, made it perfectly safe. 'Le Balafre' has been in hiding. He emerges!"

Stuart had secret reasons for knowing that Max's logic was not at fault, and this brought him to the matter of the sealed paper. He took up the envelope.

"I have here," he said slowly, "a statement. Examine the seal."

He held it out, and Max and Dunbar looked at it. The latter laughed shortly.

"Oh, it is a real statement," continued Stuart, "the nature of which I am not at liberty to divulge. But as to-night we take risks, I propose to leave it in your charge, Inspector."

He handed the envelope to Dunbar, whose face was blank with astonishment.

"In the event of failure to-night," added Stuart, "or catastrophe, I authorise you to read this statement — and act upon it. If, however, I escape safely, I ask you to return it to me, unread."

"*Eh bien,*" said Max, and fixed that eye the whole of which was visible upon Stuart. "Perhaps I understand, and certainly" — he removed his hand from Dunbar's shoulder and rested it upon that of Stuart — "but certainly, my friend, I sympathise!"

Stuart started guiltily, but Max immediately turned aside and began to speak about their plans.

"In a bag which Inspector Dunbar has thoughtfully left in the cab," he said ——

Dunbar hastily retired and Max laughed.

"In that bag," he continued, "is a suit of clothes such as habitues of 'The Pidgin House' rejoice to wear. I, who have studied disguise almost as deeply as the great Willy Clarkson, will transform you into a perfect ruffian. It is important, you understand, that someone should be inside the house of Ah-Fang-Fu, as otherwise by means of some secret exit the man we seek may escape. I believe that he contemplates departing at any moment, and I believe that the visit of Miguel means that what I may term the masters of the minor lodges are coming to London for parting instructions — or, of course Miguel may have come about the disappearance of 'Le Balafre.'"

"Suppose you meet Miguel!"

"My dear friend, I must trust to the Kismet who pursues evil-doers! The only reason which has led me to adopt this daring disguise is a simple one. Although I believe 'The Pidgin House' to be open to ordinary opium-smokers, it may not be open on 'lodge nights.' Do you follow me? Very well. I have the golden scorpion — which I suppose to be a sort of passport."

Stuart wondered more and more at the reasoning powers of this remarkable man, which could lead him to such an accurate conclusion.

"The existence of such a passport," continued Max, "would seem to point to the fact that all the members of this organisation are not known personally to one another. At the same time those invited or expected at present *may* be known to Ah-Fang-Fu or to whoever acts as concierge. You see? Expected or otherwise, I assume that 'Le Balafre' would be admitted — and at night I shall pass very well for 'Le Balafre' — somewhat damaged as a result of my encounter with the late Charles Malet, but still recognisable!"

"And I?"

"You will be 'franked' in. The word of 'Le Balafre' should be sufficient for that! Of course I may be conducted immediately into the presence of the Chief — 'The Scorpion' — and he may prove to be none other than Miguel, for instance — or my Algerian acquaintance — or may even be a 'she' — the fascinating Zara el-Khala! We do not know. But I *think* — oh, decidedly I think — that the cowled one is a male creature, and his habits and habitat suggests to me that he is a Chinaman."

"And in that event how shall you act?"

"At once! I shall hold him, if I can, or shoot him if I cannot hold him! Both of us will blow police-whistles with which we shall be provided and Inspectors Dunbar and Kelly will raid the premises. But I am hoping for an interval. I do not like these inartistic scrimmages! The fact that these people foregather at an opium-house suggests to me that a certain procedure may be followed which I observed during the course of the celebrated 'Mr. Q' case in New York. 'Mr. Q.' also had an audience-chamber adjoining and opium den, and his visitors went there ostensibly to smoke opium. The opium-den was a sort of anteroom."

"Weymouth's big Chinese case had similar features," said Inspector Dunbar, who re-entered at that moment carrying a leathern grip. "If you are kept waiting and you keep your ears open, doctor, that's when your knowledge of the lingo will come in useful. We might rope in the whole gang and find we hadn't a scrap of evidence against them, for except the attempt on yourself, Dr. Stuart, there's nothing so far that I can see to connect 'The Scorpion' with Sir Frank Newcombe!"

"It is such a bungle that I fear!" cried Max. "Ah! how this looped-up lip annoys me!" He adjusted the bandage carefully.

"We've got the place comfortably surrounded," continued Dunbar, "and whoever may be inside is booked! A lady, answering to the description of Mlle. Dorian, went in this evening, so Sowerby reports."

Stuart felt that he was changing colour, and he stooped hastily to inspect the contents of the bag which Dunbar had opened.

"*Eh bien!*" said Gaston Max. "We shall not go empty-handed, then. And now to transfigure you, my friend!"

CHAPTER VII
IN THE OPIUM DEN

Interrupting a spell of warm, fine weather the night had set in wet and stormy. The squalid streets through which Stuart and Gaston Max made their way looked more than normally deserted and uninviting. The wind moaned and the rain accompanied with a dreary tattoo. Sometimes a siren wailed out upon the river.

"We are nearly there," said Max. "*Pardieu!* they are well concealed, those fellows. I have not seen so much as an eyebrow."

"It would be encouraging to get a glimpse of some one!" replied Stuart.

"Ah, but bad — inartistic. It is the next door, I think...yes. I hope they have no special way of knocking."

Upon the door of a dark and apparently deserted shop he rapped.

Both had anticipated an interval of waiting, and both were astonished when the door opened almost at once, revealing a blackly cavernous interior.

"Go off! Too late! Shuttee shop!" chattered a voice out of the darkness.

Max thrust his way resolutely in, followed by Stuart. "Shut the door, Ah-Fang-Fu!" he said curtly, speaking with a laboured French accent. *"Scorpion!"*

The door was closed by the invisible Chinaman, there was a sound of soft movements and a hurricane-lantern suddenly made its appearance. Its light revealed the interior of a nondescript untidy little shop and revealed the presence of an old and very wrinkled Chinaman who held the lantern. He wore a blue smock and a bowler hat and his face possessed the absolute impassivity of an image. As he leaned over the counter, scrutinising his visitors, Max thrust forward the golden scorpion held in the palm of his hand.

"Hoi, hoi" chattered the Chinaman. "Fo-Hi fellers, eh? You hab got plenty much late. Other fellers Fo-Hi pidgin plenty much sooner. You one time catchee allee same bhobbery, b'long number one joss-pidgin man!"

Being covertly nudged by Max:

"Cut the palaver, Pidgin," growled Stuart.

"Allee lightee," chattered Ah-Fang-Fu, for evidently this was he. "You play one piecee pipee till Fo-Hi got." Raising the lantern, he led the way through a door at the back of the shop. Descending four wooden steps, Stuart and Max found themselves in the opium-den.

"Full up. No loom," said the Chinaman.

It was a low-ceilinged apartment, the beams of the roof sloping slightly upward from west to east. The centre part of the wall at the back was covered with matting hung from the rough cornice supporting the beams. To the right of the matting was the door communicating with the shop, and to the left were bunks. Other bunks lined the southerly wall, except where, set in the thickness of the bare brick and plaster, a second strong door was partly hidden by a pile of empty packing-cases and an untidy litter of straw and matting.

Along the northern wall were more bunks, and an open wooden stair, with a handrail, ascended to a small landing or platform before a third door high up in the wall. A few mats were strewn about the floor. The place was dimly lighted by a red-shaded lamp swung from the centre of the ceiling and near the foot of the stairs another lamp (of the common tin variety) stood upon a box near which was a broken cane chair. Opium-pipes, tins, and a pack of cards were on this box.

All the bunks appeared to be occupied. Most of the occupants were lying motionless, but one or two were noisily sucking at the opium-pipes. These had not yet attained to the opium-smokers Nirvana. So much did Gaston Max, a trained observer, gather in one swift glance. Then Ah-Fang-Fu, leaving the lantern in the shop, descended the four steps and crossing the room began to arrange two mats with round head-cushions near to the empty packing-cases. Stuart and Max remained by the door.

"You see," whispered Max, "he has taken you on trust! And he did not appear to recognise me. It is as I thought. The place is 'open to the public' as usual, and Ah-Fang-Fu does a roaring trade, one would judge. For the benefit of patrons not affiliated to the order we have to pretend to smoke."

"Yes," replied Stuart with repressed excitement — "until someone called Fo-Hi is at home, or visible; the word 'got' may mean either of those things."

"Fo-Hi," whispered Max, "is 'The Scorpion!'

"I believe you are right," said Stuart — who had good reason to know it. "My God! what a foul den! The reek is suffocating. Look at that yellow lifeless face yonder, and see that other fellow whose hand hangs limply down upon the floor. Those bunks might be occupied by corpses for all the evidence of life that some of them show."

"Morbleu! do not raise your voice; for some of them are occupied by 'Scorpions.' You noted the words of Ah-Fang? *Ssh!"*

The old Chinaman returned with his curious shuffling walk, raising his hand to beckon to them.

"Number one piece bunk, lo!" he chattered.

"Good enough," growled Stuart.

The two crossed and reclined upon the uncleanly mats.

"Make special loom," explained Ah-Fang-Fu. "Velly special chop!"

He passed from bunk to bunk, and presently came to a comatose Chinaman from whose limp hand, which hung down upon the floor, the pipe had dropped. This pipe Ah-Fang-Fu took from the smoker's fingers and returning to the box upon which the tin lamp was standing began calmly to load it.

"Good heavens!" muttered Stuart — "he is short of pipes! Pah! how the place reeks!"

Ah-Fang-Fu busied himself with a tin of opium, the pipe which he had taken from the sleeper, and another pipe — apparently the last of his stock — which lay near the lamp. Igniting the two, he crossed and handed them to Stuart and Max.

"Velly soon-lo!" he said and made a curious sign, touching his brow, his lips and his breast in a manner resembling that of a Moslem.

Max repeated the gesture and then lay back upon his elbow, raising the mouthpiece of the little pipe to his lips — but carefully avoiding contact.

Ah-Fang-Fu shuffled back to the broken cane chair, from which he had evidently arisen to admit his late visitors.

Inarticulate sounds proceeded from the bunks, breaking the sinister silence which now descended upon the den. Ah-Fang-Fu began to play Patience, constantly muttering to himself. The occasional wash of tidal water became audible, and once there came a scampering and squealing of rates from beneath the floor.

"Do you notice the sound of lapping water" whispered Stuart. "The place is evidently built upon a foundation of piles and the cellars must actually be submerged at high-tide."

"Pardieu! it is a death trap. What is this!"

A loud knocking sounded upon the street door. Ah-Fang-Fu rose and shuffled up the steps into the shop. He could be heard unbarring the outer door. Then:

"Too late! shuttee shop, shuttee shop!" sounded.

"I don't want nothin' out of your blasted shop, Pidgin!" roared a loud and thick voice. "I'm old Bill Bean, I am, and I want a pipe, I do!"

"Hullo, Bill!" replied the invisible 'Pidgin.' "Allee samee dlunk again!"

A red-bearded ship's fireman, wearing sea-boots, a rough blue suit similar to that which Stuart wore, a muffler and a peaked cap, lurched into view at the head of the steps.

"Blimey!" he roared, over his shoulder. "Drunk! *Me* drunk! An' all the pubs in these parts sell barley-water coloured brown! Blimey! Chuck it, Pidgin!"

Ah-Fang-Fu reappeared behind him. "Catchee dlunk ev'ly time for comee here," he chattered.

"'Taint 'umanly possible," declared the new arrival, staggering down the steps, "fer a 'ealthy sailorman to git drunk on coloured water just 'cause the publican calls it beer! I ain't drunk; I'm only miserable. Gimmee a pipe, Pidgin."

Ah-Fang-Fu barred the door and ascended.

"Comee here," he muttered, "my placee, all full up and no other placee b'long open."

Bill Bean slapped him boisterously on the back.

"Cut the palaver, Pidgin, and gimme a pipe. Piecee pipe, Pidgin!"

He lurched across the floor, nearly falling over Stuart's legs, took up a mat and a cushion, lurched into the further corner and cast himself down.

"Ain't I one o' yer oldest customers, Pidgin?" he inquired. "One o' yer oldest, I am."

"Blight side twelve-time," muttered the Chinaman. "Getchee me in tlouble, Bill. Number one police chop."

"Not the first time it wouldn't be!" retorted the fireman. "Not the first time as you've been in trouble, Pidgin. An' unless they 'ung yer — which it ain't 'umanly possible to 'ang a Chink — it wouldn't be the last — an' not by a damn long way...*an'* not by a damn long way!"

Ah-Fang-Fu, shrugging resignedly, shuffled from bunk to bunk in quest of a disused pipe, found one, and returning to the extemporised table, began to load it, muttering to himself.

"Don't like to 'ear about your wicked past, do you?" continued Bill.

"Wicked old yellow-faced 'eathen! Remember the 'dive' in 'Frisco, Pidgin? *Wot* a rough 'ouse! Remember when I come in — full up I was: me back teeth well under water — an' you tried to Shanghai me?"

"You cutee palaber. All damn lie," muttered the Chinaman.

"Ho! a lie is it?" roared the other. "Wot about me wakin' up all of a tremble aboard o' the old *Nancy Lee* — aboard of a blasted wind-jammer! Me — a fireman! Wot about it? Wasn't that Shanghaiin'? Blighter! *An'* not a 'oat' in me pocket — not a 'bean'! Broke to the wide an' aboard of a old wind-jammer wot was a coffin-ship — a coffin-ship she was; an' 'er old man was the devil's father-in-law. Ho! lies! I *don't* think!"

"You cutee palaber!" chattered Ah-Fang-Fu, busy with the pipe. "You likee too much chin-chin. You make nice piece bhobbery."

"Not a 'bean'," continued Bill reminiscently — "not a 'oat.'" He sat up violently. "Even me pipe an' baccy was gone!" he shouted. "You'd even pinched me pipe an' baccy! You'd pinch the whiskers off a blind man, *you* would, Pidgin! 'And over the dope. Thank Gawd somebody's still the right stuff!"

Suddenly, from a bunk on the left of Gaston Max came a faint cry.

"Ah! He has bitten me!"

"'Ullo!" said Bill — "wotcher bin given' *'im*, Pidgin? *Chandu* or hydrerphobia?"

Ah-Fang-Fu crossed and handed him the pipe.

"One piecee pipee. No more hab."

Bill grasped the pipe eagerly and raised it to his lips. Ah-Fang-Fu returned unmoved to his Patience and silence reclaimed the den, only broken by the inarticulate murmuring and the lapping of the tide.

"A genuine customer!" whispered Max.

"Ah!" came again, more faintly — "he...has...bitten...me."

"Blimey!" said Bill in a drowsy voice — "'eave the chair at 'im, Pidgin."

Stuart was about to speak when Gaston Max furtively grasped his arm. "Ssh!" he whispered. "Do not move, but look...at the top of the stair!"

Stuart turned his eyes. On the platform at the head of the stairs a Hindu was standing!

"Chunda Lal!" whispered Max. "Prepare for — anything!"

"Chunda Lal descended slowly. Ah-Fang-Fu continued to play Patience. The Hindu stood behind him and began to speak in a voice of subdued fervour and with soft Hindu modulations.

"Why do you allow them, strangers, coming here to-night!"

Ah-Fang-Fu continued complacently to arrange the cards.

"S'pose hab gotchee pidgin allee samee Chunda Lal hab got? Fo-Hi no catchee buy bled and cheese for Ah-Fang-Fu. He" — nodding casually in the direction of Bill Bean — "plitty soon all blissful."

"Be very careful, Ah-Fang-Fu," said Chunda Lal tensely. He lowered his voice. "Do you forget so soon what happen last week?"

"No sabby."

"Some one comes here — we do not know how close he comes; perhaps he comes in — and he is of the *police*."

Ah-Fang-Fu shuffled uneasily in his chair.

"No police chop for Pidgin!" he muttered. "Same feller tumble in liver?"

"He is killed — yes; but suppose they find the writing he has made! Suppose he has written that it is *here* people meet together?"

"Makee chit tell my name? Muchee hard luck! Number one police chop."

"You say Fo-Hi not buying you bread and cheese. Perhaps it is Fo-Hi that save you from hanging!"

Ah-Fang-Fu hugged himself.

"Yak pozee!" (Very good) he muttered.

Chunda Lal raised his finger.

"Be very careful, Ah-Fang-Fu!"

"Allee time velly careful."

"But admit no more of them to come in, these strangers."

"Tchee, tchee! Velly ploper. Sometime big feller come in if Pidgin palaber or not. Pidgin never lude to big feller."

"Your life may depend on it," said Chunda Lal impressively. "How many are here?"

Ah-Fang-Fu turned at last from his cards, pointing in three directions, and, finally, at Gaston Max.

"Four?" said the Hindu — "how can it be?"

He peered from bunk to bunk, muttering something — a name apparently — after scrutinizing each. When his gaze rested upon Max he started, stared hard, and meeting the gaze of the one visible eye, made the strange sign.

Max repeated it; and Chunda Lal turned again to the Chinaman. "Because of that drunken pig," he said, pointing at Bill Bean — "we must wait. See to it that he is the last."

He walked slowly up the stairs, opened the door at the top and disappeared.

CHAPTER VIII
THE GREEN-EYED JOSS

Sinister silence reclaimed the house of Ah-Fang-Fu. And Ah-Fang-Fu resumed his solitary game.

"He recognised 'Le Belafre'" whispered Max — "and was surprised to see him! So there are three of the gang here! Did you particularly observe in which bunks they lay, doctor. *Ssh!"*

A voice from a bunk had commenced to sing monotonously.

"Peyala peah," it sang, weird above the murmured accompaniment of the other dreaming smokers and the *wash-wash* of the tide — *"To myn-na-peah-Phir Kysee ko kyah..."*

"He is speaking from an opium-trance," said Stuart softly. "A native song: 'If a cup of wine is drunk, and I have drunk it, what of that?'"

"Mon Dieu! it is uncanny!" whispered Max. *"Brr!* do you hear those rats? I am wondering in what order we shall be admitted to the 'Scorpion's' presence, or if we shall see him together."

"He may come in here."

"All the better."

"Gimme 'nother pipe, Pidgin," drawled a very drowsy voice from Bill Bean's corner.

Ah-Fang-Fu left his eternal arranging and rearranging of the cards and crossed the room. He took the opium-pipe from the fireman's limp fingers and returning to the box, refilled and lighted it. Max and Stuart watched him in silence until he had handed the second pipe to the man and returned to his chair.

"We must be very careful," said Stuart. "We do not know which are real smokers and which are not."

Again there was a weird interruption. A Chinaman lying in one of the bunks began to chant in a monotonous far-away voice:

> *"Chong-liou-chouay*
> *Om mani padme hum."*

"The Buddhist formula," whispered Stuart. *"He* is a real smoker. Heavens! the reek is choking me!"

The chant was repeated, the words dying away into a long murmur. Ah-Fang-Fu continued to shuffle the cards. And presently Bill Bean's second pipe dropped from his fingers. His husky voice spoke almost inaudibly.

"I'm ... old ... Bill ... Bean ... I ..."

A deep-noted siren hooted dimly.

"A steamer making for dock," whispered Max. *"Brr!* it is a nightmare, this! I think in a minute something will happen. *Ssh!"*

Ah-Fang-Fu glanced slowly around. Then he stood up, raised the lamp from the table and made a tour of the bunks, shining the light in upon the faces of the occupants. Max watched him closely, hoping to learn in which bunks the members of 'The Scorpion's' group lay. But he was disappointed. Ah-Fang-Fu examined *all* the bunks and even shone the light down upon Stuart and Max. He muttered to himself constantly, but seemed to address no one.

Replacing the lamp on the box, he whistled softly; and: ——

"Look!" breathed Max. "The stair again!"

Stuart cautiously turned his eyes toward the open stair.

On the platform above stood a bent old hag whose witch-eyes were searching the place keenly! With a curiously lithe step, for all her age, she descended, and standing behind Ah-Fang-Fu tapped him on the shoulder and pointed to the outer door. He stood up and shuffled across, went up the four steps and unbarred the door.

"Tchee, tchee," he chattered. "Pidgin make a look-out."

He went out and closed the door.

"Something happens!" whispered Max.

A gong sounded.

"Ah!"

The old woman approached the matting curtain hung over a portion of the wall, raised it slightly in the centre — where it opened — and disappeared beyond.

"You see!" said Stuart excitedly.

"Yes! it is the audience-chamber of 'The Scorpion'!"

The ancient hag came out again, crossed to a bunk and touched its occupant, a Chinaman, with her hand. He immediately shot up and followed her. The two disappeared beyond the curtain.

"What shall we do," said Stuart, *"if you* are summoned?"

"I shall throw open those curtains the moment I reach them, and present my pistol at the head of whoever is on the other side. You — *ssh!"*

The old woman reappeared, looked slowly around and then held the curtains slightly apart to allow of the Chinaman's coming out. He saluted her by touching his head, lips and breast with his right hand, then passed up to the door communicating with the shop, which he opened, and went out.

His voice came, muffled:

"Fo-Hi!"

"Fo-Hi," returned the high voice of Ah-Fang-Fu.

The outer door was opened and shut. The old woman went up and barred the inner door, then returned and stood by the matting curtain. The sound of the water below alone broke the silence. It was the hour of high tide.

"There goes the first fish into Dunbar's net!" whispered Max.

The gong sounded again.

Thereupon the old woman crossed to another bunk and conducted a brown-skinned Eastern into the hidden room. Immediately they had disappeared:

"As I pull the curtains aside," continued Max rapidly, "blow the whistle and run across and unbar the door...."

So engrossed was he in giving these directions, and so engrossed was Stuart in listening to them, that neither detected a faint creak which proceeded from almost immediately behind them. This sound was occasioned by the slow and cautious opening of that sunken, heavy door near to which they lay — the door which communicated with the labyrinth of cellars. Inch by inch from the opening protruded the head of Ah-Fang-Fu!

"If the Chinaman offers any resistance," Max went on, speaking very rapidly — *"morbleu!* you have the means to deal with him! In a word, admit the police. *Sh!* what is that!"

A moaning voice from one of the bunks came.

"Cheal kegur-men, mas ka dheer!"

"A native adage," whispered Stuart. "He is dreaming. 'There is always meat in a kite's nest.'"

"Eh bien! very true — and I think the kite is at home!"

The head of Ah-Fang-Fu vanished. A moment later the curtains opened again slightly and the old woman came out, ushering the brown man. He saluted her and unbarred the door, going out.

"Fo-Hi," came dimly.

There was no definite answer — only the sound of a muttered colloquy; and suddenly the brown man returned and spoke to the old woman in a voice so low that his words were inaudible to the two attentive listeners in the distant corner.

"Ah!" whispered Max — "what now?"

"Shall we rush the curtain!" said Stuart.

"No!" Max grasped his arm — "wait! wait! See! he is going out. He has perhaps forgotten something. A second fish in the net."

The Oriental went up the steps into the shop. The old woman closed and barred the door, then opened the matting curtain and disappeared within.

"I was right," said Max.

But for once in his career he was wrong.

She was out again almost immediately and bending over a bunk close to the left of the masked opening. The occupant concealed in its shadow did not rise and follow her, however. She seemed to be speaking to him. Stuart and Max watched intently.

The head of Ah-Fang-Fu reappeared in the doorway behind them.

"Now is our time!" whispered Max tensely. "As I rush for the curtains, you run to the shop door and get it unbolted, whistling for Dunbar — — "

Ah-Fang-Fu, fully opening the door behind them, crept out stealthily.

"Have your pistol ready," continued Max, "and first put the whistle between your teeth — — "

Ah-Fang-Fu silently placed his bowler hat upon the floor, shook down his long pigtail, and moving with catlike tread, stooping, drew nearer.

"Now, doctor!" cried Max.

Both sprang to their feet. Max leapt clear of the matting and other litter and dashed for the curtain. He reached it, seized it and tore bodily from its fastenings. Behind him the long flat note of a police whistle sounded — and ended abruptly.

"Ah! Nom d'un nom!" cried Max.

A cunningly devised door — looking like a section of solid brick and plaster wall — was closing slowly — heavily. Through the opening which yet remained he caught a glimpse of a small room, draped with Chinese dragon tapestry and having upon a raised, carpeted dais a number of cushions forming a *diwan* and an inlaid table bearing a silver snuff vase. A cowled figure was seated upon the dais. The door closed completely. Within a niche in its centre sat a yellow leering idol, green eyed and complacent.

Wild, gurgling cries brought Max sharply about.

An answering whistle sounded from the street outside...a second...a third.

Ah-Fang-Fu, stooping ever lower, at the instant that Stuart had sprung to his feet had seized his ankle from behind, pitching him on to his face. It was then that the note of the whistle had ceased. Now, the Chinaman had his long pigtail about Stuart's neck, at which Stuart, prone with the other kneeling upon his body, plucked vainly.

Max raised his pistol...and from the bunk almost at his elbow leapt Miguel the quadroon, a sand-bag raised. It descended upon the Frenchman's skull...and he crumbled up limply and collapsed upon the floor. There came a crash of broken glass from the shop.

Uttering a piercing cry, the old woman staggered from the door near which she had been standing as if stricken helpless, during the lightning moments in which these things had happened — and advanced in the direction of Ah-Fang-Fu.

"Ah, God! You kill him! You *kill* him?" she moaned.

"Through the window, Sowerby! This way!" came Dunbar's voice. "Max! Max!"

The sustained note of a whistle, a confusion of voices and a sound of heavy steps proclaimed the entrance of the police into the shop and the summoning of reinforcements.

Ah-Fang-Fu rose. Stuart had ceased to struggle. The Chinaman replaced his hat and looked up at the woman, whose eyes glared madly into his own.

"*Tche', tche'e,*" he said sibilantly — "*Tchon-dzee-ti Fan-Fu.**"

* "Yes, yes. It is the will of the Master."

"Down with the door!" roared Dunbar.

The woman threw herself, with a wild sob, upon the motionless body of Stuart.

Ensued a series of splintering crashes, and finally the head of an axe appeared through the panels of the door. Ah-Fang-Fu tried to drag the woman away, but she clung to Stuart desperately and was immovable. Thereupon the huge quadroon, running across the room, swept them both up into his giant embrace, man and woman together, and bore them down by the sunken doorway into the cellars below!

The shop door fell inwards, crashing down the four steps, and Dunbar sprang into the place, revolver in hand, followed by Inspector Kelly and four men of the River Police, one of whom carried a hurricane lantern. Ah-Fang-Fu had just descended after Miguel and closed the heavy door.

"Try this way, boys!" cried Kelly, and rushed up the stair. The four men followed him. The lantern was left on the floor. Dunbar stared about him. Sowerby and several other men entered. Suddenly Dunbar saw Gaston Max lying on the floor.

"My God!" he cried — "they have killed him!"

He ran across, knelt and examined Max, pressing his ear against his breast.

Inspector Kelly reaching the top of the stairs and finding the door locked, hurled his great bulk against it and burst it open.

"Follow me, boys!" he cried. "Take care! Bring the lantern, somebody."

The fourth man grasped the lantern and all followed the Inspector up the stair and out through the doorway. His voice came dimly:

"Mind the beam! Pass the light forward...."

Sowerby was struggling with the door by which Miguel and Ah-Fang-Fu unseen had made their escape and Dunbar, having rested Max's head upon a pillow, was glaring all about him, his square jaw set grimly and his eyes fierce with anger.

A voice droned from a bunk:

"Cheal kegur men ms ka-dheer!"

The police were moving from bunk to bunk, scrutinising the occupants.

The uproar had penetrated to them even in their drugged slumbers.

There were stirrings and mutterings and movements of yellow hands.

"But where is 'The Scorpion'?"

He turned and stared at the wall from which the matting had been torn. And out of the little niche in the cunningly masked door the green-eyed joss leered at him complacently.

PART IV
THE LAIR OF THE SCORPION

CHAPTER I
THE SUBLIME ORDER

Stuart awoke to a discovery so strange that for some time he found himself unable to accept its reality. He passed his hands over his face and eyes and looked about him dazedly. He experienced great pain in his throat, and he could feel that his neck was swollen. He stared down at his ankles, which also were throbbing agonisingly — to learn that they were confined in gyves attached by a short chain to a ring in the floor!

He was lying upon a deep *diwan,* which was covered with leopard-skins and which occupied one corner of the most extraordinary room he had ever seen or ever could have imagined. He sat up, but was immediately overcome with faintness which he conquered with difficulty.

The apartment, then, was one of extraordinary Oriental elegance, having two entrances closed with lacquer sliding doors. Chinese lamps swung from the ceiling, illuminated it warmly, and a great number of large and bright silk cushions were strewn about the floor. There were tapestries in black and gold, rich carpets and couches, several handsome cabinets and a number of tall cases of Oriental workmanship containing large and strangely bound books, scientific paraphernalia, curios and ornaments.

At the further end of the room was a deep tiled hearth in which stood a kind of chemical furnace which hissed constantly. Upon ornate small tables and pedestals were vases and cases — one of the latter containing a number or orchids, in flower.

Preserved lizards, snakes, and other creatures were in a row of jars upon a shelf, together with small skeletons of animals in frames. There was also a perfect human skeleton. Near the centre of the room was a canopied chair, of grotesque Chinese design, upon a dais, a big bronze bell hanging from it; and near to the *diwan* upon which Stuart was lying stood a large, very finely carved table upon which were some open faded volumes and a litter of scientific implements. Near the table stood a very large bowl of what looked like platinum, upon a tripod, and several volumes lay scattered near it upon the carpet. From a silver incense-burner arose a pencilling of blue smoke.

One of the lacquer doors slid noiselessly open and a man entered, Stuart inhaled sibilantly and clenched his fists.

The new-comer wore a cowled garment of some dark blue material which enveloped him from head to feet. It possessed oval eye-holes, and through these apertures gleamed two eyes which looked scarcely like the eyes of a human being. They were of that brilliant yellow color sometimes seen in the eyes of tigers, and their most marked and awful peculiarity was their unblinking regard. They seemed always to be open to their fullest extent, and Stuart realized with anger that it was impossible to sustain for long the piercing gaze of Fo-Hi...for he knew that he was in the presence of "The Scorpion"!

Walking with a slow and curious dignity, the cowled figure came across to the table, first closing the lacquer door. Stuart's hands convulsively clutched the covering of the *diwan* as the sinister figure approached. The intolerable gaze of those weird eyes had awakened a horror, a loathing horror, within him, such as he never remembered to have experienced in regard to any human being. It was the sort of horror which the proximity of a poisonous serpent occasions — or the nearness of a scorpion....

Fo-Hi seated himself at the table.

Absolute silence reigned in the big room, except for the hissing of the furnace. No sound penetrated from the outer world. Having no means of judging how long he had been insensible, Stuart found himself wondering if the raid on the den of Ah-Fang-Fu had taken place hours before, days earlier, or weeks ago.

Taking up a test-tube from a rack on the table, Fo-Hi held it near a lamp and examined the contents — a few drops of colourless fluid. These he poured into a curious long-necked yellow bottle. He began to speak, but without looking at Stuart.

His diction was characteristic, resembling his carriage in that it was slow and distinctive. He seemed deliberately to choose each word and to give to it all its value, syllable by syllable. His English was perfect to the verge of the pedantic; and his voice was metallic and harsh, touching at time, when his words were vested with some subtle or hidden significance, guttural depths which betrayed the Chinaman. He possessed uncanny dignity as of tremendous intellect and conscious power.

"I regret that you were so rash as to take part in last night's abortive raid, Dr. Stuart," he said. Stuart started. So he had been unconscious for many hour!

"Because of your professional acquirements at one time I had contemplated removing you," continued the unemotional voice. "But I rejoice to think that I failed. It would have been an error of judgement. I have useful work for such men. You shall assist in the extensive laboratories of my distinguished predecessor."

"Never!" snapped Stuart.

The man's callousness was so purposeful and deliberate that it awed. He seemed like one who stands above all ordinary human frailties and emotions.

"Your prejudice is natural," rejoined Fo-Hi calmly. "You are ignorant of our sublime motives, but you shall nevertheless assist us to establish that intellectual control which is destined to be the new World Force. No doubt you are conscious of a mental hiatus extending from the moment when you found the pigtail of the worthy Ah-Fang-Fu about your throat until that when you recovered consciousness in this room. It has covered a period roughly of twenty-four hours, Dr. Stuart."

"I don't believe it," muttered Stuart — and found his own voice to seem as unreal as everything else in the nightmare apartment. "If I had not revived earlier, I should never have revived at all."

He raised his hand to his swollen throat, touching it gingerly.

"Your unconsciousness was prolonged," explained Fo-Hi, consulting an open book written in Chinese characters, "by an injection which I found it necessary to make. Otherwise, as you remark, it would have been prolonged indefinitely. Your clever but rash companion was less happy."

"What!" cried Stuart — "he is dead? You fiend! You damned yellow fiend!" Emotion shook him and he sat clutching the leopard-skins and glaring madly at the cowled figure.

"Fortunately," resumed Fo-Hi, "my people — with one exception — succeeded in making their escape. I may add that the needless scuffling attendant upon arresting this unfortunate follower of mine, immediately outside the door of the house, led to the discovery of your own presence. Nevertheless, the others departed safely. My own departure is imminent; it has been because of certain domestic details and by the necessity of awaiting nightfall. You see, I am frank with you."

"Because the grave is silent!"

"The grave, and...China. There is no other alternative in your case."

"Are you sure that there is no other in your own?" asked Stuart huskily.

"An alternative to my returning to China? Can you suggest one?"

"The scaffold!" cried Stuart furiously, "for you and the scum who follow you!"

Fo-Hi lighted a Bunsen burner.

"I trust not," he rejoined placidly. "With two exceptions, all my people are out of England."

Stuart's heart began to throb painfully. With two exceptions! Did Miska still remain? He conquered his anger and tried to speak calmly, recognising how he lay utterly in the power of this uncanny being and how closely his happiness was involved even if he escaped with life.

"And you?" he said.

"In these matters, Dr. Stuart," replied Fo-Hi, "I have always modelled my behavior upon that of the brilliant scientist who preceded me as European representative of our movement. Your beautiful Thames is my highway as it was his highway. No one of my immediate neighbours has ever seen me or my once extensive following enter this house." He selected an empty test-tube. "No one shall see me leave."

The unreality of it all threatened to swamp Stuart's mind again, but he forced himself to speak calmly.

"Your own escape is just possible, if some vessel awaits you; but do you imagine for a moment that you can carry me to China and elude pursuit?"

Fo-Hi, again consulting the huge book with its yellow faded characters, answered him absently.

"Do you recall the death of the Grand Duke Ivan?" he said. "Does your memory retain the name of Van Rembold and has your Scotland Yard yet satisfied itself that Sir Frank Narcombe died from 'natural causes'? Then, there was Ericksen, the most brilliant European electrical expert of the century, who died quite suddenly last year. I honor you, Dr. Stuart, by inviting you to join a company so distinguished."

"You are raving! What have these men in common with me?"

Stuart found himself holding his breath as he awaited a reply — for he knew that he was on the verge of learning that which poor Gaston Max had given his life to learn. A moment Fo-Hi hesitated — and in that moment his captive recognised, and shuddered to recognise, that he won this secret too late. Then:

"The Grand Duke is a tactician who, had he remained in Europe, might well have readjusted the frontiers of his country. Van Rembold, as a mining engineer, stands alone, as does Henrik Ericksen in the electrical world. As for Sir Frank Narcombe, he is beyond doubt the most brilliant surgeon of today, and I, a judge of men, count you his peer in the realm of pure therapeutics. Whilst your studies in snake-poisons (which were narrowly watched for us in India) give you an unique place in toxicology. These great men will be some of your companions in China."

"In China!"

"In China, Dr. Stuart, where I hope you will join them. You misapprehend the purpose of my mission. It is not destructive, although neither I nor my enlightened predecessor have ever scrupled to remove any obstacle from the path of that world-change which no human power can check or hinder; it is primarily constructive. No state or group of states can hope to resist the progress of a movement guided and upheld by a monopoly of the world's genius. The Sublime Order, of which I am an unworthy member, stands for such a movement."

"Rest assured it will be crushed."

"Van Rembold is preparing radium in quantities hitherto unknown from the vast pitchblend deposits of Ho-Nan — which industry we control. He visited China arrayed in his shroud, and he travelled in a handsome Egyptian sarcophagus purchased at Sotherby's on behalf of a Chinese collector."

Fo-Hi stood up and crossed to the hissing furnace. He busied himself with some obscure experiment which proceeded there, and:

"Your own state-room will be less romantic, Dr. Stuart," he said, speaking without turning his head; "possibly a packing-case. In brief, that intellectual giant who achieved to much for the Sublime Order — my immediate predecessor in office — devised a means of inducing artificial catalepsy — — "

"My God!" muttered Stuart, as the incredible, the appalling truth burst upon his mind.

"My own rather hazardous delay," continued Fo-Hi, "is occasioned in some measure by my anxiety to complete the present experiment. Its product will be your passport to China."

Carrying a tiny crucible, he returned to the table.

Stuart felt that his self-possession was deserting him. Madness threatened...If he was not already mad. He forced himself to speak.

"You taunt me because I am helpless. I do not believe that those men have been spirited into China. Even if it were so, they would die, as I would die, rather than prostitute their talents to such mad infamy."

Fo-Hi carefully poured the contents of the crucible into a flat platinum pan.

"In China, Dr. Stuart," he said, "we know how to *make* men work! I myself am the deviser of a variant of the unduly notorious *kite* device and the scarcely less celebrated 'Six Gates of Wisdom.' I term it The Feast of a Thousand Ants. It is performed with the aid of African driver ant, a pair of surgical scissors and a pot of honey. I have observed you studying with interest the human skeleton yonder. It is that of one of my followers — a Nubian mute — who met with an untimely end quite recently. You are wondering, no doubt, how I obtained the frame in so short a time? My African driver ants, Dr. Stuart, of which I have three large cases in a cellar below this room, performed the task for me in exactly sixty-nine minutes."

Stuart strained frenziedly at his gyves.

"My God!" he groaned. "All I have heard of you was the merest flattery. You are either a fiend or a madman!"

"When you are enlisted as a member of the Sublime Order," said Fo-Hi softly, "and you awaken in China, Dr. Stuart — you will work. We have no unwilling recruits."

"Stop your accursed talk. I have heard enough."

But the metallic voice continued smoothly:

"I appreciate the difficulty which you must experience in grasping the true significance of this movement. You have seen mighty nations, armed with every known resource of science, at a deadlock on the battlefield. You naturally fail to perceive how a group of Oriental philosophers can achieve what the might of Europe failed to achieve. You will remember, in favour of my claims, that we command the service of the world's genius, and have a financial backing which could settle the national loans of the world! In other words, exhumation of a large percentage of the great men who have died in recent years would be impossible. Their tombs are empty."

"I have heard enough. Drug me, kill me; but spare me your confidences."

"In the crowded foyer of a hotel," continued Fo-Hi imperturbably, "of a theatre, of a concert-room; in the privacy of their home, of their office; wherever opportunity offered, I caused them to be touched with the point of a hypodermic needle such as this." He held up a small hypodermic syringe.

"It contained a minute quantity of the serum which I am now preparing — the serum whose discovery was the crowning achievement of a great scientist's career (I refer, Dr. Stuart, to my brilliant predecessor). They were buried alive; but no surgeon in Europe or America would have hesitated to certify them dead. Aided by a group of six Hindu fanatics, trained as *Lughais* (grave-diggers), it was easy to gain access to their resting-places. One had the misfortune to be cremated by his family — a great loss to my Council. But the others are now in China, at our headquarters. They are labouring day and night to bring this war-scarred world under the sceptre of an Eastern Emperor."

"Faugh!" cried Stuart. "The whole of that war-scarred world will stand armed before you!"

"We realise that, doctor; therefore we are prepared for it. We spoke of the Norwegian Henrick Ericksen. This is his most recent contribution to our armament."

Fo-Hi rested on long yellow hand upon a kind of model searchlight.

"I nearly committed the clumsy indiscretion of removing you with this little instrument," he said. "You recall the episode? Ericksen's Disintegrating Ray, Dr. Stuart. The model, here, possesses a limited range, of course, but the actual instrument has a compass of seven and a half miles. It can readily be carried by a heavy plane! One such plane in a flight from Suez to Port Said, could destroy all the shipping in the Canal and explode every grain of ammunition on either shore! Since I must leave England to-night, the model must be destroyed, and unfortunately a good collection of bacilli has already suffered the same fate."

Placidly, slowly, and unmoved from his habit of unruffled dignity, Fo-Hi placed the model in a deep mortar, whilst Stuart watched him speechless and aghast. He poured the contents of a large pan into the mortar, whereupon a loud hissing sound broke the awesome silence of the room and a cloud of fumes arose.

"Not a trace, doctor!" said the cowled man. "A little preparation of my own. It destroys the hardest known substance — with the solitary exception of a certain clay — in the same way that nitric acid would destroy tissue paper. You see I might have aspired to become famous among safe-breakers."

"You have preferred to become infamous among murderers!" snapped Stuart.

"To murder, Dr. Stuart, I have never stooped. I am a specialist in selective warfare. When you visit the laboratory of our chief chemist in Kiangsu you will be shown the whole of the armory of the Sublime Order. I regret that the activities of your zealous and painfully inquisitive friend, M. Gaston Max, have forced me to depart from England before I had completed my work here."

"I pray you may never depart," murmured Stuart.

Fo-Hi having added some bright green fluid to that in the flat pan, had now poured the whole into a large test-tube, and was holding it in the flame of the burner. At the moment that it reached the boiling point it became colourless. He carefully placed the whole of the liquid in a retort to which he attached a condensor. He stood up.

Crossing to a glass case which rested upon a table near the *diwan* he struck it lightly with his hand. The case contained sand and fragments of rock, but as Fo-Hi struck it, out from beneath the pieces of rock darted black active creatures.

"The common black scorpion of Southern India," he said softly. "Its venom is the basis of the priceless formula, *F. Katalepsis,* upon which the structure of our Sublime Order rests, Dr. Stuart; hence the adoption of a scorpion as our device."

He took up a long slender flask.

"This virus prepared from a glandular secretion of the Chinese swamp-adder is also beyond price. Again-the case upon the pedestal yonder contains five perfect bulbs, three already in flower, as you observe, of an orchid discovered by our chief chemist in certain forests of Burma. It only occurs at extremely rare intervals — eighty years or more — and under highly special conditions. If the other two bulbs flower, I shall be enabled to obtain from the blooms a minimum quantity of an essential oil for which the nations of the earth, if they knew its properties, would gladly empty their treasuries. This case must at all costs accompany me."

"Yet because you are still in England," said Stuart huskily, "I venture to hope that your devil dreams may end on the scaffold."

"That can never be, Dr. Stuart," returned Fo-Hi placidly. "The scaffold is not for such as I. Moreover, it is a crude and barbaric institution which I deplore. Do you see that somewhat peculiarly constructed chair, yonder? It is an adaptation, by a brilliant young chemist of Canton, of Ericksen's Disintegrating Ray. A bell hangs beside it. If you were seated in that chair and I desire to dismiss you, it would merely be necessary fro me to strike the bell once with the hammer. Before the vibration of the note had become inaudible you would be seeking your ancestors among the shades. It is the throne of the gods. Such a death is poetic."

He returned to the table and, observing meticulous care, emptied the few drops of colourless liquid from the condenser into a test-tube. Holding the tube near a lamp, he examined the contents, then poured the liquid into the curious yellow bottle. A faint vapour arose from it.

"You would scarcely suppose," he said, "that yonder window opens upon an ivy-grown balcony commanding an excellent view of that picturesque Tudor survival, Hampton Court? I apprehend, however, that the researches of your late friend, M. Gaston Max, may ere long lead Scotland Yard to my doors, although there has been nothing in the outward seeming of this house, in the circumstances of my tenancy, or in my behaviour since I have — secretly — resided here, to excite local suspicion."

"Scotland Yard men may surround the house now!" said Stuart viciously.

"One of the two followers I have retained here with me, watches at the gate," replied Fo-Hi. "An intruder seeking to enter by any other route, through the hedge, over the wall, or from the river, would cause electric bells to ring loudly in this room, the note of the bell signifying the point of entry. Finally, in the event of such a surprise, I have an exit whereby one emerges at a secret spot on the river bank. A motor-boat, suitably concealed, awaits me there."

He placed a thermometer in the neck of the yellow bottle and the bottle in a rack. He directed the intolerable gaze of his awful eyes upon the man who sat, teeth tightly clenched, watching him from the *diwan*.

"Ten minutes of life — in England — yet remain to you, Dr. Stuart. In ten minutes this fluid will have cooled to a temperature of 99 degrees, when I shall be enabled safely make an injection. You will be reborn in Kiangsu."

Fo-Hi walked slowly to the door whereby he had entered, opened it and went out. The door closed.

CHAPTER II
THE LIVING DEATH

The little furnace hissed continuously. A wisp of smoke floated up from the incense-burner.

Stuart sat with his hands locked between his knees, and his gaze set upon the yellow flask.

Even now he found it difficult to credit the verity of his case. He found it almost impossible to believe that such a being as Fo-Hi existed, that such deeds had been done, were being done, in England, as those of which he had heard from the sinister cowled man. Save for the hissing of the furnace and the clanking of the chain as he strove with all his strength to win freedom, that wonderful evil room was silent as the King's Chamber at the heart of the Great Pyramid.

His gaze reverted to the yellow flask.

"Oh, my God!" he groaned.

Terror claimed him — the terror which he had with difficulty been fending off throughout that nightmare interview with Fo-Hi. Madness threatened him, and he was seized by an almost incontrollable desire to shout execrations — prayers — he knew not what. He clenched his teeth grimly and tried to think, to plan.

He had two chances:

The statement left with Inspector Dunbar, in which he had mentioned the existence of a house "near Hampton Court," and...Miska.

That she was one of the two exceptions mentioned by Fo-Hi he felt assured. But was she in this house, and did she know of his presence there? Even so, had she access to that room of mysteries — of horrors?

And who was the other who remained? Almost certainly it was the fanatical Hindu, Chunda Lal, of whom she had spoken with such palpable terror and who watched her unceasingly, untiringly. *He* would prevent her intervening even if she had power to intervene.

His great hope, then, was in Dunbar...for Gaston Max was dead.

At the coming of that thought, the foul doing to death of the fearless Frenchman, he gnashed his teeth savagely and strained at the gyves until the pain in his ankles brought out beads of perspiration upon his forehead.

He dropped his head into his hands and frenziedly clutched at his hair with twitching fingers.

The faint sound occasioned by the opening of one of the sliding doors brought him sharply upright.

Miska entered!

She looked so bewilderingly beautiful that terror and sorrow fled, leaving Stuart filled only with passionate admiration. She wore an Eastern dress of gauzy shimmering silk and high-heeled gilt Turkish slippers upon her stockingless feet. About her left ankle was a gold bangle, and there was barbaric jewellery upon her arms. She was a figure unreal as all lose in that house of dreams, but a figure so lovely that Stuart forgot the yellow flask...forgot that less than ten minutes of life remained to him.

"Miska!" he whispered — "Miska!"

She exhibited intense but repressed excitement and fear. Creeping to the second door — that by which Fo-Hi had gone out — she pressed her ear to the lacquered panel and listened intently. Then, coming swiftly to the table, she took up a bunch of keys, approached Stuart and, kneeling, unlocked the gyves. The scent of jasmine stole to his nostrils.

"God bless you!" he said with stifled ardour.

She rose quickly to her feet, standing before him with head downcast. Stuart rose with difficulty. His legs were cramped and aching. He grasped Miska's hand and endeavoured to induce her to look up. One swift glance she gave him and looked away again.

"You must go — this instant," she said. "I show you the way. There is not a moment to lose...."

"Miska!"

She glanced at him again.

"You must come with me!"

"Ah!" she whispered — "that is impossible! Have I not told you so?"

"You have told me, but I cannot understand. Here, in England, you are free. Why should you remain with that cowled monster?"

"Shall I tell you?" she asked, and he could feel how she trembled. "If I tell you, will you promise to believe me — and to go?"

"Not without you!"

"Ah! no, no! If I tell you that my only chance of life — such a little, little chance — is to stay, will you go?"

Stuart secured her other hand and drew her toward him, half resisting.

"Tell me," he said softly. "I will believe you — and if it can spare you one moment of pain or sorrow, I will go as you ask me."

"Listen," she whispered, glancing fearfully back toward the closed door — "Fo-Hi has something that make people to die; and only he can bring them to life again. Do you believe this?"

She looked up at him rapidly, her wonderful eyes wide and fearful. He nodded.

"Ah! you know! Very well. On that day in Cairo, which I am taken before him — you remember, I tell you? — he...oh!"

She shuddered wildly and hid her beautiful face against Stuart's breast. He threw his arms about her.

"Tell me," he said.

"With the needle, he...inject..."

"Miska!"

Stuart felt the blood rushing to his heart and knew that he had paled.

"There is something else," she went on, almost inaudibly, "with which he gives life again to those he had made dead with the needle. It is a light green liquid tasting like bitter apples; and once each week for six months it must be drunk or else...the living death comes. Sometimes I have not seen Fo-Hi for six months at a time, but a tiny flask, one draught, of the green liquid, always comes to me wherever I am, every week...and twice each year I see him — Fo-Hi... and he..."

Her voice quivered and ceased. Moving back, she slipped a soft shoulder free of it s flimsy covering.

Stuart looked — and suppressed a groan.

Her arm was dotted with the tiny marks made by a hypodermic syringe!

"You see!" she whispered tremulously. "If I go, I die, and I am buried alive...or else I live until my body..."

"Oh, God!" moaned Stuart — "the fiend! the merciless, cunning fiend! Is there *nothing* ..."

"Yes, yes!" said Miska, looking up. "If I can get enough of the green fluid and escape. But he tell me once — it was in America — that he only prepares one tiny draught at a time! Listen! I must stay, and if he can be captured he must be forced to make this antidote...Ah! go! go!"

Her words ended in a sob, and Stuart held her to him convulsively, his heart filled with such helpless, fierce misery and bitterness as he had never known.

"Go, please go!" she whispered. "It is my only chance — there is no other. There is not a moment to wait. Listen to me! You will go by that door by which I come in. There is a better way, through a tunnel he has made to the river bank; but I cannot open the door. Only *he* has the key. At the end of the passage some one is waiting — — "

"Chunda Lal!" Miska glanced up rapidly and then dropped her eyes again.

"Yes — poor Chunda Lal. He is my only friend. Give him this."

She removed an amulet upon a gold chain from about her neck and thrust it into Stuart's hand.

"It seems to you silly, but Chunda Lal is of the East; and he has promised. Oh! be quick! I am afraid. I tell you something. Fo-Hi does not know, but the police Inspector and many men search the river bank for the house! I see them from a window — — "

"What!" cried Stuart — "Dunbar is here!"

"*Ssh! ssh!*" Miska clutched him wildly. "*He* is not far away. You will go and bring him here. No! for me do not fear. I put the keys back and he will think you have opened the lock by some trick — — "

"Miska!"

"Oh, no more!"

She slipped from his arms, crossed and reopened the lacquered door, revealing a corridor dimly lighted. Stuart followed and looked along the corridor.

"Right to the end," she whispered, "and down the steps. You know" — touching the amulet which Stuart carried — "how to deal with — Chunda Lal."

But still he hesitated; until she seized his hand and urged him.

Thereupon he swept her wildly into his arms.

"Miska! how can I leave you! It is maddening!"

"You must! you must!"

He looked into her eyes, stooped and kissed her upon the lips. Then, with no other word, he tore himself away and walked quickly along the corridor. Miska watched him until he was out of sight, then re-entered the great room and closed the door. She turned, and:

"Oh, God of mercy," she whispered.

Just within the second doorway stood Fo-Hi watching her.

CHAPTER III
THE FIFTH SECRET OF RACHE CHURAN

Stricken silent with fear, Miska staggered back against the lacquered door, dropping the keys which she held in her hand. Fo-Hi had removed the cowled garment and was now arrayed in a rich mandarin robe. Through the grotesque green veil which obscured his features the brilliant eyes shone catlike.

"So," he said softly, "you speed the parting guest. And did I not hear the sound of a chaste salute?"

Miska watched him, wild-eyed.

"And he knows," continued the metallic voice, "how to deal with Chunda Lal'? But it may be that Chunda Lal will know how to deal with *him!* I had suspected that Dr. Keppel Stuart entertained an unprofessional interest in his charming patient. Your failure to force the bureau drawer in his study excited my suspicion — unjustly, I admit; for did not I fail also when I paid the doctor a personal visit? True, I was disturbed. But this suspicion later returned. It was in order that some lingering doubt might be removed that I afforded you the opportunity of interviewing my guest. But whatever surprise his ingenuity, aided by your woman's wit, has planned for Chunda Lal, I dare to believe that Chunda Lal, being forewarned, will meet successfully. He is expecting an attempt, by Dr. Stuart, to leave this house. He has my orders to detain him."

At that, anger conquered terror in the heart of Miska, and:

"You mean he has your orders to kill him!" she cried desperately.

Fo-Hi closed the door.

"On the contrary, he has my orders to take every possible care of him. Those blind, tempestuous passions which merely make a woman more desirable find no place in the trained mind of the scientist. That Dr. Stuart covets my choicest possession in no way detracts from his value to my Council."

Miska had never moved from the doorway by which Stuart had gone out; and now, having listened covertly and heard no outcry, her faith in Chunda Lal was restored. Her wonderful eyes narrowed momentarily, and she spoke with the guile, which seems so naive, of the Oriental woman.

"I care nothing for him — this Dr. Stuart. But he had done you no wrong — —"

"Beyond seeking my death — none. I have already said" — the eyes of Fo-Hi gleamed through the hideous veil — "that I bear him no ill will."

"But you plan to carry him to China — like those others."

"I assign him a part in the New Renaissance — yes. In the Deluge that shall engulf the world, his place is in the Ark. I honor him."

"Perhaps he rather remain a — nobody — than be so honored."

"In his present state of imperfect understanding it is quite possible," said Fo-Hi smoothly. "But if he refuses to achieve greatness he must have greatness thrust upon him. Van Rembold, I seem to recall, hesitated for some time to direct his genius to the problem of producing radium in workable quantities from the pitchblend deposits of Ho-Nan. But the *split rod* had not been applied to the soles of his feet more than five times ere he reviewed his prejudices and found them to be surmountable."

Miska, knowing well the moods of the monstrous being whose unveiled face she had never seen, was not deceived by the suavity of his manner. Nevertheless, she fought down her terror, knowing how much might depend upon her retaining her presence of mind. How much of her interview with Stuart he had overheard she did not know, nor how much he had witnessed.

"But," she said, moving away from him, "he does not matter — this one. Forgive me if I think to let him go; but I am afraid — —"

Fo-Hi crossed slowly, intercepting her.

"Ah!" said Miska, her eyes opening widely — "you are going to punish me again! For why? Because I am a woman and cannot always be cruel?"

From its place on the wall Fo-Hi took a whip. At that:

"Ah! no, no!" she cried. "You drive me mad! I am only in part of the East and I cannot bear it — I cannot bear it! You teach me to be like the women of England, who are free, and you treat me like the women of China, who are slaves. Once, it did not matter. I thought it was a part of a woman's life to be treated so. But now I cannot bear it!" She stamped her foot fiercely upon the floor. "I tell you I cannot bear it!"

Whip in hand, Fo-Hi stood watching her.

"You release that man — for whom you 'care nothing' — in order that he may bring my enemies about me, in order that he may hand me over to the barbarous law of England. Now, you 'cannot bear' so light a rebuke as the whip. Here, I perceive, is some deep psychological change. Such protests do not belong to the women of my country; they are never heard in the *zenana,* and would provoke derision in the *harems* of Stambul.

"You have trained me to know that life in a *harem* is not life, but only the existence of an animal."

"I have trained you — yes. What fate was before you when I intervened in that Mecca slave-market? You who are 'only in part of the East.' Do you forget so soon how you cowered there amongst the others, Arabs, Circassians, Georgians, Nubians, striving to veil your beauty from those ravenous eyes? From *what* did I rescue you?"

"And *for* what?" cried Miska bitterly. "To use me as a lure — and beat me if I failed."

Fo-Hi stood watching her, and slowly, as he watched, terror grew upon her and she retreated before him, step by step. He made no attempt to follow her, but continued to watch. Then, raising the whip he broke it across his knee and dropped the pieces on the floor.

At that she extended her hands towards him pitifully.

"Oh! what are you going to do to me!" she said. "Let me go! let me go! I can no more be of use to you. Give me back my life and let me go — et me go and hide away from them all — from all...the world...."

Her words died away and ceased upon a suppressed hysterical sob. For, in silence, Fo-Hi stood watching her, unmoved.

"Oh!" she moaned, and sank cowering upon a *diwan* — "why do you watch me so!"

"Because," came the metallic voice, softly — "you are beautiful with a beauty given but rarely to the daughters of men. The Sublime Order has acquired many pretty women — for they are potent weapons — but none so fair as you. Miska, I would make life sweet for you."

"Ah! you do not mean that!" she whispered fearfully.

"Have I not clothed you in the raiment of a princess!" continued Fo-Hi. "To-night, at my urgent request, you wear the charming national costume in which I delight to see you. But is there a woman of Paris, of London, of New York, who has such robes, such jewels, such apartments as you possess? Perhaps the peculiar duties which I have required you to perform, the hideous disguises, which you have sometimes been called upon to adopt, have disgusted you."

Her heart beating wildly, for she did not know this mood but divined it to portend some unique horror, Miska crouched, head averted.

"To-night the hour has come to break the whip. To-night the master in me dies. My cloak of wise authority has fallen from me and I offer myself in bondage to *you*, my slave!"

"This is some trap you set for me!" she whispered.

But Fo-Hi, paying no heed to her words, continued in the same rapt voice:

"Truly have you observed that the Chinese wife is but a slave to her lord. I have said that the relation of master and slave is ended between us. I offer you a companionship that signifies absolute freedom and perfect understanding. Half of all I have — and the world lies in my grasp — is yours. I offer a throne set upon the Seven Mountains of the Universe. Look into my eyes and read the truth."

But lower and lower she cowered upon the *diwan*.

"No, no! I am afraid!"

Fo-Hi approached her closely and abject terror now had robbed her of strength. Her limbs seemed to have become numbed, her tongue clave to the roof of her mouth.

"Fear me no more, Miska," said Fo-Hi. "I *will* you nothing but joy. The man who has learned the Fifth Secret of Rache Churan — who has learned how to control his will — holds a power absolute and beyond perfectability. You know, who have dwelt beneath my roof, that there is no escape from my will." His calm was terrible, and his glance, through the green veil, was like a ray of scorching heat. His voice sank lower and lower.

"There is one frailty, Miska, that even the Adept cannot conquer. It is inherent in every man. Miska, I would not *force* you to grasp the joy I offer; I would have you *accept* it willingly. No! do not turn from me! No woman in all the world has ever heard me plead, as I plead to you. Never before have I *sued* for favours. Do not turn from me, Miska."

Slightly, the metallic voice vibrated, and the ruffling of that giant calm was a thing horrible to witness. Fo-Hi extended his long yellow hands, advancing step by step until he stood over the cowering girl. Irresistibly her glance was drawn to those blazing eyes which the veil could not hide, and as she met that unblinking gaze her own eyes dilated and grew fixed as those of a sleep-walker. A moment Fo-Hi stood so. Then passion swept him from his feet and he seized her fiercely.

"Your eyes drive me mad!" he hissed. "Your lips taunt me, and I know all earthly greatness to be a mirage, its conquests visions, and its fairness dust. I would rather be a captive in your white arms than the emperor of heaven! Your sweetness intoxicates me, Miska. A fever burns me up!"

Helpless, enmeshed in the toils of that mighty will, Miska raised her head; and gradually her expression changed. Fear was smoothed away from her lovely face as by some magic brush. She grew placid; and finally she smiled — the luresome, caressing smile of the East. Nearer and nearer drew the green veil. Then, uttering a sudden fierce exclamation, Fo-Hi thrust her from him.

"That smile is not for *me*, the man!" he cried gutterally. "Ah! I could curse the power that I coveted and set above all earthly joys! I who boasted that he could control his will — I read in your eyes that I am *willing* you to love me! I seek a gift and can obtain but a tribute!"

Miska, with a sobbing moan, sank upon the *diwan*. Fo-Hi stood motionless, looking straight before him. His terrible calm was restored.

"It is the bitter truth," he said — "that to win the world I have bartered the birthright of men; the art of winning a woman's heart. There is much in our Chinese wisdom. I erred in breaking the whip. I erred in doubting my own prescience, which told me that the smiles I could not woo were given freely to another…and perhaps the kisses. At least I can set these poor frail human doubts at rest."

He crossed and struck a gong which hung midway between the two doors.

CHAPTER IV
THE GUILE OF THE EAST

Her beautiful face a mask of anguish, Miska cowered upon the *diwan,* watching the closed doors. Fo-Hi stood in the centre of the great room with his back to the entrance. Silently one of the lacquered panels slid open and Chunda Lal entered. He saluted the figure of the veiled Chinaman but never once glanced in the direction of the *diwan* from which Miska wildly was watching him.

Without turning his head, Fo-Hi, who seemed to detect the presence of the silent Hindu by means of some fifth sense, pointed to a bundle of long rods stacked in a corner of the room.

His brown face expressionless as that of a bronze statue, Chunda Lal crossed and took the rods from their place.

"*Tum samajhte ho?*" (Do you understand?) said Fo-Hi. Chunda Lal inclined his head.

"*Main tumhari bat manunga*" (Your orders shall be obeyed), he replied.

"Ah, God! no!" whispered Miska — "what are you going to do?"

"Your Hindustani was ever poor, Miska," said Fo-Hi.

He turned to Chunda Lal.

"Until you hear the gong," he said in English.

Miska leapt to her feet, as Chunda Lal, never once glancing at her, went out bearing the rods, and closed the door behind him. Fo-Hi turned and confronted her.

"*Ta'ala hina* (come hither), Miska!" he said softly. "Shall I speak to you in the soft Arab tongue? Come to me, lovely Miska. Let me feel how that sorrowful heart will leap like a captive gazelle."

But Miska shrank back from him, pale to the lips.

"Very well." His metallic voice sank to a hiss. "I employ no force. You shall yield to me your heart as a love offering. Of such motives as jealousy and revenge you know me incapable. What I do, I do with a purpose. That compassion of yours shall be a lever to cast you into my arms. Your hatred you shall conquer."

"Oh, have you no mercy? Is there *nothing* human in your heart? Did I say I hate you!"

"Your eyes are eloquent, Miska. I cherish two memories of those beautiful eyes. One is of their fear and loathing — of *me*; the other is of their sweet softness when they watched the departure of my guest. Listen! Do you hear nothing?"

In an attitude of alert and fearful attention Miska stood listening.

Fo-Hi watched her through the veil with those remorseless blazing eyes.

"I will open the door," he said smoothly, "that we may more fully enjoy the protests of one for whom you 'care nothing' — of one whose lips have pressed — your hand."

He opened the door by which Chunda Lal had gone out and turned again to Miska. Her eyes looked unnaturally dark by contrast with the pallor of her face.

Chunda Lal had betrayed her. She no longer doubted it. For he had not dared to meet her glance. His fear of Fo-Hi had overcome his love for her... and Stuart had been treacherously seized somewhere in the corridors and rendered helpless by the awful art of the thug.

"There is a brief interval," hissed the evil voice. "Chunda Lal is securing him to the frame and baring the soles of his feet for the caresses of the rod."

Suddenly, from somewhere outside the room, came the sound of dull, regular blows... then, a smothered moan!

Miska sprang forward and threw herself upon her knees before Fo-Hi, clutching at his robe frantically.

"Ah! merciful God! he is there! Spare him! spare him! No more — no more!"

"He is there?" repeated Fo-Hi suavely. "Assuredly he is there, Miska. I know not by what trick he hoped to 'deal with' Chunda Lal. But, as I informed you, Chunda Lal was forewarned."

The sound of blows continued, followed by that of another, louder groan.

"Stop him! Stop him!" shrieked Miska.

"You 'care nothing' for this man. Why do you tremble?"

"Oh!" she wailed piteously. "I cannot bear it... oh, I cannot bear it! Do what you like with me, but spare him. Ah! you have no mercy."

Fo-Hi handed her the hammer for striking the gong.

"It is *you* who have no mercy," he replied. "I have asked but one gift. The sound of the gong will end Dr. Stuart's discomfort... and will mean that you *voluntarily* accept my offer. What! you hesitate?" A stifled scream rang out sharply.

"Ah, yes! yes!"

Miska ran and struck the gong, then staggered back to the *diwan* and fell upon it, hiding her face in her hands. The sounds of torture ceased.

Fo-Hi closed the door and stood looking at her where she lay.

"I permit you some moments of reflection," he said, "in order that you may compose yourself to receive the addresses which I shall presently have the honour, and joy, of making to you. Yes — this door is unlocked." He threw the keys on the table. "I respect your promise... and Chunda Lal guards the *outer* exits."

He opened the further door, by which he had entered, and went out.

Miska, through the fingers of her shielding hands, watched him go.

When he had disappeared she sprang up, clenching her teeth, and her face was contorted with anguish. She began to move aimlessly about the room, glancing at the many strange objects on the big table and fearfully at the canopied chair beside which hung the bronze bell. Finally:

"Oh, Chunda Lal! Chunda Lal!" she moaned, and threw herself face downward on the *diwan,* sobbing wildly.

So she lay, her whole body quivering with the frenzy of her emotions, and as she lay there, inch by inch, cautiously, the nearer door began to open. Chunda Lal looked in.

Finding the room to be occupied only by Miska, he crossed rapidly to the *diwan,* bending over her with infinite pity and tenderness.

"Miska!" he whispered softly.

As though an adder had touched her, Miska sprang to her feet — and back from the Hindu. Her eyes flashed fiercely.

"Ah! *you! you!*" she cried at him, with a repressed savagery that spoke of the Oriental blood in her veins. "Do not speak to me — look at me! Do not come near me! I hate you! God! how I hate you!"

"Miska! Miska!" he said beseechingly — "you pierce my heart! you kill me! Can you not understand — —"

"Go! go!"

She drew back from him, clenching and unclenching her jewelled fingers and glaring madly into his eyes.

"Look, Miska!" He took the gold chain and amulet from his bosom. "Your token! Can you not understand! *Yah Allah!* how little you trust me — and I would die for one glance of your eyes!

"*He* — Stuart Sahib — has gone, gone long since!"

"Ah! Chunda Lal!"

Miska swayed dizzily and extended her hands towards him. Chunda Lal glanced fearfully about him.

"Did I not," he whispered, with an intense ardour in his soft voice, — "did I not lay my life, my service, all I have, at your feet? Did I not vow to serve you in the name of *Bhowani!* He is long since gone to bring his friends — who are searching from house to house along the river. At any moment they may be here!"

Miska dropped weakly upon her knees before him and clasped his hand.

"Chunda Lal, my friend! Oh, forgive me!" Her voice broke. "Forgive..."

Chunda Lal raised her gently.

"Not upon your knees to *me,* Miska. It was a little thing to do — for you. Did I not tell you that *he* had cast his eyes upon you? Mine was the voice you heard to cry out. Ah! you do not know; it is to gain *time* that I seem to serve *him!* Only this, Miska" — he revealed the blade of a concealed knife — "stand between Fo-Hi and — you! Had I not read it in his eyes!"

He raised his glance upward frantically.

"*Jey Bhowani!* give me strength, give me courage! For if I fail..."

He glared at her passionately, clutching his bosom; then, pressing the necklet to his lips, he concealed it again, and bent, whispering urgently:

"Listen again — I reveal it to you without price or hope of reward, for I know there is no love in your heart to give, Miska; I know that it takes you out of my sight for always. But I tell you what I learn in the house of Abdul Rozan. Your life is your own, Miska! With the needle" — yet closer he bent to her ear and even softer he spoke — "he pricks your white skin — no more! The vial he sends contains a harmless cordial!"

"Chunda Lal!"

Miska swayed again dizzily, clutching at the Hindu for support.

"Quick! fly!" he said, leading her to the door. "I will see *he* does not pursue!"

"No, no! you shall shed no blood for me! Not even *his.* You come also!"

"And if he escape, and know that I was false to him, he will *call me back,* and I shall be dragged to those yellow eyes, though I am a thousand miles away! *Inshalla!* those eyes! No — I must strike swift, or he robs me of my strength."

For a long moment Miska hesitated.

"Then, I also remain, Chunda Lal, my friend! We will wait — and watch -and listen for the bells — here — that tell they are in the grounds of the house."

"Ah, Miska!" the glance of the Hindu grew fearful — "you are clever — but *he* is the Evil One! I fear for you. Fly now. There is yet time..."

A faint sound attracted Miska's attention. Placing a quivering finger to her lips, she gently thrust Chunda Lal out into the corridor.

"He returns!" she whispered: "If I call — come to me, my friend. But we have not long to wait!"

She closed the door.

CHAPTER V

Stuart had gained the end of the corridor, unmolested. There he found a short flight of steps, which he descended and came to a second corridor forming a right angle with the first. A lamp was hung at the foot of the steps, and by its light he discerned a shadowy figure standing at the further end of this second passage.

A moment he hesitated, peering eagerly along the corridor. The man who waited was Chunda Lal. Stuart approached him and silently placed in his hand the gold amulet.

Chunda Lal took it as one touching something holy, and raising it he kissed it with reverence. His dark eyes were sorrowful. Long and ardently he pressed the little trinket to his lips, then concealed it under the white robe which he wore and turned to Stuart. His eyes were sorrowful no more, but fierce as the eyes of a tiger.

"Follow!" he said.

He unlocked a door and stepped out into a neglected garden, Stuart close at his heels. The sky was cloudy, and the moon obscured. Never glancing back, Chunda Lal led the way along a path skirting a high wall upon which climbing fruit trees were growing until they came to a second door and this also the Hindu unlocked. He stood aside.

"To the end of this lane," he said, in his soft queerly modulated voice, "and along the turning to the left to the river bank. Follow the bank towards the palace and you will meet them."

"I owe you my life," said Stuart.

"Go! you owe me nothing," returned the Hindu fiercely.

Stuart turned and walked rapidly along the lane. Once he glanced back. Chunda Lal was looking after him...and he detected something that gleamed in his hand, gleamed not like gold but like the blade of a knife!

Turning the corner, Stuart began to run. For he was unarmed and still weak, and there had been that in the fierce black eyes of the Hindu when he had scorned Stuart's thanks which had bred suspicion and distrust.

From the position of the moon, Stuart judged the hour to be something after midnight. No living thing stirred about him. The lane in which now he found himself was skirted on one side by a hedge beyond which was open country and on the other by a continuation of the high wall which evidently enclosed the grounds of the house that he had just quitted. A cool breezed fanned his face, and he knew that he was approaching the Thames. Ten more paces and he came to the bank.

In his weak condition the short run had exhausted him. His bruised throat was throbbing painfully, and he experienced some difficulty in breathing. He leaned up against the moss-grown wall, looking back into the darkness of the lane.

No one was in sight. There was no sound save the gently lapping of the water upon the bank.

He would have like to bathe his throat and to quench his feverish thirst, but a mingled hope and despair spurred him and he set off along the narrow path towards where dimly above some trees he could discern in the distance a group of red-roofed buildings. Having proceeded for a considerable distance, he stood still, listening for any sound that might guide him to the search-party — or warn him that he was followed. But he could hear nothing.

Onward he pressed, not daring to think of what the future held for him, not daring to dwell upon the memory, the maddening sweetness, of that parting kiss. His eyes grew misty, he stumbled as he walked, and became oblivious of his surrounding. His awakening was a rude one.

Suddenly a man, concealed behind a bush, sprang out upon him and bore him irresistibly to the ground!

"Not a word!" rapped his assailant, "or I'll knock you out!"

Stuart glared into the red face lowered so threateningly over his own, and:

"Sergeant Sowerby!" he gasped.

The grip upon his shoulders relaxed.

"Damn!" cried Sowerby — "if it isn't Dr. Stuart?"

"What is that!" cried another voice from the shelter of the bush. *"Pardieu! say it again!...* Dr. Stuart!"

And Gaston Max sprang out!

"Max!" murmured Stuart, staggering to his feet — "Max!"

"Nom d'un nom! Two dead men meet!" exclaimed Gaston Max. "But indeed" — he grasped Stuart by both hands and his voice shook with emotion — "I thank God that I see you!"

Stuart was dazed. Words failed him, and he swayed dizzily.

"I thought *you* were murdered," said Max, still grasping his hand, "and I perceive that you had made the same mistake about me! Do you know what saved me, my friend, from the consequences of that frightful blow? It was the bandage of 'Le Balafre'!"

"You must possess a skull like a negro's!" said Stuart feebly.

"I believe I have a skull like a baboon!" returned Max, laughing with joyous excitement. "And you, doctor, you must possess a steel wind-pipe; for flesh and blood could never have survived the pressure of that horrible pigtail. You will rejoice to learn that Miguel was arrested on the Dover boat-train this morning and Ah-Fang-Fu at Tilbury Dock some four hours ago. So we are both avenged! But we waste time!"

He unscrewed a flask and handed it to Stuart.

"A terrible experience has befallen you," he said. "But tell me — do you know where it is — the lair of 'The Scorpion'?"

"I do!" replied Stuart, having taken a welcome draught from the flask. "Where is Dunbar? We must carefully surround the place or he will elude us."

"Ah! as he eluded us at 'The Pidgin House'!" cried Max. "Do you know what happened? They had a motorboat in the very cellar of that warren. At high tide they could creep out into the cutting, drawing their craft along from pile to pile, and reach the open river at a point fifty yards above the house! In the damnable darkness they escaped. But we have two of them."

"It was all my fault," said Sowerby guiltily. "I missed my spring when I went for the Chinaman who came out first, and he gave one yell. The old fox in the shop heard it and the fat was in the fire."

"You didn't miss your spring at me!" retort Stuart ruefully.

"No," agreed Sowerby. "I didn't mean to miss a second time!"

"What's all this row," came a gruff voice.

"Ah! Inspector Dunbar!" said Max.

Dunbar walked up the path, followed by a number of men. At first he did not observe Stuart, and:

"You'll be waking all the neighborhood," he said. "It's the next big house, Sowerby, the one we thought, surrounded by the brick wall. There's no doubt, I think... Why!"

He had seen Stuart, and he sprang forward with outstretched hand.

"Thank God!" he cried, disregarding his own counsel about creating a disturbance. "This is fine! Eh, man! but I'm glad to see you!"

"And *I* am glad to be here!" Stuart assured him.

They shook hands warmly.

"You have read my statement, of course?" asked Stuart.

"I have," replied the Inspector, and gave him a swift glance of the tawny eyes. "And considering that you've nearly been strangled, I'll forgive you! But I wish we'd known about this house — —"

"Ah! Inspector," interrupted Gaston Max, "but you have never seen Zara el-Khala! I have seen her — and *I* forgive him, also!"

Stuart continued rapidly:

"We have little time to waste. There are only three people in the house, so far as I am aware: Miska — known to you, M. Max, as Zara el-Khala — the Hindu, Chunda Lal, and — Fo-Hi — —"

"Ah!" cried Max — "'The Scorpion.' Chunda Lal, for some obscure personal reason, not entirely unconnected with Miska, enabled me to make my escape in order that I might lead you to the house. Therefore we may look upon Chunda Lal, as well as Miska, in the light of an accomplice — — "

"*Eh, bien!* a spy in the camp! This is where we see how fatal to the success of any enterprise, criminal or otherwise, is the presence of a pretty woman! Proceed, my friend!"

"There are three entrances to the apartment in which Fo-Hi apparently spends the greater part of his time. Two of these I know, although I am unaware where one of them leads to. But the third, of which he alone holds the key, communicates with a tunnel leading to the river bank, where a motorboat is concealed."

"Ah, that motor-boat!" cried Max. "He travels at night, you understand — — "

"Always, I am told."

"Yes, always. Therefore, once he is out on the river, he is moderately secure between the first lock and the Nore! When a police patrol is near he can shut off his engine and lie under the bank. Last night he crept away from us in that fashion. Tonight is not so dark, and the River Police are watching all the way down."

"Furthermore," replied Stuart, "Chunda Lal, who acts as engineer, has it in his power to prevent Fo-Hi's escape by that route! But we must count upon the possibility of his attempting to leave by water. Therefore, in disposing your forces, place a certain number of men along the bank and below the house. Is there a River Police boat near?"

"Not nearer than Putney Bridge," answered Dunbar. "We shall have to try and block that exit."

"There's no time to waste," continued Stuart excitedly — "and I have a very particular request to make: that you will take Fo-Hi *alive.*"

"But of course," said Gaston Max, "if it is humanly possible."

Stuart repressed a groan; for even so he had little hope of inducing the awful veiled man to give back life to the woman who would have been instrumental in bringing him to the scaffold... and no compromise was possible!

"If you will muster your men, Inspector," he said, "I will lead you to the spot. Once we have affected an entrance we must proceed with dispatch. He has alarm-bells connected with every possible point of entry."

"Lead on, my friend," cried Gaston Max. "I perceive that time is precious."

CHAPTER VI
"JEY BHOWANI!"

As the door closed upon Chunda Lal, Miska stepped back from it and stood, unconsciously, in a curiously rigid and statuesque attitude, her arms pressed to her sides and her hands directed outward. It was the physical expression of an intense mental effort to gain control of herself. Her heart was leaping wildly in her breast — for the future that had held only horror and a living tomb, now opened out sweetly before her. She had only to ply her native wiles for a few precious moments... and *someone* would have her in his arms, to hold her safe from harm! If the will of the awful Chinaman threatened to swamp her individuality, then — there was Chunda Lal!

But because of his helpless, unselfish love, she hesitated even at the price of remaining alone again with Fo-Hi, to demand any further sacrifice of the Hindu. Furthermore — he might fail!

The lacquer door slid noiselessly open and Fo-Hi entered. He paused, watching her.

"Ah," he said, in that low-pitched voice which was so terrifying — "a *gaziyeh* of Ancient Egypt! How beautiful you are, Miska! You transport me to the court of golden Pharaoh. Miska! daughter of the moon-magic of Isis — Zara el-Khala! At any hour my enemies may be clamoring at my doors. But *this* hour is mine!"

He moved at his customary slow gait to the table, took up the keys…and locked both doors!

Miska, perceiving in this her chance of aid from Chunda Lal utterly destroyed, sank slowly upon the *diwan,* her pale face expressing the utmost consternation. Suppose the police did not come!

Fo-Hi dropped the keys on the table again and approached her. She stood up, retreating before him. He inhaled sibilantly and paused.

"So your 'acceptance' was only a trick," he said. "Your loathing of my presence is as strong as ever. Well!" At the word, as a volcano leaps into life, the hidden fires which burned within this terrible man leapt up consumingly — "if the gift of the flower is withheld, at least I will grasp the Dead Sea Fruit!"

He leapt toward Miska — and she fled shrieking before him. Running around a couch which stood near the centre of the room, she sprang to the door and beat upon it madly.

"Chunda Lal!" she cried — "Chunda Lal!"

Fo-Hi was close upon her, and she turned striving to elude him.

"Oh, merciful God! *Chunda Lal!*"

The name burst from her lips in a long frenzied scream. Fo-Hi had seized her!

Grasping her shoulders, he twisted her about so that he could look into her eyes. A low, shuddering cry, died away, and her gaze became set, hypnotically, upon Fo-Hi. He raised one hand, fingers outstretched before her. She swayed slightly.

"Forget!" he said in a deep, guttural voice of command — "forget. I *will* it. We stand in an empty world, you and I; you, Miska, and I, Fo-Hi, your master."

"My master," she whispered mechanically.

"Your lover."

"My lover."

"You give me your life, to do with as I will."

"As you will."

Fo-Hi momentarily raised the blazing eyes.

"Oh, empty shell of a vanished joy!" he cried.

Then, frenziedly grasping Miska by her arms, he glared into her impassive face.

"Your heart leaps wildly in your breast!" he whispered tenderly.

"Look into my eyes…."

Miska sighed and opened her eyes yet more widely. She shuddered and a slow smile appeared upon her lips.

The lacquer screen making the window was pushed open and Chunda Lal leapt in over the edge. As Fo-Hi drew the yielding, hypnotised girl towards him, Chunda Lal, a gleaming *kukri* held aloft, ran with a silent panther step across the floor.

He reached Fo-Hi, drew himself upright; the glittering blade quivered…and Fo-Hi divined his presence.

Uttering a short, guttural exclamation, he thrust Miska aside. She staggered dazedly and fell prone upon the floor. The quivering blade did not descend.

Fo-Hi drew himself rigidly upright, extending his hands, palms downward, before him. He was exerting a superhuman effort. The breath whistled through his nostrils. Chunda Lal, knife upraised, endeavored to strike; but his arm seemed to have become incapable of movement and to be held, helpless, aloft.

Staring at the rigid figure before him, he began to pant like a man engaged in a wrestle for life.

Fo-Hi stretched his right arm outward, and with a gesture of hand and fingers beckoned to Chunda Lal to come before him.

And now, Miska, awakening as from a fevered dream, looked wildly about her, and then, serpentine, began to creep to the table upon which the keys were lying. Always watching the awful group of two, she rose slowly, snatched the keys and leapt across to the open window….

Chunda Lal, swollen veins standing out cord-like on his brow, his gaze set hypnotically upon the moving hand, dropped his knife and began to move in obedience to the will of Fo-Hi.

As he came finally face to face with the terrible Adept of Rache Churan, Miska disappeared into the shadow of the balcony. Fo-Hi by an imperious gesture commanded Chunda Lal to kneel and bow his head. The Hindu, gasping, obeyed.

Thereupon Fo-Hi momentarily relaxed his giant concentration and almost staggered as he glared down at the kneeling man. But never was that dreadful gaze removed from Chunda Lal. And now the veiled man drew himself rigidly upright again and stepped backward until the fallen *kukri* lay at his feet. He spoke, "Chunda Lal!"

The Hindu rose, gazing before him with unseeing eyes. His forehead was wet with perspiration.

Fo-Hi pointed to the knife.

Chunda Lal, without removing his sightless gaze from the veiled face, stooped, groped until he found the knife and rose with it in his hand.

Back stepped Fo-Hi, and back, until he could touch the big table. He moved a brass switch —and a trap opened in the floor behind Chunda Lal. Fo-Hi raised his right hand, having the fingers tightly closed as if grasping the hilt of a knife. With his left hand he pointed to the trap. Again he spoke.

"Tum samauhe ho?"

Mechanically Chunda La replied:

"Ah, Sahib, tumhara huken jaldi: kiya' jaega'" (Yes, I hear and obey.)

As Fo-Hi raised his clenched right hand, so did Chunda Lal raise the *kukri*. Fo-Hi extended his left hand rigidly towards the Hindu and seemed to force him, step by step, back towards the open trap. Almost at the brink, Chunda Lal paused, swayed, and began to utter short, agonised cries. Froth appeared upon his lips.

Raising his right hand yet further aloft, Fo-Hi swiftly brought it down, performing the gesture of stabbing himself to the heart. His ghastly reserve deserted him.

"Jey Bhowana!" he screamed — "Yah Allah!"

Chunda Lal, uttering a loud groan, stabbed himself and fell backward into the opening. Ensued a monstrous crash of broken glass.

As he fell, Fo-Hi leapt to the brink of the trap, glaring down madly into the cellar below. His yellow fingers opened and closed spasmodically.

"Lie there," he shrieked — "my 'faithful' servant! The ants shall pick your bones!"

He grasped the upstanding door of the trap and closed it. It descended with a reverberating boom. Fo-Hi raised his clenched fists and stepped to the door. Finding it locked, he stood looking toward the open screen before the window.

"Miska!" he whispered despairingly.

He crossed to the window and was about to look out, when a high-pitched electric bell began to ring in the room.

Instantly Fo-Hi closed the screen and turned, looking in the direction from whence the sound of ringing proceeded. As he did so, a second bell, in another key, began to ring — a third — a fourth.

Momentarily the veiled man exhibited evidence of indecision. Then, from beneath his robe he took a small key. Approaching an ornate cabinet set against the wall to the left of one of the lacquer doors, he inserted the key in a hidden lock, and slid the entire cabinet partly aside revealing an opening.

Fo-Hi bent, peering down into the darkness of the passage below. A muffled report came, a flash out of the blackness of the river tunnel, and a bullet passed through the end of the cabinet upon which his hand was resting, smashing an ivory statuette and shattering the glass.

Hurriedly he slid the cabinet into place again and stood with his back to it, arms outstretched.

"Miska!" he said — and a note of yet deeper despair had crept into the harsh voice.

Awhile he stood thus; then he drew himself up with dignity. The bells had ceased.

Methodically Fo-Hi began to take certain books from the shelves and to cast them into the great metal bowl which stood upon the tripod. Into the bowl he poured the contents of a large glass jar. Flames and clouds of smoke arose. He paused, listening.

Confused voices were audible, seemingly from all around him, together with a sound of vague movements.

Fo-Hi took up vials and jars and dashed them to pieces upon the tiled hearth in which the furnace rested. Test-tubes, flasks and retorts he shattered, and finally, raising the large glass case of orchids he dashed it down amid the debris of the other nameless and priceless monstrosities unknown to Western science.

CHAPTER VII
THE WAY OF A SCORPION

A black cloud swept past the face of the moon and cold illumination flooded the narrow lane and patched with light the drive leading up to the front of the isolated mansion. Wrought-iron gates closed both entrances and a high wall, surmounted by broken glass and barbed wire, entirely surrounded the grounds.

"This one also is locked," said Gaston Max, trying the gate and then peering through the bars in the direction of the gloomy house.

All the visible windows were shuttered. No ray of light showed anywhere. The house must have been pronounced deserted by anyone contemplating it.

"Upon which side do you suppose the big room to be?" asked Max.

"It is difficult to judge," replied Stuart. "But I am disposed to believe that it is in the front of the house and on the first floor, for I traversed a long corridor, descended several stairs, turned to the right and emerged in a part of the garden bordering the lane in which Inspector Kelly is posted."

"I was thinking of the window and the balcony which 'The Scorpion' informed you commanded a view of Hampton Court. Hampton Court," he turned half-left, "lies about yonder. Therefore you are probably right, doctor; the room as you say should be in front of the house. Since we do not know how to disconnect the alarms, once we have entered the grounds it is important that we should gain access to the house immediately. Ah! *morbleu!* the moon disappears again!"

Darkness crept over the countryside.

"There is an iron balcony jutting out amongst the ivy just above and to the right of the porch!" cried Stuart, who had also been peering up the moon-patched drive. "I would wager that that is the room!"

"Ah!" replied Max, "I believe you are right. This, then is how we shall proceed: Inspector Kelly, with the aid of two men, can get over the wall near that garden door by which you came out. If they cannot force it from inside, you also must get over and lead the way to the entrance you know of. Sowerby and two more men will remain to watch the lane. The river front is well guarded. We will post a man here at this gate and one at the other. Dunbar and I will climb this one and rush straight for that balcony which we must hope to reach by climbing up the ivy. Ah! here comes Inspector Dunbar...and *someone* is with him!"

Dunbar appeared at the double around the corner of the lane which led riverward, and beside him ran a girl who presented a bizarre figure beside the gaunt Scotsman and a figure wildly out of place in that English riverside setting.

It was Miska, arrayed in her flimsy *harem* dress!

"Miska!" cried Stuart, and sprang towards her, sweeping her hungrily into his arms — forgetful of, indifferent to, the presence of Max and Dunbar.

"Ah!" sighed the Frenchman — "yes, she is beautiful!"

Trembling wildly, Miska clung to Stuart and began to speak, her English more broken than ever, because of her emotion.

"Listen — quick!" she panted. "Oh! do not hold me so tight. I have the house-keys — look!" — she held up a bunch of keys — "but not the keys of the gates. Two men have gone to the end of the tunnel where the boat is hid beside the river. Someone — he better climb this gate and by the ivy he can reach the room in which Fo-Hi is! I come down so. You do not see me because the moon goes out and I run to the side-door. It is open. *You* come with me!"

She clung to Stuart, looking up into his eyes.

"Yes, yes, Miska!"

"Oh! Chunda Lal" — she choked down a sob. "Be quick! be quick! *He* will kill him! he will kill him!"

"Off you go, doctor!" cried Max. "Come along, Dunbar!"

He began to climb the ironwork of the gate.

"This way!" said Miska, dragging Stuart by the arm. "Oh! I am wild with fear and sorrow and joy!"

"With joy, dear little Miska!" whispered Stuart, as he followed her.

They passed around the bend into the narrower lane which led toward the river and upon which the garden-door opened. Stuart detained her. If the fate of the whole world had hung in the balance — as indeed, perhaps it did — he could not have acted otherwise. He raised her bewitching face and kissed her ardently.

She trembled and clung to him rapturously.

"I *live!*" she whispered. "Oh! I am mad with happiness! It is Chunda Lal that gives me life — for he tells me the truth. It is not with the living-death that *he* touches me; it is a trick, it is all a trick to bind me to him! Oh, Chunda Lal! Hurry! he is going to kill him!"

But supreme above all the other truths in the world, the joyous truth that Miska was to live set Stuart's heart on fire.

"Thank God!" he said fervently — "oh, thank God! Miska!"

At the garden-door a group of men awaited them. Sergeant Sowerby and two assistants remaining to watch the entrance and the lane, Miska led Stuart and the burly Inspector Kelly along that path beside the wall which Stuart so well remembered.

"Hurry!" she whispered urgently. "We must try to reach him before..."

"You fear for Chunda Lal?" said Stuart.

"Oh, yes! He has a terrible power — Fo-Hi — which he never employs with me, until to-night. Ah! it is only Chunda Lal, who saved me! But Chunda Lal he can command with his *Will.* From it, once he has made anyone a slave to it, there is no escape. I have seen one in the city of Quebec, in Canada, forget all else and begin to act in obedience to the will of Fo-Hi who is thousands of miles away!"

"My God!" murmured Stuart, "what a horrible monster!"

They had reached the open door beyond which showed the dimly lighted passage. Miska hesitated.

"Oh! I am afraid!" she whispered.

She thrust the keys into the hand of Inspector Kelly, pointing to one of them, and:

"That is the key!" she said. "Have your pistol ready. Do not touch anything in the room and do not go in if I tell you not to. Come!"

They pressed along the passage, came to the stair and were about to ascend, when there ensued a dull reverberating boom, and Miska shrank back into Stuart's arms with a stifled shriek.

"Oh! Chunda Lal!" she moaned — "Chunda Lal! It is the trap!"

"The trap!" said Inspector Kelly.

"The cellar trap. He has thrown him down... to the ants!"

Inspector Kelly uttered a short laugh; but Stuart repressed a shudder. He was never likely to forget the skeleton of the Nubian mute which had been stripped by the ants in sixty-nine minutes!

"We are too late!" whispered Miska. "Oh! listen! listen!"

Bells began to ring somewhere above them.

"Max and Dunbar are in!" said Kelly. "Come on, sir! Follow closely, boys!"

He ran up the stairs and along the corridor to the door at the end.

A muffled shot sounded from somewhere in the depths of the house.

"That's Harvey!" said one of the men who followed — "Our man must have tried to escape by the tunnel to the river bank!"

Inspector Kelly placed the key in the lock of the door.

It was at this moment that Gaston Max, climbing up to the front balcony by means of the natural ladder afforded by the ancient ivy, grasped the iron railing and drew himself up to the level of the room. By this same stairway Chunda Lal had ascended to death and Miska had climbed down to life.

"Mind the ironwork doesn't give way, sir!" called Dunbar from below.

"It is strong," replied Max. "Join me here, my friend."

Max, taking a magazine pistol from his pocket, stepped warily over the ledge into the mysterious half-light behind the great screen. As he did so, one of the lacquer doors was unlocked from the outside, and across the extraordinary, smoke-laden room he saw Inspector Kelly enter. He saw something else.

Seated in a strangely-shaped canopied chair was a figure wearing a rich mandarin robe, but having its face covered with a green veil.

"Mon Deiu! at last!" he cried, and leapt into the room. "'The Scorpion'!"

Even as he leapt, and as the Scotland Yard men closed in upon the chair also, all of them armed and all half fearful, a thing happened which struck awe to every heart — for it seemed to be supernatural.

Raising a metal hammer which he held in his hand, Fo-Hi struck the bronze bell hung beside the chair. It emitted a deep, loud note....

There came a flash of blinding light, and intense crackling sound, the crash of broken glass, and a dense cloud of pungent fumes rose in the heated air.

Dunbar had just climbed in behind Gaston Max. Bother were all but hurled from their feet by the force of the explosion. Then:

"Oh, my God!" cried Dunbar, staggering, half blinded, *"look — look!"*

A deathly silence claimed them all. Just within the doorway Stuart appeared, having his arm about the shoulders of Miska.

The Throne of the Gods was empty! A thin coating of grey dust was settling upon it and upon the dais which supported it.

They had witnessed a scientific miracle... the complete and instantaneous disintegration of a human body. Gaston Max was the first to recover speech.

"We are defeated," he said. "'The Scorpion,' surrounded, destroys himself. It is the way of a scorpion."